# THE
# BILLIONAIRES

ALSO BY CALISTA FOX

*Burned Deep*

*Flash Burned*

*Burned Hearts*

# THE BILLIONAIRES

## CALISTA FOX

ST. MARTIN'S GRIFFIN
NEW YORK

THE BILLIONAIRES. Copyright © 2017 by Calista Fox. All rights reserved. Printed in the United States of America. For information, address St. Martin's Press, 175 Fifth Avenue, New York, N.Y. 10010.

www.stmartins.com

Designed by Omar Chapa

The Library of Congress Cataloging-in-Publication Data is available upon request.

ISBN 978-1-250-09640-1 (trade paperback)
ISBN 978-1-250-09641-8 (e-book)

Our books may be purchased in bulk for promotional, educational, or business use. Please contact your local bookseller or the Macmillan Corporate and Premium Sales Department at 1-800-221-7945, extension 5442, or by e-mail at MacmillanSpecialMarkets@macmillan.com.

First Edition: April 2017

10  9  8  7  6  5  4  3  2  1

*For my readers. I love writing steamy romances for you and giving you a sexy alpha hero to get your pulse racing. Here are two of them, to double your reading pleasure—Rogen Angelini and Vin D'Angelo . . . and the heroine, Jewel Catalano, who has a heart big enough to love them both.*

# ACKNOWLEDGMENTS

I would have been excited to write one billionaire ménage story, but was given the opportunity to write three! The Lovers' Triangle series is a sexy foray into the world of the polyamorous. But beyond the sensuousness and the seductions, there are very real and sometimes raw emotions my characters have to face and fears they must overcome in order to fulfill their hearts' desires. One of my favorite things about working with my editor, Monique Patterson, is that she's very astute when it comes to getting to the heart of the matter in a romance. And when it comes to three characters entangled in that romance, I felt I had the absolute right partner to guide me through the process. So, once again, I offer my gratitude to Miss Patterson—it is always fantastic working with you!

My agent, Sarah Younger, is the one who pitched the initial series idea and wove it into a higher concept with Monique. Something I love about Sarah is that she knows I will do everything in my power to go the extra mile for my editor and for my readers. I deeply appreciate her faith in me, and that she embraces the way I enthusiastically bend and flex with changing romantic elements. This series has been an enthralling one to write that has certainly challenged me—and I've loved every moment of it!

As usual, I have to thank everyone at St. Martin's Press who touches the book, keeps the entire process neat and orderly, and never leaves a tie dangling. From the cover art that I always love to the PR and marketing efforts to keeping all of my editing stages on track, I am always in great hands. You all make it much easier to breathe when I'm under tight deadlines!

Finally, I've met so many new and incredible readers since my first St. Martin's Press series, Burned Deep, launched, and I look forward to hearing from more of you! I write from the heart in hopes of sparking something in the people holding my books in their hands. I also have an amazing family/friend support group standing behind me, and I thank all of you.

This series started out as a three-book deal. I was so happy to pull out an old idea I hadn't fully developed of wine country royalty vying over land in a Montague/Capuletesque feud, and loved writing Rogen, Jewel, and Vin's story. A modern-day Romeo and Juliet saga with a ménage twist! When I was asked to write five spin-off billionaire ménage romances (my Bayfront Billionaires) that are offered in e-book format, I got to expand this universe of hot, dynamic heroes and the heroines who love them. I sincerely hope you enjoy reading about their journeys as much as I've enjoyed writing them!

# THE
# BILLIONAIRES

# ONE

"You realize you're crashing the Angelinis' party, despite having an invitation."

Jewel Catalano glanced up from the gorgeous ecru-colored and gold-embossed gala announcement she held in her hot little hands. A very unexpected gift from her assistant, Cameron Valens, who sat next to her in the back of a limo as they traveled the rising and falling slopes of road that cut through endless acres of ripe, rowed vineyards and tree-lined, grass-covered hills leading to the wine community of River Cross, California. Home to two internationally acclaimed vineyards that had sparked the town's growth and stimulated its economy over the past century: the Catalano winery and the Angelini distillery.

Both cellars of exceptional reputation. Both owners bitter rivals.

"If I'm going to make a major power play for that deadlocked land the Angelinis co-own with my parents," Jewel contended, "this is my only hope for gaining an audience with Gian Angelini and attempting to strike a deal."

"You have a bargaining chip to take into the lion's den?"

Jewel smiled, even though her stomach knotted over how accurate a picture Cameron painted. Yet Jewel truly did have an ace up her sleeve. "Came across it while I was in Paris. I intend to make an offer the Angelinis can't refuse."

She'd spent the past six years trying to ascertain what Gian Angelini didn't have that he might want to get his hands on. Jewel believed she'd *finally* hit upon it.

As a Senior Vice President of Acquisitions for Catalano Enterprises, Jewel thrived on securing rare possessions to help seal her most lucrative deals. Her experience was that transactions didn't always boil down to how much money one offered during negotiations. Sometimes it helped to find whatever unicorn was most elusive to the person on the other side of the table and use that to sweeten the pot.

Luckily, she had help in this area from two lifelong friends, Bayli Styles and Scarlet Drake. Bayli was a research hound, and Scarlet had the uncanny ability—and all the right connections— to track down unique treasures. Jewel just had to provide the scent and the girls picked up the trail.

"You are tenacious. I'll give you that much," Jewel's assistant said in her smoky voice. "Gian Angelini is not a man I'd want to go toe to toe with."

"I'm not exactly looking forward to invading his turf, especially unannounced. But what choice do I have? He hasn't taken any of my calls or answered my e-mails. When we're in a roomful of people, however, he won't be able to ignore me. He might be intimidating as hell, but he has impeccable manners when in the midst of polite society."

"I still wouldn't want to be in your Jimmy Choo shoes."

With a snicker, Jewel said, "I don't blame you. Thanks, by the way, for finagling this invitation from the printer."

"How convenient that I'm sleeping with him." Cameron winked.

"Indeed." Jewel laughed softly. "And I appreciate you bringing all these documents I needed to sign." She handed over the stack of papers and Cameron tucked them into a slim black leather portfolio.

Jewel's assistant had come in from San Francisco, where Catalano Enterprises was headquartered, to meet her at the private hangar on the edge of River Cross that housed CE's corporate jets so that they could catch up on business.

Jewel had been in France for nearly a week, working a different deal to procure the only building left on Paris's stunning Avenue des Lamond not owned by CE. Her father, Anthony Catalano, had plans to develop an even more prestigious Champs-Élysées. She was convinced he wouldn't be satisfied until he'd left his footprint on every major city in the world.

Jewel's main objective was more localized. She didn't need her own Champs-Élysées or Taj Mahal. Just a small slice of heaven that was rightfully hers.

Well, *almost* rightfully hers. For Jewel was heir to property that also belonged to the Angelini estate, making their one and only beneficiary, Rogen, equally entitled.

And it wasn't exactly *a small slice*. The massive acreage Jewel wanted full custody of for her own business purposes stretched between the Catalano estate and the one owned by the Angelinis.

But the tract of land was tied up in messy legalities and a vicious feud between her family and Rogen's. So all that prime real estate sat undisturbed and undeveloped. A complete waste, in Jewel's mind.

A thought that festered 24/7 in the back of her head.

The very reason she was currently in River Cross.

"You really think you can sway Gian Angelini?" Cameron asked. She was an attractive woman of forty-six with sophisticatedly coiffed short brown hair and an eye for fashion.

By contrast, Jewel had long sleek blond hair and sapphire eyes that caught the light in the reflection as her gaze shifted to the side windows while she considered the probability of pulling off this latest endeavor.

The driver of the limo took the turn toward the northwestern portion of the county, winding through the manicured township of stylish boutiques, restaurants, and wine bars, with bistro sets dotting pavered patios. There were plenty of lush, verdant courtyards boasting fountains and freshly varnished park benches.

The sun began its gradual descent on the horizon, casting vibrant shades of blood orange, vermilion, and gold across the landscape, turning the mountain range in the distance into a fiery sentinel looming above the river that ran along the base, then weaving its way through the countryside.

Though Jewel had lived in San Francisco since she was eighteen, she'd always loved the elegantly rustic community of River Cross. Yet as the limo traveled farther north she turned away from the mesmeric scenery—before they passed the Angelini estate and distillery on their way to her family's manor. Her stomach already churned enough over her decision to attend the gala this evening. A tricky, potentially volatile affair that left her on edge and slightly breathless.

She didn't need to torment herself further over what she might encounter when she set foot on Angelini property for the first time in fifteen years. The mere thought called forth voices from the past. Handsome faces. Stolen kisses. Love, longing, and loss.

Trying to reel in emotions that threatened to get the best of her, Jewel returned to her previous conversation with Cameron, saying, "I believe I can get Gian to see that it makes no sense to keep the land in a stranglehold because of one argument." Which had erupted over venomous accusations and tenuous emotions shortly after the Angelinis' young daughter had passed, when Jewel was thirteen. "My parents and Gian and Rose-Marie Angelini used to be the best of friends. Now they despise each other."

"Such a shame. Do you ever speak with their son?"

"Not in years."

Rogen was her age, twenty-eight. They'd been close growing up. More than that, really. He'd been her first . . . *everything*.

But he'd spent half of his life away from River Cross, only having moved back about six months ago, or so the grapevine reported. Actually, there'd been quite a few rumors whispered of late by a high school friend or two of Jewel's, mostly about how Rogen's best friend, Vincent D'Angelo, had returned as well and the two men were currently pleasing several of the pampered "ladies who lunch." It was hinted the men were experts at doing this *at the same time*.

Jewel waved a dismissive hand at the gossips. But, admittedly, certain forbidden thoughts cropped up. She fought their elusive pull, including the old memories creeping in on her now.

She tried to shake the remembrance of her past with Rogen from her head. Yet she couldn't block the mental flash of his vibrant cerulean eyes and wicked grin, which instantly ignited her nerve endings.

Precisely why she didn't allow herself to indulge in reveries of him.

That and the fact that their family situations did not bode well for any sort of wishful reconciliation. Both fathers had held their grudge to such great extent, they'd done everything in their power to separate Jewel and Rogen when they were teenagers. Gian had shipped his son off to the highest-ranking prep school in the country, Trinity, in Manhattan. Jewel had been prohibited from seeing him, though they'd found sequestered moments together when Rogen had flown in for holidays. Until their junior year. That was when the Angelinis had begun vacationing in Europe, not giving Rogen much chance to come home.

For the most part, Jewel had had to rely on the *out of sight, out of mind* mentality . . . or she'd never get past her heartbreak. Both of them. Because her disconnection from Rogen had eventually led her into Vin's arms. That had gone horrifically wrong around graduation. She hadn't seen him since. Didn't speak to him.

And though she'd secretly visited Rogen once at Trinity and then one more time in Italy during a college break, she'd opted to sever the ties with him, too. It'd been excruciating to see each other on such a limited basis. To have to be so sneaky about it. That had never felt right.

Then again, her split from Vin hadn't sat well with her, either. But it was all a complicated mess that had never been straightened out. Just like the family feud that had started with mourning, morphed into misunderstandings, and then exploded into a vindictive backlash—with the two heirs, Rogen and Jewel, caught in the cross fire. And Vin suffering along with them.

Diverting her thoughts as the limo passed through the massive gates of the Catalano estate, she told Cameron, "Take the car back into the city and enjoy a night out with Spence, on me." They wove their way through the plush setting of velvety-green grass, voluptuous trees, and gently flowing streams before pulling under the vast porte cochere of the main house.

The driver opened the door for Jewel.

"I'll see you in the office on Monday morning," she told her assistant.

"Wait." Cameron gingerly clasped Jewel's arm, a hint of warning in her tone. "What about your parents?"

"Not here to grill me over why I'm in River Cross. Thank God. Daddy's plane hasn't landed yet from his trip to Aspen and I arranged a day at the spa for Mother."

"Clever girl," Cameron said with a conspiratorial grin.

Jewel nodded. It was a huge relief her parents wouldn't be around to talk her out of attending a party she wasn't actually invited to. They would make the attempt to thwart her efforts not just because of the difficulty and sensitivity of this impending real estate negotiation—if they suspected anything, that was, because Jewel hadn't told them her plans, they'd come about so quickly— but also because Rogen would be there.

Her breath caught at the prospect of seeing him after so many years. Chased by a blazing fire in her veins that Vin could be on hand as well. He was the family's Chief General Counsel now. She'd read that in the *Wall Street Journal*.

Vin was the last person she wanted to run into this evening. One smug word out of his mouth and she knew her temper would flare. She couldn't afford that. Jewel had to play this hand calmly and coolly. Which basically meant avoiding Vin D'Angelo at all costs.

It also meant she had to continue greasing the wheels in order to get what she wanted. So she told Cameron, "Send over two cases of our Meritage to the Angelinis, my compliments." It was the Catalanos' prized merlot-sauvignon-cabernet blend. "Mrs. Angelini has always favored that variety. We used to provide it for all of her events as a hostess gift. Back in the day."

"Consider everything taken care of." Cameron's manicured fingers slid away, though the concern still rimmed her hazel eyes. "And good luck with your new mission."

"Thank you." Jewel exited the car. Adrenaline over the prospect of coming to acceptable terms with Gian mixed with anxiety over seeing Rogen.

And possibly Vin.

She couldn't argue with the wary voice inside her head that told her this might all be a gigantic mistake on her part. But no one else was making a move on that land. It was high time someone did.

Even if it put her in a prickly situation with three men she wasn't exactly primed and ready to confront . . .

But Jewel lived and breathed the adage of *no guts, no glory*.

She prayed her motto would not fail her tonight!

"If I recall correctly," Vin D'Angelo said to Rogen Angelini as Vin checked his diamond-studded cuff links to ensure they were secure, "there's a gala about to commence in half an hour. And you're still in jeans. *Dusty* jeans and boots, to be exact." He sniffed the air and added, "You also smell like the stables."

"Smart-ass." Rogen dropped his saddlebags on the kitchen table in his three-bedroom house on the Angelini estate and extracted several containers. "I was out riding the adjacent property, collecting more soil samples to keep testing what grapes will grow best on that land. What hybrids I can work with."

"First of all," Vin said in his deep, lawyerly voice, "there's a *no trespassing without written consent* clause in the contracts your parents and the Catalanos signed when they jointly purchased the property. It even applies to you."

Rogen smirked.

"Second," Vin continued, unfazed, "Anthony Catalano will never consent to a sale—and the binding agreements specifically state that Catalanos can only sell their portion of the land to Angelinis and vice versa. Which clearly is never going to happen. So testing the soil is pretty much a waste of time."

"Doesn't hurt to be prepared for any opportunity that might come along, my friend." Rogen had wanted to grow on that property since he could walk the lot line.

Perhaps a slight exaggeration, but still. It was his dream.

"The only thing you need to be concerned about right now is this ostentatious shindig your mother is throwing," Vin reminded him. "There are over six hundred VIPs from San Diego to San Francisco—and all the Sans and Santas in between—about to fill the mansion and spill out onto the grounds. The Golden Boy son needs to look a little less Lone Ranger and a lot more James Bond."

"I'll leave the latter to you. You've got that whole Pierce Brosnan thing going on."

Vin stood six-foot-four and had dark, strategically tousled hair. He had deep-green eyes and broad shoulders women seemed to go for.

Rogen was his direct opposite. A couple inches shorter, though still over six feet, with short, dark blond hair and blue eyes. He currently sported two days' of stubble along his strong jawline. He was solidly built and athletic, whereas Vin was more sculpted in a refined, sophisticated way.

"I do look damn good in a tux," Vin conceded as he admired himself in the mirror mounted on the wall beyond the kitchen table.

"Spare me," Rogen said, the sarcasm dripping from his tone. "Your ego won't fit in this house with the both of us."

His best friend chuckled under his breath. "Good point."

"Who'd you decide to bring as the date du jour?" Rogen asked.

Vin flashed a mischievous grin. "As it turns out, Holly McCormick is back in town. She'll be on my arm this evening."

"And no doubt in your bed."

"Feel free to join us. You know how insatiable she is."

"The woman doesn't have an off switch."

"She certainly enjoys her multiple orgasms. And we enjoy giving them to her." He winked.

"Tempting," Rogen mused. "Chances are very good I'll be taking you up on that offer."

Several months ago, he and Vin had swapped their corporate offices at Angelini, Inc. headquarters in Tuscany for ones in River Cross. That was when they'd met Holly and spent one overly decadent night in her *casita*, pleasuring her until the sun came up. And she'd still wanted more.

The ménage had been a going-away present for her, at both men's suggestion. Holly hadn't even batted a lash at the risqué proposition. She was a curvy redhead with a hearty sexual appetite and zero inhibitions, which had made for a very memorable evening, with Rogen and Vin working in tandem to get her off. Repeatedly.

Though Holly was not, by any stretch of the imagination, their first foray into threesome territory. Being such close friends all their lives and having such vastly different personalities and dispositions lent to their special talent and innate desire to share a woman in that way.

The discovery of their particular gift had come sophomore year at Yale. Rather accidentally, since Rogen had been at the library when Vin had gotten Amber Halston between the sheets. Rogen had slipped into the dorm room to grab some study notes just as Amber had been hitting *her* high notes. Things had escalated from there.

Both men had maintained a modicum of discretion with their forbidden affairs in college. When they'd started working in the Italy offices after Rogen received his MBA and Vin graduated from law school, they'd come upon several gorgeous European women who were more than amenable to a ménage à trois.

Both Rogen and Vin had immediately realized that making a woman come with two pairs of hands and lips on her body and two cocks to satisfy her was a heady rush. And they were damn good at racking up the orgasms.

But always on a temporary basis.

"Holly's aware you're not looking for any sort of commitment, right?" Rogen had to lob the cautionary sentiment out there, since women flocked to Vin's commanding presence and latched on quickly. Held on tight.

Rogen had his fair share of admirers, but he'd been told on numerous occasions that he exuded a razor vibe that apparently told women he wasn't interested in a permanent love connection without him even saying a word.

"I trust my reputation precedes me," Vin said. "I have neither the time nor the desire to get involved. In fact, this is the first night I've taken off in weeks. Your family keeps me busy, no doubt there."

"Dad doesn't believe in resting on his laurels. *Conquer the world* is his current mission."

"Are you sure it's not to rank even higher on the *Forbes* billionaires list?"

"It does annoy him that he flip-flops with Anthony Catalano on that damn list."

"Well, I'll bet he's feeling a bit of vindication, throwing another extravaganza the Catalanos aren't invited to."

"They wouldn't come if they were invited, out of sheer principle. Neither side cares about appearances when it comes to this feud, which I think everyone has long since forgotten how it even started." He shook his head. "It'd be nice if they just fucking got over it already."

"That'd certainly make things easier on the heirs." Vin scowled. "Or maybe not. You and Jewel are nothing but a rose garden filled with thorns."

Rogen didn't allow himself to travel the path of wishful thinking when it came to her. Despite wanting to see her. Jewel Catalano lived in the city and, from what he'd heard, she didn't visit River Cross all that often.

A moot point, really. They were long over. Still, Rogen would be lying to himself if he denied she was the reason he didn't date any more seriously than Vin did. Both men had been hooked on her in one way or another since they were kids. And both men knew all that had ever brought to either of their lives was more complication.

Vin didn't typically speak of Jewel, and Rogen respected his privacy on the matter. Rogen had no idea what had happened between the two of them after he had been sent to Trinity, a year after the dispute over the untouched land had flared. The exile from California had happened right around the time Rogen and Jewel had fallen in love—a huge source of contention for their parents, who'd proven they would do anything to keep the two away from each other. And had succeeded, for the most part.

Rogen had his suspicions as to how Jewel and Vin's friendship had progressed after he'd left but wasn't really sure he wanted to know the actual details. Vin's intensity when the subject came up was a loud and clear warning for Rogen to avoid the topic entirely. Vin clearly felt the same. Hence the scowl.

Rogen said, "I'd better get around. I'll see you in a little while."

"I'm taking one of the limos to pick up Holly. We'll be along shortly."

"Don't get that particular party started without me." He grinned.

Vin chuckled again, on his way out the door. Rogen hit the shower and shaved. As Chief Operating Officer of Angelini, Inc., which housed its auxiliary offices within the estate, Rogen was usually on the clean-cut side. But he didn't mind the scruffy jaw when working the vineyard or doing his soil testing.

He dressed in an Armani tux, then raked a hand through his hair, making it stand a little on end. He took an all-terrain Rhino to the service entrance of the mansion and joined the festivities as they were getting under way.

He grabbed a glass of champagne from a passing server. There were numerous food stations and seafood towers, plus hot- and cold-passed hors d'oeuvres. Free-flowing champagne and the distillery's top-notch cognacs.

A pianist and a harpist were set up in one of the courtyards. A steel-drum band played in the gardens. An eighteen-piece orchestra took requests on the event lawn. And a contemporary band rocked the grand ballroom.

Tree trunks outside were all lit with clear twinkling lights. Candles burned in hurricanes and decorative lanterns. Inside, the chandeliers glowed brilliantly, sending glittery rays across the cream-colored marble floors. All of the rooms designated for entertaining flowed into one another, making it easy for groups to mix and mingle.

Rogen greeted guests, accepted pecks on the cheek, shook

hands, and chatted everyone up as he moved toward the spacious great room by the entryway. There he dropped off his empty glass and was served another before strolling closer to the foyer to ensure there was a welcoming committee at the front door.

He drew up short when he caught sight of a striking blonde wearing a one-shouldered sparkling dress in ice blue that set off her sapphire irises. She stood on the landing of the steps that led down into the great room, adjacent to the twin staircases that stretched and curved to the second floor and beyond to two more floors.

Rogen did a double take. He absorbed the sight of her from head to toe, including the slit in the left side of her dress that started at her slim ankle and ran clear up to the top of her shapely thigh, where a diamond-encrusted brooch was pinned.

His cock sprang to life. His pulse shot through the roof.

It was *her*.

Rogen handed over his crystal flute to another server and worked his way through the crowd, his heart hammering. He took the three steps up to the landing and asked, "Are you a mirage?"

Jewel gave him a beautiful bright-white smile. "Not that I'm aware of."

"Because I've fantasized about you appearing out of thin air when I least expect it."

"Sorry to catch you off-guard. It couldn't be helped."

"Do you hear me complaining?"

Her smile softened. "I wasn't sure how you'd feel about me showing up."

"Like I just took a dive out of an airplane and am free-falling without a chute."

"Interesting." She stared up at him, her big blue eyes shimmering under the chandeliers. "I know the feeling." Her voice was low and evocative. Breathy.

"Good." He mentally shook his head. Maybe it wasn't so good they still reacted so strongly to each other. Especially after what

Vin had said about the thorns. Rogen changed the subject. "I don't recall seeing your name on the guest list."

"Nor would you. I'm crashing. For a good cause, I promise."

"I don't care that you're crashing," Rogen said with conviction in his tone. "It's fucking incredible to see you, Jewel."

*So much for changing the subject . . .*

But, damn—it'd been seven long years since he'd last seen her.

His gaze slid over her from head to toe and back up. Slowly, as he once again took in the long, sculpted leg on display, the gentle rounding of her hips, the dip of her waist where the material clung to her feminine curves, her enticing breasts, her bare shoulders.

He soaked in all that creamy, silky-looking skin. The long column of her neck. Her full, glossy lips, which were slightly parted as she drew in wispy breaths.

Shiny blond hair was swept away from her delicate features to fall in a sleek curtain between her shoulder blades. Her dark irises continued to glow seductively.

Rogen's chest pulled tight. His cock pulsed with erratic beats.

"You're sensational," he said, completely blown away by the sight of her.

The corners of her mouth quivered. A hint of mist covered her eyes. "I'm not really sure I prepared myself enough for a reunion."

Her fingers curled around her silver satin clutch as though that would keep her from touching him.

Frustration tore through him. Rogen *burned* for her touch. Instantly. Fervently.

"Jesus, Jewel," he murmured. "You could stop a man's heart looking like that."

"Rogen . . ." She stared deep into his eyes. Searching them. Likely looking for all the elusive answers even he'd never found when it came to the two of them.

"I've missed you," they said in unison. Each took a stride closer to the other, then instinctively stepped back.

Rogen let out a low growl, annoyed with himself. "We're not fucking teenagers, Jewel. If I want to hug you, it's no one's goddamn business but mine."

"I know. You're right. Of course."

He closed the gap. His head dipped and his lips brushed over her cheek. He inhaled her rich, sultry scent. And everything inside of Rogen went haywire.

"Fuck," he muttered. Moved a bit away from her. Shoved a hand through his hair. His gaze roved her body again and his jaw clenched.

Jewel seemed to swallow down a lump of emotion before she said, "You look good. C-O-O of Angelini, Inc., suits you. So does the tux."

"I prefer my jeans, but what can you do?" He tried to lighten the suddenly tense moment. Yet every muscle in his body was rigid with wanting her. That rapidly. That painfully.

She gave him another pretty smile, though it looked a bit strained. Like she felt the electric current of their unwavering attraction—and the tormenting tension it elicited.

"How'd the California cowboy make it through an East Coast prep school and Ivy League college?" she asked.

"That's the last thing I want to talk about." He stepped toward her again, held her gaze, and continued the free fall. "Tell me why you're here. And it'd better have something to do with being desperate to see me."

Desire flashed in her eyes. Along with something deeper, darker. Something elusive. Alluring. *Soul stirring.*

Yet a heartbeat later—

"Yes, Jewel. Please do tell us why you're here."

Rogen winced at his mother's smooth, cultured voice shattering the private moment he'd shared with Jewel. Too fleeting a span of time.

His father added, "This is quite a surprise, young lady."

Jewel's soft features hardened—a soldier preparing for battle. Regret replaced the desire in her sapphire irises. She appeared reluctant to drag her gaze from Rogen but turned her attention to his parents. "I apologize for the intrusion. I need to speak with you, Mr. Angelini. It's important."

Rogen's parents exchanged a curious look.

His mother said, "I trust everyone's well at your estate?"

"Yes, of course. We're all perfectly healthy. I hope the same goes for your family."

"It does," his mother assured Jewel. "And thank you for the meritage. That was . . . considerate." That last word seemed to push the boundaries of civility where Rogen's mother was concerned.

Jewel pretended not to notice. "I was pleased to hear that you were entertaining. Your parties have always been the talk of the Valley."

"I plan to host them more regularly."

"That's wonderful."

Though the conversation was cordial, there was no mistaking the underlying hostility on his parents' part, the contained aggression and bitterness exuding from them. It infuriated Rogen that they directed their angst toward Jewel. Like him, she was but a victim of circumstance when it came to the dispute.

But Rogen's admiration for her surged as Jewel squared her shoulders and lifted her chin. She boldly told his father, "I only need a few minutes of your time. Then I'll leave."

Rogen didn't like the sound of that. Though he was dying to know what business Jewel was here to discuss, he was mostly agitated that she intended to make a hasty retreat.

Hoping to stall her exit, he suggested, "Why don't I get us all some champagne?"

He headed off for a tray of glasses, his mind whirling over how to get Jewel to stick around awhile longer.

This was the first time since he'd returned to River Cross that he'd had the chance to see her, to talk to her. He sure as hell wouldn't let the opportunity to spend more time with her slip through his fingers.

His family and a fifteen-year feud be damned!

# TWO

Jewel gave herself a quick mental pep talk to try to bring her anxiety down. She wasn't sure what was more unnerving—Rogen looking too stunning for words in his tux, the fact that he'd kissed her and he exuded raw, sensual male heat, or the stare-down from his parents.

*Deep breaths, Jewel. You can do this.*

She respectfully asked, "May we step into your office, Mr. Angelini?"

Mrs. Angelini looked on the verge of protesting, but her husband raised a hand to stop her and said, "Ten minutes are all I can spare, Jewel. I have guests."

"Of course." She slid a glance to the matriarch of the family, her wheat-colored hair elegantly styled, her attractive face perfectly made up. Rose-Marie Angelini was a slim, statuesque woman who favored blue dresses and always dripped diamonds. Her husband was a sturdy sort, as tall as Rogen, with dark blond hair that had grayed at the temples. Gian Angelini was handsome in his own right but didn't hold a candle to the rugged good looks of his son.

*That* man had an earthy quality to him that made Jewel want to strip him bare and crawl all over him.

But that was currently neither here nor there.

*Focus!*

She'd won the opportunity she'd brazenly come for. She couldn't afford to spoil it by getting lost in thoughts of Rogen naked and sinking deep into her.

Which spawned a dull ache and a slow burn that spread from her belly to her core. Her pussy clenched with memories of being filled and stretched by Rogen as he set a sexy, enticing pace that always made her lose herself in the feel of him, the smell of him. Her love for him.

But that was all in the past.

*Come on, Jewel. Pull yourself together.*

She fought the allure of Rogen. Her sudden need for him. Fully realizing that, indeed, she had made a tragic mistake by coming this evening. She danced much too close to the flame where he was concerned. But at least she'd scored an audience with Mr. Angelini.

*That* was the ultimate goal—not ending up in Rogen's bed at the end of the night.

Because that would never happen, she told herself. No matter how tempting he was.

She made another apology to Mrs. Angelini for the interruption and followed Gian through the maze of marbled corridors to the back of the mansion.

The last time Jewel had been here was right after nine-year-old Taylor Angelini had died. The funeral service had been heart wrenching, most of it spent with Jewel standing graveside between Rogen and Vin, the three holding hands, not even trying to fight back tears.

During the wake in this very house, they'd left the adults and the other kids to escape to Rogen's room and put the bleak atmosphere behind them. As always, they'd settled on the big bed, Rogen and Jewel listening to music, Vin reading a book. Vin was always reading a book.

Jewel recalled how stark and grim the mansion had seemed when she and Vin had left in the morning, having fallen asleep in Rogen's room, exhausted from the emotional turmoil. The house staff had appeared somber. There'd been a lot of watery eyes and quiet consoling. Above that, the mansion had a fragile air to it. The entire place had felt brittle, like they were all standing on a treacherously thin patch of ice that could crack at any moment. Pull everyone under.

That was very reason Jewel was pleased the Angelinis had eventually begun entertaining once more. It'd taken over a decade for them to host a party, but Jewel supposed it was difficult to hear laughter echo through the vast hallways and know it would never again be your daughter's.

An incredibly dismal thought that sat heavy in Jewel's heart to this day. Yet another one she had to rise above for the sake of her business this evening.

Gian gestured for her to precede him into his enormous study, with sturdy bronze-colored leather furniture scattered about, its heady scent permeating the room along with the aroma of expensive tobacco.

He took to his chair behind his massive mahogany desk, clasped his fingers on top of the old-fashioned blotter, and wore a formidable expression that nearly made her knees knock together.

She drew in a deep breath. This was unlike any negotiation Jewel had ever entered. First, her father had no idea what she was up to—and wouldn't be pleased about being kept in the dark, or over the fact that she was here at the home of his sworn enemy. Second, the man currently brooding over her audacious move truly did intimidate the hell out of her.

Jewel held fast to a bit of false bravado and said, "I'd like to speak with you about the land our families jointly own, and something I believe I can give you that might encourage you to sell to us."

Gian let out a low chuckle that basically indicated she was a foolish girl.

Naturally, that sparked her ire.

She told him, "I happen to have the correct bargaining chip." She whipped her iPhone from her purse and set it on the desk in front of him, the photo of a gorgeous crystal decanter on the screen, courtesy of Bayli's research efforts and Scarlet's connections with auction houses and global black markets.

Jewel said, "That's the very last of the Angelini scotch produced by your ancestors' first distillery before it burned to the ground." Back in the early 1800s.

The premium whisky was currently preserved in a one-of-a-kind blown-glass decanter crafted by a renowned Italian artist from Murano. Only three bottles of the scotch had been made—all from spirits dating back to the time of the French and American revolutions.

The other two bottles were long gone, as Gian knew. She'd heard him speak of the coveted scotch at a dinner party many moons ago. Back when Taylor was still alive, the two families had held numerous lucrative business partnerships with each other and everyone had gotten along.

Continuing, Jewel said, "The scotch was sold at auction by Sotheby's for just over a million dollars to an undisclosed bidder. He wasn't you."

"I'm well aware of that, Jewel." Gian's jaw tightened the way Rogen's always did when he was restless or contemplative.

She pulled in another steadying breath at Gian's instant aggravation. She was poking the cagey lion with a stick, out of sheer necessity.

"It was suggested an error on the auction house's part kept you from winning that decanter," she said. "Though any wrongdoing couldn't be proven. And your subsequent lawsuit did not make you the victor. However, that scotch *does* belong to your family, Mr. Angelini—it's part of your heritage. And I can get it for you."

He glared at her as though she'd grown a third eye and just declared she could achieve world dominance with the snap of her fingers.

Jewel fought the outrageous thundering of her heart. She curled her fingers into her palms so that Gian Angelini wouldn't see them tremble.

It took him some time to respond. When his answer eventually came, it was simple and finite. "Impossible."

Jewel was not deterred. Here was where she excelled in the Acquisitions division of Catalano Enterprises.

"You say that because you've already tried to buy the decanter. But, Mr. Angelini . . ." She slipped into a chair before his desk and speared him with an earnest, insistent look. "You know as well as I do that anyone who has a mil in spare change to purchase scotch they won't drink, because it's meant to be put on display like a trophy, isn't interested in how much it's worth monetarily. There is no true cash value that can be placed on something so rare. The eccentric person who bid on and won that scotch would only part with it if enticed by a new possession that would yield even more significant bragging rights."

His gray eyes narrowed. "What are you suggesting, Jewel?"

She had his attention—had clearly piqued his interest. She intended to keep it.

"I've done a hell of a lot of digging," she told him. "With a hell of a lot of help. I know the identity of the winner of that auction item and I know there's something out there that he wants even more than the scotch. But, like you, he can't get his hands on it. Unless he has something substantial to barter with."

Gian gazed at her for several suspended seconds. Then he unclasped his hands and sat back in his big leather chair. "I'm listening."

Jewel didn't waste a second. Jumped right in. "It turns out that this gentleman is an art aficionado but can't procure two rare paintings that would complete one of his priceless collections. My team has tracked down the owner of those paintings, and I know what *he* desires—something currently out of his reach as well. I can make the deals, connect the dots, and put that decanter of scotch in *your* trophy case. I've done it before, with much less motivation."

Their gazes remained locked. He didn't say a word.

"I can do it again."

Gian took endless minutes to consider her proposal. They'd gone well over the time he'd allotted her, but he didn't seem to notice or care. His mind apparently churned over the possibility she'd presented him.

Jewel sat perfectly still, riveted, her heart pounding. Fast. Ridiculously fast.

Still not speaking, but schooling his features so that he didn't give away a goddamn thing, Gian pushed back his chair and paced behind his desk.

Jewel watched him. Her heartbeats wouldn't slow and her fingers coiled into the arms of the chair.

The fact that this man deliberated over her daring proposal encouraged Jewel. Conversely, she wondered if he was trying to figure out some way to break it to her that she was all kinds of crazy for coming to him and that he also intended to spill the beans to her father.

But then Gian drew up short, gripped the back of his chair, and pinned her with an intent look.

He took her *seriously*!

Yet no sigh of relief escaped her. Because he hadn't delivered his verdict.

She fought the urge to gnaw her lower lip—a nervous habit.

A couple more minutes passed.

Finally—*finally*—Gian Angelini told her, "I'm intrigued. What is your full offer?"

She hastily retrieved a small, sealed envelope from her clutch and placed it on the leather blotter on his desk. "I think you'll find that very appealing, in addition to the scotch."

He snatched the packet and slid a silver letter opener under the flap. Extracting the card, he studied it while Jewel's pulse raged in her ears, because she wanted this deal to go through so badly.

Gian made her suffer further as he seemed to run numbers through his mind, debate this or that.

Pure torture.

*He's torturing me.*

And for what? What the hell had she ever done to him that he'd be this cruel to her? That he'd drag out a decision so that she was just about to—

"You get me the scotch, young lady," he suddenly said, "and I'll get you the three signatures required on the bill of sale for the land. Mine, my wife's . . . *and* Rogen's."

Jewel's heart nearly burst from her chest.

She'd done it!

Leaping to her feet, she managed to ask, "I have your word?"

"Yes, Jewel." He extended his hand to her, across the desk. "You have my word."

They shook. Excitement coursed through her, wild and effervescent.

Granted, it wasn't a done deal until she'd fulfilled her end of the bargain, but it was absolutely the "in" she needed. And, sure, her father would have heart palpitations over how much money it would cost, in the end, to acquire that land.

But it would be theirs. Which was what he'd wanted for nearly two decades.

"Thank you, Mr. Angelini," she said in the most professional tone she could muster, given that her body practically vibrated from exhilaration. "I promise, you won't be disappointed. Give me two weeks, tops. And I'll be back."

There was a shrewd look on his face—as though a part of him doubted she could accomplish her side of the transaction. Yet admiration rimmed his eyes. She'd earned his respect.

Jewel collected her iPhone and left the office, floating on a cloud.

She'd taken a huge risk by coming here—and it had miraculously paid off. This was her biggest coup d'état to date. Nothing could bring her down even a single notch. Nothing could taint her euphoria in the tiniest way.

Not tonight.

"Well, well, well," came the all-too-familiar, deliciously rich and intimate voice of Vin D'Angelo. Stopping her dead in her tracks.

Vin was the exception. The only thing that could burst her bubble.

"So, the prodigal daughter returns to River Cross. And goddamn, aren't you a sight to behold, Jewel Catalano?"

Her head whipped around. Her heart launched into her throat so that she couldn't speak. Whereas seeing Rogen after all this time had left Jewel emotionally charged and drowning in desire, seeing the devilishly handsome Vin ignited an inferno, not solely related to lust. Though that did play a major part.

Like Rogen, he was a mesmeric force with which to be reckoned.

And one look at him catapulted Jewel into a past where love and hate walked hand in hand.

Vin stood midway down one of the grand staircases, hands shoved into the slant pockets of his tailored tux.

Jewel glared up at him.

With fire and fury in her eyes.

A powerful combination. An erotic one that complemented her drop-dead gorgeous appearance. He unabashedly absorbed every inch of luscious female, decked to the nines in a stunning gown that did everything to show off her sensational body—and make him insanely hard. In an instant.

Not necessarily a good thing.

Lust mixed with the bittersweet taste of wanting something he knew he could never have. The only woman he'd ever burned to possess. The one who belonged, heart and soul, to his best friend.

Her body, on the other hand . . .

Well, he actually had possessed that for a time. Too fleeting a span of time, but long and scorchingly hot enough for it to be ingrained in his brain. Entrenched within him.

And seeing her now . . . It did things to him. Made him think of all the ways he'd once pleasured her.

But . . . *uh-huh.*

He mentally shook his head.

*No need to have* those *thoughts.*

She was the one female considered off-limits when it came to his and Rogen's penchant for satisfying a woman at the same time. They'd never even discussed it; neither had dared to suggest it. Sharing Jewel was an unspoken no-no. A completely forbidden notion.

Even if it would be the ultimate threesome for the two men.

But aside from the inherent complications related to entangled feelings and relationships, Rogen didn't really know what had gone on between Vin and Jewel after he'd left for Trinity. No one knew, that Vin was aware of. Perhaps Bayli and Scarlet. As far as everyone in River Cross was concerned, she'd been Rogen's. *Only* Rogen's.

All of this sparked Vin's own fury.

But he tamped down the edgy sensation and, instead, shot for nonchalance. He wouldn't let Jewel see how deeply, how quickly, she had affected him after all this time. He had to play this cool.

So he gave her a slow grin and continued to admire the view. She looked a bit dazed at the sight of him, a bit off-kilter as those plump, glossy lips of hers parted and she inhaled sharply.

Glad to know he wasn't the only one suffering the side effects of an unexpected reunion.

Forcing a neutral tone so desire and long-buried emotions didn't betray him, he said, "Look who's all grown-up."

*And absolutely breathtaking.*

Jewel crossed the marbled entryway to the first step. She started a gradual, sexy ascent toward him, her hips swaying provocatively, the flash of bare legs driving him wild.

Vin added, "Very nice, Jewel." His gaze fixated on her ample chest, rising and falling with her agitation, or excitement. Maybe both? The fact that she evoked *his* excitement and need so vehemently made him just frustrated enough to goad, "You've finally filled out in all the right places."

She'd been a bit on the skinny side as a teen, though still striking enough to star in all of his fantasies. Now she was—

*Fuck.*

She was more riveting than anything he'd ever known. And the constant, fiery yearning for her that had roared through his veins for longer than he could remember was just as bright and searing tonight. More so, he couldn't deny. Because they weren't eighteen-year-olds exploring mutual attraction and trying to sate raging hormones.

This was something altogether different. The heat flaring in Jewel's eyes as she feasted on him while cresting the last step told Vin the magnetism was just as strong on her end. Whether she wanted it to be or not.

Truly the bane of her existence as much as his.

Knowing how to keep the upper hand, his grin turned cocky.

He said, "My fantasy woman come to life. Aren't I suddenly the lucky bastard?"

Jewel was the epitome of *the one who got away*. His fault as much as it was hers, which had left them at an impasse years ago. Something that ate at him like a piranha trying to consume his very soul.

Her gaze flitted from him to the second-floor mezzanine and then back.

Vin fought a scowl. He suspected Holly stood there, likely using a compact from her handbag to apply a fresh coat of lipstick after giving him a stellar blow job on the private terrace adjacent to his office.

A hint of betrayal crept in on him. Not because he and Holly actually *had* "started the party" without Rogen—she'd been quite the eager beaver.

No, this particular tension was wrapped wholly around Jewel. But Vin reminded himself that he had nothing to feel guilty about when it came to being with another woman. Holly, in this case. He and Jewel weren't a couple. Hadn't been for some time.

Yet the slight watering of her eyes as her gaze held his—and several strides separated them—made his gut twist.

"Jewel—" His teeth ground. What the fuck was he supposed to say to her?

They'd always been the equivalent of two ships passing in the night. Potentially destined for something great, but always hindered by circumstance. Her endless love for Rogen. Her decision to live in San Francisco rather than River Cross. Her anger toward Vin, which she obviously had not let go of.

She didn't give him the chance to discern how he was supposed to mend the fence—if that was even possible. She stepped closer, raised her hand, and slapped him soundly across the face.

No lie, it stung like hell.

But as Vin hastily recovered, he realized if she'd hurt him, she'd hurt herself tenfold.

"Jesus," he whispered, and reached for her hand.

Tears flooded her eyes.

"Jewel. *Shit*," he hissed out.

He held her hand gently in both of his, her palm engulfed by his larger ones as she visibly reeled. Tried to pull in a full breath. Trembled from head to toe.

"That was stupid," he scolded in a low tone so that only she heard.

"Asshole," came her quiet retort.

His jaw tightened a moment. Then Vin said, "Yes. But always for a reason." He lifted her hand to his mouth and tenderly kissed her reddened flesh.

It looked as though she still couldn't catch her breath. She stared at him, clearly taken by surprise. And . . . *touched* . . . if the softening of her expression was any indication.

One corner of his mouth jerked up. "I always did like your feisty spirit."

She was at a loss for words as their gazes held. Then she came around. A bit too jarringly.

"Don't suddenly play nice, Vin." She yanked her hand from his. "I've wasted more time trying to figure out your game than I care to admit. It's just not worth it."

She whirled around and stalked off, making her way so quickly down the stairs that Vin's body went on high alert in preparation for having to rescue her from a horrific Scarlett O'Hara fall. But she made it safely to the foyer and continued on her way, out of his sight.

Under his breath, Vin murmured, "There never was a game."

His head dropped and he shook it slowly.

She hated him.

He knew why.

But again . . . he wasn't the only one to blame.

From behind him, Vin heard Holly approach. His head snapped up—and he snapped out of his sudden funk, not interested in anyone discovering he'd never gotten over his first and only love.

Holly said in her whisky voice, "What a spectacle the two of you make. Enough fireworks and drama to excite innocent bystanders."

"There's nothing innocent about you," he reminded her.

"So true," she drawled, a southern belle from Savannah. "I am just *dying* to know who that was."

"Jewel Catalano."

"Ah. The wine heiress Rogen has reportedly pined over." She sighed wistfully. "Forever and a day."

Vin's body turned even more rigid. There was nothing convenient about best friends falling in love with the same woman. Even if their desire for Jewel had never impacted their friendship—because it had never fully been laid on the table—Rogen had to have known that Vin's interest in Jewel had gone well beyond childhood pals. There'd always been an underlying current of sexual and emotional tension amongst the trio. Something none of them had ever discussed. It was just easier that way. Safer. Saner.

"She's definitely peeved," Holly continued. "What'd you do to get on her shit list?"

*Breathe?*

He fought a growl. Then confessed, "I stood her up on prom night."

Holly let out a hearty laugh. "Good Lord, Vin. Why would you do such a thing? That's sacrilege in the mind of a teenage girl."

"So I've learned."

Holly was quiet a moment, then said, "I don't get it. Why's she still so upset? That was ten years ago, right?"

"The woman knows how to hold a grudge. Runs in her family."

"Apparently with the Angelinis as well." Holly whistled softly. "'Hell hath no fury' and all that. But holy Christ . . . Isn't she quite the tigress?"

"You have no idea."

And now Vin was tormented with the rush of memories of naked bodies entwined and hips bucking. Jewel moaning and begging for more as he explored every conceivable way in which to pleasure her. Took her hard and fast, with no boundaries established. Owning her in the only way he could—the one way Rogen had not. Because even though Rogen had been her first, he'd never fucked her like Vin had.

And desperately wanted to again.

*No.* It was worse than that. Because between his last time with Jewel and seeing her this evening he'd learned enough about how he and Rogen could satisfy her *together.*

The ultimate fantasy.

Which, despite it being completely inconceivable, was now rooted deep in his mind. Lodged in his soul.

*Goddamn it.*

Rogen caught sight of Jewel as she wove through the crowd, briefly greeting the guests she knew yet decidedly on a mission. Though she wore a brave face, he could see sheer agony in her eyes.

What the hell had happened between her and his father? And why had she been so adamant about seeing Gian tonight—after all this time?

Rogen met her at one of the bars as she asked for ice. The tuxedo-clad bartender used silver tongs to place several cubes in a doubled-up napkin and passed the tidy packet to her. Jewel placed it in her palm and squeezed.

"What's going on?" Rogen asked.

Jewel just shook her head.

He said to the bartender, "Send someone out to the terrace with two cognacs. The alcove on the far side of the library, by the patio doors."

"Certainly, sir."

Rogen gently placed a hand at the small of Jewel's back and silently directed her through the opened wall of floor-to-ceiling pocket doors, across the terrace, and to a private spot shrouded by rich, blooming foliage. The intimate space only dimly illuminated with golden up-lighting edging the garden that abutted the veranda. Thick vines wound along the black wrought-iron railing and the faint scent of jasmine in bloom wafted on a gentle breeze.

"What happened?" he demanded in a quiet voice.

She sucked in a breath, then simply said, "Vin."

Rogen's anger flared—or perhaps it was alpha tendencies? A natural instinct where Jewel was concerned. The only time they ever truly kicked in with a woman. "What'd he do to you?"

"This time, it's not what he did to me. It's what *I* did to him."

Rogen's brow crooked.

Jewel rolled her eyes. "I slapped him. Hard."

"Oh, fuck. That wasn't smart."

"No shit." Her gaze dropped to her hand holding the ice. "But he deserved it. I couldn't resist."

"Christ, Jewel. What went on between the two of you?"

Her attention shifted to the server who approached and dropped off the cognac on one of the glass end tables accompanying the outdoor sectional.

Rogen collected the snifters and offered one to Jewel. She took it with her good hand and sipped slowly.

Then she said, "This is incredibly helpful, thank you."

"You still look a little flushed."

"Vin pisses me off."

"After all this time?"

She sighed. "His very existence just makes me . . . *crazed*." She ground out the last word.

Rogen's chuckle was a strained one, holding no humor. "He's always known how to push your buttons. But the two of you are . . . ?" His brow rose again with curiosity.

"We aren't *anything*, Rogen. Don't conjure any delusions. He walked out on me, without a word, without the chance for discussion. With no explanation. So . . . That's that. And honestly, it was so long ago that—"

"You should be over it by now?" he offered and challenged at the same time.

Jewel's dark blue irises clouded. "I should be over a lot of things by now." Gazing up at him, she said, "Clearly, I'm not meant to be freed from the past."

"Jewel." Rogen downed a big gulp of cognac. The alcohol that seared his insides came nowhere close to the sizzling sensation of Jewel standing so near that he breathed in her captivating scent and his body flamed with the intense desire to shed his tux and her dress and finally feel her supple skin and soft curves against his hard body.

"I know I shouldn't have just popped in without warning," she confessed, her tone compelling. "But if I had told someone I was coming, I fear I never would have made it through the front doors. And it was imperative that I speak with your father." With another shake of her head, she added, "Unfortunately, I've turned everything upside down for you, me, and Vin. I swear there's some cosmic force dedicated to keeping the three of us in constant turmoil whenever we're together."

"I think the collective nemesis is a bit more localized. Our parents have done a great job of derailing our association in every form it's taken. Vin's been stuck in the middle."

"There's so much anger between me and him."

"And what's between us?" Rogen softly commanded. "Because the second I saw you, Jewel, it was like a jump start to a dead battery—and I had no idea my heart was the dead battery."

Her eyelids fluttered closed. "Rogen."

"Come on, Jewel," he urged as he cupped her elbow and coaxed her toward him. "Don't fuck around here. You feel it, too, right?"

Her eyes flew open. "*Of course*," she said with conviction. Tears crested the rims. "It's the very reason I've avoided River Cross all this time. The very reason I rarely ever come home. When I do," she told him with unmistakable agony in her tone as fat drops tumbled down her cheeks, "I always, *always* look the other way as we pass the distillery and this estate. I can't stand to think about what exists beyond those huge wrought-iron gates that's so far out of my reach. You, Rogen." She stared hard, didn't blink. "*And* Vin."

# THREE

This evening was taking all kinds of wayward turns.

Jewel's heart felt constricted, as though a big fist squeezed it tight. Her breathing had yet to return to normal. From the moment she'd walked into the mansion and almost straight into Rogen's arms, she'd been on the roller-coaster ride of her life—and couldn't get her emotions, her physical responses, or her pulse under control.

Breaking their intense gaze, she took a long sip of cognac. Then another. Her hand shook.

"Jewel," he ground out in apparent frustration over her slight retreat. The reprieve she needed from the razors slicing through her, bringing back past pains that suddenly felt fresh and raw.

Rogen whisked away some of her tears from one cheek. Then he palmed the side of her face and his thumb swept away more from the other.

His head dipped and his lips grazed her temple as he said, "You're killing me here, sweetheart."

A small cry wrenched from somewhere deep within her.

"I know it got difficult among the three of us," he murmured. "I'm sorry it hurt so much when I left for Trinity."

"And every day thereafter," she told him. "Vin helped me through it. For a little while. Then he just . . . disappeared."

"I remember he went off the grid at the end of senior year. I didn't hear from him for months. He never told me what that was all about. Just said he had something to work through in his mind, and left it at that."

Jewel gnawed her bottom lip a moment. Stepped away. Put a little space between them so that she could think straight, not get lost in Rogen's vibrant blue eyes and ruggedly handsome face. The feel of his lips and fingertips on her skin. The intimate moments drawing out between them. The electric current humming through her veins.

"I don't want to talk about it, either," she said. "I should go."

"Slow down," he insisted. "Not so fast. You haven't been here that long. And, Christ . . ." He shoved a hand through his hair. "When am I going to see you again?"

Jewel set aside her snifter and the crumpled napkin that was now soaked, since the ice had melted. Her palm still smarted, but that was the least of her worries.

The least of her torment.

She hadn't crashed the Angelinis' gala as a means to start something up with Rogen. Certainly not Vin. She was here for business, not romance.

Yet Rogen was a powerful undertow. He took her tenderly by the hand she hadn't used to slap Vin and turned to leave the terrace. She willingly went with him.

Over one impossibly broad shoulder, he said, "I'm going to take you someplace that will instantly cheer you up." His roguish grin stole her breath. So, no chance of getting it back while she was still in his presence.

They took the short flight of steps down to the manicured event lawn and along the west wing of the mansion, toward the service entrance. Rogen directed her to a Rhino parked outside the building and helped her into the passenger seat. Her gaze followed him as he rounded the front of the all-terrain vehicle. She admired his confident strides, his virility.

He climbed in next to her and cranked the key in the ignition. Jewel wasn't quite sure what he was up to or whether it was wise to play along. Really, the more time she spent here—and with him—the more difficult it would be to reconcile her feelings when she returned to San Francisco and tried to erase from her mind the sight of Rogen. And Vin.

Not to mention the yearning and heartache they both sparked.

Jesus, why'd they have to be so devilishly handsome? So damn tempting?

They each possessed significantly different qualities that called to Jewel. Rogen was the rough-and-tumble type. Tough as nails, steely nerved, masculine, solid as oak physically and emotionally. He was also gentle, soft-spoken at just the right moments, heartwarmingly amiable, sensitive when the situation warranted. She'd cried on his shoulder plenty of times, and he'd never seemed to mind. Had never gotten antsy or appeared the least bit uncomfortable with her family drama, her girly feelings.

By contrast, Vin was dark and broody. Even as a kid. More so after his parents had died in a horrific plane crash when he, Rogen, and Jewel were all sixteen and he'd ended up moving into the Angelini mansion. He had a refined look, but raw intensity oozed from his every pore. While he liked to project his arrogant nature, Jewel had been privy to his fiercely compassionate side.

The man would save puppies from a burning building. He'd brag about it afterward, of course. That was Vin. Whereas Rogen would simply shrug off any hero worship if he'd been the one to swoop in to save the day, and say, *Anyone would have done the same.*

It was no wonder the two men were still best friends—their

yin and yang complemented each other. And Jewel was wholly, inexplicitly, and irrevocably affected by both of them. *Drawn* to both of them.

Which made her night at the Angelinis' even more complex.

As her stomach remained knotted over the events of the evening, Rogen parked the Rhino on the cobblestone pathway that led to a large white stucco building almost completely shrouded by tall foliage and topped with a red-tiled roof.

Jewel grinned, despite her consternation. "The Angels' Share Room," she commented, knowing her spirits were about to be lifted.

Rogen escorted her to the front doors while he talked on his iPhone, evidently to someone in Security, because a few interior lights came to life and the blinking crimson dots on the alarm pad alongside the main doors turned to green. She heard the distinct sound of a latch springing free and Rogen disconnected the call.

Turning to Jewel, he said in his low, rumbling voice, "Guaranteed to put you in a better frame of mind. Take a couple of deep breaths."

She inhaled and exhaled slowly, methodically.

Then Rogen told her, "Once more, with a big exhale, and then don't breathe until we're inside."

Jewel did as instructed. Rogen swung open one of the thick wood-and-glass doors and guided her through the entryway. Jewel pulled up short. She sucked in a long stream of air, filling her lungs with the glorious scent of rich, aromatic cognac. She held the breath, warmth and relaxation seeping through her veins, curling around her like a cozy blanket, sealing all the gaping holes within her that had been ripped open this evening.

She let the breath out slowly, then inhaled again. Deeply. She repeated this numerous times, letting the fragrance calm her, soothe her. Along with the soulful aria floating from hidden speakers, the dimly lit chandeliers hanging from the polished beams overhead, and the gorgeously designed wooden floor, with cherub angels fluttering their wings and singing the praises of the heavens with skinny bugles and voluptuous harps.

This was the room that inspired inner peace. That salved old wounds. That reminded Jewel of the beautiful world in which she'd been raised. The wine world.

She crossed to the wide ledge between two curving staircases that led down to the VIP tasting room, cellar, and storage floor. She looked out at all the oak casks stacked high and recalled how as a kid, she'd always been fascinated with not only the distilling process but also the aging one.

Rogen stood next to her, an elbow casually propped on the ledge, his other hand at the small of her back.

She slid a glance his way. Smiled softly. She was fairly certain her eyes glowed with gratitude . . . and her deep affection for Rogen. "Thanks for bringing me here."

"Always cheered you up when you were blue."

"And I've missed it."

He nodded. "Separating us is something I've never reconciled with my parents. I don't know that I ever will."

"It was wrong," she agreed. "My parents played a part, too. That damn feud—"

"Yes. But we're not teenagers anymore, Jewel." His cerulean eyes deepened in color. "They can't control us. They can't lay down any laws between us."

She swallowed the emotion bubbling in her throat. "Rogen, I—"

"Come on." He shoved away from the split railing and took her hand again. "Let's sample the expensive stuff."

"And you'll tell me the story I want to hear?"

Now his eyes sparkled. "Of course."

He unhooked a gold-velvet rope at the top of one staircase and she passed through and descended the steps. They crossed to the far end, to the elegantly appointed tasting room with plush furniture and more elaborate chandeliers. A pool table. High-top tables and leather-padded stools. Lots of ornately framed mirrors.

She took one of the stools and Rogen punched in the key code to unlock the cellar and disappeared for a few minutes. When he returned, he set out three Baccarat crystal-cut decanters and matching snifters. He also grabbed two small bottles of water from the cooler and a silver bucket to cleanse their palates and rinse their glasses in between tastings.

He poured the first sample and handed it over. "I know you favor a hint of vanilla."

They'd snuck more than a few sips while growing up. "Yes, I still do." Gently swirling the dark-amber liquid in the bowl of the snifter, she dipped her head and pulled in the bold bouquet that further stimulated her senses. As did the incredibly sexy man sitting across from her.

She took a small drink, loving the slight burn over her tongue, down her throat, and to her belly, where heat spread slowly, deliciously, through her.

The daring notes ended with a smooth vanilla finish that was a pleasant surprise.

With a nod, Jewel said, "Sensational flavors. Now, tell me my story."

Rogen sipped his cognac while she enjoyed the rest of hers. Then he rinsed their glasses and poured another sample.

He unraveled his bow tie to get comfortable. Jewel's gaze fixated on his strong fingers, deftly working the tie until the ends fell against his crisp white shirt. It'd been a hell of a long time since she'd felt his hands on her naked body. Remembering how lovingly, how sensually, he'd always touched her sparked an intense craving deep within her.

Rogen shrugged out of the tuxedo jacket, removed and pocketed his cuff links, and rolled up his sleeves.

Jewel was held spellbound, her arm suspended in the air, her snifter lifted midway to her lips, as she eyed Rogen over the rim. Exhilaration shimmied down her spine. Flames of desire licked her clit, sending a sizzle straight to the core of her being.

Rogen's gaze smoldered as he watched her watch him. As though he knew exactly what he did to her. How his nearness, how his fluid movements, how the sight of his large hands and powerful forearms, ignited her insides.

When he slipped the first few buttons of his flap through their holes, Jewel's jaw slackened. She had no doubt her irises blazed with appreciation of his considerable assets, the memory of what he looked like stripped bare, hard and wanting her.

Her mouth watered. Her pulse reverberated within her, a measured cadence that thrummed against all of her erogenous zones, heightening her arousal.

Rogen said, "You keep staring at me like that and I'm gonna skip right over the story you want me to tell you and get straight to the kissing."

Her heart jumped. Her pussy clenched. Lust and need hitched her pulse further. Though she told him, "I didn't come here for kissing."

His brow crooked. "Being with me hasn't crossed your mind since you arrived? Because I have to say, sweetheart, the way you devour me with those big blue eyes of yours . . . Well, kissing you is about the *only* thing I've been able to think of from the moment I saw you."

"I . . . Rogen." She shook her head. Fought to find the right words.

Hell, yes, she wanted him to kiss her. She wanted him to do so much more than that.

Jewel wanted him to peel away her dress. Touch her everywhere. With his hands, his mouth, that very talented tongue of his. She was desperate to feel him buried deep inside her, doing that slow, steady pumping of his cock that felt as though he were stroking her very soul as he rubbed against her most sensitive spot and made throaty moans fall from her lips.

"Sip," he quietly prompted, reminding her that she still held her snifter in mid-air as every nerve ending went haywire.

Jewel did as instructed, operating strictly on autopilot, because she was now lost somewhere in his heated gaze, somewhere in her heart, somewhere that had once been a safe haven for their love and desire for each other.

Rogen gave her his easy grin and said, "When the monks first started making wine, they anxiously awaited the day their varietals aged to the point where they could sample the Lord's sacrament. The time eventually came, and they cracked open a cask, tapping the wine with excitement and gratitude for the blessed rite. But something was amiss. . . ."

One corner of Jewel's mouth quirked as Rogen's gaze turned mischievous. She loved this story.

He said in a curious tone, "'What's this?' the monks asked, bewildered to find that a portion of their sacred wine was missing. They tapped several more casks to see if the other barrels were low on wine as well. Indeed they were." Rogen's brow jerked up again. "'But how could this be?' Unless . . . They glanced around, suddenly suspicious that perhaps their brothers had been sneaking wine in the middle of the night. Wine meant for divine consumption, not one's personal pleasure."

"Those naughty monks," Jewel teased.

Rogen's grin widened. "It wasn't in the monks' nature to be accusatory, of course, but what other explanation could there be? Mistrust rippled through the monastery, and the monks set up nightly watches to make sure no one violated the agreement to only serve the precious offering as Eucharist and Communion. Yet each cask they checked, they found more of their wine missing."

"Well, wine does beat the hell out of holy water."

"Sacrilege!" He feigned shock. Though there was a twinkle in his eye.

Jewel laughed. Rogen had always been good at lightening her heart.

"So, what happened?" she asked, leaning forward in her seat, listening intently, though she'd heard this tale a thousand times before. She loved how Rogen got caught up in the telling of it, his mesmerizing facial expressions, the octave his voice dropped.

"Naturally, the accusations grew, until the monks were fighting amongst themselves, even though none could prove their brothers were the offenders. Then a rainy day brought with it a leak in the roof. So a couple of the monks climbed onto the red tiles to replace the damaged ones and discovered something intriguing. . . ."

Jewel sucked in a breath for effect. "Whatever could it have been?"

"The entire roof was shielded with the clay tiles. However, only the ones directly above the casks were covered with a thick moss. They found this curious. They reported back to their brothers and they all pondered the mystery of it. And suddenly came to the stunning conclusion that no one was stealing their wine—at least not anyone within the walls or under the roof of the monastery."

"Then the culprit would be . . . ?"

"Evaporation," he said in an astonished tone. "You see, a small portion of the wine evaporated during the aging process and escaped through the roof, producing the growth of moss on the tiles."

"Fascinating," she said, as though this were the first time he'd ever told her of this phenomenon.

"Indeed," Rogen said with a nod. "And because the monks were so blessed with their sacrament, they made amends with each other and agreed that the angels in heaven deserved *their* share of the wine."

"Aw." Jewel fanned her face with a hand as mist covered her eyes. A genuine response. "I just love a happy ending."

"I love how you still get emotional when you've heard this story your entire life."

"It's sweet."

"Mm." He slipped from his stool and stepped toward hers. He uncrossed her legs. Spread them to accommodate his hard body in the V created, the high slit in her skirt working to his advantage. "I think those lips of yours are sweet."

A thrill ribboned through Jewel.

Rogen's gaze landed on her slowly rising and falling chest. Then lifted to meet hers. The blue pools were hypnotic . . . and Jewel found herself drowning in them.

"I came back to River Cross six months ago, Jewel. After years in Manhattan, then Yale, then the Tuscany headquarters. Every day that I've been home, I've thought of you. Hell." He let out a sharp laugh. "I've thought of you every day no matter where I was."

"Rogen." They couldn't start something that couldn't be finished. Regardless of how much she wanted him. Jewel had plans that might adversely affect Rogen. And what about Vin? She'd never shared with Rogen things he really ought to know about her past with his best friend.

Still, she felt the intensity of the moment, the yearning that enveloped them both.

Rogen's head lowered to hers and he whispered, "I'll never claim we were fated in a good way, because of all the bullshit we've endured. But you can't deny our current destiny."

His lips brushed hers. The warmest, most sensual kiss. One that made her heart soar.

He said, "We naturally gravitate to each other. We naturally find ourselves in each other's arms. Doesn't matter where we are or how long we've been apart. We *need* each other, Jewel."

His mouth sealed with hers, his tongue sweeping over hers, then delving deeper, twisting and tangling until she was captured, enrapt, lost.

Rogen's arms slipped around her waist. Her breasts pressed below the hard ledge of his pectoral muscles. She let the sensations consume her. The sexy ones, the sentimental ones.

A part of her wanted to swing from the chandeliers as pleasure raced through her. The other part wanted to cry a river for the years gone by—and the uncertainty of everything that stretched beyond this one night.

But she clung to Rogen, her arms around his neck, holding him tight. He owned half her heart, half her soul. Always had. Always would.

And he was right—there was no denying their powerful connection. Or the fiery sensations he so easily invoked.

Breaking their kiss, she simply said, "Take me someplace where we can get naked."

# FOUR

Rogen had temporarily forgotten there were surveillance cameras everywhere. He'd been too caught up in the heat of the moment with Jewel. Too wrapped up in her.

Damn, it was crazy how she ensnared him so completely that nothing registered in his mind except her.

He stepped away. Collected the silver satin clutch she'd had tucked under her arm for most of the evening but set on the table when they'd settled in. With his other hand, he cupped her elbow and helped her off the stool.

Her expression was a complicated one to decipher. There were questions in her eyes. Uncertainty. And blatant arousal. No mistaking it.

He wound an arm about her waist and led her back to the stairs. The staff would clean the remnants of their samplings in the morning. Jewel didn't say a word as they left the Angels' Share Room and took the Rhino on more cobblestone pathways winding through the vast property to his house. He guided her inside, through the great room, and toward the wall of glass doors where the patio lay beyond.

Snatching the remote from an end table they passed, Rogen hit a button that made the doors slide apart and into pockets along the edges, so that the entire wall opened onto the patio. He then selected the dim setting of accent lamps. Flipped the switch for the huge planters filled with chunks of lava and drilled-holes for copper tubing underneath that allowed the gas flames to illuminate the rocks in the decorative pots that sat atop the half wall surrounding the terrace. There was also a fireplace in the corner and a lit pool. Chaise longue chairs and other furniture and table settings covered the pavered area.

"Nice setup," Jewel said as she surveyed it all. "Quite beautiful under a diamond-studded night sky and a crescent moon. The vineyard in the backdrop."

Rogen turned on music at a low level.

She shot a look over her shoulder. "Your patio of seduction?"

"Hardly."

Rogen was no monk. That was for damn sure. But he'd never brought a woman here. Whether he was on his own or pairing with Vin, Rogen only ever scratched the itch with one-night stands. He didn't engage in serious involvements, relationships, whatever. The mere notion seemed false, because he was wholly hooked on one woman.

He said, "I had the house built last year, when I made plans to come back to River Cross and run operations from the mansion."

"But you didn't want to live in the mansion?"

"Too many memories in that bedroom."

She turned to face him. "Yeah," she said in a quiet voice. "I have that problem, too."

She stepped toward him, and her manicured nails skated over the line of buttons on his shirt, up to where he'd undone the first few. Her fingers brushed the inner swells of his pecs. It would have been a light, flirty touch, but he caught the tremble in her hand. He covered it with his. Gave a gentle squeeze.

His head dipped head and he kissed her. Softly at first. Tasting her, teasing her, tempting her.

Passion sparked instantly and Rogen let it consume them both. He raised her arm to wrap around his neck. His other hand slid to her ass and he palmed a cheek, pressing her body firmly to his.

He deepened the kiss, their tongues tangling, their breaths becoming one.

Adrenaline pumped through his veins. His cock thickened, straining against the confines of boxer briefs and his tuxedo pants.

When they finally came up for air, Jewel gazed at him with an urgency in her eyes that likely mirrored his own. She worked the buttons on his shirt, then shoved the material over his shoulders and down his arms. It dropped to the pavers.

Her hands splayed over his stomach.

"Jesus, Rogen," she said in a husky voice, "you are so gorgeous."

His muscles flexed beneath her touch and admiring gaze. She traced a fingertip over the ridges of his abs, then reached for the fastenings at his waist, unbuttoning, unzipping, while he toed off his shoes.

His raging pulse echoed throughout his body and his cock throbbed in wild beats. His heart pounded erratically.

God, he wanted her. More than ever before. And that was saying something, because he'd always had it bad for her.

Jewel shifted away as he divested himself of his clothing. She released the clasp at her shoulder and eased her dress downward, revealing her teardrop breasts with taut, rosy nipples. Then her stomach, her shapely hips, her long legs.

Holding Rogen spellbound.

She stepped out of the sparkly ice-blue garment and draped it over the back of a chair. Then kicked off her sandals.

Rogen hadn't thought his dick could get any harder. He'd been wrong.

She was stunning. He was captivated.

With the crooking of her finger, she said, "Take my panties off."

"Always willing to."

Rogen knelt before her. He curled his fingers behind the thin strands at her hips and dragged the thong down her thighs. He leaned in close, at the apex of her legs, and inhaled the scent of her.

"Fuck, you smell good," he told her in a rough voice. His tongue swept over her slick folds. "You taste even better."

Her flesh quivered. Her fingers threaded through his hair. "You get me so hot."

He glanced up at her. "What do you think you're doing to me?"

"Let's go skinny-dipping. Like we used to in the river."

Rogen stood. Jewel whirled around and strolled over to the pool, taking the tiled steps into the shallow end. He dove into the deep end. When he surfaced, she dove under and swam toward him, meeting him in the middle. Her arms circled his neck as their legs swirled in the water. Her blond hair was slicked back from her sculpted face and her eyes glimmered in the firelight.

Her nipples brushed his chest, taunting him. He pulled her more tightly to him, her breasts pressing below his pecs again, her stomach cradling his erection.

He kissed her, loving the feel of her soft body against his, savoring the sizzle along his nerve endings, the need mounting with every second that passed. Rogen hadn't wanted a woman this intensely since the last time Jewel had been in his arms.

As desperately as he yearned to be buried inside her, though, he was glad she'd suggested the quick dip. Might help to cool him down just enough so that he didn't come the second he entered her.

Watching her strip away her dress and then tasting her pussy had revved him a bit too much.

He felt a little more under control now.

*A little.*

Her fingers glided over the tattoo on his left biceps. "This is new."

"Senior year of Yale. I was feeling rebellious."

She traced the black-inked blade of a dagger stabbed into a chunk of ground, a trio of vines entwined, braided as they coiled around the edges up to the hilt, where they split. Two veering off to twine around the respective arms, one snaking around the handle. All left straggling as though a breeze might carry them anywhere. Separate from one another.

"Pretty symbolic," she said, catching on quick to what the graphic represented. "Our threesome is a bit twisted, isn't it?"

So unlike any of his and Vin's threesomes, at least in the tormented sense . . .

"I'm not sure exactly how twisted," Rogen told her. "Vin doesn't talk about you, as a rule."

"There's nothing to talk about," she said. "We severed ties. He went off in one direction; I went off in another. As did you. So . . . accurate depiction with the tattoo."

"Maybe. Maybe not." She was here with him now, wasn't she?

"Remember the first time we did this in the river?" she asked, changing the subject.

"How could I forget?" They'd been sixteen and Rogen had come home for a long weekend. Vin had not been with them that day. He'd been getting his driver's license, just weeks before his parents had died. "You were nervous as hell to take off your clothes. Even though I'd seen you in a bikini dozens of times."

"That's not naked."

It'd taken some coaxing to get her to slip out of her lacy bra and thong. A bit of goading, actually. The effort on Rogen's part had been well worth seeing all of her for the first time. The water had been chilly and her nipples had been hard. Rogen had been mesmerized.

After their dip, she'd tried to hide behind a towel as they'd lain on a blanket spread beneath a tree while the sun set. Her head had been resting on his shoulder and he'd tugged at the end of the towel that was tucked between her breasts, unraveling the material. She'd gasped, shocked by his audacity but also turned on by it, he'd suspected. He'd whisked the pad of his thumb over a pebbled bead and felt the shiver down her spine.

"Have you ever done it?" she'd asked in her breathless tone.

"Who would I have done it with, if not you?"

She'd nibbled her lower lip, as she was prone to do when anxiety got the best of her. "Some girl at Trinity?"

"Not a chance. I love *you*, remember?"

"Then maybe we should do it."

He'd grinned. "I was hoping you'd say that."

He'd kissed her endlessly. Felt her body relax. Sensed the need and desire blooming within her.

When she'd eventually broken the kiss, she'd said, "I want to feel you inside me."

He'd stared into her eyes, entranced. Then his lips had grazed hers and he'd said, "I only want you, Jewel. Even if we can't really be together. Distance and all that. It doesn't matter. You're all I think of."

"You say the sweetest things." Her eyes had misted, but then she'd told him, "We can't make any promises to each other, Rogen. All I'm asking is that right this very moment you know in your heart that this is real and special and memorable."

"Jewel." He'd swept another kiss over her lips as emotion gripped him. "*Every* moment with you is real and special and memorable."

She'd given him a look of gratitude and said, "Make love to me. Slowly."

It'd been one of the best damn days of his life.

Now Rogen asked, "Are you still on the pill?"

She gave him a soft smile. "Mm-hmm. Keeps my cycles regular."

"When's the last time you were with someone?"

There was a hint of hesitation from her. Then she said, "You were my last time. When I visited you in Italy, while you were doing a summer internship between your junior and senior years of college."

Rogen's gut clenched. "Jewel, that was seven years ago."

"Yes."

*Whoa.*

"Don't worry," she continued, a tinge of melancholy in her voice. "I don't expect you to say the same. You are much too virile for celibacy. And we're just . . . star-crossed lovers."

"Yeah, well, don't go thinking I've been sleeping my way around the county since I got back. I'm selective. And, actually, it's been a while."

"I've heard whispers. Of you. Of . . ." Her voice trailed off. She sighed. Shook her head. Said, "Hopefully you haven't been with anyone I know."

"No." He kissed her. "No one you know. No one who really knows about us."

"Rogen." She smoothed a hand over his wet hair. "There is no *us.*"

This time it was his heart that clutched fiercely. Painfully.

"There's always going to be an *us,* sweetheart. Our history keeps repeating itself."

"That makes us masochistic."

"Yes. Now," he said as he guided her to wind her legs around his waist before he waded through the water toward the steps. "For the record, I just had my annual physical a couple weeks ago. Got tested. All good there."

Her fingers grazed his cheek. "You want to make love to me without a condom."

"I want to come inside you. You're the only one."

Desire and affection for him flared in her eyes. "I want that, too. It feels so good." Her mouth skimmed over his. Against his lips, she murmured, "The rush of heat. The very essence of you flowing through my pussy."

"Your very tight, wet pussy." His groin blazed. He recalled exactly how she felt surrounding him, holding him in a vise grip. Milking his cock until he came. "Christ, Jewel. I was trying to slow this down. But that's impossible." He had to have her. *Now.*

"I want your mouth on me first," she told him. "You are so, so good at making me come."

He reached the steps and carried her up them, snagging a rolled bath sheet from the supply stacked on a glass-topped end table. He snapped it open with the flick of his wrist and tossed the oversize towel haphazardly onto a double chaise longue chair.

Rogen rested a knee on the thick sienna-colored cushion and guided Jewel down so she was sprawled on her back and he was positioned between her parted legs. He spread them farther with his hands on her inner thighs. His thumbs stroked her dewy folds and she sucked in a breath. Propped herself up on one elbow to watch him as his head dipped and his tongue fluttered over her clit, already swollen from her arousal.

"Rogen," she said on a lusty sigh. Her free hand slid along his shoulder before her fingers threaded through his hair. "It's been forever and a day. Too fucking long to go without this."

He used the tip of his tongue to lightly, quickly flick the little bud. Butterfly wings against her clit, she used to say.

His thumbs kept her pussy lips spread as he alternately flicked and suckled the pulsating pearl.

Jewel's shallow breath turned into erotic whimpers that drove him wild. He loved hearing her moan. Loved knowing he was getting her all worked up.

His lips tugged on hers, making her gasp. Then he licked slowly. Circled his tongue around her clit, increasing the pressure, the pace.

"Yes," she muttered. "Sooo good." Her hips rose and she pressed herself to his mouth, silently demanding more.

His hands slipped under her and he cupped her ass. He returned to the lightning-quick flickers of his tongue against the knot of nerves, then suckled feverishly.

"Rogen," she panted. "You're going to make me come."

He shifted a hand and eased a finger into her dripping pussy.

A cry fell from her parted lips.

He worked in a second finger and massaged her inner walls while his mouth pleasured her. Tremors ran through her body, the telltale sign of how close she was to climaxing.

His tongue circled again, more aggressively. His fingers plunged deep, finding that special spot that he rubbed vigorously.

"Oh, Christ," she said. "Oh, God. That's it, Rogen. Right fucking *there*!"

Her hips jerked. Her hand at the back of his head held him to her.

"Yes," she whimpered. "Yes, *yes*."

He drew her clit into his mouth.

Her body tensed, held suspended for several seconds.

*"Oh!"* She quaked with her release as she called out, "Rogen!"

Her harsh breaths filled the quiet night. Her pussy clenched his fingers. Her hand kept his head to the apex of her legs, his mouth still on her.

"Oh, God," she gushed. "That was incredible."

"Fuck, I love listening to you come."

Jewel's grip on him loosened and she fell against the slightly angled lounger. She gazed at the stars overhead, not entirely convinced they were just celestial ones she saw. Rogen had made her come hard. *So hard*. And so damn fast.

Lord, he was a master at bringing her to orgasm with his mouth.

His fingers withdrew from her body and she shuddered with delight at how every tiny sensation registered in her mind, in her heart. She was ridiculously aware of him, hypersensitive to his touch and his wicked grin.

Which he gave her, satisfaction lighting his gorgeous cerulean eyes.

"You look quite pleased with yourself," she told him as he dropped kisses over her stomach and up her ribs to her breasts.

He teased the inner swells with his warm breath when he murmured, "I do enjoy getting you off." He shifted slightly and his tongue swept over her puckered nipple. Her body jolted, the titillation shooting straight to her core.

Taking her reaction as encouragement, his lips closed around the taut bead and he suckled it the way he had her clit.

She wriggled beneath him, her pussy rubbing against his strong thigh. His erection pressed along her stomach.

She clasped one rock-hard upper arm and a solid shoulder. She closed her eyes and let him take her to a beautiful place with his thumb whisking over one nipple and his tongue doing sinfully delicious things to the other one.

"You could make me come again," she said. "Just like this."

His hips rocked slightly so that his cock slid along her damp skin and his muscular leg stroked her slick folds.

Jewel loved the foreplay, despite the incessant need she had to feel him inside her. She wanted another orgasm. Barreled toward it as Rogen diligently continued his stroking and suckling and whisking. They moved together, their breathing escalating, their bodies melding and writhing.

Excitement trilled down her spine. The first of the tremors that raced through her.

"Don't stop," she quietly commanded.

"You're making me half out of my mind, sweetheart," he said against her flushed and tingling flesh. "Come again for me."

He kissed his way up her neck, to that erogenous zone below her ear that he apparently remembered made her lose all control. He pressed his tongue to it. Stroked. Then gently bit.

"Oh, God." The tremors intensified. Her leg twined with his, keeping him anchored, his thigh rubbing her clit, the slight bit of wet, silky hair on his skin adding a hint of friction, though mostly it was a feathery effect that aroused her deeply.

His muscles bunched and Jewel reveled in all the hard angles of his body against her curves. He was chiseled to perfection. Magnificent.

And Jewel was drowning in lust again.

"Rogen," she whispered, her eyes fluttering open, her gaze locking with his. "You feel amazing and you're not even inside me yet."

"We fit together," he said, his voice strained with his own desire. "We've always been this good together."

He moved with a quicker tempo and Jewel lost her breath as everything within her pulled taut and then released in a sensational orgasm that blazed through her.

"Oh, fuck!" she cried out. "Rogen!"

He shifted and his cock thrust into her while her pussy quavered and clenched.

"Damn. Jewel. Oh, goddamn, you're tight. So *fucking* tight."

Rogen filled her. Stretched her. And kept the climax burning.

Her hips rose and she continued to squeeze him firmly, eliciting a low, sexy growl from him. His hand slipped around to her backside and then down to her thigh. He lifted her leg and slung it over his waist. Plunged deeper.

She couldn't catch her breath. He pumped in short, steady beats, the head of his cock massaging her G-spot, his shaft stroking her inner walls.

"Like that," she said on a sliver of air. "Oh, God. Rogen. Just like that."

He knew to grip her ass, tilt her hips, gradually pick up the tempo until she was clinging to him, inside and out, and panting heavily.

"Yes," she said. "Only you could do this to me. Right where I need to feel you the most."

Her hips rolled with his. Their bodies were melded together and Rogen was huge within her.

Her last orgasm had barely dimmed when the next one swelled and taunted her. An exquisitely alluring sensation as he pumped heartily.

Her moans of pleasure echoed around them. Heat and desire consumed her. She dug her nails into Rogen's muscles, holding on as he took her right to the precipice.

"I'm going to come again," she said. "So hard. Oh, God, I'm going to come so fucking hard."

The sensations collided and erupted and she called out his name.

Her pussy pulsated from the scorching orgasm and an electric current hummed beneath her skin, keeping her charged, keeping her hungry for more.

"Jewel." He groaned. "You have no idea what you do to me. Christ. When you lose it for me . . ." He shook his head. "Nothing feels better than you."

He rolled onto his back, bringing her with him, their bodies still joined. Jewel straddled him, brimming from the thrills Rogen elicited.

She flattened her palms against his sculpted chest as his hands on her hips guided her into a quick, sexy rhythm.

"You are insanely beautiful," he told her, emotion in his voice. "*So* beautiful. Riding me hard, all those blond waves tumbling down your back, your eyes glowing." His hands shifted to her breasts and he caressed her with a hint of urgency and excitement. "Damn, Jewel. I should never have to go this long without being inside you."

Her heart skipped a few beats. "You've got all the right moves and all the right words, cowboy."

He sat up suddenly, his cock thick and throbbing in her pussy. His arms slid around her waist; hers circled his neck. They moved together, him thrusting smoothly, Jewel rocking her hips in time with each fluid pump that pushed him deeper, made her hotter. He drew one of her nipples into his mouth. Her head fell back on her shoulders and her eyelids drifted closed. She let out a low moan.

The intense emotion he sparked along with all the carnal cravings coalesced into overwhelming feelings. There were no perfect answers to their situation. Only perfect moments they stole on occasion. Like this one.

"I want to feel you come inside me," she said as another orgasm bloomed.

"Yes . . ." His tongue flitted over her nipple. One of his hands returned to her hip and he led her into a faster pace, pressing her downward so that she ground against his pelvis.

Exhilaration shot through her. Her eyes opened. Her head dropped slightly forward.

And her gaze landed on Vin.

Her body jolted.

He stood in the shadowy depths of the house. Watching Jewel as Rogen made love to her. As she was about to come.

The roar of sensations couldn't be quelled. Was amplified, in fact, as Vin held her gaze, his hands in his pockets once again, the expression on his face impossible to discern.

Rogen was sending her to that pinnacle of desire, pushing breathy whimpers from low in her throat. Nothing could slow the speeding train. His mouth was on her breast; his cock was rigid and surging within her. His muscles and heat engulfed her.

All the while, Vin maintained the eye contact, giving her another wicked thrill as thoughts of him naked and right there with them, kissing her as Rogen fucked her, her hand pumping Vin's cock, filled her head.

Jewel's excitement escalated . . . and erupted.

"*Yes*! Rogen!"

"Oh, fuck," Rogen said on a harsh breath. "Squeeze me tight, sweetheart. Oh, goddamn."

He exploded, and the liquid heat coursing through her kept her orgasm radiating. Kept the sharp sobs of release falling from her lips. Kept her body quaking.

It was a perfect storm of erotic and elusive desires. A love triangle that would never be resolved—or wholly explored. But which now burned bright in her mind.

Jewel's eyes closed once more and she pressed her forehead to Rogen's shoulder as she savored the climax and his hot seed inside her.

She had no idea how long it took to return to herself. For her breathing to slow. For Rogen's to reach some semblance of normalcy, too.

Eventually, her lids lifted and her head came up. She stared into the empty great room of Rogen's house.

Vin was gone.

# FIVE

Rogen collapsed against the slanted chaise longue, once again bringing Jewel with him.

"Christ, you are something else," he told her. "It's never better than with you. Fuck. You feel incredible."

Jewel snuggled close, her breasts pressed to his chest. His arms were around her and he was still nestled in her pussy. A gentle breeze ruffled her nearly dried hair, the previously straight, sleek strands now holding a natural curl.

She left feathery kisses along his neck and said, "It was always so easy between us. Even our first time. You were so gentle, so caring. So romantic."

"I wouldn't intentionally hurt you, Jewel. Not for any reason. Some things were just beyond our control when we were growing up."

"And now?" she asked.

Rogen wasn't sure what she was getting at but felt compelled to say, "If you think it'd be simple for either of us to walk away again, you're wrong."

She was quiet a moment, then said, "I wasn't really looking to rock the boat tonight, Rogen. I didn't come here to hook up with you." Her head rose. "You're just that irresistible."

He grinned. "So stay the night and let me make you come a half-dozen more times."

She stared into his eyes and Rogen felt myriad emotions. He wanted her again. Wanted her in his arms when he fell asleep. Wanted her to still be there when he woke in the morning.

But she wiggled out of his embrace and slipped from the lounger. She used one of the towels to tidy herself and then tossed it in the rattan linen basket.

She stood with her back to him, her skin golden in the moonlight.

He didn't have to see the look on her face to know how conflicted she was. He felt it himself, to the depths of his soul. Watched with a heavy heart as she crossed the patio to their discarded clothes and pulled on her thong. Stepped into her dress and secured it at the shoulder. Put her heeled sandals on.

She collected her purse and retrieved her cell. Phoned her driver to meet her at the house up the hill from the mansion.

Disappointment snaked through Rogen. Coiled low in his gut.

Apparently, it *was* simple for her to walk away.

"You really have to leave so soon?" he asked as he hauled himself up and wrapped a towel around his waist.

She turned to him. Gave a faint smile. "We'd only make it harder on ourselves if I stayed any longer."

"Am I supposed to pretend this didn't happen?" Damn the torment in his voice.

Jewel gave a slight shake of her head. "No. And you know I could never pretend it didn't happen, either. I just don't know what it means. What to do about it." She sighed. "I'm having a very bizarre evening."

"Yeah, I get that."

"I would stay," she confessed, "but I want to speak with my parents first thing tomorrow morning. I haven't seen them in a couple of weeks. Mother's visits to the apartment Daddy keeps in the city have become less frequent, since her volunteering efforts now transcend counties and keep her busier than ever."

"When are you going back to San Fran?"

"Sunday night."

"Then meet me at Bristol's before that. Three o'clock."

She hedged, her teeth clamping down on her plump, tempting bottom lip.

He crossed his arms over his chest. "Three o'clock," he reiterated. Not taking *no* for an answer.

Jewel nodded. "All right. I'll be there."

Rogen unfolded his arms and stalked toward her. He brushed his fingers over her cheek and she trembled at his touch. Her eyes shimmered with the hint of tears.

His head lowered and he kissed her tenderly, lips tangling, no tongue. Then he pulled away ever so slightly. She moved with him, wanting more.

Rogen bit back a triumphant grin. Instead, he kissed her more fervently. Which she responded to, twining her arms around his neck. Sealing her body to his.

It seemed she couldn't get enough of him any more than he could of her.

But, inevitably, she broke the kiss. She said, "I really do have to go."

He let out a low growl of frustration. "What's the rush, Cinderella?"

Her thumb swept over his furrowed brow. "Not so much Cinderella. More Juliet, don't you think?"

"I refuse to believe we're meant to end in tragedy," he adamantly told her.

Jewel stepped away. "We already have. Multiple times."

She left. While he stewed.

In her bedroom at the estate, Jewel fought the urge to drag out photo albums and yearbooks to reminisce about her teenage years with Rogen and Vin. Nostalgia was a real bitch. It could comfort her at times, shred her at others. She feared the latter this evening. So she showered, checked her e-mails, and called it a night.

Unfortunately, thoughts of Rogen making love to her wouldn't leave her mind. Nor would Vin's piercing green eyes. It had excited her to discover him standing in the shadows, staring at her. It hadn't really shocked her to realize she'd desperately wanted Vin kissing her in his passionate, fiery way while she came.

But that was just the wildest damn idea! Even if some of those hush-hush comments about the two men having a knack and a proclivity for making love to a woman together were true, there was no way in hell it could ever come about with this particular trio.

They might be fated, but in a very disastrous way, as she'd contended earlier. Rogen's tattoo said it all.

She thought of how his calls and e-mails had become less frequent as he'd prepped for Yale. All the schoolwork, the community service and volunteering, the clubs and sports. And then his parents deciding to vacation elsewhere during his breaks so that Rogen was rarely ever in River Cross.

Jewel had missed him like crazy. Had been so grateful she'd had Vin to help fill the void.

One Saturday, a month or so after Vin had turned eighteen, ahead of her, the two of them had gone fishing riverside. Then they'd sprawled on a blanket and Vin had read while Jewel had e-mailed with Bayli and Scarlet on their BlackBerries. Her head had rested on Vin's hard stomach as she'd lain perpendicular to him, soaking up the sun in shorts and a tank top.

Bayli had been in the midst of a meltdown because she and her boyfriend had finally decided to make love—and were desperate for advice. Prompting Jewel to ask Vin, "What kind of condoms do you use?"

"Where the hell did that come from?" he'd retorted, not bothering to set aside *War and Peace*.

"Bay's wigging at present. She and Jonathan are actually planning out a whole *shred the V-card* event, right down to the time they arrive at the hotel he's booked, have a glass of smuggled wine, and then . . . do it. Like, no spontaneity whatsoever."

"That's because Jonathan plans *everything*. He probably schedules time in his calendar for when he should take a piss or pop the top on a Mountain Dew."

She'd laughed softly. "Funny. But having an agenda for first-time sex? Seems too premeditated for such a special occasion. I'm not saying break out the rose petals and violins, but still. Choreographing every move to be made seems . . . anti-climactic. Definitely unromantic."

Vin had scoffed. "It doesn't always have to be romantic."

"Sure it does," she'd insisted. Then asked, "What should I tell her about the condoms?"

"You and Rogen have had sex, right?"

"Of course." She'd put down her phone and sat up. "He didn't tell you?"

Eyes glued to the page he was reading, Vin had absently said, "Not something I've ever wanted to discuss with him. And he likes to keep things like that to himself."

"True."

"So you two don't use condoms?"

"*Didn't* is the proper tense." Her heart had wrenched when she'd confessed, "It's been a long time. I haven't seen him in eight months, you know?"

"Fine. You *didn't* use protection?"

"I've been on the pill since I was sixteen. And given that neither of us had ever been with anyone else, it didn't exactly seem necessary to raid the stash at the local convenience store. Besides, I liked . . . Never mind."

"What?" he'd asked, sounding slightly exasperated with the topic of conversation. Had remained somewhat engrossed in his novel.

"I liked how it felt when he came inside me."

Vin had let out a strange grunt. Not exactly a condemnation. More like . . . she'd finally intrigued him.

"Anyway. I'm guessing since you can't answer my question," she'd goaded, "you still haven't had sex. I mean, I rarely ever see you with a girl other than me."

"I've done it plenty of times, Jewel."

"With who?" she'd demanded.

He spared a glance her way and his grin dripped wickedness. "Shayla Harding."

"*What?!*" She'd ripped the book from his hand and glared. "You are such a liar!"

Shayla Harding was a popular wine-country artist with long brown hair and—reportedly—surgically enhanced breasts.

Vin had given Jewel a smug look. He'd known from the age of seven that he was a handsome devil, and didn't hide that he was perfectly aware of the fact.

"Shayla taught me everything I know. And, trust me, I know a lot."

He'd winked.

She'd gaped.

With a chuckle, Vin had added, "A very hot divorcée. No need to say more."

"Except that she's, like, twenty-five. Or thirty."

"Twenty-eight."

"Vin! That's way too old for you!"

He'd sighed. "Yeah. That's why she called it off."

"Oh, my God." Jewel had stared again, for endless seconds. Had then snickered. "You're bullshitting me. Shayla would never—"

"Ah, but she did." He'd crooked a brow at Jewel and asked, "How many positions have you and Rogen tried? Two?"

"None of your business." She'd scowled. Then: "He really hasn't told you?"

"He's not one for sharing juicy details."

"But we all know that you are. So exactly how did you and Mrs. Robinson hook up?"

"Ha-ha." He'd sat up and moved in close, pinning Jewel with a burning look. "Isn't the question you're really dying to ask me more along the lines of exactly *how many* different positions are there?"

Excitement had shot through her, headed straight to her clit. "I don't need to know that."

His gaze had dropped to her slightly parted, glossy lips. Then his emerald eyes had met hers again. They'd blazed. "Sure you do."

She'd swatted playfully at him to break the sudden sexual tension. "Perv."

"Give me my book."

"Tell me what to e-mail Bay and you can have it back."

He'd given her his bad-boy smirk. "You don't get to make ultimatums."

"Why not?" she'd challenged.

"Because I'm bigger than you. Stronger than you. Older than you now, too. *And* I happen to know that you're ticklish." He'd reached for her.

"Vin!" she'd squealed. "Don't you dare!"

They'd wrestled a little, laughing heartily. And then Vin had grabbed her around the waist and hauled her over his body and onto her back on the other side of him, her legs draped across his thighs as he lay on his hip facing her, leaning over her.

The laughter had instantly died on the vine. To be replaced with an electric current arcing between them as they'd both breathed heavily. Stared into each other's eyes.

"Not only have you not seen Rogen in eight months," Vin had said, "but you two hardly talk anymore. Does that mean you're broken up?"

"I don't know," she'd admitted, her chest rising and falling quickly as heat had rimmed Vin's glowing irises. "I kind of think so. Since he's going off to Yale after he graduates from Trinity. And I'm not smart enough to get in."

"You're plenty smart," Vin had said. Then he'd kissed her. Not in the soft, sweet way Rogen always had, which started tender and turned into something deeper, soul stirring.

No, Vin's kiss had been hot and searing and downright lethal. Passionate. Erotic.

Precisely how he'd taken her that day. . . .

Naturally, having experienced what both men had to offer, Jewel could understand why they were allegedly so good at satisfying a woman when they were both with her. And Jewel couldn't deny that had Vin stepped in when she'd been with Rogen at his house earlier in the evening it would have made for one scorching encounter. Not that she really comprehended how that would fully work out—or what impact it would have on their relationships.

Definitely a repercussion to be wary of—they'd suffered enough already, and the bonds were still tenuous in many respects.

In addition, if word got around the inner circle Jewel would have to face the consequences of being a woman who let two men pleasure her at the same time. How would that affect her reputation? What if the rumor spread to her parents? To the Angelini estate? To her colleagues at work?

There were plenty of concerns to take into consideration, beyond the mechanics of a sexual threesome.

Yet . . . Jewel suspected the combination of Rogen's intense lovemaking and Vin's aggressive fucking would be explosive. She could imagine their hands and mouths on her body. Could hear in her mind the men's sexy groans, her throaty moans—all mingled together. Could envision Vin taking her in the way he preferred, anally, while Rogen's thick cock pumped steadily deep in her pussy.

She knew so little about ménages. But suddenly craved one with Rogen and Vin.

So much so, the fantasy of seducing them into agreeing to share *her* began to weave in Jewel's mind, despite all of the reasons it was a dangerous idea that she'd just mentally ticked off.

She wanted them both. No sense in denying it.

In the morning, Jewel joined her parents on the east patio.

It wasn't easy putting her fantasy on the back burner but absolutely necessary. She had important business to tend to now.

"Mother." She dropped a kiss on Sophia Catalano's cheek, then rounded the glass-topped table to where her father sat, reading the paper. "Daddy." Another peck. "How was your trip?"

"Successful," he said. "The Everton Lodge in Aspen is now part of our real estate portfolio."

"Congratulations. I have good news as well." She took her seat across from them and tried to contain her enthusiasm. Her meeting with Gian Angelini and her night with Rogen had her exhilarated—and ravenous. When the buffet attendant, Stella, approached the table, Jewel told her, "Load me up, please."

Jewel's fit and trim mother eyed her curiously. Sophia, a tall, striking brunette with sculpted brows and tight, dewy skin, ate only grapefruit for breakfast and worked out with a personal trainer. Never went a day without time on her elliptical machine.

"I'll spend an extra hour on the tennis courts with you today," Jewel promised her mother. "I skipped dinner last night."

"Calories have never been my concern when it comes to you, darling," her mother said adoringly. "It's just that you typically don't favor breakfast."

"Yes, well, I'm pretty excited this morning, so eggs Benedict, southwestern potatoes, and sausage sounds fabulous." She sipped the coffee Stella delivered for her.

The exchange seemed to pique her father's interest. He folded over the *USA Today* and set it aside. Anthony was a handsome man with an athletic build and sandy-brown hair. Eyes a rich midnight-blue color. "Care to tell us what's got you so worked up? You don't come to River Cross often. Does your visit have something to do with the Angelinis' party?"

"As a matter of fact, it does." Jewel dug into her food, momentarily leaving her parents in suspense. She washed down a large bite with orange juice and then announced, "I struck a deal with Mr. Angelini for the property you jointly own with him."

Sophia's jaw slacked and her peridot eyes popped.

Anthony speared Jewel with a sharp look and said, "Surely you're mistaken."

"No." Perhaps her smile *was* a bit smug. She said, "Bayli and Scarlet came through once again on their hunting mission. They located something Mr. Angelini had once waxed poetic about when you two were business partners. Something he hasn't been able to procure. But I can get it for him, with a little help from my friends."

Her parents were well versed in her high-end bartering system. While her father would prefer—in his own words—to just write the damn check for his transactions, Jewel held fast to the power of her unicorn theory. It was certainly panning out in this instance.

Slowly recovering, her mother said, "We've made numerous offers to Gian and Rose-Marie. They haven't entertained a single one, despite it being fruitless to hold on to land they can't do anything with unless they receive our consent."

Jewel told her parents, "Bay researched a decanter of scotch I told her about, and the owner of it lives in Paris. I visited him while I was working on my Avenue des Lamond deal. He wants something other than money—and Scarlet also tracked down those possessions. It's a little tricky, I'll admit. But Mr. Angelini gave me his word that if I can get him the scotch he'd accept my cash offer and sell his portion of the property to us. So . . . surprise!"

Jewel's heart thumped a bit fast, because it was a mishmash of wily deals. But she had to believe the incongruent pieces would all fall into place.

"I'm impressed," her father said. "Though you realize Gian will never follow through. He'll find a way to keep the scotch *and* the land." Anthony picked up his paper and went back to reading.

Jewel's stomach plummeted. She pushed her plate aside. It really wasn't like her father to give up so quickly.

Then again, he knew Gian better than Jewel ever would.

"Now, Jewel," her mother said, patting Jewel's hand. "You know how proud your father is of your acquisitions. But this is Gian Angelini you're talking about. He'll do anything to twist the knife, even if it means baiting you and walking away with all the cards still in his hand."

Frustration tore through her. So, too, did the burning desire to prove her parents wrong. Because she'd executed some amazing transactions in her six years at CE, with men as powerful as Gian Angelini. Sure, she'd learned a few painful lessons along the way. Not every contract had been signed. Not every "original" treasure had been acceptably authenticated by her specialists. Yet she still had a fantastic track record to give her the confidence that she could pull off this deal with Gian.

She lifted her chin a notch and asked, "If I can make this happen, would you two deed the property to me? Outside of the living trust?"

The paper crinkled as her father returned it to the table. "What's your sudden interest in that land?"

"It's not so sudden. Just something that seemed too far out of my reach to attempt. Then the girls found the scotch for me, and now I want to pursue this."

In an uncharacteristically tight tone, her mother asked, "What would you do with all that acreage, Jewel?"

"I want to build an inn. A big, beautiful inn, with event lawns for weddings and parties. And an award-winning golf course. I've already made inquiries with Jack Nicklaus's people. In fact, I took all the specs on the land that you collected, Daddy, and gave them to an architectural firm I selected to design the inn."

"Jewel," her mother said on a long, dramatic breath. Much more her custom. "You're creating a dream around property you'll never own. Gian won't—"

"Perhaps he *won't* follow through," Jewel's father repeated. Then added, "But if he does . . . if you can reach terms with him, Jewel, that land is yours. *All* yours."

Now her heart launched into her throat. Tears stung the backs of her eyes. She could see from her father's steely gaze that he wasn't humoring her. He'd always admired her verve, and Jewel knew she'd impressed him with this latest ambition. Enough so that he'd reward her greatly if she succeeded.

Well, that—and he likely relished the idea of severing the last tie with the Angelinis.

Jewel didn't want that to be the end result. Rather, she hoped her plans would bridge the gap between the Catalanos and the Angelinis. But that was a whole missing piece to the puzzle that she had to work on. *After* she'd gotten her hands on that land.

Jumping up from the table, she kissed her mother again, then her father. "Thanks, Daddy. You won't be disappointed."

Vin was in a shitty mood as he turned into the bustling parking lot of Bristol's on the opposite end of the aisle that Jewel's sparkling, powder-blue convertible BMW entered at the same time. They both spotted the SUV backing out of the spot—the only one available on this side of the building. She switched on her turn signal. Vin ignored it. The SUV blocked her, and Vin pulled into the coveted space.

Jewel whaled on the horn. He glanced at her over his shoulder, out of the side of his convertible Maserati, and grinned. She flipped him off.

With a chuckle, he killed the engine and climbed out. She drove off and rounded the facility in search of another spot. He waited for her at the main door.

When she eventually stalked toward him, looking hotter than hell with blistering irritation and wearing a lavender strapless minidress, she said, "Didn't you see my blinker?"

"Sorry, no."

She scowled. "And God forbid you'd do the manly thing and let me have the space."

"I don't exactly consider that manly. Gallant, sure. But that's not really up my alley, is it? That's more Rogen's thing."

Shaking her head, she said, "You're getting a kick out of antagonizing me."

"Who slapped who?" he countered.

"And who was spying on who?" she demanded, not backing down. One of the many things he'd always loved about her.

He said, "I wasn't spying. I was looking for Rogen, because he'd disappeared and there were some people who wanted to talk business with him. I didn't actually believe he'd be making love to you within an hour of you crashing the party. By the way"—he leaned in close as an elderly couple exited the restaurant, and whispered in her ear—"you scream my name *much* louder when I make you come."

She glared at him. But Vin didn't miss the wicked flash in her sapphire eyes.

She could be pissed to high heaven at him. She still wanted him.

He knew it, because he'd read the signs on her face and in her gaze a million times before. And felt exactly the same.

Yes, he'd been upset that their reunion had been a volatile one at the gala. He'd been annoyed and frustrated that she'd ended up with Rogen that night. Not just because she hadn't even given Vin a chance, but because she always, *always* went back to Rogen.

Which was why Vin was in such a shitty mood.

Jewel was too feisty to let him win, though. She said, "I'm sure the redhead screamed plenty loud."

His jaw clenched briefly.

Vin had no idea what possessed him, but he admitted, "It was just a blow job in my office. I took her home after I saw you. Kissed her on the cheek and returned to the mansion."

"Yeah, right," Jewel scoffed as she headed toward the door, which Vin yanked open for her. She preceded him; he enjoyed the view. The sassy sway of her hips, those long, sleek legs. An ass he wanted to fuck. She added, "Is that because Rogen wasn't there to help you heat things up?"

Vin's gut twisted. "I have no idea what you're talking about," he lied.

She *knew?*

*How?*

Jewel said, "For the record, I didn't just fall off the turnip truck."

"I never really did understand that saying," he muttered as he followed her into the busy Saltillo-tiled entryway.

She tossed a sassy look over her shoulder and boldly informed him, "I've heard it murmured here and there that you both like to be in on the same action. Not necessarily *separately*." Her gaze remained on him a moment more, as though challenging him to deny it.

Vin merely smirked.

She kept strutting through the entryway. Vin's groin tightened as he suddenly thought of Jewel naked and sprawled across his bed. She'd been willing to let him experiment years ago. Not establishing any limitations. Getting off on everything he did to her.

Sure, she'd had some insecurities, some uncertainty, when he'd gotten particularly daring. But the chemistry between them had sizzled to the point of distracting her from her inhibitions.

God, how he'd loved making her come.

So, too, did Rogen.

The conundrum grew.

Was she still as adventurous as she'd once been?

Was it even a possibility that she was mentioning the "murmurs" for a specific reason? Planting the seeds in his mind—possibly Rogen's, too?

*Oh, fuck.*

His cock twitched.

Jewel interrupted his errant thoughts, asking, "What are you doing here, anyway?"

*Ah, thank God.* A much-needed distraction.

Back to the business at hand.

He said, "Rogen wanted me here as his general counsel."

"It's only champagne and charcuterie, Vin," she flippantly said. "Hardly requires legal representation."

He gave a half snort. "That's subjective."

"Hey. There you two are." Rogen suddenly appeared as they stood in a throng of tourists hoping for a table. The locals knew to make reservations well in advance on the weekends. Or possess the proper last name. "We're set up out back."

Rogen swooped in and kissed Jewel on the cheek. Vin fought a scowl, his temper simmering as they skirted the large fountain and made their way through the bar and lounge area and onto the patio.

It had always been so easy-breezy between Rogen and Jewel. And always so damn tumultuous between Vin and Jewel.

The bane of his existence was that he'd never gotten over her. Had never gotten her out of his system.

They'd kept their romance to themselves. Mostly because the Angelinis had taken Vin in after his parents' deaths and Jewel had worried over Gian sending Vin off to Trinity, too, if he found out about them.

Vin had always been torn between attending the prep school with his best friend and staying in River Cross. With his best friend's girlfriend.

In the end, she'd been impossible to leave. She'd been heartbroken and devastated when Rogen had left. Vin had sworn *he'd* never leave her. He'd sworn she could always count on him.

That had turned out to be another lie.

But again . . . not entirely his fault.

The trio crossed the threshold of opened glass doors and Rogen directed them to a collection of oversize armless patio chairs with thick cushions and a round glass-topped coffee table with a decorative black wrought-iron frame positioned in the middle of the seating area. The way the chairs were arranged created a inverted triangle with Vin and Rogen at the top and Jewel at the bottom.

Or maybe Vin just couldn't get threesome connotations out of his mind.

Had it been Holly McCormick Rogen was making love to the

other night, Vin would have joined them. And vice versa. But no. It had been Jewel.

And that was different.

So very, *very* different.

Yet . . . tempting.

So very, *very* tempting.

The two of them with her . . . Yeah. That'd pretty much comprise the *be-all, end-all* of ménages. And no fooling himself, he burned for it. Wanted more than anything for him and Rogen to do what they did best—work together to make her come, over and over, in the most dynamic ways.

But again . . . *Not* a fantasy that would ever become a reality. *Let it go, man.*

Their server greeted them as she set out the charcuterie board with an assortment of cheeses, breads, pâtés, and olive oil–soaked almonds, while someone from the bar rushed over with a free-standing chiller, both Jewel and Rogen being wine-country royalty. The server popped the cork on a bottle of Cristal and the men deferred to Jewel to sample the champagne. With her nod of approval, the server poured.

When the trio was left alone, they raised their glasses, said "*Salut*," in unison, and sipped.

Then Vin got right down to business. Once more latching on to the fact that it was the safe, sane thing to do.

He told Jewel, "Rogen and I figure the reason you came to the mansion was to make a play for the property your family co-owns with the Angelinis."

She sipped again. "You could have gone straight to the source for confirmation—Gian."

"He left for Italy this morning," Rogen informed her. "And it was a pretty easy assumption to make, considering you said everyone's fine at your estate. What other reason would you have to speak with my father?"

"It's true," she told them. "And he agreed to the sale."

Vin sucked down more champagne as his blood boiled. What was it about Jewel Catalano that held him enrapt—and chipped away at him at the same time?

It wasn't just the nearly palpable sexual tension that naturally sparked between her and Rogen. Hell, it flamed between Vin and her as well.

Maybe that was what put him so on edge. How could she be so addictive to both men? And why the hell could none of them fully break free of the web they'd woven years ago? For that matter, why were they spinning and twining fresh threads now?

Vin set aside his glass. There was raw agitation coursing through his veins that wasn't entirely related to this land deal Jewel was trying to pull off. He was too damn caught up in her for his own good. The smart, savvy woman she'd become. The sweet, shattered girl she'd once been.

For Christ's sake, how many tears had he brushed from her cheeks?

How many times had he told himself it was pointless to fall for her? How many times was he going to tell himself now that she could never be a part of his and Rogen's current sexual lifestyle? While in the back of his mind he wondered if she actually *could* be.

With a mental shake of his head, he tried to steer clear of all the emotions she evoked, all the desire. All the landmines inherent to their situation.

He said, "You're forgetting that it's not just Gian's and Rose-Marie's signatures you need on a bill of sale, Jewel. You have to get Rogen's, too. And I've advised him not to sign."

Vin pushed to his feet and stalked off, not wanting to see the look of defeat on Jewel's face.

That *he'd* put there.

# SIX

"What the hell?" Rogen questioned as Vin stormed off.

Jewel's gaze was on Vin's back. Her stomach knotted. Her heart wrenched.

Vin's hostility was wrapped in pain.

She'd experienced it enough in her lifetime to recognize the signs. To hear it in his voice. See it in his eyes.

But what, exactly, was his full source of contention? It was clearly directed at her. Yet Jewel had no idea why he was so razor-sharp with her.

Sure, the fact that he'd come across her and Rogen making love the other night might have something to do with it. Might have cut deep.

Though it really shouldn't.

Vin had walked out on *her*. Not the other way around.

Obviously, she was missing something.

"Here I thought this was going to be a civilized afternoon," she lamented. Cocktails and appetizers. Vin in black pants and a robin's-egg blue dress shirt, the sleeves rolled up his impressive forearms. Rogen in black pants as well with a magenta polo shirt from the local country club, the hems of the short sleeves straining against his bulging biceps. Her in her mini and sandals.

She sighed. Polished off her champagne and deposited the crystal flute on the table. To Rogen, she said, "This is unresolved angst. I need to speak with him." Clear the air. Once and for all.

Jewel followed after Vin, through the dining room toward the restrooms. She found him at the end of the long hallway, by the windows, talking on his iPhone and pacing agitatedly.

He caught sight of her, disconnected the call, and sauntered toward her.

"What business is it of yours if I make a deal with Gian for the property?" she asked.

"Maybe Rogen has plans for that land, Jewel. Ever occur to you?"

"No, actually. He's never personally come to my family to buy us out."

Vin shoved a hand through his dark, tousled hair. "He's equally entitled. By inheritance."

"Jesus, Vin. We could be sixty or seventy before that property passes to us. It's just going to sit undeveloped for the next thirty, forty years because of some absurd argument?"

"If that's what both your parents choose."

Her gaze narrowed on him. "And what did you advise, exactly? Surely you're not passing judgement because it's *me* who wants that land?"

"You're pretty damn good at getting everything you want—"

"I've gotten *nothing* that I wanted!" she erupted, not giving a damn who heard her. Luckily, the hallway was currently empty. "There were only two things, *ever*. And I lost them both, so—"

His hand shot out and he clasped her upper arm. He dragged her into an unoccupied restroom and slammed the door behind them. Locked it. Pressed Jewel's back against the smooth wood.

"You didn't lose me," he insisted, his eyes full of rage . . . and red-hot desire. Stealing Jewel's breath. "I was just never enough for you."

Emotion roared through her. Tears burned her eyes. "That is absolutely *not* true." Her chest rose and fell quickly, her body instantly responding to the nearness of him. The heat and intensity that always lit her up. "I'm not the one who left."

"Goddamn it, Jewel."

Anger radiated from him.

Exciting her.

A heartbeat later his mouth crashed over hers in a hungry, demanding kiss. A greedy one that immediately commanded her passion and ignited a firestorm within her.

She'd never forgotten how crazed Vin made her—not just in an infuriating way but also in a sexy way. How powerful the attraction was between them. The need . . . the fever. Her fingers plowed through his thick hair as his arms wrapped around her and he hauled her up against him. Held her tight.

She remembered how sometimes the insanity and intensity of the moment would scare her—not because of anything she feared Vin doing to her. But because of how vehemently she responded to him. How willingly she gave herself over to him. How she let the inferno consume her, let him have her in any way he wanted her.

It was irrational, illogical, how she became someone else with Vin D'Angelo. How she became a wild creature that wanted to claw at him. To rip open his shirt and *literally* claw at him.

Jewel knew he felt the same.

He shoved her skirt up, pushed her thong to the side, and thrust two fingers into her. Rocking her to the core of her being. Not just from the sudden, scorching invasion, but because he knew— *he'd always known*—she'd be wet for him, dripping and ready for whatever he did to her.

He stroked aggressively, confidently. Masterfully. Owning her as all the sizzling sensations flamed within her.

The pad of his thumb rubbed her clit with just the right amount of pressure. He didn't release her from their sizzling kiss, making the fire burn brighter.

Her orgasm was seconds away. She wondered if he'd let her have it. Or if he intended to punish her for her night with Rogen.

But then he stroked faster, with sheer determination. Jewel tore her mouth from his and cried out as the climax burned through her. She instantly bit into Vin's shoulder to quiet herself.

*Oh, God!* He'd been right—he did make her scream!

Her body quaked from her release and she clung to Vin, her breath coming in heavy pulls. As did his.

Getting her off turned him on. Melded to him, she could feel his steel erection.

"You want my cock inside you, don't you?"

It was so fucking risky to get tangled up with both men. She'd already forewarned herself.

But it was also inevitable.

"Yes," she said on a lust-filled breath.

Vin let out a low, sensuous growl at her immediate consent. Her instant surrender.

"Can you take me the way you used to?"

Magma replaced the blood in her veins. "Yes." She had a well-stocked goody drawer at home that kept her primed. Even though there hadn't been anyone in her life these past several years to be primed for.

Vin reached in his pocket for his wallet. He extracted a condom. *Extra Lubricated* the packet read.

"Bend over the vanity," he quietly demanded. His devilishly handsome face was a mask of hard angles, etched with need and desire. That need was centered on possessing her. She had no doubt.

Jewel crossed the room and did as instructed, propping her forearms on the granite counter. She watched Vin in the large oval rattan-framed mirror. He stood behind her, his gaze locked with hers as he undid his pants and shoved them and his black boxer briefs to mid-thigh. He tore open the foil square and Jewel's breath hitched. Exhilaration flooded her veins. Tinged with anxiety. Because Vin was huge.

"Spread your legs wider for me," he said.

She inched them apart as he rolled on the condom. Then he jerked the sliver of lace from her thong over one ass cheek. His fingers massaged her cleft, rubbing slowly from the small hole of her anus to the opening of her pussy. Back and forth. Teasing her.

"Vin," she urged as a familiar, though long-buried, restlessness took hold of her. She was desperate to feel him, desperate to see all the emotions play on his strong features as he fucked her. And that was exactly what he'd do. Unapologetically. Assertively. Not sweet and romantic like Rogen, but forcefully. Fiercely.

She desperately yearned for it.

His fingers dipped into her pussy, stroking deeply. Her inner muscles clutched and released involuntarily, her body wanting more. So much more.

"You get so damn wet for me. Do you get this wet for him?"

"Yes," she said.

Angst flashed in Vin's hypnotic green eyes.

"Do you want me to lie?" she asked.

"No."

He continued to stroke.

"Do you both really enjoy one woman at the same time?" she challenged.

His jaw worked rigorously. Then . . . "Yes."

She blinked, actually taken aback. When she shouldn't have been.

*Ask the question, expect the answer. . . .*

"Do you want me to lie?" he taunted.

"No. I want you to fuck me."

He withdrew from her and used the cream that coated one of his fingers to rim her anus, pressing in to lubricate her with her own juices. Her knees nearly buckled at the searing sensation. The intensity of Vin's expression. All his dark edges and his powerful presence.

"Are you okay?" His gaze continued to hold hers in their reflection. "Is this going to be too much?"

"I want you," she repeated. The anticipation mounted, seizing her, making her crazed for him.

Vin removed his finger and nudged the hole with the tip of his cock.

The anticipation nearly burst her wide open, to the depths of her soul.

"Jesus, Vin," she pleaded in a breathy voice. "Do it. Let me feel you."

He very slowly, very carefully entered her.

Jewel let out a small cry of pleasure. There was something incredibly enticing about the discomfort. The pinching. The raw sensations.

Though Vin had thoroughly educated her the first time he'd taken her this way and she'd known what to expect, in theory, there really was no describing, no preparing for, the purely primal heat and lust invoked by the forbidden act.

"Breathe, baby," he said in a strained tone.

Jewel sucked in a slice of air, not even realizing she'd been holding her breath.

He pulled out of her, then pushed back in, a bit hastier this time. The action jolted her and he wound an arm around the front of her, at the waist, to steady her. To keep her hips from hitting the granite.

Jewel's spine bowed and she lifted her ass higher.

Vin let out a carnal grunt. "You really do want me to fuck you."

"You know I do," she shamelessly said.

Vin pulled out once more. Plunged in. Pumped steadily.

"Oh, Christ," she whimpered. She reached for his free hand and covered her mouth with his palm as her moans bounced off the river rock–trimmed walls, only slightly diffused by the jazz music piped in. She would have turned on the water faucet for more camouflage if California weren't in the middle of a drought.

"Goddamn, Jewel." Vin's voice was tight, gruff. "You feel incredible."

She kept her hand over his at her mouth and slipped the other one between her legs to rub her clit. Quickly. Like the way he moved inside her. Sliding along the narrow walls, not thrusting all the way in but far enough to send them both soaring.

His jaw clenched again. His chest heaved. She watched him barrel toward orgasm right along with her.

"Oh, yeah," he ground out. "This is good. So damn good."

He fucked her faster, his hips jerking. Her muffled cries were more frequent now as the pressure built. The searing mixed with the sheer pleasure of having him inside her in this incredibly forbidden, decadent way. And knowing he was about to explode. As was she.

"Come for me, baby," he insisted, need blazing in his eyes.

She was *so* close.

His hips continued to buck. Her hard nipples ached for his touch. Her pussy wept. Her clit tingled. Every fiber of her being was caught in the sensuous heat and she knew she was going to come hard. Feared the scream that would wrench from her lips. But there was no turning back. No stopping.

Vin worked her into a blissful frenzy, setting her off with explosive potency. Her wail was barely stifled. Her eyes squeezed shut and her legs shook as the feverish climax took her.

"Fuck, yes," Vin said in a rough tone. "I love it when you lose it for me, baby."

His cock surged. His body convulsed. And then Vin let out a low roar as he came inside her, pushing just a bit deeper and prolonging her orgasm.

Jewel couldn't breathe. She quaked and flamed to the core. Rocked by Vin's intensity and aggression.

"Jesus," he muttered. "You make me so fucking hot."

She pulled his hand from her mouth and tried to inhale beyond slight wisps of air. Vin took his time riding out his own release. He looked as dazed as she felt. Slowly collected himself.

Eventually, he withdrew from her and peeled off the condom. Wrapped it in a tissue and tossed it in the trash. Then he cleaned himself up and dried his hands with a plush towel. His breathing was still labored.

Jewel was afraid to move. Wasn't sure her weak knees and trembling legs would support her.

Vin eyed her curiously. Stepped toward her and shifted her thong back into place. Worked her tight skirt along her backside.

She gazed at him over her shoulder.

"Did I hurt you?" he asked, appearing genuinely concerned.

Jewel finally rallied the strength to straighten. She turned to him. "No. You know I liked it. Though I probably won't be able to sit properly for a week." Her gaze narrowed on him. "Why'd you do it that way?"

His expression darkened. "Because Rogen never has, right?"

She shook her head.

"No one ever has, right?"

Another slight shake.

"That's why. I want to own you like no other man ever has. And"—his head lowered to hers and he murmured, "I wanted you to feel me long after we were done."

Damn him for stealing her breath again.

Yet she managed to ask, *"Are* we done?"

Vin dragged a hand down his face. Sighed with exasperation. And a notable amount of irritation.

"I don't fucking know, Jewel." Pain flitted across his chiseled face, making her heart hurt. "I take one look at you and I want you like nothing I've ever known before. Every single time. I'm held hostage by it, trapped. And I can't tell whether or not I ever want to escape. But all that comes of it is me getting screwed over."

*"You?"* she softly demanded, her own pain swelling in her throat.

"You always go back to Rogen, Jewel. *Always.*"

"I'm not the one who disappeared," she reminded him in a sharp voice. "If you're held hostage, how could you have ever left me? Especially when you swore you never would."

More tears stung her eyes. Memories of Vin going off the grid with no explanation whatsoever made her stomach coil.

"You walked away *so* easily," she accused. "What . . . did you get bored with me, Vin? Had you fucked me every way you knew how and were just plain finished with me?"

Now the tears fell. The lump in her throat grew, nearly choking her.

"You'd be insane to believe that, Jewel. Even for a second."

"You broke my heart!" she cried.

Vin's jaw set. Agony filled his eyes as he said with controlled fury, "You fucking broke mine."

Then he walked past her and out the door.

Leaving Jewel reeling.

She stared at the door he'd slammed shut behind him. Figuratively as much as literally?

She didn't know.

Jewel swiped at her tears, but they kept coming. She needed a really good sobfest at the moment. Wanted to weep for all the shit they'd gone through as teens. The disaster that still haunted them, still existed between her, Vin, and Rogen.

But she didn't have time for that.

*Come on, Jewel. Pull it together.*

She splashed water on her face. Dabbed at her skin with a hand towel. Inhaled deeply. Exhaled slowly. Over and over. Until the flow of tears stopped. Until she was no longer shaking.

As she gazed at herself in the mirror, she could see she looked wholly off-kilter, yet for contradictory reasons. There was a certain glow to her directly related to two amazing orgasms. But the pain was still visible.

With a sigh, she left the restroom. Only to run smack into Francine Hillman, a high school friend. One of the "murmurers" who thrived on top-secret gossip.

"Oh, my God, Jewel!" she blurted in her exuberant voice. Francine was a perky thing with short, sassy blond hair and big hazel eyes. "So it's true—you *are* back in town for the weekend. Why didn't you call me?"

"Nice to see you, France." They hugged. Then Jewel said, "I was with Bayli and Scarlet last night before Bay takes off on her big New York adventure."

"I'm so happy for her. Now . . . about *you*. Inner-circle confidants say you're having cocktails with Vin and Rogen this afternoon. Leslie Stevens saw you on the patio earlier." Her sculpted brows wagged. "I swear you are the luckiest woman in the world to have those two men so hopelessly devoted to you."

"I don't know about that," she grumbled, her heart compressing.

"You mean the three of you aren't . . . *you know*?" Francine's eyes lit with excitement.

"Oh, hell, no," Jewel was quick to say. "It's *definitely* not like that!"

*Who would even think that for a second?*

*Oh, yeah.* Jewel would.

She bit back a groan. *Do not go there. Do not go there. Do not—*

Could she actually seduce them into agreeing to be with her? It was sooo tempting!

*Do not—*

"Well, anyway," Francine said, "perhaps someday you'll finally choose between them? Free up one of their hearts for the rest of us to vie for?" She winked.

"I'm not holding anyone back, France." Though Vin's words instantly returned to her. . . . *I can't tell whether or not I ever want to escape.*

What the hell was she supposed to make of that? *Do* with that?

Jewel had no idea. She told Francine, "I'm heading back to the city tonight. I don't intend to make it a habit to come home."

All the memories wrecked her, so what was the point? Well, until she got hold of that land she wanted. Then she'd be so damn busy with her plans for the inn that she wouldn't have time to think about Rogen and Vin. Or get mired in the past.

The inn was her future—*that* needed to be her focus. Not whether two hot and hunky men would concede to sending her to sexual heights the likes of which she'd never known.

"Look, I've got to run," Jewel said. "The guys are waiting for me." They hugged again.

"Try not to be too much of a stranger, huh?"

Jewel smiled. "We'll see. It was good bumping into you." She continued on her way.

Joining Rogen and Vin, she slipped into her seat and tried to appear collected. Strictly a facade, because she was a mess inside. And it didn't help matters that Rogen studied her a bit too closely, making her squirm as she propped herself partially on her hip to avoid any discomfort and reached for her freshly poured champagne.

Vin looked equally tense. Rogen's gaze slid from her to him, and back.

Then he said, "This is an interesting turn of events. Seems we all have something the other wants. Question is, what are we going to do about it?"

Jewel swallowed hard.

*Oh, Christ.*

Was this opportunity knocking?

Was this the moment Jewel was supposed to mention that she was fully amenable to a different definition of *their* "threesome"?

# SEVEN

Jewel took a long drink from her glass. Averted her gaze.

Rogen's gut clenched. She and Vin had been gone for some time. When Vin had returned, he'd still appeared uptight, but with a smug, satisfied air about him that had made Rogen wonder if he'd just had Jewel in a bathroom of Bristol's. After all, Rogen was quite familiar with his friend's triumphant expression when he'd just made a woman scream so loud she shook the rafters.

And since Jewel suddenly wouldn't make eye contact with either of them and her breaths came in sharp pulls—not to mention her neck and cheeks were flushed—Rogen had a feeling his suspicion was dead-on.

*Fucking fantastic.*

All that avoidance they'd done for the past decade was about to come to a head.

Perhaps that was a good thing. Get it all out in the open.

The past pains. And current desires.

Except that Vin drained his Cristal, set the flute aside, and stood. "There's nothing to discuss here. That land is going to remain deadlocked until the two of you inherit it, and then you can decide what you want to do. Leave me the hell out of it." To Jewel, he said, "Go back to San Francisco." His attention shifted to Rogen. "I'll see you at the estate tomorrow morning."

Then he sauntered off.

Rogen shook his head. Yeah, there was definitely something going on that he'd turned a blind eye to for far too long. He wasn't one to bury his head in the sand as a rule. He didn't mind confrontation, always chose to stand his ground. In business and with his parents as well, now that he was an adult and they didn't have a say in how he lived his life—or what woman he ended up with.

But sharing Jewel with Vin?

He bit back a disconcerted growl. First, he'd punch Vin in the face. Then . . . well, then he didn't know what the fuck he'd do.

Because the thought of the three of them together *together* had been on his mind since the party. Yet it was a notion wrapped in prickly feelings and risky complexities. Too volatile a subject to ever broach.

Jewel finished her champagne before getting to her feet. She smoothed a hand over her short skirt while holding her small handbag in the other. She said, "I really have to be getting back."

So Vin and Jewel wanted to keep playing the avoidance game, too. How smart was that, really? Aside from maintaining the peace amongst them? For the most part, at any rate. It was obvious there was still something wrong between Vin and Jewel.

Rogen said, "I'll walk you out."

"No, that's fine. I'm going to make the rounds in the bar and say hi to whoever might be there so I don't appear anti-social. France already caught me in the hallway." She pulled in a deep breath, squared her shoulders, and attempted a smile, though he could see that the corner of her mouth quivered with emotion. "See you around, cowboy."

She left him. Rogen let her go.

No easy feat.

But sometimes holding on too tight didn't get you where you

wanted or needed to be and letting go was necessary to preserve your sanity. And your friendships. Even if all the signs screamed that Rogen wasn't the only one in love with Jewel Catalano.

Which could lead to one seriously explosive situation—in a lot of different ways.

Rogen beat the hell out of his punching bag Sunday afternoon. Immersed himself in work Monday and Tuesday. Cornered his father Wednesday evening, when Gian had returned from a quick trip to the Tuscany operations.

Rogen dropped a file folder on his father's desk in his massive study and said, "Our highest-end cognacs are now on the premium lists at the Bellagio and Caesars Palace. Three more country clubs in Santa Barbara, Dana Point, and Palm Springs. That's just this week."

"Excellent," Gian told him with a nod of approval. "We want to maintain exclusivity with the new line, but we do need to be hitting those VIP rooms. Create a buzz."

"Ha. Puny." Rogen smirked.

His father didn't look amused.

So Rogen simply said, "Agreed." He slid his hands into the pockets of his dress pants and got down to other business. "I spoke with Jewel. She thinks we're going to sell the land to her."

Gian didn't glance up from the paperwork he perused. "I have no intention of relinquishing that property."

Rogen's gaze narrowed. "She seemed pretty confident you'd come to terms."

"I let her buy into that. Clever girl, that one. She knew better than to just come at me with a check and a smile. She's located a vintage brand of scotch from our family's first distillery that I haven't been able to acquire. She's convinced she can secure it, and damned if I'm not a believer. Clever *and* tenacious." He whistled under his breath.

"Pretty ballsy, too, to have come here without her father."

"It's her own deal, I think. But again . . . I'm not selling."

This confused Rogen. It didn't surprise him, yet . . . "What about the scotch you want?"

"Oh, I intend to end up with it. I have a plan."

"And that plan would be?"

Gian finally looked up from his desk and gave Rogen a conspiratorial grin. "When I send it out for authentication, the decanter will get lost in transit. I'll compensate Jewel for her trouble and regretfully inform her that without the scotch the deal's off. It'll eventually turn up and sit on my shelf."

Rogen folded his arms over his chest. "You're going to double-cross her."

"It's business, Son. Jewel is smart enough to know that anything could go wrong. That this could all fall apart for her. She might be out time and effort but, as I said, she'll be compensated."

Stewing over this, Rogen asked, "What's the point in keeping that property in a stranglehold? If we can't develop it, nor can the Catalanos, what's the purpose of it still being part of our portfolio?"

Gian pushed his chair back and stood, planting his hands on his desk. Spearing Rogen with an intense look. "I refuse to let Catalanos encroach on my lot line. Keeping that tract between our estate and theirs is the purpose of it still being part of our portfolio."

"Then why don't *we* make an offer?"

"Because Anthony Catalano feels the exact same way. We might have to coexist in this town, but not as direct neighbors."

*Oh, for fuck's sake!*

"I understand that Anthony broke your pact," Rogen said. "That he moved autonomously on that land when it was supposed to be a joint venture. And he took advantage of the situation during a vulnerable time for our family." Right in the middle of Taylor's illness and subsequent death. Rogen's younger sister had been diagnosed with late-stage cancer, had suffered horrifically, and had died not more than four weeks later. It had wrecked everyone under this roof.

So yes, Rogen could fully understand his father's anguish. The unfortunate aspect was that the situation had never been resolved. The two men had never even tried to make amends.

Rogen hadn't been privy to all the details, but from what he'd gleaned, Anthony Catalano had made the split decision to employ Plan B for the land, rather than the Plan A he and Gian had finally agreed upon. Anthony had brought surveyors onto the property, had conducted environmental tests, and intended to break ground on an Italian village of art galleries, restaurants, and specialty markets with imported goods—rather than the viticulture center and international tasting room previously agreed upon with Gian.

Anthony had later contended that Gian was not of the frame of mind to make sound business decisions while dealing with his daughter's severe illness and treatments and the ensuing grief of her death. Taylor had only been nine, after all. A beautiful, precocious girl who'd easily wrapped everyone around her little finger from the very beginning.

Rogen in particular. He'd been devastated by her dire diagnosis alone. It had also rocked the very foundation of the Angelini estate. The entire community of River Cross. Making it particularly shortsighted on Anthony's part to swoop in with his favored plans for the property.

Later, Anthony had asserted that he'd had everyone's best interests at heart. But despite the fact that his business schematic would have made the two families a shitload of money, it was the principle of the matter that led to Gian not reconciling with him. And forbidding his wife and his son from associating with Catalanos.

A huge clusterfuck all the way around.

For God's sake, Rogen's parents had staff call whatever restaurant they chose to dine out at in order to ensure Anthony and

Sophia didn't have a reservation there within a two-hour time frame of their visit.

Gian said, "If Jewel is interested in that land, Anthony will grind over the fact that they can't get their hands on it. That's the only vengeance I get. But I'll take it." He returned to his seat.

Rogen didn't bother to mention he'd been grinding himself, for years, because he wanted his own vineyard. He already knew what his father would say: *So find some other land to grow on.*

But the point was to keep the distillery and a new winery connected, not divided by a county or two.

"If that's all," Gian said, "I've got a lot of work to catch up on."

Rogen nodded. "I'll see you at dinner, then."

His mind churned with a way to acquire that land himself, but the Catalanos had not been receptive to Gian's offers in the past, so the Angelinis had stopped making them. And Rogen's father was right. Anthony clearly wanted the property and would leave it sitting if he couldn't have it. The men wouldn't even consider subdividing, each taking a slice. Because, yes, they'd border each other's estates. And, apparently, they preferred to have mass quantities of acreage separating them.

Yet there had to be a reasonable solution.

Perhaps it was time Rogen found it.

"You realize you're constructing a house of cards?" Bayli asked on a three-way videoconference call with Jewel and Scarlet on Thursday morning.

Ignoring the ominous warning for the moment, Jewel gazed past Bayli's slender shoulder and said, "Please tell me that's *not* your new apartment in the background?"

"Yippers, this is the one." She flashed a bright smile, then informed them, "I'm scrubbing and disinfecting every square inch of it. Pretty disgusting, right? But a fresh coat of paint is cheaper than just about every other place I looked at. And I really don't want to live in Hoboken. I need to be in Manhattan. This city has such an amazing vibe to it—I totally love it here!"

Scarlet said, "All well and good, but seriously, Bay. I think I see something crawling along the wall behind you."

"Oh, yeah. That." Bayli shrugged. She was a gorgeous tawny-eyed brunette hoping to spark her flailing modeling career. She was a year younger than Jewel and Scarlet, but the three had been friends most of their lives. This was the first time the girls had truly been separated.

Bayli said, "If I could get the cockroaches sharing my space to pay rent, I'd let the little suckers live." She reached for something out of the screenshot of her propped-up tablet and then moved back into place. Holding up a can of Raid, she added, "Give me a week and this place will be completely bug-free. I'm spraying *everything*! The inner and outer door frames, all the baseboards, the garbage chute down the main hall. I promise, I *will* prevail!"

Her enthusiasm couldn't be contained.

Meanwhile, Jewel's spirits plummeted. "I offered you a loan, Bay."

"One I can't pay back, Jewel."

"Then don't pay it back." Jewel knew her friend was flat broke. The plane ticket to Newark, the shuttle ride into the city, the rent and deposit, and bare necessities were about all she could afford at this point.

Bayli had made it through two years of college before the expense of her mom's heart surgeries and at-home care had depleted all of her savings and Bayli had had to get a job. Unfortunately, she wasn't the type to settle on just one thing, so she'd worked a bunch of odd, part-time jobs rather than finding something full-time. Even though she had tried at first. But landing a position in San Francisco's Financial District that would pay her the kind of salary she needed for medical and living expenses required the degree she'd never gotten. A vicious Catch-22 for her.

"Try not to worry about me," Bayli said, ever the optimist. "Everyone in this business has to pay their dues. Once I meet some other models, I might be able to find one or two of them to room with and that'll be a huge help. In the meantime, let's talk about this little plot of yours, Jewel."

"Bay's right, Jewel," said Scarlet, a fiery redhead who worked in River Cross as an independent insurance-fraud investigator. She had an inquisitive mind and a voracious appetite for solving mysteries, a trait that came from her famous crime-novelist grandmother. "One card gets out of whack and your house comes crumbling to the ground."

"I have the agreements all drawn up," Jewel told them. "Everything's in place. I just need my itinerary from Cameron, which she's finalizing as we speak. I leave tomorrow for the whirlwind trip to collect all the cards." Her own enthusiasm was as strong as Bayli's.

The girls had helped Jewel connect the dots, and by this time next week she ought to be at the Angelini estate with her legal team to execute the sale with Gian.

Scarlet said, "Let us know if there's anything else we can do to help."

"You've been fantastic. I owe you big-time."

"Are you kidding?" Bayli gushed. "This is the high point of my day! I love researching all this stuff. And watching Scarlet hunt it all down."

"You're geniuses," Jewel said. "Now, Bay, I'm really worried about—"

"Ah-ah-ah." Her friend waggled a finger onscreen. "Do not stress about me in New York City. I am *thrilled*! I already landed fifteen hours a week at a public library, so you know that puts me in heaven right there. I also have ten hours on weekends at a gelato stand in Central Park—now doesn't that sound fun for the summer? And, oh! I totally forgot to tell you that Christian Davila is opening up a steakhouse with the very brilliant celebrity chef Rory St. James along the subway line from where I live—just a hop, skip, and a jump away. One of Christian's first restaurants was Bristol's and it's apparently very near and dear to his heart, so I thought that me being a River Cross 'hometown girl,' it'd be pretty easy to land a waitressing job there."

"Yeahh," Scarlet said, drawing out the word with notable skepticism. "Um. Let us not forget that the last time you tried serving was at Alioto's on the Wharf, and you spilled a glass of red wine on the mayor's wife. Who happened to be wearing all white that evening."

"Oh, please," Bayli scoffed. "Everyone spills at some point in their career. Yesterday, I was talking with a server at a place around the corner and she said she took home a tray and piled books on top of it and carried it around her apartment, figuring out the correct weight placement and getting used to hauling the load all with one hand. I can totally do this. And how great would it be to work at a premier restaurant with a celebrity chef while I'm trying to break out as a model? I'm sure to get discovered, right?"

Now she gnawed her bottom lip.

Jewel's heart constricted at her friend's hint of insecurity. "Bay, you are totally going to be discovered. You're sensational. So, *so* beautiful. And the most photogenic person I've ever known. No offense, Scarlet, but there's no camera angle under the sun that captures the two of us in a good light. We always look like we've just tasted a bad Bordeaux."

"Or our eyes are closed," Scarlet lamented. "I swear, when the three of us are in a photo together, it's as though whoever's taking the picture is focused solely on Bay and doesn't give a rip how shitty we come out."

Jewel laughed. "You're so right!"

"Aw, you guys." Bayli dabbed at the corner of her eye. Fanned her face with a hand. "You're gonna make me cry."

"No tears," Jewel insisted. She was still on the verge of her own sobfest over Rogen and Vin. She couldn't afford anything sparking it. "Just promise me that if you need anything—anything at all—"

"Like dental floss," Scarlet quipped, stealing a line from one of their favorite movies, *Pretty Woman*.

"Yes," Jewel agreed. "Like dental floss. Or rent. Call me instantly." She pinned Bayli with a stern look. "I'm deathly serious here, Bay. Do *not*, under any circumstances, hesitate to call. And for the love of God, please don't forsake a single meal. You are absolutely perfect, and missing dinner because you can't afford it is *not* an option."

Now fat drops tumbled down Bayli's cheeks. "You know I can take care of myself, girls. This might not be a mansion in River Cross, Jewel, but it already feels like home. Like I found my place. So please, *please* trust that I can handle this and believe that someday soon I'm going to be squealing on one of our calls that I've landed the cover of *Vanity Fair*."

"Oh, we're counting on it," Scarlet said. "And you're immediately autographing two copies and sending them our way. *Immediately*."

"If not sooner," Bayli said as she whisked away tears.

Jewel said to Scarlet, "All's well with you, too?"

"Well, I wasn't spotted on the patio of Bristol's having champagne and charcuterie with Rogen Angelini and Vin D'Angelo over the weekend, but yes. All's well."

Bayli gasped. "What was *that* about, Jewel? You haven't seen either one of them in years."

Waving a dismissive hand in the air, because Jewel did not want to travel this twisted path—she had not told Bayli or Scarlet about her encounter with either man at the gala—she said, "It was strictly business. Related to the house of cards."

"So, Rogen knows you want the land?" Scarlet asked.

"Yes. And Vin has advised him to not provide the third signature I need."

*"What?!"* Bayli blurted.

"It's a long and complicated story," Jewel told them with a shake of her head.

"Jesus," Scarlet added. "Isn't it always that way with the three of you?"

"Yes. Unfortunately, it hasn't gotten any easier." However, Jewel had returned to the adage of *out of sight, out of mind.* For her own sanity. "It doesn't matter, really. I'm extremely close to getting what I want, and that's where my focus is."

Granted, even coveted real estate was a sorry second to Rogen and Vin. But there was no way she could ever choose between the two of them. And there might not even be the possibility of it, especially with Vin so angsty toward her. So why deliberate over a potentially nonexistent scenario?

If Jewel had her inn to concentrate on and preoccupy every waking minute, that would make her happy. She could live with that as the main fulfillment in her life.

*Hopefully.*

One erotic thought did continue to sizzle and snap in her mind, though.

She asked her friends, "Either of you know Holly McCormick?"

"Not well," Scarlet said. "She was in town for about a year, then left for six months. Just now returned. She's a Realtor, but I think she has some other business ventures elsewhere."

"Hmm."

"Why do you ask?" This from Bayli.

"Just curious. Have you ever heard of her mentioned along with Rogen . . . or Vin?"

"Sure," Scarlet said with a devious smile. "France says Holly has the hots for both guys. And they've both dated her."

"Just dated?" Jewel innocently ventured.

"Apparently, anything's possible with those two," Scarlet said. And winked.

*All righty, then. Nuff of that line of questioning.*

Luckily, Cameron entered the office, giving Jewel an excuse to get off the topic of her two favorite men. She told her friends, "I have to go, ladies. I've got one crazy whirlwind escapade to embark on."

"Good luck," Bayli said.

"If you need us for anything, let us know," Scarlet added. "Fingers and toes crossed. Not the legs, though. I seriously need to get laid."

"I'm so certain my assistant needed to hear that." Jewel laughed.

They said their good-byes and Jewel disconnected the call.

Cameron told her, "I don't understand why they're both still single. You, either. Except, well . . . I know your history."

"Don't you mean my *hang-ups?*"

"I was trying to be polite. Now, I have your flight schedule all mapped out. Cabo San Lucas, Las Vegas, Paris. Joseph and Lars are taking a second plane to accommodate security and shipping of the paintings and scotch, but the yacht is to be transported by the new owners' designated people. Jack from Legal will be on hand, too, in the event any issues with the agreements pop up. Accounting will handle the initial electronic transfer of funds immediately at your request."

"God, you're efficient." Jewel collected her laptop and packed up.

"You do understand that if even one deal falls through you're not getting that land."

"I love that you're a realist. Truly, I do," Jewel said. "But let's all have a little faith here. Bayli and Scarlet laid some awesome groundwork, and I put everything systematically in place. This *is* going to work."

Cameron handed over the itinerary. Jewel slipped it into her bag as well. Then she left the office, took the elevator to the ground floor, and climbed into the town car waiting outside the lobby of the Catalano Enterprises building on Sacramento and Davis Streets. The early-evening fog had rolled in. The gray haze ribboned through the skyscrapers and the Embarcadero Center, filled with restaurants, shops, and galleries. A light mist fell.

Jewel had always found the weather in San Francisco sultry and provocative, adding a mysterious element to a city already brimming with alluring personality.

The first flat she'd rented with Bayli and Scarlet, who'd both gone to San Francisco State University with her, had been on Columbus Avenue and Greenwich Street along the edge of North Beach. Rumor had it scenes from a Dirty Harry movie had been filmed there, and the front rounded windows had a straight shot to Alcatraz Island. The Powell-Mason cable car line ran just outside her door, and she'd gotten a kick out of the *ching-ching* of the bell every time a cable car stopped at her corner.

She'd loved the unique view and the energetic ambience. The sunsets over the bay and the foghorns from ships in the early morning.

Now she owned a Victorian house in the upper-crust Pacific Heights neighborhood, per her parents' request, since they deemed it safer. The street she lived on was beautiful and well maintained but admittedly lacking the character of the Wharf and Columbus Avenue, which held the sinfully delicious aromas of roasted garlic cloves and fresh seafood from the multitude of Italian restaurants and the sounds of music and laughter echoing through the corridor of the avenue from the pubs and bars she missed frequenting.

Actually, she missed all of artsy, lively North Beach. Mostly its zesty, mouthwatering, mozzarella-dripping pizza slices.

She considered whether she'd move back to River Cross once she broke ground on the inn. It'd likely behoove her to establish an office there and be on-site on a daily basis. She just wasn't sure how that decision would sit with her father. He liked having her in the San Francisco headquarters, keeping her finger on the pulse of the company.

But Jewel contended that even if he wanted her to eventually take over, that wouldn't be for another two decades, since her father was only forty-eight. And she had three older, male cousins currently serving as executive vice presidents who might be better suited to run the organization when the time came—and if her inn panned out. . . .

Jewel contemplated that scenario as the car wound through the city and then pulled into her drive. Behind a pewter-gray Range Rover.

"Were you expecting company?" her chauffeur asked.

"No. But I think I know who it is, so it's okay."

*Rogen.*

She had no idea what vehicle he drove, though this one seemed befitting of him. Elegantly rugged.

But what was he doing here?

# EIGHT

Rogen was sprawled in a chair on the porch when Jewel ascended the steps and propped a hip against a tall column along the railing.

"How'd you find me?" she asked.

"Wasn't too difficult."

"Yet you've been back in California for six months and this is the first time you've shown up outside my house."

"Yeah, well." He hauled himself out of the chair. "You haven't exactly called, now have you?" He gave her a pointed look.

She said, "I lost my phone years ago and had to reprogram a new one. I didn't have all the old numbers written down anywhere."

"The 'old' numbers." Contacts from the past—her main connection to the past.

He couldn't tell if her excuse was just that or legitimate.

Did it matter?

Probably not. They'd willingly and consciously split paths.

"So what are you doing here this evening?" she asked as she unlocked the double doors with crystal-cut glass insets and pushed one open.

Following her into the large foyer, Rogen said, "Need to talk business with you."

Jewel disengaged the alarm, then dropped her keys into a decorative bowl on a narrow table against the wall and set her laptop bag at its base. Another table—a large, round one—sat in the middle of the foyer with a fresh bouquet of calla lilies in a slender, cylinder crystal vase. Rogen helped her out of her full-length coat and hung it on the rack in the corner, along with his brown distressed-leather jacket.

He took in the wide-open space of her home, with glossy hardwood floors, thick molding, rich wood accents. Three steps off the vast entryway led up to the bedrooms on the right, and three led down into the living room on the left.

He eyed the fireplace and the aspen logs stacked neatly next to the hearth and said, "Why don't I make a fire and you go change into something comfortable? Get out of those five-inch heels you seem to love wearing."

She gestured toward the fireplace and said, "It's gas. The logs are just decorative. The switch is under the mantle."

"Fine. I'll pour wine instead."

He wandered into the cavernous room while she went in the opposite direction. He lit the fire, then crossed to the wet bar and studied the impressive labels in the wine rack, selecting a Sangiovese. He pulled the cork and splashed a healthy amount into two glasses. Took a deep sip. Nearly spewed wine when he glanced over his shoulder at the sound of Jewel's approach.

Turning to her, he said, "Jesus Christ. Do you always have to take my breath away?"

"It's just lingerie."

"Hardly."

He set aside the glass and closed the gap between them. His fingers grazed the silky black material at her shoulders. "I don't really see the need for the robe."

He eased it down her arms and tossed it toward one of the sofas. She wore a black lace nightie with a tight, demi-bra bodice that plumped up her breasts and had crimson satin woven through it. A tiny matching bow sat between the valley of those enticing globes that nearly spilled over the scalloped edging. The rest of the material was clingy, sheer lace, hugging the dip of her waist and the curve of her hips, ending at the tops of her thighs. He wouldn't be surprised if he caught a glimpse of ass cheek in the back.

Rogen's muscles bunched and his cock sprang to life.

The woman did things to him. And she hadn't even touched him. But he could tell she wanted to. Could see it in her eyes as her gaze roved his body, taking in his navy-colored T-shirt, the short sleeves straining against his biceps, a small portion of the bottom hem tucked behind a belt buckle. He was dressed in jeans and his dusty-tan suede boots.

Her gaze lifted to his face and her breath caught.

Reaching a hand out to him, Jewel grazed his abs with manicured fingernails. Then slipped her palm beneath his shirt to lightly caress his skin. Turning every inch of him rigid.

"Why does it feel like time just melts away when we're together?" she asked in a quiet voice. "As though seven years apart don't even exist."

"Because we're comfortable with each other. Aware of each other on every level."

"Right." She inhaled deeply, held the breath in for a few moments. "I love how you smell. So masculine. So tough, resilient." She let out a soft laugh. "Those aren't actual scents, are they?"

"I think I get it."

"I think so, too. You always get me."

Her sapphire eyes held myriad emotions. Some of them easy to peg. Longing. Adoration. Others not so simple to decipher. Because they ran deeper. Were more complicated.

Rogen grabbed a fistful of material at his nape, hauled his shirt over his head, and dropped it to the floor.

"Touch me," he murmured, his own longing intensifying with every second she devoured him with her hungry gaze.

Her hands grazed his hot skin, up to his chest, along his shoulders. Down his arms. Back up, her nails trailing across his collarbone. Then her palms splayed over his pecs as Rogen's head dipped. His lips swept over hers. His insides ignited.

He pulled her to him so that she had to shift her hands to his back, allowing their bodies to press together. He kissed her deeply, their tongues tangling. One hand combed through her silky hair. The other cupped an ass cheek and squeezed.

She returned his kiss with equal fervor, her fingertips digging into his solid muscles. Her body rubbed against his, making him hotter. Harder.

When Rogen finally tore his mouth from hers, he slipped a hand between them and unfastened his belt, his jeans.

"Suck my dick," he told her, urgency tingeing his rough voice.

Jewel shoved his pants and briefs downward, then knelt before him. Her fingers circled his shaft and he pulled in a sharp breath.

She pumped slowly, at his root. Then her tongue ran the length of him to his tip, which she flicked playfully, making his hips jerk. Jewel smiled.

"You little tease."

Gazing up at him, she said, "*Teasing* would imply I don't intend to follow through. I have *every* intention of following through."

Her tongue swept along the groove of his head. Then her lips closed around him. She drew him into her mouth, inch by inch. Down to where she still firmly gripped him. Sucked hard. So fucking hard.

A low growl escaped him. Rogen whisked away strands of hair from her face and held them off her shoulders, wanting to watch her pleasure him with her luscious mouth. Her eyes closed and she worked him good. His cock slid along her tongue, her teeth lightly scraping as she nearly released him and then took him deep again.

"Oh, hell, yes," he said on a sliver of air.

She picked up the pace, her head bobbing as she stroked him and sucked with amazing skill. Her free hand cupped his balls and gently rolled and tugged, pushing him closer to the edge. Then the heel of her hand massaged his sac as her fingers grazed his cleft. The tip of one rimmed his anus.

Not something Rogen was familiar with, but goddamn, did it feel good. He let her have at it, stroking and massaging and rimming. Suctioning him. Milking him. Until he was on the verge of losing it.

He held her head in place, steady as he took over and fucked her mouth, his hips bucking, his breaths coming in heavy pulls.

"Ah, damn," he mumbled. "Jesus, you're good."

She continued her ministrations and the pressure mounted within him. "Swallow me down, sweetheart."

At that very moment her finger pressed in and the sensation rocketed through him. Rogen exploded in her mouth. "Fuck, Jewel!"

His body jolted. Tremors raced down his legs.

His orgasm was a powerful one. Nearly bringing him to his knees.

"Son of a bitch," he ground out. His heart thundering and his cock throbbing.

It'd easily been the best blow job of his life. Though, in the back of his mind, he recalled she'd not been such an expert the times he'd asked her to get him off this way.

Jewel got to her feet, a triumphant look on her beautiful face. "See? No teasing." She licked her lips saucily and then whirled around and sauntered off, likely to the restroom.

His pulse still roaring in his veins, Rogen zipped up but yanked the belt from the loops and hung it over the arm of a chair.

Left the top button of his jeans undone and his shirt off. He wasn't finished with her.

Though he couldn't release the notion eating a hole in his brain. When Jewel returned, he said, "That was sensational. Vin teach you how to do that?"

Jewel skirted around him and lifted one of the glasses Rogen had poured. They were *definitely* dancing around the flame. She sipped the Sangiovese as she contemplated her answer.

Indeed, Vin had instructed her on exactly how to make a man come fast and hard. He'd taught her a lot of things in bed. Things Rogen had no idea she knew.

But something else took precedence. Facing him, she asked, "What business do we have? You said that's why you're here."

Rogen groaned. Because she hadn't validated his suspicion? Or because of the new topic on deck?

He said, "Just when we thought things couldn't get stickier between us, I have to break some bad news to you."

"You're still not going to sign the bill of sale." Disappointment sat heavy in her belly. "Rogen. There's no point in—"

"Hear me out before you get pissed off. I'm actually on your side."

"Sorry, but I find that very hard to believe when it comes to this transaction."

He reached for his glass and pulled in a long drink. Then he told her, "My father's going to renege on the deal."

She gaped.

Rogen continued. "The scotch will disappear for a time but will eventually end up in his possession. He'll have paid you, so *no harm, no foul* in his mind. And the Angelini portion of the land will stay in our portfolio." He appeared contrite as he added, "It's no consolation, Jewel, but he's impressed with your resourceful-ness. He just refuses to part with that property."

"Goddamn it," she said, her heart sinking. Her dreams evaporating like the monks' wine. "Fuck me." She let out a humorless half snort. "In every conceivable way."

"Sweetheart." Rogen tucked a few strands of hair behind her ear. "I'm sorry."

Gazing up at him, she simply said, "Sure."

His expression turned tormented. His fingertips brushed gently over her cheek. "It's the truth, Jewel. I am sorry that my father would do something so underhanded, especially when you're making a valiant effort to free up that land."

"It's not just that, Rogen." She stared at him imploringly. "There has to be a way to get our families to let go of the past and move on. Be friends again. *Trust* each other. They're neighbors in a small community!"

His caressing hand fell away. He stepped around her. Went back to attempting to wear a hole in her floorboards.

But his apparent frustration and deliberation over the predicament was actually moot. Her big coup was dead in the water and there was nothing Rogen could do to help her salvage it.

Her eyes squeezed shut. She'd like to have said she'd gotten *so close* to succeeding and feel a modicum of pride for attempting something bold and daring. But she hadn't come even remotely close. She'd been stonewalled before she'd even shaken Gian Angelini's hand.

And should have known it.

"Jewel."

Her lids fluttered open. Her eyes were a bit misty, and her pride took another hit. What a fool they all must think she was. Gian. Rose-Marie. Rogen. Vin.

She turned away and sipped her wine, her nerves now frayed.

She wanted to scream. Instead, she said, "I'll bet Vin's getting a good laugh out of this."

"Vin doesn't know. And, for the record, *no one's* getting a laugh out of it. I don't even think my father's happy with his strategy. But it's the only one he's got, and it's the only way he's going to feel a little vindication over what your father tried to pull off when Taylor got sick and my family's attention was elsewhere."

"My father always contended he was doing right by the two businesses. That his projected profit margin was much wider than with a viticulture center and tasting room, to everyone's benefit."

"And he had all the proof to back it up; that can't be disputed. But the fact still remains, he cut my parents out of the decision-making and operated on his own."

Jewel turned back to Rogen. "Yes. You're right. And all of this bullshit is just supposed to be chalked up to best practices? What was supposed to be most advantageous for the bottom line? Except there is no bottom line with that property I want, as long as we all remain in a stalemate. So my father might as well have built his marketplace fifteen years ago and split the profits with your family. They would have made money—not lost it. Not continued to lose it."

"In a roundabout way . . . yes. That is true." Rogen stopped his pacing and asked, "What do you want with that land?"

"An inn. With plenty of room for events and weddings. Plus a Nicklaus– or Jim Engh–designed golf course. But what does it matter?"

*It's a dead stick now.*

She winced inwardly.

"So much for progress," Jewel said. "And trying to bridge our families. It was a stupid idea, wasn't it?" She stared up at Rogen again, her heart aching.

He gave her a solemn look, which only made her hurt more.

"It wasn't a stupid idea, sweetheart. In fact, it's a fantastic idea. Very smart, Jewel."

She fought the emotion crushing in on her. Latched on to

what Vin had said at the restaurant. She asked, "Was there some-thing *you* wanted to do with all that acreage?"

Rogen rubbed the back of his neck, as though tension had knotted the nerves. She was momentarily distracted by his bulging biceps and tanned skin.

He told her, "I want to grow on it. Mostly hybrids. Have my own winery."

"Wow." She was a bit blown away. "You never mentioned that."

"Because I was supposed to become Chief Operating Officer of Angelini, Inc., and juggle headquarters in Tuscany and second-ary operations in River Cross. I never imagined there'd be time left over for anything else. But all five distilleries have been in my family for generations and it's fairly smooth sailing."

He paced a little more.

Jewel regarded him thoughtfully, wondering what all he had yet to tell her.

Rogen said, "Sure, like everyone else, we suffer from the threat of frost and freezing, wildfires, infestations, the economy, labor dis-putes, all that. But in the grand scheme of things, we've been a well-oiled machine for centuries. Yes, evolution throws a wrench in the works from time to time. It's never anything critical . . . just proper advancement with new technologies. I want a *different* challenge."

She took a few steps toward him. "Along with your own con-tribution to the dynasty? Your own legacy?"

"I will admit, I never felt my destiny was just to feel content to be born with a silver spoon in my mouth. I work hard, no doubt. But not as hard as I would if I had to build something from the ground up and its success was my sole responsibility."

"Proof we're not just heirs, but entrepreneurs."

His gaze locked with hers. "Yes."

"And you'd like to see an end to this feud, too. Right?"

"Absolutely. Our parents were incredibly close once upon a time. It's disturbing to see them hold a grudge for so long. And I could tell when you showed up unexpectedly at the gala, their first concern was that something had happened at your estate. They were worried, even if they couldn't admit it out loud."

"I agree."

Mere inches separated them and they stared into each other's eyes while the air shifted and something new brewed between them.

Jewel couldn't keep herself from taking a huge leap of faith as a fresh idea sprang to mind and exhilaration chased down her spine. "You came here to warn me that I was going to get screwed out of my deal. Your father won't be pleased to know you tipped me off."

"No, he won't be."

"But you did it anyway."

"You don't deserve to get thrown under the bus any more than I do."

"True. Still . . ." She pressed a palm to his chest, over his heart. His muscles bunched at her touch, making all her intimate parts tingle. Somehow, she remained focused on the issue at hand. She said, "You chose me over him in this instance."

Rogen's teeth ground. Jewel saw the defining moment for what it was. They'd each had to do a hell of a lot of fighting to break free of some of the ideals of two powerful families and hadn't fully achieved that. There were some concessions Jewel still had to ask her parents for—land that she wanted to build on, for example.

But then again . . . no. She wasn't just asking to be handed something for nothing. She'd been willing to do whatever was necessary to get the Angelinis to consent to a sale. She was willing to work for what she wanted. To create something meaningful for herself, for her future, and for her family name.

And potentially reunite old friends in the process.

Rogen was willing to do the same.

So . . .

Her gaze turned hopeful, she was sure.

Rogen looked suspiciously at her. "What are you thinking?"

"That an inn and a winery are a fabulous combination."

"Jewel—"

"Just wait. Listen." She started to do some pacing of her own.
It helped her to think more clearly, sort out all the details. Not get
caught up in the delicious sight and scent of him. "If we could keep
this deal from falling apart and I sold you half of the land after I
acquired it from my parents, you could grow and I could build.
And we could prove to everyone that Catalanos and Angelinis *can*
trust each other and partner together. It'd be our own joint venture."

Because Jewel believed in Rogen enough to know that he
would never cheat her out of a transaction. She had a lifetime of
reasons to rely on that intuition, and one more that had occurred
this evening because he'd come here to warn her about his father's
intentions. Rogen had sacrificed a bit of family loyalty for her sake.
That couldn't have been easy for him, a man who prided himself
on loyalty and integrity.

Clearly, he felt loyalty toward her as well.

"Rogen," she said insistently. "We could *both* create our own
legacies. There's no reason why we can't do this together."

"Aside from our parents *not* signing on the dotted line?"

"My father agreed. If there's some way to keep your father
from double-crossing me, then all you have to do is provide the
final signature and we're in business."

He mulled this over. She could practically see his brain churning. With possibilities. Hope. Excitement.

Jewel's pulse raced.

"We could totally do this," she assured him. "I'll dump the

golf course in lieu of a vineyard. Think of the events we could host with an inn and a winery!"

Rogen nodded. "You're right. It'd be a great combo."

"And the perfect location."

He gave it further thought. A slow grin spread across his tempting lips. "Damn, Jewel. It's a fucking incredible idea." His enthusiasm grew with every passing second. His hands cupped her face. He stared deep into her eyes. Still grinning. Then he said, "We're gonna need Vin's help."

Jewel's racing pulse came to an abrupt halt. Her stomach took a serious dive south.

"No," she said. "Not Vin."

"We need legal counsel, Jewel," Rogen said. "Someone who can free that property from all the restrictions placed on it and ensure we execute a solid, loop-free deal all the way around."

"Rogen . . ." She shook her head. "*Not* him."

Rogen's brow furrowed. The snapping of the fire filled the quiet room as he seemed to wade through her adamant response. Finally, he asked, "Why not Vin? We've been friends with him since we were kids. It makes total sense."

"I don't trust him!" she blurted. Then pressed a hand to her mouth. Tried to collect herself. Dragging her hand away—stepping away—she attempted to explain. "It's not that I don't trust him in general. I *do*."

For God's sake, she'd let him fuck her ass in the bathroom at Bristol's. Knowing he'd be careful. And hadn't he been concerned when he'd first entered her? Then worried over whether he'd hurt her?

It was that whole broken-hearts thing that she couldn't get past. How had she broken Vin's heart? Had he actually been in love with her back then? He'd never once said the words. But that could have been because of her association with Rogen. And for that matter . . .

She pinched the bridge of her nose with her finger and thumb. She was going in wayward directions. So she told Rogen, "I just don't think I can trust him with my future plans. He's got some serious issues with me that I can't even begin to dissect or fix."

Rogen frowned. "That might be my fault, sweetheart."

# NINE

"No," Jewel asserted. "It's circumstance and teenage drama. Let's face it. We were kids who grew up fast and did some mature things we weren't exactly mature enough to handle or understand. I'm not even sure I'm experienced enough right now to reconcile all the intricate nuances when it comes to the three of us."

Rogen looked a bit taken aback. Because he didn't know the extent of her involvement with Vin?

She said, "I'm being honest here. There is so much spiraling out of control inside me from seeing you and Vin the other night . . . and these subsequent meetings."

"You two need to work this all out. Especially if we're going to move forward with our plans." Rogen extracted his iPhone from his front pocket, hit a contact in the list, and handed over the device.

Jewel stared at a smirking Vin onscreen, knowing he'd probably flipped Rogen off after Rogen had taken the photo. Again, she thought of how well the two men complemented each other and how close they'd always been, even with her thrown into the mix.

"Do it, Jewel. You two can't go on like this. I can see it's tearing you up as much as it is him. And, damn it, we *do* need him."

She took a deep breath. Her heart picked up several extra beats. It took a hell of a lot of courage, but she connected the call. Wholly uncertain of how much more conflict she was about to create for the three of them. How much more she could take.

"Hey, man," Vin came on the line, his enticing tone sending shivers down her spine, despite her trepidation. "I was ready to hit a bar for a beer, but Lane said you'd already left the office for the night."

"It's Jewel," she said, her voice cracking slightly. She cleared her throat in hopes of covering it up.

Vin was silent for a few tense moments, then said in a gruffer voice, "Since you're calling me on Rogen's phone, I can assume you just wanted to let me know you were with him?"

Jewel's brow dipped. That wasn't anger in his voice. That was pain. *Again.*

A curious thought ribboned through her mind, but she couldn't clutch it tightly enough to discern its full meaning.

She said, "Try to be a little less hostile. We're discussing business. And we'd like your help."

"You're trying to talk him into selling to you, aren't you? Or"—Vin's tone now held the anger she'd been expecting—"*seduce* him into selling?"

"Stop being so agitated. We've decided to go into business together. Sort of." She didn't want to elaborate over the phone. Rogen was right about her needing to work things out with Vin. Just to set all the records straight, at the very least. "Rogen came into the city tonight. He was waiting for me when I got home from work. Can you meet us?"

More silence. It was nerve-wracking. She wished she could see Vin's expression, look into his eyes. Maybe somehow convince him that releasing the sexual tension between them had done absolutely nothing to alleviate the emotional turmoil. And that was necessary, as Rogen contended.

Though it was going to take some serious effort on her and Vin's parts.

"Vin," she said. "It's important."

"Fine," he retorted in a steely tone. She could practically feel the angst exuding from him. And it turned her on—when it really shouldn't.

His dark and broody disposition, the intensity of his moods and desires, had always called to her. Even over the phone.

*Urg.*

*Who's the one who can't escape?*

A flicker of heat against her clit, because Vin's commanding presence was powerful enough to transcend satellite technology, had Jewel a bit breathy as she gave him the address.

Then Vin said, "It'll be about an hour and a half."

"I'll put a pot of sauce on the stove."

He was quiet again.

"Vin?" Her breath was held suspended. Was he going to change his mind?

He tortured her for endless moments, then eventually told her, "I really should muster some willpower when it comes to you."

He disconnected the call.

*Okay. Still pissed.*

She returned the phone to Rogen. "He's on his way. Not in a good mood. Be forewarned."

Grabbing her wineglass, she left the living room, passing the long dining table that sat twelve, and entered the kitchen. Rogen followed. He set the bottle of wine on the island and surveyed the space while she lifted a pot from its hook on the overhead rack and placed it on the six-burner stove. She then retrieved three frying pans and laid them out.

Rogen fell right in step with her, since they'd made pasta to-

gether dozens of times before. They'd all spent a significant amount
of time in one kitchen or another when growing up.

He located her flour container while she went to the fridge and
collected eggs for him, then grabbed the coiled links of hot and
sweet Italian sausage wrapped in butcher paper and ground beef for
her Bolognese sauce. She started browning the meat in the pans
while Rogen made a mound of flour on the granite countertop with
a dip in the middle where he dropped the yolks and drizzled olive
oil. Then he whisked eggs and kneaded the dough, which had to
rest at least an hour, so she greatly appreciated his help while she
worked her tasks. She also knew Rogen loved to cook.

She set out plastic wrap for the resting period and the old-
fashioned crank-handled pasta maker for when the dough was
ready, so everything was on hand for him. Then she dumped crushed
tomatoes into her pot and added fresh herbs, letting the sauce
simmer. Rounding the counter across from Rogen, she grabbed a
bamboo cutting board and used a new razor blade to shave slivers
of garlic.

He said, "Maybe it's time we address the elephant in the
room."

She let out a hollow laugh. "Vin's not even here yet."

Rogen smirked at her. She took a break from slicing and sipped
her wine. Preparing herself to jump from yet another high cliff.

She said, "When I visited you at Trinity . . . I had a specific
reason for being there."

"Seeing me wasn't enough?" He tried to jest; she could tell.
But his rugged features were set in stone.

"Always," she admitted. "But some things had changed and I
needed to tell you about them."

"What changed?"

She swallowed down a little more wine. This was about to get
prickly.

Jewel scraped the garlic into a small bowl and began chopping red and green bell peppers. She said, "I went to see you at Trinity because I wanted you to know Vin and I had started dating. Secretly—we really didn't want your parents to know, since he was living under their roof at that point. And . . . I was falling for him. I wanted you to hear that from me."

She paused. Glanced up.

Rogen stared at her, his expression difficult to read. Not exactly shocked, yet still stunned. A look she couldn't quite reconcile.

The betrayal in his tone, however, said it all. "Falling in *love*?"

Her stomach instantly became a tangled mess. "Yes."

She chopped some more, concentrating on not lopping off a finger, while he digested her words. Then she gazed at him again and said, "It happened sort of out of the blue. I mean, we spent all of our time together, yes. But we didn't plan it, Rogen. We didn't talk about it even as we were growing closer. The relationship just . . . evolved."

*Oh, shit.* Was that the right word? *Evolved?*

*No.*

Because she and Vin hadn't morphed from friends to lovers. They'd literally been thrust into it. Like a switch had been thrown. One day they were trying to wade through Rogen being gone and Vin's parents dying and Jewel was just waiting, waiting, waiting for the other shoe to drop.

Then they'd been discussing Bayli and Jonathan plotting out their *let's finally do it!* date, and Vin had challenged Jewel about positions and tempted her with his extensive knowledge and . . . well . . . when he'd kissed her down by the river, she'd been out of her mind with wanting him.

That clawing sensation—that was the first time she'd experienced it.

She'd broken the kiss. Their eyes had locked. And Vin had *known*. He'd known exactly what to do to her. Things Rogen never had.

Honestly, Vin possessed a skill set to boggle a girl's mind.

The brooding had been something a little more complex to deal with, yet Jewel had somehow convinced herself that she understood Vin in a way no one else could, particularly following the harrowing deaths of his parents. And maybe it'd been true. For a while.

In a tight voice, Rogen said, "So you went to New York to tell me you were fucking my best friend."

He deserved to be pissy.

She calmly—so she hoped—repeated, "No, I went to tell you I was falling in love with him. Vin and I had both agreed to go to San Francisco State together. He had yet to tell you he wasn't going to Yale with you. It felt as though we actually had a future, Vin and I. Whereas with you . . . well, you had internships in Italy and college on the opposite coast, and come on, Rogen. That whole star-crossed-lovers thing . . . At some point, you have to admit that we're on completely different trajectories."

Which had broken her heart wide open. Vin had helped to heal it.

*Look how that turned out.*

Karma, like nostalgia, could also be a bit of a bitch sometimes.

Rogen asked, "So, what—you and Vin were fated?"

She felt his agitation across the five feet separating them. "Clearly not."

"Jewel." He reached for the Saran to wrap the dough but then just stared at her. "The three of us haven't hung out as a group since we were sixteen. Okay, yeah, I doubt anything was going on between the two of you then—"

"*Nothing* was going on then, Rogen," she assured him. "When you and I were actually together, that was it. Just us."

"But the other day at Bristol's. He fucked you, didn't he?"

She went back to chopping.

They were entering sketchy territory here. The problem with

this direction of conversation was that, yes, the air needed to be cleared. But it also meant that they were tiptoeing toward that forbidden notion Jewel had been toying with.

Did she have the courage to broach that subject?

"Jewel." Rogen interrupted her mental debate. "I know what you look like after you've had an orgasm. Your neck gets flushed. Your eyes dance a little. I *know*, okay?"

"But you don't *really* know. When it comes to me and Vin, you don't know. Nor do I. Because after I left Trinity, and you and I hadn't slept together that night—"

"We did sleep together. In the same bed. I snuck you into my dorm room."

"But we didn't have sex."

"You said you were having your period."

She groaned. "I told you that so you wouldn't wonder why I couldn't make love with you. I couldn't cheat on Vin."

"And yet," Rogen challenged, "you never actually got around to telling me about the two of you."

"Correct." She dumped the peppers into another bowl and collected fresh mushrooms to cut up. She was halfway through the container when she glanced over at him and said, "I took one look at you and I just couldn't do it. All the old feelings, all the memories, flooded me and I just . . . I couldn't do it. I couldn't think of anything other than how great it was to see you. How much I missed being with you."

Fat drops welled in her eyes. Jewel shut them, ashamed.

She'd never understood at the age of eighteen how she could be in love with two men at the same time. It hadn't seemed logical. Certainly not practical. Completely selfish.

*Aha!*

Perhaps *that* was the primary cause between her push and pull with the very tempting ménage concept when it came to Rogen and Vin.

But that wasn't currently the issue at hand. Just a festering thought that taunted her.

She opened her eyes and stared at Rogen. "I spent the weekend with you, because I wanted one last bit of time together," she said. "Vin and I were going to prom and then graduating. Then we were both supposed to be at SFSU. But none of that happened."

Jewel rounded the island to tend to the meat on the stove, draining the grease, putting links in the food processor to grind into fine pieces, and then pouring it and the ground beef into her pot of sauce. She sprinkled in hot pepper flakes and stirred. Rogen cleaned the counter and washed his hands.

She returned to the island to mince onion and then started to sauté the vegetables. Rogen set up the pasta machine.

When she felt a modicum of composure, because cooking was therapeutic for them both, she told him, "Vin never showed up on prom night. I tried calling, e-mailing. Didn't hear a peep. I had to phone the estate, I was so worried about him. Thank God one of the housekeepers answered, not your mom. Georgina said Vin had packed a bag and left that morning. Your father arranged for Vin to take his final exams and he'd graduated, though he'd not attended the ceremony. I had no idea where he went—no one seemed to know. Even you told me he hadn't shared his plans with you. And he didn't ever respond to me. I don't know why he left. I don't know why he left . . . *me*."

The pain returned. Escalating.

*So much for culinary therapy.*

"I screwed the whole damn thing up," she said miserably.

Rogen let out a long breath. Planted his hands on his waist. "No, it wasn't you, Jewel. It was me."

Her gaze narrowed on him. He'd suggested that earlier.

"Fuck." Rogen winced. "I didn't know. I didn't . . . *goddamn it*. I didn't know—about the two of you." He shook his head. "Sure, I had some suspicions. But nothing concrete. Until now. He and I didn't talk about you—and I couldn't afford to buy into any thoughts of you and Vin. . . . It would have sucked the soul right from me if he'd gone on and on about the two of you at school, at the movies, at parties, whatever. When I couldn't be there with you."

Rogen's raw emotions sliced through her. He'd initially fought the idea of prep school when his father had enrolled him. He didn't want to leave River Cross, Vin, Jewel. But, invariably, she knew Rogen had felt the exact same about the mansion that she had—it was too frail and breakable an environment to exist in. Rogen's mother had taken to her room (and, rumor had it, pills), and Gian was a bear to be around. Not to mention, Rogen had found it next to impossible to be there without Taylor.

So for his own mental well-being, and to keep the peace in his already-ravaged family, he'd eventually conceded to Trinity.

Continuing, Rogen said, "Vin sent an e-mail to my Black-Berry that Sunday you were in New York. Said you'd gone MIA for the weekend and he couldn't reach you. Asked if I'd heard from you. I replied that you were fine, that you'd been with me at Trinity, and that I'd just dropped you off at the airport and you were on your way home. That was when the communication went dark. I couldn't reach him, either. Not after that."

"Oh, Jesus." Jewel's heart wrenched. Guilt slammed into her. Vin had known? All this time? He'd known she'd gone to see Rogen—but he had no clue why. And that must have been what sent him over the edge.

Vin's declaration when they were alone at Bristol's flashed in her mind.

*You didn't lose me . . . I was just never enough for you.*

Her stomach lurched. Jewel instantly felt sick.

"Fuck," she whispered.

"Jewel, I'm so sorry."

She believed him. Because this meant Rogen had inadvertently hurt Vin, too. And that wasn't in Rogen's nature.

"It's not your fault," she assured him, her head still spinning. "I should have told Vin up front what my plans were, or had him go with me. I just didn't want us coming at you as a couple without giving you some advance warning. And it never really occurred to me when he didn't respond to my calls that that was the reason he didn't want to speak with me. If Vin thought you and I were getting back together or were seeing each other behind his back, he would have confronted us. That's the way he is. Instead, he just . . . vanished. So I didn't think it was because of us."

"I figured it had something to do with his parents."

"That's exactly what I thought, at first. He was graduating high school, entering another phase of his life—and they weren't there to see how great he'd turned out, to celebrate his perfect GPA and the fact that he'd gotten into all the Ivy League schools he'd applied to, even though he'd decided to stay in state."

Jewel fought a wave of emotion. Sure, Vin could have been feeling uncharacteristically vulnerable at that pivotal point of his life. But the bottom line was, he'd found out about her trip to see Rogen. It all made sense now. How Vin had distanced himself from her, and from Rogen for a time. How Vin had taunted her at the gala. Why he'd been so angry and hurt at Bristol's. Why he'd advised Rogen against giving her the land she wanted.

"Oh, goddamn," she said on a heavy breath. "Rogen . . . we called him to come see us tonight, to help us with a joint venture between the two of us. How much more in-the-face is *that*? And . . . there's no way in hell he's going to agree to represent us."

"This is a professional issue, Jewel. Not a personal one."

"How can you say that?" she demanded. "*Everything* about the three of us is personal. Rogen, one of the reasons Vin was so hostile toward me on Sunday was because . . . he sort of . . . he was . . ." She tripped over the words. "He was *there*. At your house. The night of the party. He saw us—he *watched* us."

Rogen stopped cranking dough through the pasta maker, flattening it into narrow sheets. He stared at her.

She gave a slow nod. "I opened my eyes and he was standing just inside the doors."

Rogen's jaw clenched. He went back to working the dough. Jewel poured more Sangiovese and kept self-medicating in hopes of easing her tension while Rogen laid out sheet after sheet on parchment paper. He appeared deep in thought and it ate at her to not know what he was thinking.

Finally, he told her, "Had I been with any other woman that night, Vin would have joined us. Vice versa."

Her eyes popped.

*Didn't see that blatant honesty coming.*

He said, "You're not the first woman we've 'shared,' Jewel. But this is not the same thing. Not the same scenario. At all."

She recovered and eyed him curiously. "The redhead?"

"Yeah. Holly McCormick. I'd taken her out for dinner one night, when we first met. A week or so later, Vin brought her into the city for an opera. We'd both slept with her separately, then . . ."

The word *together* was one that had become lodged in Jewel's brain.

Rogen continued his work, not saying anything further. As though he *wanted* her to process what all a ménage might entail. *Was* it something he wanted to engage in with her? Had he and Vin discussed this after the night of the gala?

Before she could digest all of that, Jewel had to battle a serious bout of jealousy because Rogen and Vin had been with other women. She'd accepted that long ago—in theory. The reality of them making love to someone else was actually a jagged pill to swallow. It made everything inside her pull tight until it was difficult to breathe.

Rogen gave her more to chew on. "Holly liked Vin's aggressiveness. And she liked my—"

"Natural instinct. I'm well aware of the contrasts." They were going to need more wine to get through this discussion. She left the kitchen to retrieve another bottle from the wet bar. She'd turned one of the spare bedrooms into a full-blown cellar and tasting room for when she entertained clients or Bayli and Scarlet came into the city for a girls' night. But she kept a dozen or so of her favorites close at hand. Some women collected shoes; Jewel collected award-winning reds.

She returned to the island where Rogen was now running the dough through the attachment he'd snapped on, cutting long strands of linguine. Jewel poured for them both, then crossed to the far wall and pulled out the mounted wooden rods that looked like rolling pins framed by decorative black wrought-iron arms. There were three staggered tiers and she dusted them with flour, then started to hang the pasta to dry, evenly spacing out the thin strips.

Her mother had always preferred to leave the pasta in small spiraled piles on the counter. Jewel's grandmother had used racks similar to the ones Jewel had installed in order to drape the dough. It felt more authentic that way, though Jewel really wasn't sure there was any difference in the outcome.

When she was done, she popped a loaf of Italian bread in the oven while Rogen stirred the sauce. The fragrance of the herbs and meats filled the room. Though all the activity provided absolutely no distraction from her new obsession over what it might be like to be with Rogen and Vin.

*At the same time.*

Nor did the sight of Rogen, so skilled and helpful alongside her, looking so *right* in her kitchen, make it easy to push her forbidden thoughts aside. He kept her pulse thumping erratically. Especially since he hadn't put his shirt back on.

As she watched him clean up again, her gaze on his large hands, rock-hard biceps, and broad shoulders, she couldn't think of much beyond her bare chest melded to his . . . and Vin's pressed to her back. Their hands and mouths all over her.

What must that feel like?

And how was it that Holly McCormick had experienced it all—and Jewel had not?

She dragged her gaze from Rogen's shirtless form, his well-defined pecs, his ripped abs on full display and making her mouth water, and went back to the sauce. Before sensory overload made it impossible for her to function.

Rogen said, "If I wouldn't have answered Vin's e-mail that day, the two of you would've stayed together. You'd still be together."

Jewel found it oddly difficult to fully validate that notion.

"Maybe," she said. "Vin's very unpredictable. Impulsive. Daring. I'm not so sure staying in California and going to SFSU would have panned out for him. Chances are good he would have changed his mind when he realized all he was missing out on by not going to Yale with you."

"But then he would have been missing out on *you*. I don't think he would have chosen Yale, Jewel. Under different circumstances."

"Doesn't matter," she said with a sigh. "Speculating doesn't alter the course our lives took. It's all in the past."

"Really?" He gave her a pointed look. "Or is it all staring you in the face now?"

She moved away, unable to meet those mesmerizing blue eyes of his. Especially without seeing Vin's piercing green ones as well, in her mind.

Wine was her current escape.

So she'd hoped.

Rogen joined her at the island and asked, "Did you want to end up with Vin?"

Her hand shook, so she set the glass aside. What a loaded question he'd lobbed her way!

"Jewel," he prompted in a tight tone. "You didn't tell me about the two of you when you'd intended to do just that. What did you really want when you visited me at Trinity? For *me* to change my mind about Yale? Come back to California?"

She blinked a couple of times. That was a dream she'd never allowed herself to weave, because it'd seemed too far-fetched. Why torture herself over something that would never be? And she and Vin had had plans to—

The doorbell rang.

Jewel and Rogen stared at each other for several suspended seconds.

Then Rogen tossed aside the dish towel he'd used to dry his hands and said, "I'll get it. You—" He let out a strangled sound as disconcertion etched his strong visage. "Try to look a little less devastated."

# TEN

Vin had no fucking clue what Rogen and Jewel were up to, but he was cagey, regardless. It wasn't so much that Jewel had called him on Rogen's phone. Or that she'd mentioned a business venture. It was that Rogen was here at her house. That his Range Rover was parked in her driveway. That they were together.

*Again.*

In Vin's mind, it made him ten kinds of a fool.

*Again.*

Because he'd wanted her the night of the gala—had even forsaken his own after-party with Holly in hopes of hooking up with Jewel. Yet she'd ended up in Rogen's bed.

*Again.*

Vin had wanted her despite that. Had literally not been able to stop himself from taking her at Bristol's. In a bathroom, goddamn it.

Yeah. That was classy.

But the woman sparked something so explosive and carnal within him that Vin couldn't help but respond to it. And the fact that she never, ever said no to him . . . that was enough to make him do crazy-stupid shit like fuck her in a public restroom.

And drive into the city to see her.

When he knew she never, ever said no to Rogen, either.

Vin had always considered himself of decent intellect and sound reasoning. Then Jewel Catalano would show up in a short skirt and high heels . . . and he instantly became a colossal idiot.

He fell apart for her every single fucking time.

Therefore, he should have been relieved to see it was Rogen who answered the door, not Jewel, so that Vin had a few more minutes to bring his agitation down a notch or ten.

Except that Rogen was yanking the hem of his T-shirt down his stomach and the top button of his jeans was undone.

Vin scowled. "I see I've interrupted. You two have turned into horny rabbits?"

"It was just a blow job."

"There's no such thing when it comes to Jewel," Vin said irritably as he stepped into the foyer. So much for dialing down the intensity of his emotions.

"You're right about that," Rogen said in an equally tight voice. "Nice technique, by the way."

Vin shot him a look.

Rogen smirked.

*Okay, there's a little vindication.*

Shedding his black leather jacket, Vin added the garment to Jewel's and Rogen's on the rack. Gloated inwardly over having taught Jewel a thing or two that likely made Rogen stew.

Granted, Rogen also benefited from the tutelage. But still. It had to rub him raw that she did certain things *Vin's* way.

Then again . . . She likely did certain things Rogen's way when she was with Vin.

That left Rogen one up on him, since he'd gotten the blow job tonight.

*Ten kinds of a fool.*

*Gonna multiply that number with every minute that passes?*

If he were as wise as he claimed to be, Vin would get his ass back in his Maserati and return to River Cross. Let Rogen have Jewel.

*Precisely what you should do.*

But then he entered the kitchen and she stepped into his arms and clung to him.

*What the fuck?*

Of course, he hugged her back. Held on tight. He might be a fool, but he'd never pass up a chance to hold her.

Though it really didn't help matters that she wore a skimpy, curve-hugging black lace nightie that did everything to evoke a man's desire. Made him hard in an instant.

She didn't say anything, just kept her arms wrapped around him and her body pressed to his. Her face burrowed in the crook of his neck and Vin felt the distinct wetness of tears on his skin.

*Aw, hell.*

His throat tightened. His gut clenched. What happened to his heart was just too painful to accept. Because it meant he still cared about this woman. To the depths of his soul.

It wasn't just lust. It was *everything*. Every little thing about Jewel Catalano. Some shit he couldn't even begin to grasp or explain, but mostly . . . her very essence consumed him. Made him restless. Made him hot. Made him want to say whatever the hell he had to say in order to *not* be the source of her tears. To not be the bad guy to Rogen's knight in shining armor.

He spared a glance at Rogen, who dragged a hand down his face, apparently experiencing some peculiar emotions himself. Then Rogen grabbed a mitt and crossed to the double oven along the back wall and pulled out a baking sheet with bread. He set the loaf on the counter and retrieved a stockpot from one of the large racks over the island.

Rogen shook his head, obviously lost in his own consternation. Eventually, he said to Vin, "I didn't know the two of you were together when she came to see me at Trinity. That e-mail I sent you—"

"Fuck, Rogen. That was ten years ago." And not anything Vin wanted to discuss with his best friend. Or anyone else, for that matter. *Ever.* "Let it pass."

Vin unraveled himself from Jewel. Whisked away the trickles on her cheeks. Kissed her on the forehead. Then he said, "Tell me what's happening now. With whatever business you two have drummed up."

Because he honestly couldn't rehash that day when Rogen had sent him the simplest, most innocent message—and it had turned Vin's life upside down. Just when he'd righted it following his parents' tragic and shocking deaths.

Jewel sniffled and went for a tissue. Rogen hacked off a chunk of bread and tore it into small pieces. Vin joined him and snagged one, dipping it into the spicily aromatic sauce. He sampled it and told Jewel, "One of your best pots."

She'd always been great with sauces.

"I know Bolognese is your favorite," she said, pain still clouding her eyes. Continuing to hold Vin hostage.

Rogen told him, "We struck up our own deal related to the property."

Vin bit back a groan. "No, you did not."

"Yeah. We did." Rogen let out a strained laugh. "It's a bit on the risky side, but it'll be worth it in the end."

Jewel set the table in the bay window that created a good-size alcove. Rogen brought water to a boil on the stove and Vin washed his hands, then started collecting the dried pasta that would take only a minute or two to cook. For him, it was a bit unnerving how they were all so simpatico in the kitchen. Not tripping over one another or wondering what to do next. They just picked up whatever slack there was and the result was always some fantastically executed meal.

The kitchen staff at the estates had never been too thrilled when the trio would take over from time to time, but that was usually when a grandparent would swoop in and smooth the waters. And partake in the food.

Rogen said, "My father is going to renege on his verbal agreement."

Vin glanced at Jewel. "Always get it in writing, sweetheart."

"Yes, I know. Except . . ." She shook her head. "I didn't have anything concrete until I hooked him with scotch that's, like, a gazillion years old. It has sentimental value. And the entire transaction is contingent on me procuring that decanter, so . . . first things first."

Vin tamped down the legal lecture. Instead, he said, "Without the senior Angelinis' signatures, you're back to square one."

"We'll get those signatures," Rogen asserted. "I know my father's plan and I'm going to prevent him from jerking her around. He'll get his scotch and the money Jewel proposed. The signatures will follow. Including mine."

Vin brought the wine and glasses over and took a seat at the table, opposite Rogen. Jewel set out bowls of the pasta and the sauce and served her guests.

"Not to harp," Vin said, trying to keep all the errant feelings and tension from his voice—and not so sure he succeeded, "but I advised you against that, Rogen."

"For good reason," his friend conceded.

Temporarily derailed by Jewel's sexy body—those curves and plumped-up breasts, not to mention an ass that never failed to tempt him—Vin suggested to her, "Perhaps you should put some clothes on. Let us drool over the Bolognese, not you."

"I'm sure you both can handle it." There was a hint of mischief in her tone, overriding whatever had made her cry on his shoulder. She brought over the bread, then sat between the two men.

They toasted and sipped before digging into their plates.

Rogen took a few bites before saying, "I came to Jewel to find out why she wants the property. For an inn." He shared a smile with her, and Vin had to look away. Rogen added, "I want a vineyard. They go perfectly together. So why shouldn't we go into business together? In one form or another."

"Meaning?" Vin asked with a crooked brow, not certain he liked the direction in which this conversation was headed. For numerous reasons.

"Meaning," Jewel chimed in, "we could either subdivide and Rogen could buy half of the land from me for his own purposes. Or . . ." She pulled in a long breath and stole a glance at Rogen before returning her attention to Vin. "We could partner up. Fifty-fifty in procuring the land, developing it, and managing the inn and the winery."

"Jesus Christ." Vin dropped his fork on his plate and reached for his wine. He sucked down a healthy amount. "You're shitting me."

"No," Rogen and Jewel said in unison.

Vin piled a second heap of pasta on his plate and ladled the sauce over it. Jewel topped it with freshly grated Parmesan from a stainless-steel grater.

"Seriously, the best Bolognese I've ever had," Vin commended her. "But, honestly? You two are fucking out of your minds."

Jewel returned the grater to the table and pushed her food aside. She stood and paced. Her crimson-painted toes distracted Vin for a moment.

"It's not going to be easy," she said. "We already know that. And like Bay and Scarlet have told me a dozen times before, the whole idea is a house of cards. One false move and Rogen and I could come up empty-handed. But—" She halted abruptly and speared Vin with a solemn look. "No guts, no glory, right?"

She smiled. Though it was a bit shaky.

His stomach wrenched.

No, that might have been his heart.

*Damn it.*

Vin didn't say anything for a while. Finished his pasta so that he didn't immediately discount the business-plotting effort on Rogen and Jewel's part. They were smart and worked for their respective family empires. Neither would hastily or recklessly come to terms with each other after all the Angelini–Catalano feuding. And all they'd been through personally.

Sure, Vin recognized that Rogen and Jewel's history would play a part in their decision. The fact that they'd once been in love. Not to mention they obviously still held each other in high regard. The attraction and affection were clearly still there.

No doubt emotion influenced them, but again . . . Vin knew them well enough to know that neither would propose something this audacious if they didn't fully believe they could pull it off.

Provided they procured the land.

Vin sat back and sipped some more, still contemplative.

Rogen said, "We could use your help, man. We need that property free of all the restrictions the current contracts have placed on it, and we need to make sure we have new contracts drawn up that are solid—so that Jewel and I don't lose this opportunity because of a parental vendetta."

"They'll all go through the roof when they find out you want a joint venture," Vin told him. "How many times did we hear your father say there will never be an Angelini and Catalano partnership again? He and Anthony even went to the extent of declaring you and Jewel will never marry, never have 'mixed-blood' heirs. Then you were sent off to Trinity, in hopes you'd get over each other."

Vin shoved back his chair, took his plate to the sink, and rinsed it off.

Rogen said, "We were fourteen when I left for Trinity. Now

we're twenty-eight. He's not shipping me anywhere. And if Jewel and I want to go into business together, then goddamn it, that's what we're going to do."

"While I admire your spirit and tenacity," Vin told them both, "I wouldn't get my hopes up if I were you. And you'll need to find an independent attorney, because this would be a conflict of interest for me."

"Vin—" Jewel began.

He held up a hand. "I work for Angelini, Inc. For Gian Angelini, ultimately. And not only does he sign my paycheck, but he took me in after my parents' plane crashed. I owe him a lot, Jewel."

"And you've achieved a lot for him," Rogen reminded Vin. "You've worked your ass off for him. For the family. I understand what you're saying, because I face the same dilemma. But let's not forget that, one, he's willing to double-cross Jewel. Two, that land is a part of both our inheritances, so it will eventually pass to us. But it'll continue to sit there for the next four decades. I'm not really interested in starting a vineyard when I'm seventy. Third, we—"

"Hey," Vin said, cutting him off. "I'm aware of all the reasoning."

"Maybe not," Jewel interjected. "Because one thing that only Rogen and I might be considering is that proving we can be partners and build something together could be a great way to get our families to bury the hatchet."

Vin's gaze locked with hers. "And then you can marry Rogen."

# ELEVEN

Jewel stared at Vin, aghast.

"That just came out," he said crossly, and turned away. He wrapped up the remainder of the bread as Jewel tried to wade through the dynamic in her kitchen. All the surface stuff they'd addressed—the new deal, the reasons it didn't sit right with Vin to be involved—and the underlying issues. The room was sexually and emotionally charged. It was hard to ignore either, and it ratcheted her own internal tension.

Jewel said, "It's not like you to blurt out something you haven't fully given consideration to, Vin." She tried to reel in her own emotions. "For the record, Rogen and I getting married is something that hasn't been a topic of discussion since we were thirteen or fourteen. And what did we know at that age?"

Rogen shrugged. "Seemed to be a good plan at the time."

"Sure," she agreed. "And then a feud erupted and you wound up all the way across the country—then on another continent."

"Be that as it may," Vin interrupted, "you're no longer subjected to the will of patriarchs when it comes to your love lives."

"We're not really subjected to *anyone's* will when it comes to that," Jewel tacked on to the sentiment. "Are we?" She gave both men a direct, knowing look.

Here they all were. Together. At pivotal crossroads.

Honestly, all the cards had been revealed, so what good did it serve them to avoid one extremely crucial element to their love triangle?

The truly wicked one. The one that was . . .

*Wrong?*

No. Enticing.

*So very wrong?*

No. So . . . *Delicious.*

Jewel grabbed her glass and headed out of the kitchen and into the living room. Flames from the fire cast flickering shadows over the furniture and against the walls. She hadn't put on music and the quiet air made her hear every little thing—like Rogen and Vin joining her. Their breaths a bit heavy, as was hers.

Okay, perhaps she'd had a bit too much of the Sangiovese. Because her blood had turned molten, and exhilaration hummed through her.

Or maybe she'd just fully accepted the fact that she wanted—*needed*—them both.

They were two incredibly sensual, incredibly talented men. Both experts in varying techniques, so that Jewel always felt as though sex was a whole new experience with each of them.

For those techniques and expertise to collide . . . ?

It. Would. Be. *Amazing!*

She smiled. Perhaps a bit deviously.

"Jewel," Rogen ventured in a tentative voice. "Care to explain the cat-that-ate-the-canary grin?"

Vin shifted from foot to foot, eyeing her as though he could read every single lascivious thought suddenly racing through her brain.

Knowing Vin, he probably could.

And Rogen was likely able to interpret every physical response she had to those thoughts. The way her nipples tightened behind her nightie. The way she pressed her thighs together because her clit tingled. The sudden hitch in her breath.

No doubt her eyes also shimmered with lust over the possibility that suddenly consumed her mind.

"I was just thinking," she brazenly began, "that this past week, I've been with both of you. And I'm not trying to hide it from either of you. We might as well be open about it, right?"

Vin's jaw set. Rogen's brow furrowed.

To Vin, she said, "I know about Holly McCormick. Rogen explained."

"Oh, fuck," Rogen grumbled. "I told you, Jewel. It's not the same."

"You can't actually be suggesting . . . ?"

She caught the flicker of excitement in Vin's emerald eyes. He'd thought of this, too—she could see it on his face.

Jewel fought to keep her grin from widening. Yes, it was bold of her to put this sexy idea on the table. To put *herself* on the table. But Jewel knew both men wanted her. She was allowing them to have her. Because she wanted *them*.

"I understand there's a lot of residual conflict," she admitted. "It just seems that rather than get pissed off at each other because one of you has just fucked me or made love to me, keeping it all aboveboard will spare some feelings."

Rogen exchanged a look with Vin. Silence ensued. Jewel's nerves jumped.

"She does make a good point," Rogen eventually said. "And since it's Jewel we're talking about . . . That would make what we do best even better, don't you think? More powerful? Because it's *her*."

Her stomach flipped.

*Oh, my God!*

He was agreeing as well!

Jewel was more and more aroused by this concept—and these men—as the discussion continued. Her entire being burned for them. Her skin flamed.

She longed to see both men stripped bare. To touch them. Taste them. And let them do the same to her.

How she wanted it!

The forbidden had always been a huge aphrodisiac for her, although this particular guilty pleasure had never occurred to her until their recent reunion.

The wine coursing through her veins gave her just the verve she needed to take a step toward Rogen, closing the gap between them.

*Time to seal the deal.*

She gazed into his beautiful blue eyes and said, "Let's face facts. I know about the two of you. Can you honestly say you haven't thought of *me* as the woman you share?"

Another look passed between the two men. This one secretive.

A question? A . . . consent?

Jewel's pulse shifted into high gear. "I want you both. It's no mystery, no new revelation. Well, relatively speaking. But it is the truth. I want you both," she repeated. "Not one more over the other, but equally." Her fingers skimmed along Rogen's abs, up to his chest. Then she went on tiptoe to sweep her lips over his. Against them, she added, "And you can both have me." She kissed him. Suspecting he wouldn't be able to resist her.

She was right.

Rogen's arms instantly circled her waist, crushing her to his hunky body as her arms wound around his neck.

He took over the kiss. Jewel would forever be astounded by how she got lost in his strong embrace, his smoldering kisses.

He was erect and obviously teeming with desire. When she

eventually pulled away from him, his expression was a heated, sexy one as he asked in his rumbling voice, "When did you learn to play dirty?"

She gave him a coy smile and breathlessly said, "Right this very second."

She slipped from his arms. Turned to Vin. Who appeared equally turned on. As though he were already two steps ahead of them in his mind. Already contemplating how this new situation amongst them might play out.

That excited her all the more.

Yet because it was Vin and he loved to make her work for his affection, he quietly demanded, "You don't seriously think that trick is going to have an effect on me?"

Moving toward him, she slid her gaze over six feet, four inches of lean-muscled male, up to his commanding facial features. Lust flared in his eyes. Spurring her on.

"Yes, I do." Her fingers curled around the opening of his white dress shirt at the neck and she yanked the material apart, popping buttons, sending them flying.

"Goddamn it, Jewel. This is an expensive shirt."

"I bet you've got an entire closetful of expensive shirts, Vin." She pulled the tails from his pants and politely slipped the disks through the holes of the remaining buttons while peering up at him from under long lashes, certain there was a hint of goading stamped across her face.

His jaw worked. In anticipation.

She had to do more than go up on tiptoe for him. Her hand pressed to the back of his head and she coaxed him to lower it until their mouths met in a hard, searing kiss. Vin shoved off his shirt and hauled her up against his naked chest, his ridged abs.

He gave in quickly. Fire rushed through her veins.

His aggressive kiss spoke volumes. Telling her what she'd set in motion just might overwhelm her. Be too much for her.

Valid concerns.

But there was no mistaking how aroused he was over this turn of events. That stoked the inferno inside her and kept Jewel from backing down.

When he eventually broke the kiss, she was light-headed. Scarcely able to pull in even the tiniest of breaths.

The combination of Rogen's need to please and Vin's need to possess was as sensational as she'd expected.

On slightly shaky legs, she returned to Rogen. She gripped his tee at his stomach and pushed the material upward. He dragged it over his head, and Jewel leaned toward him, inhaling his earthy, masculine scent. Her lips glided over his hot skin, up his torso, her tongue flicking a small nipple. Her teeth scraped, making his body jolt. She continued the path, her mouth sliding along the thick cords of his neck, over his jaw.

Her palms flattened against his waist. His hands clasped her arms, as though knowing to hold her steady, knowing she'd begin trembling at any moment. He was intuitive that way.

His gaze was glued to hers, and she tried to read all the emotions swirling in his glowing blue irises. He wanted her. Bad. But like Vin, his expression held a hint of foreboding, belying the danger inherent to her quest.

If she was going to back down, now would be the time to do it. Before they went any further. Before they got swept away by passion and her potentially horrible judgement that could later be blamed on the Sangiovese, but only in a cowardly way.

Yet this was Rogen. And Vin. They'd never hurt her. What they would do was everything in their power to give her exactly what she desired. Many, *many* orgasms.

She needed them—the men and the orgasms. Desperately.

She nipped at Rogen's bottom lip and whispered, "You like it when my nipples are ridiculously hard. So do I. Make them that way."

His grip on her biceps tightened. He was trying to keep himself in check. That just wouldn't do. She wanted him to unleash his passion. She wanted them both out of control—because of her.

"Rogen," she urged in a soft voice. "Do it."

He released her arms. His large hands slid up her rib cage and cupped her breasts, massaging confidently, the pads of his thumbs whisking over the tight centers. Exactly what she wanted. A small whimper fell from her lips.

Vin stepped behind her and she felt his heat at her back, his smooth skin against hers, above the straight line of her nightie at her shoulder blades. He held her hips as Rogen's head dipped and he tongued her nipple through the lace, the material creating a hint of friction. The erotic sensation coursed through every inch of her. Pulsated in her pussy.

She raised an arm and snaked it around Vin's neck, craning hers so that he could capture her mouth in a scorching kiss. Her other hand sought Rogen's silky, spiked strands of hair, her fingers threading through them.

Fever blazed through her as Vin's kiss deepened and Rogen peeled away the lace at her chest, tucking the cups under her breasts. His mouth closed over her nipple again and it sent a lightning bolt against her clit.

She broke her kiss with Vin.

"Oh, God," she moaned. "Yes. Suck my nipples, Rogen. Suck them hard."

He did while caressing her breasts, squeezing almost roughly, insistently. Everything inside her went haywire.

Vin's lips skimmed down her spine as he sank to his knees behind her. She shuddered from the vibrant sensation that burst against each vertebra.

His fingers hooked in the sides of her thong and he dragged the black satin down her legs and helped her out of her panties. It was a little difficult to focus on that while Rogen drove her wild with his tongue fluttering against her nipple as his finger and thumb rolled the other one, pinched lightly. A moan wrenched from the back of her throat.

Adding to the glorious sensations was Vin spreading her pussy lips and flicking his tongue over her clit.

*Oh, fuck!*

Two mouths on her body . . . two tongues!

The warm moisture against her tingling flesh in both places at the same time was sinful. Fantastic. A little overwhelming, but she concentrated on separating out the feelings and savoring the two distinctly different rhythms and textures and . . . *oh, hell*.

They both suckled at the same time—Rogen on her nipple, Vin on her clit.

Jewel cried out.

Vin's tongue dipped into her pussy. Rogen's flickered over her taut nipple. One, then the other.

"Dear God," she ground out. "That's incredible."

Sensation built upon sensation. Vin's tongue laved at her clit again. Then his lips tugged at her slick folds, pushing her right to the precipice.

"Yes. *Yes* . . ."

Vin eased two fingers into her and slowly stood. He whispered in her ear, "You are dripping wet. So fucking wet."

"How could I not be?" she asked, breathless. "The two of you know exactly how to touch me, exactly how to make me come. And I want it. I want to come for you. Both of you."

His fingers glided smoothly along the inner walls of her pussy and he pumped heartily. One of Rogen's hands slid down her belly and the pads of two fingers rubbed her clit. Quickly.

*"Oh!"* Another cry tore from her as they worked her expertly.

Vin caught her mouth with his and she tasted herself on his lips and tongue, turning her on even more. Rogen continued suckling, teasing her nipples. Both men's fingers pleasured her inside and out.

Her pulse echoed in her ears. Her heart hammered.

There was nothing more exquisite than having Rogen's sinewy body pressed to hers . . . along with Vin's sleekly powerful one melding against her so that she was completely surrounded by them. Could smell them both. Could *feel* them both.

It was decadent and beautiful.

And it sent Jewel over the edge.

She ripped her mouth from Vin's.

"Oh, God! *Yes!*"

A fiery orgasm erupted deep within and seared every inch of her. Jewel's body vibrated, her inner muscles clutching Vin's fingers. Her own fingers fisted in Rogen's hair.

"Christ!" She gasped for air as every nerve ending ignited. "Oh, God!"

Vin slid his arm around her waist to hold her steady.

The firestorm raged within her. Hot. Radiant.

So exciting.

So addictive.

Her pussy continued to clench and release Vin's fingers, drawing out every little bit of her climax.

God, it felt so good!

She rode the high as Rogen lifted his head and kissed her. Intensely. Passionately.

The tremors ran rampant. Heat danced over her skin. A restless, gnawing sensation grew in her core. A deep, dark need that demanded to be sated.

When Rogen finally dragged his mouth away so they could breathe, Vin clasped the lace clinging to Jewel, pulled it up her body, and whisked it off. Her bare breasts pressed below the ledge of Rogen's pecs while Vin's hands slid all over her flushed skin.

"Yes," she murmured. "Touch me everywhere. I want it all."

Greedy, sure, but it was a once-in-a-lifetime opportunity she did not intend to squander.

Rogen kissed her again as she was sandwiched between their muscular bodies. Vin's lips grazed her neck, his teeth nipping below her ear. He'd discovered that precious spot, too.

Her hand slipped between hers and Vin's bodies, and she stroked his cock through his pants and briefs. He was thick and full. Rogen was as well.

"You want me to fuck you," Vin confidently said.

A moan lodged in her throat as Rogen continued the sexy liplock.

Vin's warm breath tickled her skin as he added, "And you're going to come harder than you just did."

Her pussy clenched once more, this time with anticipation.

He stepped away. Rogen broke the kiss. Jewel reeled.

Vin had her by the waist once more and led her up the steps and through the foyer. Rogen followed, divesting himself of boots and clothing along the way.

Her breathing was still erratic and exhilaration flooded her veins. She vaguely pointed Vin in the direction of her master suite. He guided her to the bed and she sat on the edge. Rogen flipped on the gas fireplace, providing the only illumination in the room.

While Vin extracted a condom from his wallet and then undressed, Rogen knelt on the floor alongside the bed and pressed her thighs open with his palms.

"Yes," was all she could say, still in a passion-induced daze from how insanely good it felt to have them both pleasuring her. Rogen's mouth on her pussy was exactly what she wanted at the moment.

His tongue swept over her dewy folds. Slowly. So, so slowly. Tantalizing and teasing. A huge contrast to Vin's erotic suckling that had lit her up.

Vin stretched out beside her as she lay back, Rogen's head still between her legs.

Vin palmed a breast and caressed her with an urgency that, combined with Rogen's slow burn, had her brimming with desire. The variance between the two men actually worked in tandem to create a maelstrom of sensations that excited her.

Vin's head dipped and his tongue flickered over her nipple, both puckered centers still taut, still tingling. One of his hands roamed her body, his fingertips blazing their own trail, making her stomach quiver and her pulse race.

"I can't believe how incredible it feels to have both your mouths on me," she said in a raspy voice. Then amended, "Yes. I can."

Because it was Rogen and Vin.

"Fucking fantastic," she told them.

Rogen slipped two fingers inside her as his tongue fluttered over her clit. The little pearl was hypersensitive. The lust coursing through her made every inch of her highly responsive. More so than ever before. She felt Rogen's tongue and fingers, Vin's mouth and hands, so acutely. Inhaled their distinct scents. Reveled in their heat. Listened to their heavy breathing.

She affected them as deeply as they did her. And it didn't seem to be a competition between them but a collaborative effort to get her off.

Perhaps that was why she'd decided to jump on this opportunity. Because Rogen had always wanted to make her feel good; Vin had always wanted to make her come so hard she screamed his name.

And now Jewel was in heaven.

Rogen's fingers stroked her pussy, finding her G-spot and rubbing with just the right pressure, the right pace, while his tongue still flitted against her clit. Vin gave her a sizzling kiss.

Her excitement escalated.

She pulled her mouth from Vin's. "I'm going to come again."

"Yes," he said with anticipation in his tone. "Come for us." His head dipped and he suckled her nipple, sending her barreling toward orgasm.

"I'm so close," she told them.

Against her breast, Vin muttered, "Keep licking her pussy, Rogen. Lick it good. Make her come."

Rogen's pace hastened. Jewel's hips undulated. She felt the climax mounting, mounting, cresting . . .

"Oh, yes."

*Exploding* . . .

"Oh, fuck, yes!" Her eyes squeezed shut. Little white orbs burst behind her lids. "Oh, God!" she cried out, losing it completely.

The climax blazed through her, effervescent and intoxicating. She held fast to it, clung to the erratic beats, the heat consuming her.

Her chest heaved with her labored breaths. Her arousal didn't dim the slightest bit. Rogen's fingers were still inside her; Vin's lips still grazed her sensitive skin.

Endless moments slid by as she savored her orgasm. Savored every single second with two lovers who were clearly determined to give her everything she needed.

Making her adore them even more. Making her *want* them even more.

When she eventually opened her eyes, she simply said, "Spectacular."

Rogen withdrew from her and sprawled alongside her. One corner of his mouth quirked in that half-assed grin of his that was part cocky, part heartwarming. And which always caused her stomach to flutter. "I love that you get so into it, that you like my mouth on your pussy."

"So very, very much," she assured him.

He gave her a sexy kiss, then said, "Let Vin fuck you."

This time, her stomach flipped. She lay between the two men, on her side, facing Rogen with Vin at her back again.

Holding Rogen's gaze, she told him, "He does it differently than you." Perhaps that was more of a warning. "He fucks me hard."

Rogen murmured against her lips, "I want to be the one to watch this time." His fingers swept away strands of hair from her face. "I want to hear you moan. Beg. Come."

From behind her, Vin lifted her thigh, hooking his forearm at the underside of her knee, spreading her legs wide open.

Rogen inched closer to her, so their bodies touched. His hand cupped her breast. His gaze remained locked with hers.

Jewel's staccato breaths filled the otherwise quiet room.

He said to Vin, "Do it, man."

The head of Vin's cock rubbed the opening of her pussy. Teasing her? Preparing her? Both?

"Fuck her," Rogen urged.

"Yes," Jewel ground out as the anticipation and the need to feel Vin inside her intensified. "Please, Vin. *Now*."

He thrust in.

Hard.

Deep.

Forceful.

"Oh, God!" Jewel called out as sparks flew.

Rogen growled, low and sexy.

Vin stilled. "She's tight. So damn tight."

"I know," Rogen said in a strained tone. "Show me how she likes it with you."

Jewel gripped Rogen's shoulders for support. Vin's cock pulled almost all the way out of her.

"You want it, don't you, baby?" he whispered.

"Yes," she said on a broken breath. "Don't tease me, Vin. Fuck me. I want to feel you, hard and hot inside me."

He plunged all the way in.

"Vin!"

Her ass ground against his pelvis. His hips bucked and his

cock hammered into her, fast and furious. As though he had a point to prove.

That she'd asked for too much? That he wanted Rogen to know how he satisfied her? That he just plain needed to make her come—and come with her?

All of the above?

Jewel couldn't dissect any of it. With Rogen still staring into her eyes, his thumb toying with her nipple, and Vin thrusting heartily into her, it was a wonder she could recall her own name.

It felt good. So fucking good. In ways she couldn't yet resolve. Because it was Vin inside her and Rogen suddenly kissing her, as though he couldn't stand not being joined with her in some physical way.

His hand on her breast skated down her belly and his fingertips massaged her clit, first in a circular motion, engaging her. Then picking up Vin's tempo and rubbing fervently.

She ended the kiss. It was all too much. All too wonderful. All too insane.

She couldn't process the sensations, especially as Rogen added to them by tonguing her nipple, then drawing it into his mouth.

Jewel shifted slightly and her arm coiled around Vin's neck again. He kissed her briefly but kept his attention on fucking her. Wildly. Perfectly. His gaze on her.

Sharp whimpers of desire fell from her parted lips. She wasn't sure Vin had ever driven so deep into her, and that was saying something.

Rogen's rugged features were set, tense. His eyes burned. He told Vin, "Pump that cock into her. Damn it, Vin. Fuck her harder. Make her come."

"Yes," Jewel begged. "Please. God, Vin, please!"

The heel of Rogen's hand pressed against her clit, rubbing the entire area, a completely new sensation.

"Rogen," she gasped. "Harder." Her hand clutched his, holding him to her, making him push more firmly against her wet, sizzling flesh.

Vin's fervent fucking rocked her hips, causing her clit to rub more quickly, rhythmically, against Rogen's hand.

"Oh, God." It was like nothing she'd ever felt.

Dark, throaty moans leapt from her throat. Her eyes shut. She felt everything inside her tighten. It felt good, so damn incredible. She almost didn't want to let go. But she had no choice.

The sensations burst wide open and she screamed. Loud.

She shattered to the depths of her soul. Clenched Vin so tight that he lost it, too, and called her name as his cock surged inside her and his body convulsed.

"Oh, yeah," Rogen said. "Keep her coming."

Vin's hips jerked. The heel of Rogen's hand rubbed. Jewel continued to climax.

The two men drew out every single second. Every ounce of her orgasm.

"Goddamn," Vin said on a sharp breath. "She squeezes so fucking tight."

"Feels better than anything, doesn't it?" Rogen asked in a tone tinged with lust and yearning.

"Yes."

Jewel's lids drifted open. She tried to focus on Rogen, but her eyes wouldn't quite settle. He was staring at her, though, memorizing every stage of her orgasm.

He swallowed hard, the cords of his neck pulling. "You really are insanely beautiful."

Her fingers grazed his temple and she smiled softly, her heart soaring.

Vin withdrew from her and gently rolled her on her back, the upper part of her body sprawled across his. With Vin still holding her thigh in the crook of his arm, keeping her legs spread, Rogen slowly entered her.

Her pulse jumped. He was a little wider than Vin. Not quite as long. She'd never really noticed the subtle differences until now. But they could account for how she always felt so filled by Rogen. And how Vin always seemed to drive a bit deeper.

She liked that she could catalog the contrasts in her two lovers. That she could pinpoint what specifically stimulated her when each man was inside her. With Vin, it was how he pushed her so damn high with his hard and fast moves. With Rogen, it was that she burned from his sexy, steady pumping.

He targeted that ultra-sensitive spot within her and it was such a phenomenal sensation to feel him stroking, gradually applying more pressure.

The corrugated grooves of his stomach rubbed along her belly, and his lower body melded to hers. Vin released her leg and Rogen draped it over his hips. With Vin's rigid muscles at her back and his hands now on her breasts, she knew she'd be coming in a matter of minutes.

She glanced at Vin and said, "Kiss me. The way you do when you're really pissed at me and all those alpha tendencies take control."

His mouth crashed over hers, as it had when they were in the bathroom at Bristol's. His tongue thrusting, his kiss hungry, greedy, demanding.

Rogen filled her pussy with his thick cock and he leaned over her, his lips brushing her neck, his teeth tenderly biting.

*Yes!* she screamed in her head as Vin continued to kiss her.

Her body rocked from Rogen's solid thrusts. She lifted her hips to meet each one, clutching his shaft, releasing, clutching tighter.

"Yeah, Jewel, like that," he said against her throat. "Just like that."

He gripped her ass cheek with one hand while he was propped up on the other elbow. She wanted all of his weight on her but could barely breathe as it was. Still, having him between her legs, feeling his hard body against hers, losing herself in the exciting cadence he set, took her to all-new heights. She knew he felt it, too. Vin as well, because his sizzling kiss intensified, and once again Jewel was flying.

Rogen gave a powerful thrust that pushed her higher. She ripped her mouth from Vin's.

"Rogen!" She came just as hard as she had with Vin.

"Ah, fuck. Jewel." Rogen let out a strangled sound. "Fuck, yes. Squeeze my cock."

Seconds later he erupted inside her, his hot cum filling her, the erotic sensation titillating, exhilarating.

He kept thrusting through his climax. Still filling her. Still moving within her.

"Oh, God. Rogen," she whispered. "I'm going to come again."

The release rippled in her core, so sweet and beautiful. Different from the other orgasms that had incinerated her, but in a very alluring way. This one tickled and teased. Made her gasp.

Rogen gave her soft, tender kisses that kept her pulse racing.

When his forehead dropped to her shoulder, she glanced at Vin, who swept strands of damp hair from her temple as she enjoyed every tingle along her skin and straight to her core.

"Thank you," she murmured.

His jaw clenched briefly. Then Vin nodded. She knew he understood what she was so grateful for—not just for giving her what she'd wanted, but for the gentle gesture.

Both of which she would forever hold close to her heart. Would never forget.

No matter the ramifications she had to face in the morning.

# TWELVE

Rogen and Vin had a Board of Directors meeting at the mansion first thing the next morning. One of the reasons neither had stayed over at Jewel's house in the city. In addition to that, she'd been exhausted. Moreover, the two men needed to work out the new dynamic with Jewel.

Rogen left the meeting when it adjourned, heading to his office on the third floor. Vin followed.

Stepping inside, Rogen unbuttoned his suit jacket and stripped it off. Yanked the tie loose but left it on, in the event his father summoned him for other business.

He whirled around to hang the jacket on the coatrack in the corner and ran smack into Vin's fist.

Rogen's head snapped back from the blow.

"What the fuck?!" he erupted as blood from his split lip splattered across his white dress shirt and, goddamn it, his silk tie.

"That's for telling Jewel about Holly." Vin shook out his fist. He'd likely end up with bruised knuckles.

"Son of a bitch," Rogen grumbled. "I forgot how fucking hard you hit." He dabbed at his lip with two fingers. Pulled them away and stared at the crimson covering his skin.

Vin sauntered over to the wet bar and snagged a few cocktail napkins. He returned to where Rogen stood, still a bit dazed from having his bell rung. Vin handed over the white paper squares.

"I'd apologize," Vin said, "except that you jacked all our programs by putting ménage ideas into Jewel's head. What the hell were you thinking?"

"Oh, come on," Rogen scoffed as he gingerly pressed the napkins to his lip. Winced. Waited a few seconds. Then dropped his arm and said, "You really believe the thought never once crossed her mind?"

Vin raked a hand through his dark hair. "She's always been a bit on the adventurous side. But she's never had the look in her eyes that she did last night. It was . . ." He groaned, apparently at a loss for the right word. So not like Vin.

Therefore, Rogen offered, "Demanding?"

"Yes. And just . . . so fucking hot."

"Everything about Jewel is so fucking hot. That's our problem, man." Rogen stalked over to his desk. Swiped away more blood, then tossed the napkins in the trash bin. Draped his jacket along the back of his tall executive chair.

"Our problem is that we both fell in love with the same woman," Vin told him. "At different times of our lives—and sole and separate from each other. Now we're all reunited."

Rogen speared his best friend with a pointed look. "Was it sole and separate?"

"Absolutely." Vin dropped into a black leather chair in front of Rogen's glass-topped desk. "I was always fond of her when we were kids. That's nothing new. You understood I'd always felt protective of her, that there was just something about her that made me stick close. You experienced it, too."

"So what changed?" Rogen asked as he slid into his own seat. "When did it change?"

Vin let out a long breath. "At first, I think it was seeing her so upset that you'd been sent to Trinity. I felt . . . I don't know. Like I just wanted to let her cry on my shoulder, even though I didn't have any answers for her. So I did."

Rogen's gut roiled. "I always hated that I'd hurt her by going away."

"You really didn't have a choice, Rogen. And she knew it." Vin reached for a pen from one of the holders on the desk and tapped the end against his crossed leg. "The two of you sort of worked it out, though. You constantly e-mailed, called. Mostly using my phone so no one busted you. And when you came home, you snuck around so that you could see each other. Be together."

"With your help," Rogen conceded.

"Because you were both my best friends. At that time, that was all, Rogen. That was what I felt for her."

"She said your relationship 'evolved.' What kind of bullshit term is that?"

Vin gave a partial eyeball roll. "You got me. Except that we were really comfortable and really volatile at the same time. Any little thing could set us off and we'd bicker like an old married couple. But that'd wear us out and we'd go cook something in the kitchen or watch a movie and suddenly everything was back to normal between us."

"I sensed the underlying sexual tension, when we were teenagers," Rogen told him, wondering if Vin would fess up or not.

Vin returned the pen to its holder and pushed to his feet. "Jewel came out of the womb beautiful. I've seen the pictures. She got to us both, in a lot of different ways. Did I have a fantasy or two about her when we were growing up? Hell, yes. I also had them about Bay and Scarlet. It's just that Jewel was . . . *Jewel*."

"Yeah," Rogen said as he rubbed his chin, which only slightly stung, in comparison to his lip. "There's just something about her. Bold and tenacious. Feisty. Sweet. I don't fucking know." He shook his head. "All I know right now is that last night felt like just the tip of the iceberg when it comes to her and the two of—"

"Sorry to interrupt, Mr. Angelini," Rogen's assistant, Lane Emerson, came on the intercom of his landline. "You have a call."

Rogen sighed. "Lane, it's perfectly acceptable to call me Rogen. 'Mr. Angelini' can be reserved for my father." Rogen had only told her a hundred times in the six months he'd been in the River Cross office.

"Yes, Mr. Angelini. Now, I have a Miss Catalano on line four. Would you like to take it?"

Rogen and Vin exchanged a look. Vin appeared a bit peeved that Jewel had phoned Rogen, not him. Rogen fought the triumphant grin. If they turned this into a competition, there would be worse damage than a split lip and bruised knuckles. He had no doubt.

"Yes, I'll take it. Thank you, Lane."

Vin irritably said, "I'll give you two some privacy."

"Wait. This could be about our business deal."

"Which I'm not getting involved with," Vin reminded him. "Thought I'd made that perfectly clear."

"I'm also guessing you've always believed sharing Jewel for the evening was never an option," Rogen pointed out. "Way to stick to your guns, bro."

"Asshole."

Rogen snickered. "Let's face it. Since she blew back into our lives, it became an inevitability." He snatched the receiver and hit the button for line four. "Hey, sweetheart."

"Hey yourself," she said in her sultry tone. "I tried Vin's office, but he's not there. I wanted to ask him to reconsider his position on helping us."

Rogen told her, "Vin's here in my office."

"Oh, great. Can you put me on speaker?"

He pressed the button and returned the receiver to its cradle. "We're live."

"Wonderful." Her excited tone echoed in the cavernous room. "Hi, Vin."

"Jewel."

"I called you first, but apparently the two of you are in a pow-wow."

Unlike Rogen, Vin didn't temper his gloating. "Isn't that sweet?" he said to Rogen. "She called me first."

"Wait'll you hear why," Rogen lobbed back.

"Get right to it, Jewel," Vin told her, his shoulders bunching— because he knew she was about to test his resolve.

Rogen was relieved Vin didn't use a term of endearment with her to piss him off. Although he didn't miss the tension in Vin's voice. This was definitely a new dynamic they'd all have to get used to.

"So," Jewel said, "I have a proposition for the two of you."

Vin smirked, despite her not being able to see it. "Thought we covered that last night."

Jewel let out a soft, somewhat anxious-sounding laugh. "That's not why I'm calling. This is business."

"Then you don't need me," Vin contended. "Call me when you're looking for someone to hitch your skirt up and take you from—"

"Vin!" she scolded. "I'm on speaker in my office. With. My. Assistant."

Rogen snorted.

Unfazed, Vin said, "Fine. What's the proposition?"

"Well . . ." She suddenly sounded more tentative. "I was just fi-nalizing some details with Cameron before I head out for the week-end to collect a few items that will lead me to the scotch we need for our deal with Rogen's father and I thought that maybe you'd like to go with me. Both of you. Rogen, as my business associate. Vin, as our legal counsel."

"I'm not your legal counsel, Jewel." He shot Rogen a look and started to mouth, *Do not include*—

"He'll come," Rogen told her. "Vin wouldn't want me to spend an entire weekend alone with you." He jerked a brow as he stared at Vin. "Would you?"

"You crazy fucks," Vin growled. Then said, "My apologies, Cameron."

"No offense taken," the assistant replied. "I'm used to it. She has Bayli and Scarlet on speaker all the time. I'm well acclimated."

"Fantastic," Vin deadpanned.

"So," Jewel jumped on Rogen's hasty decision-making. "I'll have Cameron e-mail you both the itinerary. We leave at one o'clock from CE's private hangar. I anticipate we'll be back on Tuesday."

"Okay by me," Rogen said. Then considered that perhaps he was getting ahead of himself. He and Vin should probably talk this out. Rogen did not think of their threesome as a mere fling, like all the others. This was Jewel. Their ultimate fantasy woman. A woman he could actually envision them having a permanent relationship with.

Question was, could Jewel handle that sort of arrangement?

Rogen mentally shook his head. He had no answers and it was entirely possible they were all digging a deeper hole for themselves. But the idea of a long weekend with Jewel was too enticing to pass up.

Damn, it'd been exciting watching Vin fuck her. Seeing her so caught up in lust, listening to her moan, stroking her clit, staring into her eyes when she came . . . That had all been seriously arousing. Had made Rogen harder than ever before. And knowing they were both giving her something she'd never had . . . well, that had been damn thrilling, too.

There were inherent risks to the situation, no lie there. But his dick had exploded like nothing he'd experienced with any other woman. That was the sane thing to latch on to. Not all the messy emotional stuff.

For now.

Vin appeared ready to throttle Rogen for roping him into the trip, but he said, "I'll clear my schedule."

Rogen saw the e-mail from Cameron come through and he opened the itinerary. Scanned it. "Interesting combo—we'll bring tuxedos and shorts."

"Perfect," Jewel said. "I'll see you both tomorrow at one." The line went dead.

Vin ground his teeth for a moment, then asked, "What are you planning on telling your father about this impromptu scavenger hunt?"

Rogen flashed a grin. "That we're going deep-sea fishing. Cabo's our first stop." He hit *print* and handed a copy to Vin. "I haven't seen Jewel in a bikini since we were sixteen. Now that she's all shapely and womanly . . ." He sucked in a breath. "I guess you ought to bring a full box of condoms."

Vin's jaw worked. "This really isn't the best approach when it comes to her. We should discuss this."

Rogen rounded his desk and clasped his best friend on the shoulder. "I agree. And we will. But first, let's go get the scotch and set this deal in motion. Then we'll figure out where everything stands."

Vin eyed him curiously. Perhaps suspiciously? "You think she's going to choose, don't you?"

"I'm not exactly sure what's currently on her mind. And I'm not saying that I want her to choose."

They stared at each other.

Rogen added, "Though it's likely the only viable solution. I mean, could she really handle having both of us in her life—in the way we want her?"

Vin scowled. "It would be a bit unorthodox. Neither of us

knows her well enough in her adulthood to say whether or not she's cool with an unconventional relationship, now do we?"

"No, we do not. So maybe we can try to figure it out. By the way . . ." The corner of his mouth hitched again. "Guarantee I'll garner her sympathy during this trip, what with the split lip and all."

"Bastard," Vin said on a low chuckle. "You are just too much of a scoundrel for your own good."

"Look," Rogen told him, turning serious. "I don't know what the fuck is going to happen with the three of us tomorrow or Tuesday or ten years from now. All I know is that we've both waited a long time to get back together with Jewel and she wants us both. Is it sensible for the two of us to get *so* deeply involved with the same woman? Hell, no. But has it been happening our entire lives with Jewel? Yes. So. Just . . . chill for the time being and let's see where this takes us."

"Not exactly wise counsel," Vin warned.

"We've survived a lifetime friendship being in love with Jewel. We can survive this."

*Hopefully.*

Vin didn't seem to buy that sentiment, either, if his scowl was any indication.

"It is what it is for now," Rogen offered. "Let's go pack. I'll meet you at the hangar."


Jewel was a nervous wreck.

What had possessed her to invite Rogen and Vin along on her journey to secure the scotch? For the love of God! The three of them in a Gulfstream airplane, in such close proximity to one another for four days? How was she going to keep her hands off them?

And the nights . . . Sure, Cameron had booked accommodations to lodge the trio. Condos and suites with three rooms each. Could Jewel stay in her own room? Would the guys?

Flashes of *The Secret of My Success* with Michael J. Fox creeping through hallways during a weekend work retreat, trying to find his girlfriend, who had a boyfriend, who had a wife—and all of them secretly slipping in and out of beds to try to find their desired partners—made her cringe.

Not that Jewel needed to slip in and out of beds to find her desired partner. She knew exactly who she wanted.

Rogen.

Vin.

Together again.

She sighed. Left her office and took a limo to River Cross. She boarded the plane an hour before the guys were scheduled to arrive and settled in with her laptop, trying to concentrate on business. Everything for this trip was in order, but she had two other deals on her plate. So she sent e-mails and reviewed spreadsheets. In the back of her brain, however, thoughts of her two lovers simmered.

Her stomach flipped when visions of the previous evening invaded her mind. Both men naked and so, so hot. Hard. Wanting her.

And Jewel wondering if they'd only just scratched the surface.

She snapped the lid of her laptop closed. Pulled in some deep breaths.

She'd actually been relieved when they'd told her they had an early Board meeting in River Cross the night they'd all gotten together. They'd seemed to know that she needed time alone to process. And to sleep. Lord, they'd worn her out.

But in a really, really good way.

However, the morning after, as she'd stood under the hot spray of water in her shower, Jewel had encountered a serious bout of guilt. For coaxing the men to yield to her whim. It had stayed with her.

Then she'd realized that there truly was no *coaxing* either of them. Rogen and Vin were strong of mind and will as much as of body. They'd caved, yes. But because they'd both wanted her.

So that wasn't really what her guilt was about. It'd been festering, and now she considered that a part of it was due to not being able to choose between them. To adding to their internal strife in order to assuage some of hers.

It was selfish to want two men at the same time. Like, at the *exact* same time.

She tried to placate herself by contending that plenty of women filled their social calendars with more than one man during a given time period. Men did it as well. Nothing new there. Nothing to obsess over. Right?

Besides, Jewel hadn't established mutual exclusivity with Rogen after they'd made love at his house. Nor had she and Vin made any sort of commitment after Bristol's.

So what really gnawed at her had to be the emotional aspect of the threesome. The fact that she knew Rogen and Vin had had deep-seated feelings for her long ago, and clearly still held tight to them. And Jewel had intense feelings for them as well. Hence the reason she'd never be able to choose between them.

So then . . . how would that work in the grand scheme of things? If she couldn't choose, then should they all just walk away?

Now her stomach churned.

To walk away again . . .

She closed her eyes. Rested the back of her head against her seat. Tried to find a little inner peace.

She'd existed for ten years without either man being a major force, a major presence, in her life. She'd excelled at SFSU because it had been her sole focus. Ditto with Catalano Enterprises.

In the end, that had left her satisfied professionally. She loved her work, loved when she could execute transactions that made her father proud and contributed to the family legacy.

But personally? Emotionally? Sexually?

Jewel couldn't lie and say she'd had any sort of romantic fulfillment in the past decade. Including visiting Rogen in Italy that one time seven years ago. Another fleeting weekend that had left her feeling as though they were on varying planes. Again, the different trajectories of their lives that just didn't match up.

And Vin? Well. That was an excruciating scenario unto itself. To now know that he'd learned of her trip to Trinity. For him to have not realized—all this time—that she'd gone to speak to Rogen about them and that she and Rogen had not made love, had not gotten back together.

Was there any way under the sun to make that up to Vin?

The prom stand-up, his disappearance . . . none of that mattered to Jewel anymore. He'd had every right to blow her off. For his own sake. She could validate and accept that now.

What Jewel couldn't accept was that Vin hadn't confronted her. Hadn't asked her about her intentions. He'd just left.

And that was something else Jewel had to contemplate. When Vin was done with her this time around . . . could he simply leave her again?

Whether it was completely effortless or not for him to do it— could he? *Would* he?

"Fuck," she mumbled. She might as well have swallowed a box of rocks for the dead weight in her stomach.

She certainly hadn't made things easier for any of them.

But holy hell. Had it been an incredible night!

She pressed her thighs together as the tingling of her clit made her restless. Breathless. It'd been amazing to have both of them touch her, kiss her, make her come.

So, yeah . . . She wanted more.

Which made the guilt return.

A vicious cycle. But one she didn't have time to deliberate over further because there was activity in the hangar, which she heard through the opened jet door.

She jerked alert just as Vin ascended the steps and entered the cabin. She stood and moved into the aisle. Greeted him with a hug.

He held her tightly, the way he had in her kitchen. When she'd cried on his shoulder for all that they'd been through. The wounds they'd both inflicted.

"Damn, you always feel so good," he murmured.

Heat flowed through her veins. She threaded her fingers in his lush hair and said against his neck, "I like your arms around me."

*Not helping matters.*

She couldn't seem to contain her response to Vin. She knew his torment now. And suffered right along with him.

His embrace tightened. Jewel sighed contentedly.

But then, over Vin's broad shoulder, she saw Rogen enter the plane. She gasped.

"Aw, fuck," Vin grumbled, instantly releasing her. He shook his head and dropped his laptop bag into a single seat on one side of the aisle and plopped into another seat arranged in a foursome facing each other.

Jewel stared at Rogen's split and swollen lip, his slightly bruised chin.

Her heart wrenched.

"Rogen." She lifted her hand but didn't dare touch him.

Rogen shot a look toward Vin. "Isn't that sweet?" he ribbed, as Vin had done when Jewel had called the day before. "She's worried about me. Thanks for the punch, pal."

Jewel whirled around and glared at Vin. "*You* did this to him?"

With a noncommittal shrug, Vin said, "He'll survive, baby."

Her jaw slacked.

Rogen snickered.

Recovering quickly, she asked Vin, "Are we in junior high again?"

"Oh, right," Vin said with a nod, a glint in his emerald eyes.

"Rogen laid me flat for . . ." His gaze flashed to Rogen. "For what, exactly?"

"For telling Mrs. Peterson in English class that I used Cliffs-Notes when I wrote my paper on *Hamlet,* because I hadn't read the book."

"Yes, now I remember." Vin smirked. "I had to give you up on that one, man. Everyone should read *Hamlet.*"

"And *War and Peace?*" Jewel tossed in, pinning Vin with a look.

He grinned. A knowing smile that told her he instantly recalled the first time they'd realized they were hot for each other—and had done something about it.

"I offered to lend you my copy," he told her.

She gave a slight shake of her head. "It's, like, a million pages long. I didn't have the attention span back then."

"Because you were trying to help Bay and Jonathan pick out the proper condoms."

"Whoa," Rogen interjected. "Bay and Jonathan Higgins? Not a fucking chance in hell."

Jewel turned to him. " 'Fraid so. Until that night they planned to have sex. Blew up in their faces when their parents showed up at their hotel room. I told Jonathan not to leave any trails. But he used his dad's credit card, for God's sake. Pre-paid, no less, so it was already on the statement before they'd even made it into the lobby."

"Fuck." Rogen laughed. "Jonathan never was too bright. Too many concussions on the football field, I always suspected." He took a seat by the window.

Jewel sat next to him. The flight attendant, Melinda, emerged from the galley and Jewel requested an ice pack for Rogen's lip.

Vin scowled at her doting. Said, "I thought it was to the victor that went the spoils."

"Not when it's a sucker punch, asshole," Rogen told him.

"You two aren't seriously going to fight over me, are you?"

Jewel asked, consternation brewing. Then she added, "Wait. What *did* you fight over?"

"You," they both said in unison.

She grimaced.

In a serious tone, Vin said, "Rogen never should have told you about Holly."

She mulled this over, the consternation becoming a bit of a cyclone in the pit of her stomach. She dared to ask, "You both regret our night together?"

Vin shifted uncomfortably in his seat. Rogen heaved a breath.

Neither spoke as Melinda returned with the ice pack, which Jewel delicately applied to Rogen's lip.

The attendant said, "Welcome onboard, Mr. Angelini and Mr. D'Angelo. I'm Melinda. If there's anything you need, please don't hesitate to ask. We have catered food and a fully stocked bar. I habitat in the galley." Her tone was a bit flirty at her little quip, but then she turned professional again. "It doubles as an operations center. We have two laptops set up with Internet service, a laser printer, scanner, and high-speed copier. Everything is connected via satellite, so we rarely ever have any interruptions, downtime, or cycling."

"Good to know," Vin said with a nod.

Melinda smiled prettily at him and asked, "May I bring you something to drink, Mr. D'Angelo?"

"Pellegrino will be fine," he said. "Lime twist."

Her attention shifted to Jewel's other guest. "And for you, Mr. Angelini?"

"The same."

"For me as well," Jewel chimed in. "But skip the lime in Mr. Angelini's drink." She eyed his lip. "Citrus would hurt like hell."

"Good point." He grinned warmly at her. "Thanks for taking such good care of me."

Vin swore under his breath. Then said to Melinda, "Make mine a scotch. Neat."

"Of course." The attendant gave him another beguiling smile. She obviously took a liking to him.

*Not a big surprise.*

"Better make it a double," Vin added as an apparent after-thought.

"I'll be right back." Melinda left them.

Jewel was still leaning over Rogen, holding the pack to his lip. She glanced at Vin and said, "If you'll recall, I held a package of frozen peas to your shiner over the *Hamlet* debacle."

"That was before we'd slept together," Vin said in a slightly cantankerous tone. "Before you and Rogen had slept together, too."

"So me playing nursemaid has a different connotation now?" she challenged.

Vin grinned. "You never back down."

"Are you waiting for me to do just that?"

It was a question issued in jest yet it held quite a bit of meaning.

Vin appeared to give her inquiry the consideration it was due while Melinda served drinks and then returned to the galley.

Rogen sipped his sparkling water, then set the glass in the gold-plated holder in the arm of his chair. He said, "Vin had a point about Holly. I shouldn't have brought her up."

Jewel's gaze shifted to Rogen. "So you really do regret what happened, like Vin does?"

"Not a chance in hell. It was sensational." He reached toward her and his fingertips grazed her cheek. "I just regret that nothing is ever cut-and-dried with the three of us."

She frowned. "Well, there is that."

Rogen gently pulled her hand away from his mouth. Took the ice pack from her. "Better buckle up for takeoff, sweetheart."

She settled in her seat. Sipped her sparkling water. Stared at Vin.

Jewel didn't miss the mix of emotions playing across his devilishly handsome face. He wasn't feeling as glib as he was trying to project. She understood that about him. Vin had always been a bit sarcastic, sure. But after his parents' plane crash, he'd developed an edgier, rawer side. And Jewel had been fiercely attracted to it. Still was.

*For better or for worse.*

# THIRTEEN

Vin was glad he'd requested the scotch. He needed something to help dull the razor-sharp vibes he knew he exuded. Jewel sitting across from him in her tight black skirt with a hem so short she showed the majority of her long, bare legs made him hot and bothered. As did the silver satin blouse that was unbuttoned just enough for him to catch a glimpse of the scalloped trim of her black lace bra when she bent forward.

Conversely, the confused and somewhat remorseful look on her beautiful face made his gut pull tight.

She thought he and Rogen regretted sharing her when they'd been at her house. Vin couldn't ascertain whether or not it was true, even for himself. It'd been exciting. They'd all gotten caught up in erotic sensations.

And the truth was, Vin had gotten over Rogen touching her and kissing her when Jewel had started moaning. When she'd started to burn for them both.

Vin had wanted to give her whatever she needed—and he'd wanted Rogen to do the same.

But what Rogen had mentioned in his office, about whether

Jewel could accept them both in her life, as her lovers, created enough conflict to keep Vin on edge.

The sensible thing would be to have Jewel choose between them. But the more provocative and thrilling notion was to continue to share her. They were good at it. She'd obviously enjoyed herself. And well, hell. He and Rogen were nuts about her, so it wasn't at all far-fetched.

Except for that whole *unorthodox* concern.

Admittedly, a committed ménage would keep them all out of dating hell. She wouldn't have to make time for Vin. Then make time for Rogen. In this scenario, both men would know the other was sleeping with her. It'd all be out in the open, as she'd suggested.

Vin wouldn't be wondering about what went on behind closed doors with Rogen. And vice versa. If they were all together, then they'd *all* be involved.

He gulped down a healthy amount of scotch as he contemplated this further. Since law school, it was in his nature to chew over complex situations and determine the correct course of action— *before he took that action.*

Years ago, he'd been more spontaneous. Had acted on impulse when it came to Jewel on more than one occasion. That first time they'd been together by the river, for instance. Sure, he'd begun lusting after her prior to that day—he'd told Rogen as much. But Vin hadn't really allowed himself to travel a path of wicked intent with her. For all the obvious reasons.

When they'd been wrestling, though, she'd turned breathless and her hard nipples had pressed against her tank top, tempting him beyond all belief. And there'd been a distinct look of longing in her sapphire eyes. Impossible to dismiss. Impossible to turn away from.

Jewel had told him she and Rogen hadn't been together in eight months, and Vin had somehow considered that an appropri-

ate amount of time to give him the green light. He'd barreled right
through it, unable to stop.

Just like the other night.

Rogen, who was now texting on his iPhone, suddenly tossed
off his seat belt and stood, telling Jewel, "I have to take advantage
of your ops center." He stepped around her and disappeared into
the galley.

Vin eyed Jewel over the rim of his crystal tumbler as she un-
buckled as well and slipped into the seat next to him.

She said, "I need to tell you that I didn't know Rogen had
e-mailed you to say I was at Trinity that weekend before our prom."

"Jewel." He sighed. "I told him when we were at your house
that it was ten years ago. No sense in dredging it all up now."

"Yes, there is," she insisted, her dark eyes clouding. "I slapped
you at the gala because it was the first response I had to seeing you.
Anger wrapped around that one week out of our lives."

"I hurt you," he simply said.

"*I* hurt *you*."

They stared at each other for several moments.

Then Jewel added, "I didn't cheat on you. Not . . . physically."
She shook her head. "Not entirely. I didn't go to New York to be
with Rogen, to start something up with him again. I went to explain about us."

Vin's brow furrowed. "Why didn't you tell me that up front?"

"I honestly don't know. Other than to say that I figured you
would have insisted on coming along and I didn't want to spring
the news on Rogen in that way. It felt cruel for us to show up on his
doorstep and announce that we were together, that you were going
to college with me, not him. He'd suffered enough." She grimaced.
"So had you. I'm not discounting anything. It's just that . . . I
wanted to tell Rogen myself that I was falling in love with you."

Her eyes suddenly watered. Vin's gut pulled even tighter.

"You were in love with me?" he asked.

Jewel nodded. "Yeah. And I thought . . . we might have a chance. At a future. Me and you."

His gaze continued to hold hers. Vin had awaited that admission long ago. Years later, it did things to him. Made angst roar through him that he'd been so hasty in passing judgement. That he hadn't confronted her—or Rogen for that matter—about the secret tryst. He'd just assumed they were sneaking around. Because they'd done it before, behind their parents' backs. With Vin's help.

So, yes. He'd had just cause for latching on to his reason for leaving her. But he'd clearly been too hotheaded about it.

Not the first time, sadly.

"Fuck," he muttered. Then something else occurred to him. He said, "You didn't *entirely* cheat on me. What does that mean?"

And why the hell would he torture himself further by asking for details?

*Because I need to know. Once and for all.*

Jewel crossed her legs, gave a gentle tug on the hem of her skirt. Fidgeting.

She drew in a slow breath, then said, "I didn't exactly get around to telling him the reason for my visit. I just couldn't do it. Turns out, I wasn't ready to tell him about us. I wasn't ready to sever the ties with him. But I considered myself yours, Vin. Yes, Rogen kissed me. And yes, I let him. And yes, I spent the night in his bed in his dorm room. But nothing happened. I lied and said I was on my period. We didn't have sex."

"Wasn't that nice of you. Quite the sacrifice." He unhooked his belt and stood. Stepped into the aisle and paced while sucking down his scotch. The sting of the alcohol didn't override the sting of her betrayal, though. Even if that betrayal wasn't as horrific as he'd initially thought when he'd received Rogen's e-mail and Vin had been convinced they were seeing each other—sleeping with each other—and lying to him, it still grated.

Because she hadn't been able to tell Rogen about them.

Jewel got to her feet and faced Vin. Tears crested the rims of her eyes as she said, "I know what I did was wrong. I know I'm the reason we broke up. *Now* I know it, that is. Back then . . . I had no clue as to why you ditched school that last week. Why you stood me up for prom. Why you didn't attend graduation. All I knew was that you'd totally wrecked me."

"That wasn't how I saw it."

"You could have talked to me about Rogen's e-mail," she asserted. "You could have given me a chance to explain. You still would have been pissed—and you would have had the right. But maybe you wouldn't have been angry enough to leave. Maybe you would have understood. Maybe you would have stayed. Like you'd always promised you would." More drops tumbled down her cheeks.

"Low blow, Jewel," he ground out, his insides twisting over her tears. "I did make promises to you. Ones I broke. But consider that knowing you went back to Rogen wrecked *me*."

With a slight nod, she said, "I understand that now."

His eyes squeezed shut.

*Fuck. Fuck. Fuck.*

All that agonizing for both of them over nothing.

Well. Almost nothing.

Her voice cracked a little as she told him, "I was so excited to see you on prom night. More than that—I couldn't wait to see you. I was ready an hour before you were supposed to pick me up."

His lids snapped open. "You were never on time when I picked you up, let alone early."

She grinned, despite the tears. "I told you. I couldn't wait to see you."

He drained his glass. Deposited it in an armrest holder.

Jewel said, "It wasn't just a dance for me, Vin. We were graduating. We'd made plans. It was a rite of passage we were supposed to share. The ending of one of our lives and the beginning of another. It wasn't a prom for me. It was like . . . our wedding." She sobbed on a hollow laugh. "My dress was white."

"Jewel."

Christ, could she grip his heart any tighter? And if he caved to her, as he almost always did, would she rip it from his chest again?

Vin didn't know. There never seemed to be answers to all the tumultuous questions. So he did the only thing he could think of doing. He closed the gap between them in two wide strides and pulled her into his arms. Held her firmly. Let her cry. Let her apologize. Let her tell him how much she'd cared about him, how much she'd missed him.

Because deep in his soul, those were all the things *he* wanted to say.


Rogen returned to the cabin just as Vin embraced Jewel. He grunted.

On the one hand, he really did have a hard time seeing her in another man's arms. Yet Rogen would prefer it was his best friend over anyone else.

And he had a feeling Vin and Jewel had finally hashed out the whole end-of-senior-year trauma. That was a good thing, he'd allow. Too much time had passed for them to not have reconciled.

It was similar to the Angelini–Catalano family feud. Fifteen years was a long span to hold a grudge over misconstrued or even misguided intentions. Even Rogen and Vin hadn't held anything against each other when it'd come to Jewel. Not after that summer Vin had gone off on his own, then joined Rogen at college, acting as though nothing had ever happened. Just saying that he'd come to the conclusion that Yale was the place for him, not SFSU. End of story.

Rogen returned to his seat since he'd ironed out a few wrinkles with the Italy operations. Melinda had poured a scotch for him and he'd sipped while Vin consoled Jewel.

It was a past pain between Vin and Jewel that deserved a private moment to work through. Rogen could respect that.

Eventually, the plane started its descent and the two detangled from each other. Rogen was almost at the bottom of his drink. Jewel headed off to the bathroom. Vin straightened his tie and sank into his chair.

Of Rogen's silence, the fact that he hadn't intervened, Vin said, "That might have been more accommodating than I could have been."

"Don't be too sure," Rogen mused. He shook the cubes in his glass. "Our feelings for Jewel are rooted deep."

"Without doubt." Vin was quiet for a few contemplative seconds, then ventured, "Sometimes, in the end, I wonder if we've ever had her best interests at heart."

Rogen couldn't dispute that.

Vin sat back. "Still feeling guilty about going to Trinity and Yale?"

Rogen challenged, "Still feeling guilty about going MIA on prom night?"

"Yes," Vin confessed without hesitation.

"Yes for me, too." Rogen polished off the whisky. Melinda collected his glass. Asked if they needed anything else. Neither did— at least, not anything she could provide.

Jewel returned and buckled up. She looked a little unnerved but gave both men a smile.

Rogen said, "Why don't you tell us about this first transaction?" He bit back the *sweetheart* he'd almost added. What was the point in antagonizing Vin when ground rules regarding this new threesome scenario had not yet been established?

Jewel retrieved her slim laptop bag from under her seat and extracted a file folder. She handed it to Vin. Then she told them both, "Legalese. I had CE's Chief General Counsel draw up the agreements. Usually one of his representatives accompanies me on these trips, in a separate plane with Security heads and all the other pertinent players, such as appraisers and experts who can authenticate items on first glance, before they do a more in-depth analysis. I canceled Legal's presence for this trip."

Vin scanned the documents and nodded. "This all appears to be in order."

"There's some damage to the yacht I'm buying," she said. "The photos are in the back of the file. I need to verify there's nothing beyond what's visually documented and sign off on the pictorial evidence. Then my buyer will allow his people to engage in the transportation of the ship. I always insist on separate teams on both sides of the transaction, and an objective third party. That way everyone's on the same page and we all get what we're paying or bartering for."

"Very thorough of you," Rogen commended.

He'd always been impressed with her resourcefulness. Even if she hadn't had the kind of grades that would get her into an Ivy League school, Jewel had been clever in many other ways. She'd been one of the first in the community to start up crowdfunding for those in need, even before it'd become a popular concept on-line. Jewel had raised money for the animal shelter, the homeless, and even Bayli's mother, since she didn't have medical insurance.

Granted, it hadn't been enough to keep the Styles family from crumbling financially, but that was because Mrs. Styles continued to need surgeries and treatments, couldn't work, and required extensive home health care while Bayli was in school. And Mr. Styles was long gone.

Jewel said, "We're meeting with the owner of the yacht in San José, outside of Cabo." She wrung her hands in her lap. "Every single move is imperative to getting us closer to acquiring the land, Rogen. But it all starts with this first deal."

He reached over and clasped her hands. Stilled them. "My father wouldn't already have a plan in place to possess the scotch and keep the land if he thought you'd fail. So don't give in to any self-doubts, Jewel. Let's do this."

She gave him a grateful smile. Then slid her glance to Vin. "I know you feel this is a conflict of interest, but—"

He held up a hand. "It's okay right now. I didn't draw up any of these agreements, and the signatures required are between you, your sellers and buyers, and the team leads. I don't have to do more than answer any legal questions that crop up, and I'm more than willing to provide that bit of counsel, pro bono."

"Well, I wouldn't call it completely pro bono," she lightly teased, apparently overcoming some of her insecurity over the tricky transaction. "You do get a free vacation."

Vin chuckled. "I will admit, the destinations are enticing."

They chatted about the agenda as the plane landed on a narrow private airstrip. Jewel's team had arrived ahead of them and was waiting with two black SUVs to travel to San José del Cabo.

She pointed out the highlights to Rogen and Vin along the way, including the location of George and Amal Clooney's home, next door to Cindy Crawford and her husband. Rocker Sammy Hagar's retreat. The One&Only Palmilla resort, a favorite of celebrities and the ultra-affluent.

The SUVs turned into a long drive that led to a gorgeous house on the beach. Rogen watched as Jewel went into business mode, squaring her shoulders and hitching her chin, the way she'd done when she'd faced his father at the gala.

They all exited the vehicles and were met by a conglomeration of a dozen or so men. Jewel shook hands with an elderly gentleman with shockingly white hair against his tanned, leathery skin.

She said, "Señor Mendoza, a pleasure to meet you in person."

"And you."

They then proceeded to hold a discussion strictly in Spanish. Rogen caught the gist of the conversation and suspected Vin did as well, since they both spoke fluent Italian and had also taken some Spanish in school.

Jewel laid out the process of the procurement and Mendoza nodded emphatically. Then the two factions followed the older man to an enormous outbuilding that housed the yacht.

He explained to Jewel, this time in English, "The yacht was out of the water at the time Hurricane Odile hit in September 2014. She suffered much damage, as I've already shown you with the photos I e-mailed. Many of my businesses were ravaged—like so many other proprietors'. My resorts were my first consideration. I had to rebuild and that required the vast majority of my re-sources. So much so that I could not allocate money to repair the yacht. And since I'd had it out of water after I'd purchased it sometime before the hurricane, I didn't yet have insurance on it that would have covered some of the damages."

He held his hands up in the air, looking a bit devastated, a bit remorseful, a bit hopeful—the latter related to Jewel potentially alleviating him of the financial burden.

She smiled and said, "I'm sure we can mutually benefit each other."

Vin stepped in with the file folder she'd given him, and Jewel's team inspected the hull and initialed photos to attest that what was depicted in the screenshots was true in reality. Then they climbed the ladder and boarded the ship, completing the process.

Once satisfied with the inspection, Jewel and her people con-ferred. Then she and Mendoza signed the legal documents. Jewel contacted her Accounting department via speakerphone and the pre-arranged electronic transfer of funds was completed. The security and transportation specialists on both sides went into a heavy dissertation on the strategy for moving the yacht from San José to Las Vegas.

Her business concluded—and evidently feeling quite pleased with herself—Jewel linked arms with Rogen and Vin and said, "Let's celebrate."

# FOURTEEN

Jewel could almost breathe.

The first dot had been connected. So . . . yay! She'd phoned Bayli and Scarlet on the way into Cabo San Lucas and let them know she'd succeeded with stage one.

Then she, Rogen, and Vin arrived at the private condo on the marina in the heart of Cabo, overlooking the harbor, Lover's Beach, and the stunning rock formation of Land's End. They caught a spectacular sunset over the gulf and the ocean beyond. Then dressed for a casual dinner. Vin still wore dress pants but changed into a polo shirt. All in black. Which made him even more dev-ilishly handsome.

Rogen opted for board shorts, a muscle shirt, and flip-flops. So sexy.

Jewel put on a deep-teal-colored sequined string bikini. She tied a skimpy mesh sarong around her waist that matched in color. Stepped into decorative thongs. She took the men to one of her favorite beach restaurants. An open-aired *palapa*-topped establish-ment with excellent views of El Arco and the craggy walls of the far side of the harbor.

Tiki torches illuminated the beach and the crashing waves. Semi-buried railroad ties with sand filling the cracks between and partially covering the wood served as the dance floor in the restaurant. A live band entertained the crowd.

Jewel ordered a bottle of the internationally famous Cabo Wabo silver tequila and a combo of lobster tails and zesty *carne asada* "street" tacos.

The server delivered warm, crispy tortilla chips and fresh *pico de gallo* as an appetizer. He brought over the tequila for her to approve. Set out three shot glasses and a bowl of limes sliced lengthwise. She sampled the smooth tequila and then gestured for the server to pour for them all.

They toasted and slammed the first shot. Two shots later, when the lobster and tacos arrived, Jewel had a nice buzz going.

"I'm thinking this evening should *not* be featured in our 'About Us' portion of the Web site for our inn and winery," she announced.

Rogen chuckled. "Agreed. We should definitely leave the tequila and feast out of the PR materials."

"And . . ." she said before pausing to lick the crook between her index finger and thumb, sprinkle a little salt on it, down another shot, and then suck on a lime. When warmth spread through every inch of her, she continued. "The dancing."

Rogen's brow crooked. "There will be no dancing."

"Oh, but there will be." She tossed a look in Vin's direction. He scowled at her. It made her laugh. "Sometimes you're too surly when I know you want to lighten up."

"Clearly, you're reading me all wrong," he said mockingly.

She waved a dismissive hand toward Vin. Told Rogen, "We took a trip to Tijuana with Scarlet and Bay—and, yes, Jonathan. After I turned eighteen. Got completely trashed and learned how to salsa dance. Maybe lambada, too, but at that point everything was a bit fuzzy."

Rogen gave her a sexy grin. "I bet you set the dance floor on fire."

"Not sure," she said with a little shake of her head. "I only remember bits and pieces of that night. But—" She returned her gaze to Vin. Insisted, "You *did* dance."

"*Muy loco*," Vin quipped as he swirled a finger in the air, close to his temple. "She has no idea what she's talking about. It's the tequila."

Jewel reached for a packet of Wet-Naps and cleaned her hands. Then she thrust a packet toward Vin. "Tidy up there, my friend. Because we're going to show these people how it's done."

She pushed her chair back and stood. A wee bit wobbly, but she was wearing flat thongs, so she felt stable enough to dirty up the dance floor with Vin. Who never backed down from a challenge or a dare. He set aside his used Wet-Nap and got to his feet.

"You just can't fight the saucy," he said to Rogen. "Why even try?" Then he took Jewel's hand and led her to the sand-covered railroad ties.

The dance floor was packed. The music was lively. Colorful bulbs were strung along the edges of the thatched roof and wrapped around the trunks that formed the frame of the structure. It'd been forever and a day since Jewel had fallen into a perfect rhythm with a man in a sexy dance—that man being Vin.

For all his brooding and edginess, Vin's moves were fluid and sensual. His hips swayed with hers. His hand rested gingerly at the dip of her waist, to guide her if he so chose. Their gazes locked. Her pulse beat in time with the music.

At that very moment, it didn't matter that they'd fucked up their past. It didn't matter that they'd been too prideful or foolish or whatever to confront each other.

The closer they inched toward each other, the hotter the air turned between them, the more fiery the mood became. That was all that mattered.

Vin's hypnotic green eyes glimmered with lust.

Excitement shimmied down Jewel's spine.

Their bodies touched. Gyrated in time to the passionate tune. Vin's hand shifted to the small of her back, pressing her to him. His powerful thigh was between her legs. Precisely where she wanted it.

She placed a hand on his biceps. Her other palm flattened over his cut abs, feeling every ripple of sinew as he moved with her.

"I guess I do know how to dance with you," he said in a low, hungry tone.

Jewel's breathing was scarce, but she managed to jest, "Sometimes you're too obstinate for your own good."

"I'll give you that one. But," he added as his emerald eyes radiated primal heat, "sometimes *you're* too irresistible for your own good."

A spark against her clit made it even more difficult to breathe. Yet she didn't lose her footing with Vin holding her steady. "I don't think so," she told him. "I had to convince you to play along last night, didn't I?"

"No." He gave a quick shake of his head. "You only had to seduce me. Which you do so, so well. So easily."

She smiled up at him. "A man like you doesn't get seduced, Vin. He already knows what he wants. Just needs to decide if he chooses to take it."

He let out a sexy groan that lit her up. His body was hard against hers. The humidity and close physical contact had her skin glistening and her pussy aching for him. For Rogen, too.

Jewel stepped out of Vin's embrace just long enough to grab Rogen by the arm at their table and say, "Salsa with us."

"I have two left feet, sweetheart. And you know it."

"This dance has nothing to do with feet—and everything to do with hips, heart, and soul." She tugged a little harder. He stood, laughing softly. The shots were doing wonders for his mood, too.

"Don't blame me when I trip all over you," he said.

"You won't."

They joined Vin, whose eyes blazed when Jewel fell into step with the sensuous beat again.

Behind her, Rogen gripped her hips and followed along. Jewel backed up and ground her ass against his crotch. His head dipped and he suckled at her earlobe, sending a thrill down her spine.

The trio moved together, not necessarily in perfect harmony, but Jewel didn't care. She was surrounded once more by their heat and virility and it did incredibly sinful things to her body. Her senses. Her libido.

One of her hands splayed over Vin's hard chest. The other reached around to Rogen's hip. Keeping both men glued to her. Exhilaration flared low in her belly and seeped through her veins, through every inch of her.

She, Vin, and Rogen nabbed a few sideways glances from those not on the dance floor, but this was Cabo, the tequila was flowing, and the sensuality of the threesome was neither out of the ordinary, nor did it faze anyone. If anything, what Jewel noted were envious stares from women who clearly wished to be in her place, wonderfully trapped between these two seriously hot alpha males.

Jewel felt damn lucky to be the one in this position. Her nipples tightened beneath her bikini top. The ache deep in her pussy was almost unbearable to not sate immediately, but she wasn't done ratcheting the excitement amongst them. The sultry ambience, spicy music, and sexy salsa had her undulating between both men.

It was all fantastically intoxicating. She, Vin, and Rogen were melded together, and nothing else existed beyond the fire, the eroticism, the burning need.

"You're making me so fucking hard," Rogen murmured in her ear.

Jewel grinned. "I know. Vin, too. I can feel you both and it's making *me* incredibly wet."

Vin's steel-muscled chest rubbed against her breasts, pebbling her nipples further. An enticing, prickly sensation. A soft moan fell from her parted lips.

His thigh wedged between hers again and she slowly rode it under the guise of the provocative dance. His head bent to hers and he whispered, "Come for us."

She gasped. "Vin."

"Yes," Rogen added in a low tone, his warm breath on her neck, teasing her skin. He had one hand at the dip of her waist; the other covered her hand on his hip. Vin's hands were also on her, at her sides, just below her breasts. His thumbs swept over the outer swells where they were exposed beyond her skimpy top. She tingled from head to toe.

There were many other scantily clad bodies crowding them and that added to her exhilaration. The trio didn't need an excuse to be fused together, yet the more people who joined in the stimulating beat of drums and strumming of acoustic guitars provided the perfect pretext.

She stared into Vin's gorgeous green eyes, glowing with desire.

Rogen said, "You're trembling."

"That's because you're both about to get your wish."

Given her mesh sarong and bikini bottom, there just wasn't enough of a barrier between Vin's strong thigh and her pussy to lessen the sensation of him rubbing against her, stroking her clit, pushing her higher. His and Rogen's hands on her body, Rogen's lips skimming her throat, and Vin's eyes flaring with need pushed her right to the brink.

"Jesus," she muttered. "I am way too turned on by both of you."

"Is there really such a thing?" Vin countered with a roguish look.

It was just the expression to send her over the edge.

"Oh, God," she whispered, and ducked her head as the climax claimed her, stealing her breath. She clamped down on her lower lip to keep the throaty moan at bay. Her fingers curled into Vin's shirt. Her grip on Rogen's hip tightened.

Tremors ran through her, but the men had a firm hold on her. Jewel wasn't sure if she missed a few steps or not, because the delicious heat rushing straight to her core commanded her full attention. In fact, it was a damn good thing Rogen and Vin were guiding her, as pure pleasure consumed her.

"Damn," Rogen said on a sharp breath. "That's hot, sweetheart."

She peered up at Vin and said, "You are so very wicked."

His grin was a bit strained from his own arousal. "I'm not the one who just had an orgasm on the dance floor."

"You instigated it." She gave him a quick kiss. Against his lips, she added, "And it felt fabulously forbidden. Please tell me you want to taste me now."

The impish expression returned. "Hell, yes."

He exchanged a look with Rogen over her head. Then Rogen stepped away. He took her hand. She took Vin's. They left the throng of tangled bodies. Vin fished a hundred-dollar bill from his front pocket and pressed it into their server's palm.

"We'll take the bottle," Vin said as he snatched the tequila from the table. *"Muchas gracias."*

*"Adiós, mis amigos."* The waiter grinned over the generous tip.

Rogen led the way out. Jewel nearly floated on a cloud from alcohol and sexual euphoria. They made their way down the marina and to the condo.

By the time they reached the top floor of the building, she was still buzzing and ridiculously aware of both men. In need of their touches, their kisses, their cocks.

The vast living room was dimly lit. But the ocean beyond the glass balcony doors was dotted with tiny golden lights from tri-hull booze cruises, elegant dinner cruises, and commercial cruise liners.

Vin flipped on the Bose speaker and Enrique Inglesias's "Rhythm Divine" was queued. He lit a few candles and Jewel gave him a soft smile. She'd expressed the importance of romance years ago; he'd scoffed at the sentiment. Yet here he was, setting the stage. "Rhythm Divine" segued into "Bailamos," a sexy tune partially in Spanish. Enrique's sensuous voice seeped into her soul, mixing with Vin's intense gaze on her and Rogen stepping in close.

Vin poured one shot that they all shared. From behind her, Rogen pulled loose the strings at her back. His hands slipped under her top and massaged her breasts. His fingers and thumbs toyed with her nipples, hardening them.

Standing before her, Vin reached around to the nape of her neck. He untied the strings there and the bikini top dropped to the floor. His head dipped and he kissed her passionately.

Rogen's hands shifted to her waist. While he undid the knot of the sarong, Vin palmed her breasts and aggressively kneaded them. Turning her molten, while continuing the searing lip-lock.

Rogen unraveled the strands at her hips and the scant material fell away. Vin broke the kiss, gripped her around the waist, and hoisted her up. Her legs wound around him. He turned and headed toward the secluded deck that overlooked the water. Over Vin's shoulder, Jewel crooked her finger at Rogen. Knowing her smile was a seductive one.

Rogen followed and slowly stripped off his clothes while she enjoyed the show. Then Vin set her on her feet and she yanked the hem of his polo from his pants. Peeled away the shirt. Her hands roved his tapered obliques, his chiseled abs, and his wide chest, her thumbs brushing the inner swells of his defined pecs, her nails scraping his small nipples.

"Careful there, baby," he darkly warned. "I'm still rock-hard."

"And I'm still wet."

He let out a sexy grunt. "We'll make you wetter."

He unfastened his pants and divested himself of the rest of his clothing while her insides sizzled.

Rogen grabbed a towel and spread it along the edge of the sunken Jacuzzi. The music drifted from hidden speakers. Vin lit more candles. Rogen sat on the towel and gestured for Jewel to join him. She positioned herself between his parted legs, her back to his chest, her feet in the water.

His hands ran over her shoulders and down her arms, making her shiver with delight.

He didn't just touch her. He brought her skin to life. His hands glided over her, sometimes lightly. Tantalizing. Sometimes with more pressure. An insistency that silently told her of how deeply she affected him. How much he wanted her.

"I like this daring side of you," he said against her neck. Then he nipped at her skin.

"I wasn't sure you would," she confessed.

"Because Vin's the one who brought it out?"

"Yes."

Rogen tenderly bit her again. She gasped as heat sparked along her clit. He told her, "I get why you want us both at the same time. We each give you something different."

"And it's unbelievably amazing as a whole."

She slid a glance toward Vin. He stepped into the hot tub and took a quick dip. When he surfaced, she admired his solid muscles glistening in the moon- and candlelight.

Heightening her arousal was Rogen's brawn surrounding her. His powerful legs encasing hers. He continued kissing and nipping her neck as his hands caressed her breasts, squeezing enticingly, rolling the hard centers, keeping the zings running rampant. Making her restless.

The sensations were amplified as her gaze locked with Vin's. He was so gorgeous. And by the steamy look on his face and the firm set of his jaw she could tell it turned him on to see Rogen's hands on her breasts.

And that turned *her* on even more.

Vin moved stealthily through the water, toward her.

Jewel's breath caught. It was still a little difficult to separate out her feelings when it came to these two men. The emotions, certainly, because they were so intricately entwined. But aside from that were the high-voltage currents they each evoked. Vin's gaze, his intensity, inflamed her the way Rogen's touch did.

As Enrique and Whitney Houston passionately sang "Could I Have This Kiss Forever?" and the sexually charged air crackled around Jewel, Vin reached the ledge within the tub, kneeling before her.

The eye contact didn't waver as he lifted one of her legs and draped it over Rogen's thigh. Vin did the same with her other leg. So that she was spread open for him.

His hands glided over her thighs, his thumbs skimming along the inner portion. Her flesh quivered at his scorching touch. His thumbs reached the apex of her legs and stroked her slick folds.

Lust rode the magma flowing through her veins. A soft moan tumbled from her lips.

She stretched her arms behind her to wrap around Rogen's neck as his mouth found all the right spots along her throat.

Vin kept her dewy, swollen pussy lips spread as he lowered his head to her and licked the knot of nerves pulsating with need and desire.

"Yes," she sighed. "Lick my pussy."

Her eyes closed and she gave herself over to the excitement coursing through her.

The tip of Vin's tongue flickered over her clit, quickly and insistently. His hands slid under her ass and he lifted her slightly, pressing his mouth against her. He stroked with skill, suckled her lips, stroked more feverishly.

Jewel's pulse jumped.

"Vin." She really couldn't think beyond that one word. His tongue fluttered, his lips tugged, and it was all so stimulating and sinful and just plain fantastic. Hitching her breath. Pushing her toward the pinnacle that would make her scream in ecstasy when she fell from it.

Adding to her pleasure was Rogen caressing her breasts. And his racy words.

"You feel good in my hands. I want to fuck your tits."

Her stomach flipped. "While Vin fucks my ass?"

"Is that how you like it with him?" Rogen's voice was rougher than usual, tinged with lust.

"Yes." There was no point in keeping anything from him. From either of them. "He's very careful. But it's so hot."

As was what Vin continued to do to her. He slid two fingers into her pussy and pumped with a rapid pace.

"Oh, God," she said on another moan. His mouth on her clit and his fingers inside her had her close to climaxing. "Yes. That is so delicious."

Rogen teased her nipples, keeping them taut and tingling. Her hips rolled as Vin's tongue flitted and his mouth suckled. The tension built deep within her.

Then ignited.

Jewel cried out as the sensations erupted.

Her inner muscles contracted around Vin's fingers, holding them tight as her pussy thrummed vibrantly.

*So. Good.*

Vin let her ride the fiery wave before withdrawing his fingers, standing, and reaching for his discarded pants, dragging them toward him. He extracted two foil packets from a pocket. The first was a condom. He sheathed his thick cock.

While Jewel still brimmed from her orgasm, Vin leaned into her, entering her with one smooth, solid thrust.

"Vin!"

He pumped into her, aggressively. Almost . . . desperately. Like he *had* to have her. Had to make her come again.

He fucked her hard and fast. Pushing whimpers and sharp breaths of air from her lungs.

One of Rogen's hands left her breasts and he used two fingers to rub her clit, with the same assertiveness as Vin. Her arms tightened around Rogen's neck. She held on as they both worked her.

"Oh, Christ. That's just right," she encouraged. "Fuck me."

Vin's mouth captured her nipple and he drew it in, against his teeth. Her pulse spiked.

"Yes," she whispered.

"Make her come," Rogen demanded.

"Yes, Vin," she panted. "Please make me come."

"Open your eyes," he directed. "Watch me fuck you."

She did. His hips jerked and his jaw clenched. His eyes smoldered.

She unlocked her arms from Rogen's neck, one still coiled there but gripping Vin's rigid biceps with the other hand. She unclutched him tight as she held his gaze.

Rogen's fingers on her clit pressed a bit more firmly, massaged a bit faster. His erection slid along her back, aided by the light sheen on her skin from the humidity, the men's heat, the fire raging inside her.

"You're both so good at getting me off. My God. This is so incredible." She could barely breathe. Her heart beat wildly. Her inner muscles squeezed Vin's cock as he drove into her.

Jewel's throaty moans mixed with Enrique singing all in Spanish now. The song had a fervent rhythm that complemented Vin's thrusting and Rogen's stroking.

"Lose it for me," Vin commanded.

She couldn't have held back if she'd tried. The inferno burned brighter.

"Yes," she muttered. "Oh, God, yes. Oh, fuck. Vin."

His intensity only made her hotter. The erotic sensations reached the boiling point and burst forth.

Jewel screamed. Her body quaked. Her clit throbbed in an enticing, exhilarating way.

"Oh, my God." Her whimpers came on raspy breaths. "You both make me so crazed. I can't think of anything other than the two of you making me come."

Both men were highly arousing. Highly addictive.

Vin slowly slid out of her, still erect because he hadn't caved to his own release. She knew why he'd kept it together when she'd gone over the edge. Knew what he had in mind.

Jewel unraveled from Rogen and slipped into the tub. Stepped off the ledge and submerged herself in the water to help cool her down. Then she slicked her hair back and returned to where Vin stood, waiting for her. He had the other packet in his hand.

Jewel moved between Rogen's legs and leaned over him. His hands pressed to the outer swells of her breasts and his cock nestled between the full mounds.

Behind her, Vin tore the foil. She glanced over her shoulder as he drizzled lubricant along the cleft of her ass, mostly in and around the small, puckered hole.

Then he shifted slightly so that he could empty the little envelope of lube at the top of the valley of her wet breasts and Rogen's erection.

"Good thinking, man," Rogen said with a sinful grin. His hips bucked and his cock glided along her slippery skin. "Oh, yeah." He let out a harsh breath. "Fuck, yeah."

At the same time, the head of Vin's cock nudged her small hole and all the heat and erotic sensations returned in a flash.

Her palms were flattened on the deck, on the outsides of Rogen's thighs. She held herself steady as Vin eased in.

But a soft cry fell from her lips.

"Okay?" Vin asked, his tone tight.

"Yes, yes, yes," she assured him. "Oh, God. *Yes.*"

Rogen's thumbs whisked back and forth across her nipples as his dick stroked between her breasts. Vin's hands clasped her waist and he inched in. Taking her breath away.

Naturally, it was an incredibly snug fit. The tequila helped to alleviate some of the sting, making it more of a gentle searing. And the lubricant eliminated the friction so that it was a smooth motion as Vin pulled out and then pressed in again.

Jewel moaned. Vin repeated the action a few times, teasing her until she said, "Fuck me, Vin."

He slid in farther. Farther than he'd ever done before. It rocked Jewel.

"Jesus. You almost made me come," she told him.

"You're so ready for me," he said. "And I *will* make you come. Hard."

His hand moved around to the front of her, and he rubbed her clit as his cock pumped slowly into her.

Once again, Jewel was overwhelmed by the various feelings along her flesh and within her. Above what the two men did to her, her arousal was also wrapped around theirs. Knowing she was giving as much as she received. Turning them on, making them burn.

Rogen's jaw worked vigorously as he fucked her breasts, his wide shaft slipping along her slick skin, the head poking through the opening at the tops of her mounds, then disappearing between them. It sent a wicked shiver down her spine. Which made her tense up.

"Easy," Vin reminded her. "Relax, baby. Don't squeeze me."

She loved that he was so conscientious about not hurting her when he took her this way. He didn't lose control. Didn't push too deep, too hard, too fast. Instead, he kept a controlled, consistent tempo that was sexy and titillating.

His fingers on her clit circled and caressed. This wasn't the frenetic fucking that had swept her away minutes earlier. Rather, it was a scintillating mounting of pleasure and desire.

Warmth and euphoria flowed through her. Her inner thighs and stomach quivered. Her knees weakened. Her breathing picked up, as did that of her two lovers.

Rogen said, "I could get off just watching you let me fuck you like this."

"But you want to come inside me, don't you?" she tempted him.

"You know I do." So he kept the pace measured, a bit leisurely. Though she could see he was close to his own release by the shimmer in his blue eyes and the setting of his rugged facial features.

Jewel arched her back and lifted her ass higher in the air for Vin.

He let out a low, strangled sound. "You get so into this."

"Yes," she said. "And I'm about to come." She gazed at him over her shoulder once more. His entire body was rigid. "You're almost there, too."

"Impossible not to be," he told her as his cock thrust tenderly into her, but with a hint of urgency now. His fingers at her clit dipped inside her.

"Yes," she said again. "Finger my pussy while you're fucking my ass. I love how you feel. So damn hard."

His hips bucked. Jewel saw the change in him and it spurred her own anticipation of an electrifying climax.

The heel of Vin's hand rubbed the knot of nerves between her legs as his fingers and cock stroked her inner walls.

"Oh, yes." She moaned. "You both feel so damn good." Rogen's erection along the swells of her breasts and the pads of his thumbs teasing her nipples tighter were just as alluring as everything Vin did to her. She pressed a hand to Vin's at the apex of her legs, forcing him to rub harder, the way Rogen had that night at her house.

He thrust a bit faster and deeper into her. Causing louder, wilder moans of pleasure to leap from her throat.

And then everything inside her crashed head-on and tore through her.

"Oh, God!" she wailed. "Vin!"

Sensation after sensation raged.

"Oh, fuck!" She couldn't help but clench him tight as she came. Couldn't hold back the elated cries.

"Jesus, Jewel," Vin growled. "Holy hell."

Mere seconds later his body jerked, then shuddered.

"Yeah, baby," he said. "That's it. Make me come. Oh, hell, yes."

His cock surged inside her, prolonging her orgasm, keeping her falling. . . .

"Vin." She vibrated from the inside out. "Oh, God!"

It was all so fantastic. So dynamic!

"Goddamn," Rogen said with hunger in his tone. He released her breasts, freeing his cock. "You're about to make me come."

Vin withdrew from her. Gripped her at the waist again and lifted her up on the ledge of the tub. Rogen took over, pulling her to him so that she straddled his lap.

She was still lost in ecstasy when he thrust into her.

She called out, the intense feelings raging through her once again.

Still behind her, Vin's hands moved to her hips and he pushed her down against Rogen's pelvis as he pumped into her with fervor.

"Yes," she insisted, staring into Rogen's eyes. "Fuck me."

She was blinded by desire, the erratic pulsing inside her, the fierce need.

Rogen was hard and hot, deep in her pussy. Plunging and stroking feverishly. This wasn't his usual gentle lovemaking. This was him half out of his mind for her. And knowing—*knowing*—this was exactly what she needed from him.

Right. At. This. Very. Moment.

"So unbelievable," she told him. She had no other words.

Jewel's hands were splayed over his chest. His hands were on her breasts. Vin's hands were on her ass now, grinding her against Rogen so that he was buried within her and she felt him swelling and throbbing.

Then Vin circled her anus with a fingertip. Pressed in.

Another searing orgasm flashed through her and she tried to bite back a scream, but it ripped from her lips.

"Yes," Rogen nearly howled. "Oh, fuck!" And then he lost it, too.

His hot cum filled her. Her body shook and her breath was scarce. The erotic sensations hummed in her veins, straight to her core.

"Oh, God." Jewel collapsed against Rogen. He held her tight. Vin lightly stroked her back.

She couldn't help but grin. Just as Vin had brought out her adventurous side, she'd brought out his tender one. And Rogen's wicked nature.

As she'd contended earlier, as a whole they were perfect together.

# FIFTEEN

Vin didn't know exactly what the hell was happening with this no-holds-barred threesome, but he'd just come like a force of nature inside Jewel and gotten hard again when Rogen had set her off.

Definitely not a sane situation. But none of them seemed capable of or inclined to extract themselves from it.

Vin stood and snatched a towel to tidy himself. Then he returned to where Jewel was just now slowly sitting up, still straddling Rogen's lap. She held a hand to Vin and said, "Help me."

He pulled her to her feet. Wrapped an arm around her waist. She slumped against him.

Rogen hauled himself up and went for a towel.

"Wow," she said in a raspy voice. "I'm not sure I have any bones left in my body. Every bit of me liquefied. I feel limp and . . . God. So fucking good."

Vin grinned. Then scooped her into his arms. Jewel pressed a kiss to his cheek. "Aw. Now *there's* the gallant."

"Don't tell anyone," he gruffly said.

"Your secret is safe with me." Her arms tightened around his neck. Her lips grazed his jaw. "You can be very sweet when you want to be."

"Only with you."

Rogen sauntered past them. Vin carried her into the condo.

Rogen poured another shot and threw it back. Then went to the main bedroom. Vin followed. They entered the bathroom and Rogen cranked on the rain showerhead. Vin stepped into the glass-enclosed area and carefully set Jewel on her feet.

He and Rogen lathered her up, and she smiled deliriously as their hands skated over her naked body.

"I've officially discovered heaven," she murmured.

Vin chuckled. "I think it was Enrique and tequila that turned you on."

She snickered at him. "You both know *exactly* what turns me on."

She kissed Vin. Then Rogen.

They rinsed and toweled dry. Vin helped her into the bedroom, because she was apparently still limp and languid. She fell into the big bed, moved into the middle of the mattress, and slipped under the covers.

She asked, "You're both joining me, right?"

Vin slid a glance toward Rogen. Crooked a brow. "You can keep your hands off my dick?"

Rogen smirked. "It'll take some willpower, I'm sure."

Vin laughed. He climbed in next to Jewel. Rogen took the other side. She snuggled close to Vin and rested her head on his shoulder. Rogen spooned her from behind.

"Ahhh," she said on a sigh. "Bliss."

Vin's fingers lightly stroked her cheek. Her hair was still damp and the loose curls spilled over his skin, teasing his senses with the floral scent and the wispy strands. Her hand pressed against his abs. Her other arm was twined with his at Vin's side.

He breathed her in. Absorbed her nearness, her soft curves, her warm breaths.

The entire discussion on the plane over what had happened

between them ten years ago still weighed heavy on his mind, mostly because Vin wasn't a man full of regrets. He made decisions. Saw them through. Took full accountability for the outcome.

Yet what had transpired between him and Jewel long ago—and Rogen, inadvertently—left Vin with much remorse.

And some burning questions. Such as, if he'd not been so quick tempered, would things with her had turned out differently?

He couldn't say for sure, particularly because Rogen was currently wrapped around her backside. Even if Vin and Jewel had made it all work with college and beyond . . . what if Rogen had strolled back into their lives? What if Vin and Jewel had married and Rogen had suddenly shown up on their doorstep?

Would they have ended up in this exact same situation?

Because Jewel really couldn't choose?

Because he and Rogen really couldn't let her go?

Vin closed his eyes. Tried not to obsess over it all for now.

What was the point, anyway? None of them were at the right juncture to resolve the past. Maybe someday. After this trip. After Jewel and Rogen got their property.

Maybe then they could all sit down and figure this out.

*Maybe.*

Vin was just shifting from that state of deep sleep to grogginess when he heard Jewel moan.

Low. Throaty. Sexy.

Seconds later her fingers coiled around the base of his erect cock. She pumped slowly as her soft, enthralling whimpers teased his ears and his senses.

Rogen was making love to her.

Vin's eyelids drifted open. Jewel was still lying mostly on him and her body rocked gently against his.

She released him for brief seconds, licked her palm, and then slid her slick hand over the head of his cock. Rubbing enticingly.

Vin's hand covered hers and he increased the pressure. Made her slip quickly along his shaft. Up and down. More blood rushed to his dick. She continued to moan. The sound spiked his adrenaline, thickened his cock.

Her warm lips skimmed over his pecs. Her tongue flicked his nipple. Then she suckled the bud, gently nipped.

Vin let out a low growl.

"You're going to pay for that."

"Let's hope so," she said in a sultry voice.

His grip on her hand tightened. "If you're going to jerk me off while Rogen's inside you, at least be more accommodating and less sassy."

"Where's the fun in that?" She wriggled her hand free of his and licked her palm again. She rubbed it over his tip. Glided slowly down his shaft. "If you had another packet of lube, I could do some very, very naughty things to you. . . ."

"You like being naughty."

"So much."

Her body jolted against his. Rogen now hammered into her. Jewel's breath caught. Her hand pumped Vin's cock. Her whimpers fell faster, were more erratic.

"Come with us," she murmured to Vin. "Now."

Her fingers became a vise grip around his cock.

"Someday I might be able to resist you."

"Not today," she insisted. And stroked his shaft with just the right speed, just the right pressure.

Rogen pumped into her with the same tempo. Her breaths were choppy. Her lids closed. She let go.

Jewel's erotic cries filled the suite. Followed by Rogen's release. And Vin's.

He stared up at the ceiling as he wondered if he'd ever, *ever* get over this woman.

Jewel tongued his nipple again. Then playfully murmured, "Vin, honey. You made a mess."

He snorted. "So next time, make sure it's your mouth or your pussy I'm in when I come."

Jewel tried to contain a vibrant smile as she, Rogen, and Vin settled in their seats before the Gulfstream took off for Vegas. They'd cleaned themselves up. Dressed. Devoured breakfast. All politely and professionally—with an electric undercurrent so that the two men stole heated glances at her. And Jewel flamed with excitement.

Now she tried to keep an even tone as she explained her next transaction. She told them, "We're meeting Daichi Yakimoto at the Bellagio for a private gaming event. He wants the yacht we just secured. In exchange, he'll give us the two Renoirs my Paris buyer needs to complete his collection."

Rogen whistled under his breath. "Renoirs?"

"Yes," she said. "Serious stuff."

They discussed the upcoming exchange as they traveled from Cabo to Vegas. Once they landed, more SUVs took them to the Bellagio. They each showered and changed for the evening ahead of them, Jewel dressing in an ankle-length slim gown of liquid gold satin with a slit up the back and a provocative dip to her tailbone. She'd pinned her plump curls up, leaving a few strands at her temples and shoulders.

She met Vin and Rogen in the living room of their suite. Both men looked sigh worthy in tuxedos.

She fought the lust, though, and focused on business. She told Rogen, "This could be a very costly endeavor. Let me pay. Play along. It's all about appeasing Mr. Yakimoto in order to get what we want."

Rogen said, "I thought we'd considered a fifty-fifty partnership."

She smiled at him. "We can always settle up later. I trust you. You trust me." She stared deep into his cerulean eyes. "Right?"

"Right."

Jewel's heart fluttered. He always left her exhilarated.

She kissed him. Then her gaze slid to Vin, who appeared edgy because she'd shared something special with Rogen. His raw intensity lit her up.

He didn't know it, of course. And there was no way to explain it to him at present. So she simply stepped toward him and said, "You don't have to make any contributions. I know where your loyalty stands. But thank you for being here, just to answer any legalities that might arise."

He speared her with an intent look. "You think that's why I'm here?"

She gave him a kiss, too. "You came for me. And to help Rogen. I appreciate that."

Jewel collected her small clutch and they left the suite. Took the elevator to the floor where Daichi Yakimoto was hosting his private affair. Two men serving as security stood outside the double doors. One used an iPad to verify she, Vin, and Rogen were on the exclusive guest list. Then allowed them to proceed.

Inside, Jewel was informed there was a five-thousand-dollar-per-person buy-in. She handed over her credit card. They each received a chip for the buy-in amount. As they wound their way around roulette and blackjack tables that were all fully occupied, Yakimoto approached with purposeful strides. She'd spoken with him numerous times via Skype and recognized him immediately.

"Miss Catalano. A pleasure to finally meet you in person."

She bowed, as did he.

"Thank you for the invitation to this evening's festivities," she said. "I'd like to introduce Rogen Angelini, my business associate, and Vin D'Angelo, our legal consultant."

More bows. Then Yakimoto directed them through the crowd and toward a door along the far wall. "I understand from my people that the yacht is now in transit."

"I can personally confirm that the damage looks much worse in the photos than in actuality, but it is still extensive," she told him.

"I was anticipating that. But I've contacted restoration experts who are familiar with the vessel and can return it to its original state."

It was apparently a legendary ship in the yacht world. Lyle Doberman was a famous designer of luxury yachts but had never actually built any himself, despite outrageous monetary offers to do so. He'd eventually said yes when commissioned by an internationally acclaimed maritime museum for a unique project nearly seventy-five years ago. Mr. Doberman had since passed away, making his one-of-a-kind creation a valuable antiquity.

Yakimoto opened the door and gestured for her to precede him into the anteroom where his team, as well as hers, awaited them. Two large packages were laid out on a conference table—the Renoirs.

The authenticators carefully peeled away the brown-paper wrapping and began their inspections while Jewel, Rogen, and Vin engaged in idle chitchat with Yakimoto, him telling the trio that the works of art had been in his family for generations but were never a part of a complete collection. All the while, Jewel's stomach knotted with worry that something might go wrong and, as Bayli and Scarlet warned, her house of cards would crumble.

But that didn't happen. The initial assessment of the paintings affirmed they were originals. They were carefully repackaged and placed in a wooden crate with a divider in the center. It had clearly been designed specifically for these two frames, because they fit perfectly and were well protected. The crate was nailed shut and sealed with security tape to prohibit tampering. Though that was just a step meant to placate. The crate could easily be swapped out for an identical one carrying replicas, not the originals.

But Jewel's team—as well as the authenticators—would have their eyes on the prize the whole time it was being shipped to Paris in one of Catalano Enterprises' private jets.

Jewel accepted a glass of champagne while Vin handled all the paperwork. Then Yakimoto rested a hand at the small of her back and directed her to the gaming room.

"Do you play blackjack?" the refined, tuxedo-clad man asked.

"Craps is my preference, actually," she told him.

"Ah." He grinned. "I knew I liked you." He led her to a table with all male gamblers. They graciously made room for Jewel on the hook. Exactly where she liked to play.

"New shooter," one of the men said, his appreciative gaze sliding over her. She hoped like hell Rogen and Vin didn't notice as they stood behind her. But she was sure they did.

"We could use a little lady luck at this table," another gentleman told her. "How are you with the dice?"

She plunked her five-thousand-dollar chip on the pass line for the come bet. "I'll roll two or three sevens right out of the chute." With a coy smile, she added, "I like to get them out of my system up front." She winked. The men chuckled. Chances were good Rogen and Vin scowled.

Jewel was feeling a bit feisty following her successful business meeting. So she reached for the dice and tossed them against the far wall of the table. They bounced off the cushion, kissed in midair, and landed with a slight tumble.

*Seven.*

"I'll be damned," Yakimoto said, admiration in his tone.

"Now we're getting somewhere," the gambler across from her commented.

Everyone was paid. Jewel collected the chips from that roll but kept her initial bet on the pass line.

She rolled again. Another seven.

Her third roll established a point. Ten. Everyone laid out odds. She continued to throw the dice. Six. Five. Eight. Six. Snake eyes.

Then she turned to Vin and held her hand out. "Your chip, please."

His brow jumped, but he gave it over. She dropped it on the hard ten. An eight-to-one bet.

From behind her, Vin said, "Baby, that's a sucker bet."

"Not when I'm rolling." She tossed another five. Felt her point about to be delivered. She threw again.

Hard ten.

The table erupted with applause. The players were thrilled she'd made them money.

She glanced over at Yakimoto. "You won't mind if I cash out now, will you? I don't like to press my luck."

"Of course not," he said, still smiling, clearly impressed. "You will come back next time I host, though? So that I may win my money back?"

"I look forward to it." She collected her large-denomination chips from the dealer and exchanged another bow with Yakimoto.

Then she headed off to the cashier, Rogen and Vin at her sides.

"Where'd you learn craps?" Vin asked, sliding a glance her way.

"The girls and I were here in Vegas for a friend's bachelorette party that got crashed by the bachelor and his groomsmen, so we all hit the tables. I probably lost as much that weekend as I made this evening."

She handed over her chips, as Rogen did, and the cashier asked, "How would you like payment?"

Jewel requested two cashier's checks, a large percentage of her winnings to go to the charity Yakimoto was promoting, and the remainder back on her credit card, which she produced.

Once the transactions were completed, she linked arms with her two devastatingly handsome escorts and they left the gaming room behind. Since they'd had dinner on the plane, they retired to the suite. Vin popped the cork on a bottle of Dom while Jewel contentedly sank her teeth into a plump chocolate-covered strawberry. Rogen nibbled on the cheese-and-fruit tray the private butler had laid out for them.

As was their custom, they all touched the rims of their crystal flutes together. *"Salut."* They sipped.

Vin unraveled his bow tie. "Congratulations on your latest acquisition."

"I always get stressed out over the verification process. Holding my breath, praying I'm not getting duped." She could breathe much easier now.

"Has it happened before?" Rogen asked as he slipped out of his jacket.

"Twice," she confessed. "Very disappointing. But somewhat difficult to avoid, and the reason I always have a team with me. Scarlet tracks everything down and vets the items. Yet she sees the fraud enough in her own career to always warn me of the risks inherent to bartering."

Jewel had been fascinated with Scarlet's job as an insurance investigator from the time she had set up operations. With Bayli's research help, Scarlet was addicted to chasing cold cases. Jewelry, art, vases, anything worth a small mint, really, that had gone missing and caused an insurance claim to be filed hit her radar screen. She'd get tipped off on a theft scam from time to time, but mostly Scarlet liked digging on her own. And using her connections with black markets and auction houses to locate the "stolen" or secretly sold goods that owners had collected premiums on.

"This could be a very dangerous hobby," Rogen cautioned, concern in his tone.

"Yes," Jewel agreed. "And my parents were against it initially. But then I pulled off some near-impossible deals and Daddy couldn't deny it was a creative means to an end."

"Until someone double-crosses you," Rogen pointed out. And winced—over the fact that his father was trying to do exactly that to Jewel.

"The possibility always exists," she contended as she undid Rogen's tie. "But the vast majority of people I strike bargains with are genuinely interested in procuring whatever treasure is out of their reach. For instance, the yacht Mr. Yakimoto wants was auctioned off by the museum when the institution reached financial dire straits. Then the vessel changed hands through several private sales and those records were somehow lost. So with the yacht out of the water and the insurance never renewed, it was difficult to discern who possessed it. But I have very tenacious and diligent friends."

"You're also a bit of a thrill seeker," Vin commented, his rich voice tinged with desire.

She glanced over at him. "Just a bit?"

"Hmph," he snickered.

She pulled the bow tie from Rogen's neck and draped it over the chair with his jacket. Then she slowly unbuttoned his shirt while gazing into his eyes. They deepened in color.

She stripped off his shirt, then turned to Vin. Repeated the process.

God, they were just so fantastically built. It was no wonder she craved trailing her fingers and tongue all over their hot, hard muscles. Which she did, starting with Vin.

His fingers twined in her updo as her lips skimmed along his collarbone. Her hands swept over his ribs, up to his pecs, to his shoulders. He released strands of her hair and wrapped his arms around her waist. She stretched and grazed his jaw with the tip of her tongue.

"Kiss me."

One corner of his mouth lifted sexily. "I'm going to do a hell of a lot more than that. And you know it."

His mouth crashed over hers, claiming it in his usual aggressive way.

Jewel responded with equal passion. She was fairly sure she'd never come down from the high when in the presence of both men. And when they kissed her.

Dragging her mouth from Vin's, she glanced at Rogen. He'd already slipped out of his shirt. She gave him a mischievous smile.

"You like tempting me with all that brawn, don't you?" she asked.

"I wouldn't want you to get bored with Vin's wimpy physique."

Vin snickered.

Jewel unraveled from Vin and her nails skated over Rogen's torso. Her palms pressed to his chest. His head dipped and his lips tangled with hers in sizzling, tongueless kisses. Then he got serious. Sealed his mouth to hers, their tongues twisting.

When he eventually broke the kiss, she was breathless.

He said, "Let's take this into the bedroom."

# SIXTEEN

Rogen had been thinking of this moment all damn day. Imagining Vin fucking her while Rogen's hands were on her, too. She seemed to love it any way they gave it to her. And they both liked making her moan. Making her come.

Christ, she came so fucking hard. They all did.

In one of the bedrooms, Vin slipped the thin straps of her dress from her shoulders and eased them down her arms, peeling the satiny material away. She stepped out of her shoes. Vin removed her panties. Rogen shed his clothes, too, and sprawled on the enormous bed while Vin went for the condoms.

Jewel joined Rogen, crawling toward him on her hands and knees, a lascivious glint in her sapphire eyes.

She positioned herself between his legs and dragged her manicured nails along one of his inner thighs. Up to his balls. The pads of her fingers glided gingerly over his sac, brushing back and forth with a tantalizing, featherlike touch. Making him burn.

Then her fingers curled around his erection at the base. Squeezed enticingly.

He grinned. "Gonna give me another one of your world-class blow jobs?"

"If that's what you want."

"Suck me good, sweetheart. But don't make me come."

Her tongue slid along his shaft, grazing both sides, then teasing the groove at his tip. Rogen kept his gaze on her as he rested one hand at the back of his head on a pillow and threaded the other through her loose curls.

Vin climbed onto the bed, naked and hard. He moved behind Jewel, still on her knees. His hands cupped her ass cheeks, his head dipped, and he started licking her pussy. Her body jolted slightly and she let out a long breath that blew against Rogen's cock.

Then her velvety tongue whisked over his erection, making it throb in wild beats. She swiped at the drop of pre-cum, swirling it around his skin, tasting him before her lips closed over his head. She took him deep, down to where she gripped him.

Rogen pulled in a sharp breath.

"That's it," he said. "Suck my cock."

A moan at the back of her throat over Vin's mouth on her pussy reverberated along Rogen's shaft. He shuddered. Told Vin, "Keep her moaning. It feels fucking great against my dick."

Apparently, Vin put a bit more effort into his ministrations, because Jewel's whimpers came faster, were a bit heartier.

"Yeah," Rogen said to both of them. "Like that. Just like that."

Jewel's head bobbed and she worked him good, despite the tremors running through her. She palmed his balls, massaged tenderly. His hips bucked. Her teeth gently scraped. Rogen felt the sensations ripple through him. He didn't tamp them down just yet. It was too damn amazing to be in her mouth.

She clenched him a bit tighter at the root as her body rocked from Vin pleasuring her.

"Make her come," Rogen told him in a strained voice. "Keep your mouth on me when you do, Jewel."

Her suckling deepened. She tugged a little on his sac, and his hips jerked. Orgasm beckoned, taunting him. His release was close at hand. So damn close. He wouldn't give in to it, though. Not yet. Not until he was buried inside her pussy.

She moaned again. Moments later her muffled cry vibrated against his cock and Rogen nearly lost it.

"Oh, fuck," he muttered. Shifted his hand from behind his head and palmed her cheek, easing her away before he succumbed to the tension stretching tight within him.

She gasped for air, her eyes dancing a little, her neck flushing from her climax. She looked over her shoulder at Vin.

"Jesus, your thumb rimming my ass at the last second sends me flying."

His grin was a cocky one. "Glad to be of service. To both of you."

Perhaps it wasn't wise that they were all getting so into this. But Rogen really couldn't follow that logical path at the moment, because Jewel straddled him, drew him slowly in, and rode him with a gentle undulating of her hips.

Rogen clasped her waist and pressed her firmly to him as he eased into the sensual cadence with her. Lights from the Vegas Strip illuminated the large room. There was no music, no sounds other than heavy breathing, soft moans.

Rogen's thumb stroked her clit as they moved together, their gazes locked. He enjoyed their new, more fervent lovemaking, without doubt, but he would always prefer Jewel rocking with him in a seductive rhythm.

Vin was still behind her and his hands slid around her. He palmed her breasts, caressed with the same languid pace.

"Yes," Jewel whispered. Her hands covered Vin's and he massaged a bit deeper. "Don't stop. I'm going to come again."

She broke the eye contact with Rogen as her lids drifted closed. Her head fell back on Vin's shoulder. Her lips parted, her small cries falling from them.

She was the most erotic vision Rogen had ever laid eyes on. So beautiful, so consumed by passion.

Rogen had to concede that both he *and* Vin had taught Jewel to own her sexuality. To trust when to cave to it. To let it rush through her veins and into her heart and soul.

Seeing her like this not only made Rogen harder but also brought forth evocative emotions. Most of which had always stuck with him when it came to her. Some of them new and deeper. More mature. Because he and Jewel weren't sixteen years old anymore.

Vin's tongue swept over the long, graceful column of her throat.

Jewel murmured, "You both know the perfect erogenous zones."

Vin nipped at her skin just below her ear. Rogen stroked her G-spot with the head of his cock.

"Yes," she said. "Right there." Her hips rolled. Her breathing picked up.

Rogen rubbed her clit a bit faster.

"Oh, God," she whispered. "Rogen. Vin. Oh, God . . ."

Rogen felt the quivering inside her.

Vin must have felt the tremors, too. Against her neck, he said, "Come for us."

*"Yes."* And then she let out a rasping moan and nearly squeezed the life out of Rogen.

"Oh, hell," he breathed. "Goddamn, no one can keep it together when she clutches so fucking tight."

He erupted right along with her, calling out her name.


"Do you think I could take you both at the same time—inside me?"

Two sets of eyes snapped up from magazines and fixated on Jewel.

She grinned.

"Not exactly the place to be having this discussion," Vin lightly scolded.

She smirked at his lawyerly tone. They were in the Gulfstream, on their way to New York for a quick pit stop before hopping the pond to Paris.

Jewel said, "Don't worry. Melinda is in the galley listening to an audiobook on her iPad. I told her we didn't need her for a while." Jewel set aside her laptop. The guys had taken seats across from her so that she could spread out her work next to her without needing the fold-out table, since Rogen and especially Vin required extra legroom.

She couldn't concentrate on spreadsheets, profit-and-loss statements, financial forecasts. So she'd given up and then begun ruminating over the past two nights with her extremely sexy companions.

The previous evening, Vin had wanted a blow job after Rogen had made her come. Vin had told her he fantasized about it all the time, and after seeing her nearly get Rogen off with her mouth Vin had opted for the full deal. She'd swallowed him down and he'd shuddered for the longest damn time. Jewel found it incredibly heartwarming and liberating that she possessed the ability to bring the powerful man to his knees that way.

Now a different scenario ribboned through her mind.

"To clarify," Rogen slowly said, obviously not certain they should have this risqué conversation—no matter *where* they were—"you're talking about double penetration?"

"Yes," she brazenly confirmed. Though, admittedly, the concept was a little intimidating.

*A little?*

Okay. So *a lot* intimidating.

She asked, "Did you do it that way with Holly McCormick?"

"No," Rogen said, still eyeing Jewel curiously, evidently not convinced he should even remotely humor her.

"I grasp the mechanics," she explained. "I'm just wondering . . . I mean, it seems kind of as though—"

"There's not enough room?" Vin sarcastically offered.

Jewel sighed. "You don't have to be gritchy with me. You learned a hell of a lot from Shayla Harding and I was willing to let you experiment with me until you actually mastered all those techniques."

"The way you say that suggests you were just along for the ride." Vin gave her a pointed—*heated*—look. "Rather than begging me to make you come once I got started."

Rogen rolled his eyes in apparent exasperation. Or jealousy?

Jewel couldn't tell. Her two lovers were doing an excellent job sharing her without popping each other in the face anymore. That helped to alleviate some of Jewel's apprehension over wanting them both. The selfishness that wasn't really in her nature, but which strongly pertained to these two men.

As much as she'd tried to separate her feelings for each of them, she honestly couldn't. They were woven together. Every thread of desire, affection, yearning, intertwined. She'd meant what she'd said at her house the night they'd both been there. She didn't want one more than the other. She wanted them equally. Felt so much for them that it was impossible to say who she most lusted after, felt satisfied with, and cared for.

She'd contended when she'd seen Rogen at the gala that these two men each owned half her heart, half her soul.

Was that rational? Was it fair?

*No.*

*Absolutely not.*

To any of them. But her love was deep-seated. And it was unshakable.

So Jewel had to believe that whatever it was they felt for her, be it love or just lust, they could accept that she was torn. That she really and truly could not choose between them.

Wanted and needed them both. Physically and emotionally.

Which brought her right back to her question.

*Double penetration.*

Why did it lure her so?

Because it seemed so forbidden?

Because it would take everything between them to a higher level—and give her even greater pleasure?

Or . . . because it would fully join the three of them?

Jewel wasn't sure. In the back of her mind, she knew a onetime ménage held the connotation of something fun and daring. To continually have sex with two men at the same time became a riskier endeavor. And to have them both inside her at the same moment?

She stifled a small moan at the notion—and the inherent visual that flashed in her mind. It'd only make Rogen and Vin tenser.

And again . . . while the idea of having them both inside her was thrilling, the reality—the mechanics, as she'd thought of it earlier—was a bit trickier to digest.

Vin, sitting diagonal to her, stashed his new issue of *Forbes* magazine into the side pocket on the wall next to his window seat. He said, "As both Rogen and I have mentioned, it's a tight fit no matter how we fuck you. So chances are very good that, together, we'd be too much for you."

She stared at him, not quite ready to back down. Not quite ready to tuck the idea away. Mostly because it intrigued and excited her. But also because there was a fire flaring in Vin's emerald eyes over this particular topic.

Her suggestion got him going as much as it did her.

Yet he told her, "I'm willing to try new things with you, baby, but cautiously. So that you don't get hurt."

"Then we'll be cautious," she said.

Rogen pushed out of his seat and paced the aisle. Raked a hand through his hair. As usual, her stomach fluttered at the sight of his rock-hard biceps straining the hem of his T-shirt.

Vin asked her, "Where'd this idea come from? Because this time, I'm pretty sure it wasn't Rogen."

She tore her gaze from the hunky man pacing the aisle. "I read books," she told Vin. "But more than that . . . it's about the two of you surrounding me, filling me." Jewel sighed. "Maybe I can't explain it. I just feel so complete when I've got the two of you wrapped around me. Touching me. Kissing me."

She threw off her seat belt and stood. Interrupted Rogen's path and placed her hands on his obliques.

"Stop looking so agitated," she quietly said. "It was a question to be pondered. Not something to eat away at you." Jewel kissed him.

Rogen groaned. "Sweetheart, Vin's right about it potentially being painful for you, physically. Neither one of us wants to hurt you."

Her heart wrenched. Her expression softened. "I know that. And if I asked you to stop, you'd stop." She turned toward the seats and said to Vin, "You'd stop."

"Of course we'd stop," he all but snapped. A bit on the alligatorish side.

"So," she said as she returned to her chair, knowing when to let a suggestion simmer, rather than harp on it. "I'll just leave you to your thoughts."

She grabbed her laptop, opened the lid, and went back to work.

Vin shook his head. Snatched his magazine from the side pocket. Tried to focus on an article he'd been reading when Jewel had tossed out yet another erotic proposal.

Granted, it wasn't as though he hadn't already considered the possibility. How could he not be thinking two steps down the line? The truth was, they *all* got so caught up in their heated moments. And for Vin, it didn't center personally on him but on pleasuring Jewel. He was sure Rogen felt similarly.

Vin could make a lot of sacrifices for her, a lot of concessions. He wasn't the hotheaded teen who'd taken off when he'd learned she'd secretly visited Rogen at Trinity. Not that Vin was mild mannered now—not by any stretch of the imagination. But since that night of the gala, when she'd bedazzled him with her beauty and then ignited his internal fire with her impassioned slap, he'd been caught in a maelstrom of blazing desire and soul-stirring need.

And here she'd thrust him into yet another realm.

More contradictory feelings clawed at him. Vin wasn't accustomed to letting hints of the direction someone else wanted to take guide his actions. He had his own agenda, his own will. Tended to stay the course.

For Jewel, he feared he'd hop off the road paved for him every chance he got. Not wise. And to take the unbeaten path with Rogen? *Shit.* That was putting a lifelong friendship on the line, wasn't it?

Yet as Rogen appeared equally unsettled, Vin suspected he, too, deliberated over how much further they should go with this ménage. And probably felt just as anchored to it as Vin and Jewel did. Because in all honesty, the three had always been anchored to one another.

Jewel was eager to reach New York City and see Bayli, whom she'd sent a car for so that Bayli could meet the jet at a private airport.

Jewel stepped off the plane and gave Bayli a tight hug. "God, you're more beautiful than I remember!"

Bayli laughed. "Oh, stop. You saw me in River Cross a week ago. And on video on Thursday." She squeezed back, then said,

"What the hell am I saying? I could use the compliments. Tell me more!"

Jewel laughed. "Okay, I won't gush. But seriously. There is a very distinct glow to you that I've never noticed before."

"I told you, it's this city. I swear it has enough energy to light up the world—if only there was a way to channel it all."

"Through you, clearly. Wow, Bay. I'm just . . . blown away."

She nodded, suddenly looking a little guilty. "It's because I felt so stifled in California. I couldn't make anything happen for me there and I was always so tethered to my mom's needs, God rest her soul. I hated leaving her side even to just run to the grocery store or the pharmacy for her meds. Like stepping away from her for a half hour would torment me for the rest of my life if anything happened to her on my watch. If I wasn't there when . . . Well." She glanced away. "You know."

"Aw, Bay." Jewel stroked her cheek. "You did everything you could. But she wasn't well."

"And no amount of money could save her, I know. The million times your family and the Angelinis offered to pay for her care were deeply appreciated. But when her doctors said she was just too weak for another surgery . . . the only thing I could do was keep her company and try to alleviate some of her pain."

"You did just that. And now, Bay, it's your time to shine."

"Ha, well." Bayli choked on a small sob. Cleared her throat and swiped at a few tears. "Still undiscovered."

Jewel laughed softly. "You've been here a week, sweetie. I'd say give it two or three more days and *all* your dreams will come true. You'll probably be discovered in Central Park while selling gelato. That seems apropos for this city."

"From your lips to God's ears, my friend." She hugged Jewel again. "I really am glad to see you. I just didn't know you'd have company." She glanced around Jewel's shoulder and then fanned her face. "Amazingly *hot* company."

"Yes. They do provide nonstop stimulation." More than she'd ever share with Bayli. "Anyway, I brought you a little something to thank you immensely for your help with this deal-making mission I'm on."

"Jewel, I told you from the beginning, this is something I enjoy doing. Escapism, if you will. Something that my mind can grind over so I don't think about anything too depressing."

"And every time I try to compensate you, you turn me down."

"That's not true," Bayli contended. "I've never turned down dinner at an expensive restaurant in San Francisco with fancy champagne."

"Those things are barely the tip of the iceberg when it comes to expressing my gratitude. So, I want you to take this." She handed over one of the cashier's checks from the Bellagio. "I won't take 'no' for an answer."

Bayli's gaze fell to the slip of paper she held. Her eyes popped and her jaw dropped.

Jewel smiled.

"Oh! Jesus Christ!" Bayli's gaze snapped up. Locked on Jewel. "No fucking way."

"*Way.* Take it."

"Jewel! This is ten thousand dollars!"

"Yes. I have one for Scarlet, too. For all the work you both do for me that you won't accept a salary for."

"Because it's not a job, Jewel. It's a hobby. A very exciting one for me and Scarlet. And let's face it, if we didn't have the opportunity to do all this intriguing research for you, we'd be mindlessly marathon-streaming every series on Netflix and never leave our living rooms."

"Be that as it may," Jewel reiterated, "I appreciate your efforts, and CE has benefited greatly. I'm trying to pay it forward here, my friend. It's the right thing to do. So take the money. You *earned* it, Bay."

Bayli stared at the check. There was no doubt it tempted her. But she was a prideful person. So, of course, she had reservations. Which Jewel respected. She'd never had to stress over finances and parental medical expenses herself. And everything she'd done for Bayli to try to help her out had to be built around something other than a loan or a gift. Even crowdfunding donations went against Bayli's grain. Until she'd been too destitute to refuse help from a community that embraced her.

Bayli asked, "You really have a check for Scarlet, too?"

"Yes. This isn't any sort of charity or rescue mission. Bay, I swear I won the money playing craps. Vin and Rogen will attest to it."

Bayli gnawed her bottom lip for a few moments. Then let out a long sigh. "I could really use this, Jewel."

Jewel's heart constricted. She fought tears. She knew better than to get emotional with Bayli, because it would make her friend feel weak. Which she wasn't. In fact, Bayli Styles was one of the strongest, most compassionate women Jewel knew. Scarlet topped that list as well.

Yet, Bayli struggled with her own feelings. She pulled in a few deep breaths before lifting her head and meeting Jewel's gaze again. "This more than covers the research I've done. Keep asking me to help you, Jewel. But don't bring me checks like this again."

"Gotcha." They embraced once more.

Jewel continued to do everything in her power to hold her emotions inside. She understood pride. Hadn't she been so disappointed in herself when Rogen had told her his father would renege on their deal? And had instantly been consumed with humiliation that Gian, Rose-Marie, Rogen, and Vin might all think her a fool for attempting to negotiate for the land?

She *so* got Bayli's need to make things happen for herself. It was a similar sentiment that drove Jewel to realize the dream of building an inn and possibly bringing her and Rogen's parents back together.

She spent a little time catching up with Bayli while the jet was fueled and the caterers stocked the galley. Rogen and Vin joined them, and Bayli had as much trouble dragging her gaze from the men as Jewel did.

When the plane was ready, the men boarded.

Bayli asked Jewel, "How do you keep your hands off them?"

"Who says I do?" She winked.

"Jewel!"

She dropped a quick peck on Bayli's cheek, then said, "I'll let you and Scarlet know when I have the scotch. Thanks again."

Jewel crossed the narrow red carpet laid out before the steps to the Gulfstream and entered the cabin. Once they reached cruising altitude, Melinda served dinner. Then Jewel wrapped up a little more work, as Rogen and Vin did.

When exhaustion overcame her, she moved to the couch along the opposite side of the aisle and curled up with a blanket. She drifted off with all the risqué thoughts of Rogen and Vin that they'd tried to dissuade her from, but which she suspected taunted their minds as well . . .

# SEVENTEEN

*Ahh, Paris . . .*

Jewel took a quick shower, did her hair and makeup, and changed into leggings, a mock-turtleneck sweater, and suede ankle boots—all in black—before the plane made its descent. Rogen and Vin had cleaned up as well and the trio took a limo into the city.

Jewel loved Paris. Every corner they turned was more beautiful than the last, with the gorgeous white buildings and the elegant blue rooftops. The black wrought-iron-scrolled balcony railings and the flowing sheer curtains covering terrace doors. The plazas with shooting fountains, trimmed with lush green grass and vibrant flowers, and bistros with awnings over the patios and boasting tons of outdoor seating.

There were singletons typing away on laptops, likely hoping to capture the essence of Ernest Hemingway, Gertrude Stein, or F. Scott Fitzgerald. Friends celebrating life with wine and decadent desserts. Lovers huddled close, staring deep into each other's eyes.

Jewel admired them all. There was something magical and magnetic about Paris. Something ethereal that warmed her. Called to her romantic side.

And here she was. With Rogen. With Vin. Both of whom had displayed not only alpha tendencies that turned her on but also tender ones that touched her heart.

Yet Jewel couldn't get caught up in all of that at the moment. Her first order of business was the scotch, and she tried to concentrate on this latest and extremely critical transaction. Not the beautiful indulgence of Paris that lay before them.

The limo passed through tall gates of a gorgeous mansion that should rightfully be included on the registry of palaces for all its opulence. But it was much too modern, despite having been loosely modeled after the famed Fontainebleau. No royalty had resided within these walls. Still, the never-ending alabaster marble, sculpted columns and enviable paintings, chandeliers, and accent pieces were breathtaking.

Jewel, Rogen, and Vin were escorted through the lavish entryway, through patio doors, and to a verdant courtyard where Arnaud Barnier greeted them. He did the double-cheek kiss ritual with Jewel and shook hands with Rogen and Vin.

"I just uncorked an award-winning Bordeaux," Arnaud said to Jewel in French. "I understand you're a connoisseur of reds."

"Particularly vintage Bordeaux," she told him with a smile.

"Then allow me to pour?"

"I'd be honored."

Arnaud served the glasses. Meanwhile, the teams performed their duty of ensuring all was on the up-and-up with the decanter of scotch she sought.

As Jewel, Rogen, Vin, and Arnaud enjoyed the wine, Arnaud engaged Rogen in conversation about the history of the legendary scotch and the Angelini distilleries. Jewel was impressed by Rogen's knowledgeable dissertation—and Vin's informative sidebars.

She could sense the allegiance Vin held toward the Angelinis. Jewel knew losing his parents had been horrifically painful. Just like losing Taylor had been for Rogen.

Her heart had always gone out to them both. And she'd always found something awe-inspiring about how they'd embraced the pain, suffered through it, found the strength to rise above it. Perhaps it touched her so deeply because she knew their agony had been a part of them from the time they were teens to this very day. For the rest of their lives.

When the transaction was concluded and Jewel soared from the completion of connecting her dots, the threesome slipped into the limo and enjoyed some of Paris's finest offerings, including Notre Dame and a stroll along the Seine. They sat on a few patios and sipped champagne while people-watching, which was always fascinating in this city.

The sun set and they headed to dinner at Les Ombres, with a table at the window looking out onto the spectacularly lit Eiffel Tower.

Afterward, they returned to the hotel and Jewel changed into a silky red nightgown. She sent a text to Bayli and Scarlet to confirm all was in order and they'd be heading back to New York in the morning. Scarlet returned a lengthy note telling Jewel she'd be in town, since she was now investigating the disappearance of an entire art collection from an estate in the Hamptons.

Apparently, the heist had been percolating in the back of Scarlet's mind for some time. She'd consulted with her grandmother, who had numerous law-enforcement contacts, and Scarlet now strongly suspected that perhaps the two stepbrothers of the tycoon who'd owned the collection might be able to shed some light on the cold case.

Jewel made a date with the girls and invited Rogen and Vin along.

Then she settled on a sofa with sparkling water and once again broached her forbidden subject.

"So, did you both agonize over what I mentioned on the plane, or is it a nonissue?"

Vin let out a hollow laugh. "I think Paris has gone to your head."

She smiled. "Perhaps."

Rogen sipped cognac, then set his glass on an end table next to his chair. He leaned forward, resting his forearms on his thighs, and captured her gaze. "What do you want specifically, Jewel?"

"I've been mulling that over myself for the past week," she admitted. "It's incredibly difficult to reconcile, let alone articulate. Except to say that being with you both—on the plane, during a business transaction, dinner, whatever—*fixes* things inside me. The way we were torn apart from one another. The different destinies we had. The years we've spent engrossed in corporate affairs instead of personal ones. There's such a defining element to all that we've held out for these past ten years." She gave Rogen an imploring look. Then slid it toward Vin. "Right?"

Vin stood. He refreshed his cognac and sipped. She didn't press him. Though she awaited his response with bated breath.

He was halfway through his nightcap when he turned to her and said, "I'm not going to stand here and say the only reason I haven't been in a relationship since you, Jewel, is strictly related to college, law school, and work."

Rogen sat back in his chair. He let out a long breath. "I'm not interested in committing to another woman for a reason, either."

Jewel's pulse picked up. But like with Bayli, she knew to rein in her emotions and not let them intervene with the sound judgement she attempted to reach. No easy feat. Because she was wholly emotional when it came to Rogen and Vin.

But this discussion transcended emotion. Even transcended sex.

There was something more critical at stake here.

She said, "I can't be with anyone else. It's a pathetic thing to say from the standpoint of me being so bound to the two of you that I'd rather be alone than with anyone else. Yet . . ." She gnawed her lower lip. She pushed the overwhelming feelings to the depths of her soul so that she didn't appear so vulnerable that Rogen and Vin would cave to her whim strictly to placate her. That wasn't what she wanted.

This wasn't about getting her way.

It was about *finding* a way.

A way to assuage *all* the pain. To bring them together after all they'd been through.

Yes, Jewel had that innate desire to reunite people torn from each other. She didn't know from where it stemmed. All she knew was that being so intricately entwined with others' lives and then being stripped from them was excruciating. Not just for her. For *everyone*.

And it seemed that in some instances there just might be a simple answer for reconciliation. This one in particular.

So she said, "The last thing I want is for the two of you to fight over me. My intention has never been to come between you. What's happened in the past and even now . . . happened." She drew in a steadying breath and surged forward. "What I want is for you to understand that I could never love one of you more than the other. It might not make sense to anyone other than me. But in my heart, you are *both* it for me. No one else could ever replace you. And I won't ever be able to choose between you, because I am-one-hundred percent committed to both of you. *At the same time.* For all of eternity."

Jewel was a little shocked over her own confession. The acknowledgment of the finality of her feelings when it came to these two men.

Perhaps it *was* Paris that made her so forthcoming. Had her so willing to present her inevitable reality. Whether Rogen and Vin were in agreement didn't hold her back. How they felt wasn't something she could control. All she could do was be genuine. They deserved that from her. Direct and to the point. So they could make their own decisions.

Which she didn't expect them to do in one evening. The trio had reunited just over a week ago. A hell of a lot had happened in that short span of time. There was a lot to process.

She stood and deposited her snifter at the wet bar, then went into the master suite of the private executive residence she'd rented for the trip. Jewel pulled back the thick, luxurious bedcovering and slipped between sateen sheets.

Rogen and Vin joined her. She lay on her side again, this time facing Vin.

He said, "Don't take our reticence as rejection, baby."

"I'm not. In truth, I'm still absorbing the idea myself. But I'd be lying if I said taboo doesn't suddenly appeal to me."

"Mm," he murmured against her lips. "Definite thrill seeker."

"Why don't we try a little experiment?" Rogen suggested. "Take it slow."

A thrill chased through her. "As I've mentioned, I'm always willing to experiment."

Vin kissed her as Rogen's hands explored her body and his lips and tongue skated over her shoulder, along her nape, between her shoulder blades. The feathery touch of Rogen's mouth on her skin and the fiery sensation of Vin's tongue tangling with hers were the perfect combination of eroticism. A very specific example of why she felt complete when she was with them.

Rogen's hands snaked around her to cup and caress her breasts. Vin's fingers glided over her slick folds, teasing her. Both men were hard. She felt Rogen's erection against her lower back; Vin's nestled against her stomach. She writhed between them, their cocks rubbing her tingling flesh, turning her blood molten.

Her palm pressed to Vin's chest. Her other hand clasped his biceps. He continued the red-hot kiss. Rubbed her pussy lips, making her wetter.

Jewel lifted her leg and draped it over Vin's waist. Rogen apparently took that as an invitation, because he eased his cock into her from behind. Pumped slowly.

Jewel's grip on Vin tightened. Exhilaration ribboned through her. She had a feeling this was about to get a hell of a lot sexier.

"Vin," Rogen said in a low tone. He withdrew from her.

Vin entered her.

Jewel's nerve endings ignited.

Vin gave several solid thrusts, then pulled out. Rogen plunged in.

Jewel tore her mouth from Vin's. "Oh, God," she said on a lusty moan. It wasn't just the difference in their length and width. Their technique. The angles at which they each penetrated her. It was that they worked so well in unison. The tandem act of Rogen pumping into her while she ground her ass against his groin, and then Vin driving more forcefully as his fingers massaged her clit.

They took turns with her. Their breathing escalated at the same pace as Jewel's. She kissed Vin. Then Rogen. The tempo quickened and they changed up their pattern to three deep thrusts each, one after the other so that she barely noticed a void as Rogen slipped out and Vin slipped in.

"Yes," she whispered, her lids dipping, her mind going blank. She concentrated only on having them both in her pussy—*almost* at the same time. It was sensational. The technique changed to two strokes. The pace hastened. Then it was one stroke each until Jewel shattered.

"Yes!" she cried. And her body quaked.

Then Vin fucked her until he exploded. Rogen followed, filling her pussy with his hot seed. And sending a second, rippling orgasm through her.

"Are you still in love with her?" Rogen posed the question to Vin the next morning. "After all this time?"

They hunkered down at the kitchen island, Rogen eating a croissant and drinking orange juice, Vin reading a newspaper and sipping black coffee. Jewel had gone shopping.

Glancing up from the *Wall Street Journal*, Vin countered with, "We're really going to have this conversation now?"

"Well, my lip's pretty much healed, so I think I can handle a rematch. Though . . . I do owe you."

"If the mood strikes, be sure to hit me in the gut. Don't mess up this perfect face of mine."

Rogen let out a hearty laugh, despite the tension created by the touchy subject matter—his question regarding Jewel. "A black eye would be a huge improvement. Trust me."

Vin scowled.

Rogen said, "Seriously, man. Are you?"

With a sigh, Vin set aside *WSJ*. His jaw clenched briefly as he seemed to contemplate what he did or didn't want to divulge. Then offered, "For a while, after your e-mail, I thought I hated her. I honestly didn't see the betrayal coming. I guess because of all the plans we'd made. Her trip to Trinity was shitty timing and . . . I don't know." He blew out a puff of air. "As much stock as she'd put into prom and our future, so had I. There was a . . . Oh, fuck."

He slid from his stool and stepped away from the breakfast bar. Turned his back on Rogen and poured more coffee from the stainless-steel carafe.

Rogen's stomach twisted. Intuition kicked in. He had a damn good idea what Vin had just been about to say. Masochistic as it was, he prompted, "There was a . . . *what*?"

Facing Rogen, Vin wore a stony expression as he said, "A ring. I bought her a ring. A really fucking big-ass diamond ring."

"Ah, shit." Rogen's gut took a dive south. Mostly over the fact that Vin had been ready to stake a claim on Jewel—whom Rogen had considered, until recent events, *his* woman. But also because Rogen had inadvertently foiled Vin's plans. And shattered Jewel's dream.

*Son of a bitch.*

"It wasn't as though I wanted us to get married the day after graduation or anything," Vin explained. "I was going to give her the ring on prom night. Then we'd go to college and maybe after we turned twenty-one or graduated we'd tie the knot. I just wanted her to know how serious I was about her."

Vin shook his head, sighed with notable agitation. Then added, "Problem was, I flew off the handle when I found out she'd gone to you. It hurt. I wanted to hurt her back. That's irrational and petty, but then again, we were eighteen—what the hell did we know about being *rational*?"

"She was pretty devastated when she called me afterward, to see if I'd heard from you at all. But she wouldn't tell me why she was so upset. Just that she needed to talk to you and couldn't reach you."

"I ditched my phone," Vin told him. "Bought a new one. With a new number. So I didn't have to see her calls or e-mails coming through. So I didn't have her number programmed in. Hell, I even changed my e-mail address."

"That was harsh," Rogen commented. Then said, "Though I likely would have done the exact same thing in your shoes."

"The thing is," Vin told him in a darker tone, suddenly opening up, "you always let her know how you felt about her. You always complimented her. Always told her you loved her, once you'd realized it. I never did."

"You never said you loved her?"

Vin gave a sharp shake of his head. "I was much too obstinate— or maybe arrogant—about it. I wanted her to say it first, so I'd know she was really over you. Serious about moving on. With me. But I definitely felt it. Christ," he groaned. "I think I fell in love with her the first time I was inside her. She gave me this look . . . all wide-eyed and breathy. Then she smiled. Goddamn, she has the prettiest smile."

"Yeah. She does."

"As prom night was rolling around, though," Vin confessed, "I didn't care who said it first, because I was damn certain we were on the same page. So I was willing to take a chance. But then everything between us blew up. End of story."

Rogen stood and rounded the island. Slugged Vin in the gut, and he nearly doubled over.

"What the *hell*?" he roared.

"That was for fucking my girlfriend."

Vin glared. "She wasn't your girlfriend at the time. She hadn't seen you in eight months."

"That's why I didn't punch you in the face."

Jewel was already on the jet when the guys showed up. Vin yanked the hem of his polo shirt from his dress pants and flashed his ridged stomach, with a light bruise on it.

She gaped. Shot Rogen a look. Demanded, "I thought you two were done fighting over me."

"Yeah, well, it was . . . what'd you call it?" he asked her. "Residual angst?"

"*Conflict* was the term I used."

Vin plopped into a seat next to Jewel. Gave her his roguish grin. "Doesn't hurt, baby. I was just trying to gain a little sympathy from you."

"Jerk," she quipped. Then kissed him.

Rogen snickered.

Turning her attention to him, she said, "Did you get out all of your aggression?"

"For the moment."

"Rogen."

"Jewel," he countered. Then leaned forward, his elbows on his thighs, his hands dangling between his parted legs. "The fact is, we all fucked up ten years ago. You should have told me about Vin.

I shouldn't have gloated that you'd just been with me at Trinity. And he should have admitted he was in love with you."

She sucked in a breath. Whipped her head in Vin's direction. "You never once uttered those words."

"Neither did you," he challenged.

"I was going to," she assured him. "Prom night."

"Yeah. Me, too."

"Such idiots," Rogen said in a light tone, obviously trying to keep the tension from ratcheting. "Tell her about the ring."

Vin glowered.

Jewel's heart jumped. "There was a ring?"

Vin merely nodded.

"Like . . . what kind of ring?" she prompted with bated breath. Not that it mattered today. But she was dying to know.

"The kind that looks like a skating rink on a girl's finger," Vin told her.

"Of the engagement variety?" she ventured.

"It would have been a long engagement. Till we got through college. But . . . yes."

"Whoa." She sat back in her seat. Took several minutes to digest. The plane taxied to the runway and then took off. Jewel was still stunned.

Naturally, a million what-ifs wanted to infiltrate her brain. But what was the point in entertaining the idea of her and Vin actually making it to prom that night, saying the words to each other, him going down on one knee, and—

Tears instantly sprang to her eyes. She tossed off her seat belt and stood, rushing down the aisle to the bathroom.

"Jewel!" Rogen called after her. "We haven't even leveled out yet!"

She didn't care. She locked herself in the lavatory. Tried to breathe. Tried to stop the flow of tears.

Vin was going to propose.

It wasn't exactly something she'd put substantial thought into back then. She'd basically operated on a one-step-at-time, even keel. That was how she'd gotten through all the tragedies and losses.

Sure, when she was twelve, thirteen, fourteen, she'd considered Rogen asking for her hand. But then he'd been sent off to Trinity and she'd let that little fairy tale die on the vine. Following that painful experience, Jewel hadn't considered herself to be happily-ever-after material.

But she had allowed herself to fall for Vin. So maybe, deep in her heart, she'd held out some hope that they were doing more than just going off to college together.

She'd told Rogen at her house that she wasn't certain a future with Vin would have panned out, because he might have decided halfway through school that he really wanted to be at Yale. And she'd believed what she'd said at the time—she'd never hung huge hopes on what five or ten years down the road would look like with Vin. Primarily because she was accustomed to having the rug ripped from underneath her.

*But . . . wow.* Vin had bought a ring.

She fought to compose herself. Splashed water on her face. Patted her skin dry. Wondered if that little tidbit was what had set Rogen off and made him punch Vin. Probably.

So maybe this threesome was a bit more volatile than she'd ever imagined.

Then again, it was imperative to finally lay the remaining pieces of the past on the table, so that they could perhaps get over it all. Move on. Cut the cord on that one week a decade ago.

Well, and the years leading up to it.

Jewel pulled in steadying breaths. Felt a bit more collected.

She realized her heart didn't just hurt for her sake. For all that hadn't come to fruition in her life. She hurt for Vin, for how he'd been blindsided, betrayed. She hurt for Rogen, for all the choices he'd never been able to make for himself as a teenager under parental control.

She hoped getting it all out in the open was the cleanse the three of them needed.

Jewel left the bathroom and returned to her seat. Crossed her legs. Rested her hands in her lap.

Both Rogen and Vin eyed her curiously.

A few tense minutes passed. Then Rogen raked a hand through his hair and said, "This has become an all-or-nothing situation amongst us. What you said last night—that you're committed to us both . . . The thing is"—he shot Vin a look—"we're both committed to you, too. The fact is, we're all right for one another. Vin and I enjoy threesomes. You're well aware of that now. But we've never met a woman we wanted an actual relationship with, even if being partners in pleasuring her is ideal and desirable for us both."

"The question is," Vin interjected, "do you fully understand what you were saying last night, Jewel? What it would really mean to be in a permanent relationship with us . . . *both* of us. No choosing."

"No more secrets, either," Rogen added.

Jewel forced herself not to bite her bottom lip. She'd meant what she'd said to them the previous evening. But they both had a point.

A permanent ménage.

That was something that would go public.

Something she'd have to share with her family and friends. And, yes, even her coworkers. Because the relationship would never be strictly confidential.

Yet there was a bit more than that at stake. Rogen and Vin each held a claim on her. They were just territorial enough to make this risky business. They'd never fought over a woman, because they'd never both cared so deeply for the same woman—except her. She knew that.

She also knew that the last thing she ever wanted to do was hurt either one of them again. Or come between them.

Rogen was suggesting she become a part of their sexual lifestyle; Jewel heard his convictions. The men wanted this to continue beyond the whirlwind trip they were currently on.

Question was, had this evolved into a case of *be careful what you wish for*—for all parties involved?

Jewel mulled this over. She couldn't give either of them up, and they weren't asking her to. But in the grand scheme of things, in the light of day, in the harsh truth of reality beyond Cabo and Vegas and Paris . . . Was it honestly a possibility?

More than that . . . was it a *sensible* possibility?

She still didn't have an answer, so she said, "We have a lot to sort out when we get back to California."

Rogen sat back in his seat.

Vin reached for his magazine.

Jewel closed her eyes. And worked really, really hard to clear her mind. At least for a little while.

# EIGHTEEN

Unfortunately, Jewel was not meant to be freed from her tension.

The guys bailed on dinner and decided to catch a UFC fight at a bar. Jewel wasn't sure that was a grand plan, considering it would hitch their testosterone. She hoped the only brawling occurred on the big screens.

She met up with Bayli and Scarlet at a five-star Italian restaurant overlooking Central Park. The girls caught her up on their past couple of days.

Bayli bounced a little in her seat and said, "I've been saving this tidbit until we all got together. A modeling agency picked me up!"

"That's awesome!" Scarlet squealed. "Congratulations!"

"So we're celebrating tonight," Jewel enthusiastically said, grateful to have something to focus on other than her relationship drama.

"Well," Bayli contended, "it's not really *that* big a deal—until I land a gig. But yeah. I'm pretty stoked."

"It's fantastic news, Bay," Jewel assured her. "You're going to take this city by storm!"

The server came around and Jewel ordered champagne. Then she asked Scarlet, "How's your case coming along?"

"Frigid as the Alaskan frontier."

"Oh. Darn. Sorry." Jewel reached for her water glass and sipped.

Bayli asked, "Anything we can do to help?"

"Not unless you possess extensive knowledge on LoJacking a person."

Jewel nearly spewed water. "Excuse me?"

"Seriously," Scarlet said, not the least bit contrite. "I need to plant a tracking device on Michael Vandenberg. He's the most elusive man on the planet. He's supposed to be in Atlanta, Georgia, but arrives in Athens, Greece. Supposed to be in Charlotte, turns up in Chicago. I had him pegged for Manhattan today, but nope. Nowhere to be found. I'm sure I'll read tomorrow morning that he was in Madaripur, Bangladesh."

"I don't even know where the hell that is," Jewel admitted. "But why is his name so familiar?"

"You've likely tried to seal a deal with him at some point for land," Scarlet explained. "Huge real estate mogul. They call him the Wolf of Wall Street, because he's a genius with investments and flips commercial property quicker than a quarter."

"Huh." Jewel couldn't place him for sure but likely had come across information on him when exploring new acquisitions. "So who's your source for where he's purportedly going to be at any given time?"

"Previously, his assistant," Scarlet lamented. "But she's clearly been instructed to send insurance-fraud investigators on wild-goose chases."

"So I'll call his office," Bayli said, still lit up over her big news yet obviously excited by the prospect of an additional challenge.

"What are you going to say?" Jewel curiously asked. "That you're a one-night stand gone awry and the little pink plus sign showed up on the pee stick?"

"That's got potential." Bayli laughed. "But I was thinking something more along the lines of finding a pattern related to his flips and seeing if I can entice him with a potential 'deal' I'd like to make."

"Granted," Scarlet said, "there are shades of brilliance there. But this is a possible criminal we're talking about. Which makes it a bit too dangerous to toy with him like that."

"Then I'll tell him the little pink plus sign showed up on the pee stick." Bayli winked.

Jewel offered, "Let me see what Cameron can do to track him down. Maybe an assistant-to-assistant kindred-spirit kind of connection will work. And she actually is a legitimate source—Vandenberg's person can verify Cameron works for Catalano Enterprises, for the Senior Vice President of Acquisitions. That keeps everything on the up-and-up. And Bay stays out of the man's crosshairs."

"Sure, but now you've got me worried about Scarlet being in his crosshairs," Bayli said.

"She does have a point," Jewel concurred.

"Wouldn't be the first time," Scarlet told them. She paused as the server returned with the champagne, uncorked the bottle, allowed the ceremonious sample, then poured. When he left the table, Scarlet continued, "I'm well prepared. It's the nature of the beast in this particular industry."

The women toasted. Then Jewel said, "Yes, we understand that. It's risky business when I meet with my barterers and my buyers. Yet this is quite different, Scarlet. I don't go into my meetings with the accusation of wrongdoing lingering between us. *You* have targets and they get agitated when they learn you're there to grill them for suspected criminal activity."

"No worse than being a detective," Scarlet said. "I'm armed."

"Which makes me oh so comfortable," Bayli chimed in.

With a smug smile, the fiery redhead told them, "I'm an excellent marksman. And I don't poke the snakes with a stick. I have much more finesse than that." She tossed long, sleek dark-auburn strands over one bare shoulder and added, "Whatever that saying is about attracting bees with honey . . . that's me. I know to lure. Then gently probe. Then give the full-court press when I'm certain I have the home-field advantage."

"Wow. Way to mix your metaphors, girlfriend." Jewel laughed softly.

"You get my point," Scarlet retorted, the sassy dripping from her tone.

Bayli warned, "Just be careful. Anyone who's been dubbed the 'Wolf' of anything is likely not someone to trifle with."

"Agreed," Scarlet sensibly said. Then her gaze landed on Jewel and she gave a coy smile. "Soooo . . . speaking of being in some-one's crosshairs. You mentioned Holly McCormick last week. What the *hell* did you do to her to get on her snarky side?"

Jewel nearly spewed again. This time expensive champagne. "Um . . . why would you ask me that?"

"Because," Scarlet said between sips, "rumors are afoot in River Cross, my friend. You, Rogen, and Vin are burning up the grape-vine." She laughed. "Yay, me! I finally got a metaphor right! Ru-mors . . . Grapevine . . . River Cross . . . Wine country . . . Everyone with me?"

Jewel tried to play along and smirk, but the corner of her mouth quivered. Her stomach clenched. "What do you mean, we're 'burning up the grapevine'? Why?"

"Come on, Jewel." Scarlet pinned her with a knowing look. "Holly McCormick has become close personal friends with Fran-cine Hillman. She told France that you crashed the Angelinis' gala and slapped Vin when you saw him."

"Jewel!" Bayli gasped.

"He deserved it," she defended herself. Then sighed. "At the time." Things were a bit different now. *A lot* different.

"Anyway," Scarlet continued in a conspiratorial tone, leaning forward on her side of the booth while Jewel and Bayli sat on the other, "France told me the story, *and* that you left the party with Rogen. Totally disappeared and didn't come back—according to Holly."

"So?" Jewel tentatively asked, sucking down more champagne in hopes of combatting anxiety. No such luck there.

"It was also reported by Holly that Vin took her home before the party was over and very chastely kissed her on the cheek. That he was clearly pained over the hostile reunion with you, Jewel. Which apparently wasn't quite so hostile, because he kissed your hand after you slapped him."

"So he dropped Holly off without fucking her," Jewel commented, shooting for nonchalance. "Is that what's stuck in her craw?"

"I don't know," Scarlet said. "But then France shared with Holly that she'd seen the three of you on the patio at Bristol's—though I'd heard about that from Nadine Portman originally. Evidently, you and Rogen were chummy. Vin stormed off, and you followed him. France confirmed she saw both you and Vin leaving the same restroom . . . right around the same time."

Scarlet wagged her brows.

Bayli pinched Jewel's arm. "You *didn't*! In a public bathroom? My God—how horny *are* you two?"

Jewel's head spun. And it wasn't from the champagne. Holding up her hand, she said, "Wait, wait, wait. This is all *huge* conjecture."

"Are you denying any of the details as fact?" Scarlet pulled out her investigator voice.

"No," Jewel slowly said. "But it doesn't mean—"

"Jewel." Scarlet turned the big guns on her. "You crash the

party because of the land deal you want. Run into both Rogen and Vin in the same night. Disappear with one. Are seen with both two days later. Disappear with the other. For quite some time, from what I hear. And then suddenly you're traveling the world with them?"

"Oh, wow." Bayli squirmed in her seat. "This is *so* juicy!"

*Shit!*

Scarlet said, "Last little tidbit to impart. Holly phoned Vin before you all left on your trip. Likely a booty call, but whatever. He said he was on his way to Cabo. Very last-minute. Very unexpected. So she deviously called CE and learned you were out of the office until Tuesday. Cameron did not mention your whereabouts, but then Holly contacted Rogen's assistant, who congenially offered that he was on his way to Cabo San Lucas. With one Jewel Catalano."

Jewel's jaw dropped. She set aside her glass. Tried to breathe.

Bayli whistled softly.

Eventually Jewel recovered and said, "Really, none of this means anything. It doesn't confirm I'm hooking up with Rogen or Vin."

"Why wouldn't you hook up with Rogen or Vin?" Scarlet demanded. "They are seriously hot!"

"And you did say—" Bayli started to remind her of their conversation during the plane's last New York City pit stop.

"I was teasing!" Jewel cut her off.

There was a sparkle in Bayli's eyes as she asked, "*Were* you just teasing, Jewel? About not being able to keep your hands off of them?"

"Whose side are you both on?"

"Yours, of course," Scarlet scoffed. "But just so you know, word in the inner circle is that there's a ménage unfolding at thirty-five thousand feet."

"Oh, fuck!" Jewel blurted.

"Exactly." Scarlet sipped, a twinkle in her eyes as well.

"Actually"—Bayli turned contemplative, her studious nature taking over—"*ménage* doesn't necessarily have a sexual connotation. Its French origin was used to designate a household arrangement, usually the management of said household. Add the *à trois* and it's a household of three. Only in later society did the term become more widely and popularly associated with a sexual threesome."

She sat back, quite pleased with her dissertation.

A heartbeat later, Bayli jerked forward and exclaimed, "Oh, holy hell! You're having a ménage à trois with Rogen and Vin! *Contemporary* meaning!"

"I—uh—" Jewel reached for her flute. Polished off her champagne. Grabbed the neck of the bottle from the chiller and poured some more.

"Fucking delicious!" Scarlet cooed.

And Jewel knew her friend wasn't talking about the Dom.

"How was dinner with Bay and Scarlet?" Vin asked as they made their descent into River Cross around six the next morning.

Jewel had boarded the plane after her dinner with the girls, curled up on the couch, and promptly passed out. No questions asked. No answers supplied.

She really couldn't rehash the grilling Bayli and Scarlet had given her over the ménage. Both women had been way, way too excited. Way too intrigued. And had admitted to being way too envious.

Though they were the least of her worries. Jewel knew her friends wouldn't spread further rumors. Yes, Scarlet loved being looped into all the town's gossip. But that was due to her investigative nature. She didn't generate her own speculation, especially when it involved her best friends.

Bayli had burned with curiosity over how the whole sexual

situation worked, and Jewel had dodged the bullets by ordering another bottle of champagne.

Now she was ridiculously hungover—and being interrogated by Vin.

Minutes before, she'd tidied up in the lavatory and changed her clothes. Now she pulled sunglasses from her laptop bag and slipped them on, the bright light streaming through the windows nearly frying her likely bloodshot eyes.

To Vin, she said, "We've collectively made an enemy."

His brow furrowed. "Who? And why?"

Rogen tucked his iPhone into the front pocket of his jeans and joined the convo.

Jewel told them, "Holly McCormick has insinuated herself into mine, Bay's, and Scarlet's circle of friends. She's letting them know that the three of *us* have had individual hookups and are currently traveling as a cozy trio."

Rogen snorted.

Vin laughed. "Seriously?"

"I fail to see the humor in the situation," she told them. "River Cross is a small community. The inner circle is only so strong. By now, the leaks have sprung."

"So we're traveling together," Vin said. "That doesn't mean anything other than we have business to conduct. Anyone, including Scarlet, can attest to that."

"And she has. But apparently Holly's enjoying spinning yarns."

Not that they were yarns, tall tales, whatever. Because what Holly hinted at—or blatantly declared—was, in fact, truth. Clearly a jealous rant. But truth nonetheless.

"So let her talk," Rogen added in his calm, steady voice. "I will concede it's not likely anyone would fully buy the three of us conducting business together. Me being an Angelini. Jewel being a Catalano. Vin holding loyalty to my father. But so what?"

Jewel grimaced. "You're missing the entire point of a smear campaign. Holly spreading rumors about us can wreak havoc on our personal reputations, our family names, and even our new venture, Rogen."

"California's a progressive state, sweetheart," he contended.

"Sure," Jewel agreed. "Alternative lifestyles are more readily accepted here. But that mostly pertains to same-sex relationships and marriages. Not a ménage à trois."

"She's got you on that one," Vin said. Then told them, "I'll speak with Holly."

"All well and good," Jewel added. "And appreciated. However, she's already turned into the town crier." She shook her head. "If my parents hear about this . . ." She glanced at Rogen. "If *your* parents hear of this . . ."

"Play it cool for now," Vin recommended. "We don't have anything to defend, because we were, in fact, on a business trip."

"Sure," Jewel cautiously said, "but if we play that card, then you have to fess up to Gian that you provided legal counsel on mine and Rogen's joint venture."

His jaw set. Jewel could see he stewed over the reality of the situation. Yet he didn't give in to contemplation—and the challenge of his loyalty. Instead, he said, "Let me deal with that. Don't worry about me."

Jewel gnawed her lip a moment, then told him, "But I do worry about you. So you have to validate that we're all in this together." Her gaze shifted to Rogen. "Right?"

"I'm not trying to hide anything," Rogen insisted. "We're in possession of the scotch. Even if my father has heard about the three of us traveling together, even if he's already ascertained that I don't intend to let him screw you out of the deal . . . He doesn't currently have the winning hand. We do. Because we have the bargaining chip."

"Which he could effectively decide isn't worth the hassle,"

Jewel pointed out. "Or the land. So that would put us at an impasse. Kill our dreams. Leave us with the rumors."

Neither man appeared willing to confirm or deny her summation.

Because it was deeply rooted in fact.

# NINETEEN

With the information from Jewel about Holly's squawking, Rogen knew his best offensive move was to seek out his father as soon as the plane landed and he returned to the estate. It wouldn't be a smooth interaction by any stretch of the imagination, and he'd asked Vin to go directly to his own office, in hopes of leaving him out of this.

Vin didn't take the bait.

"I'm not going to pretend I wasn't on the trip," Vin said. "That I don't know what you and Jewel are up to."

"You haven't done more than help to get signatures on contracts you didn't even draw up. So, technically, you were just along for the ride."

They stalked through the enormous foyer, then toward the back of the mansion where Gian's study was located.

"I admire what the two of you are trying to do," Vin told Rogen. "I'm not particularly pleased your father wants to double-cross Jewel. Nor am I currently willing to throw away my career with Angelini, Inc. However—"

"Wait." Rogen drew up short, his arm shooting out and his

palm flattening solidly against Vin's chest, stopping him dead in his tracks. "Currently?"

Vin sighed. "I'm not of the *never say never* mind-set. Do I owe your parents for taking me in so I didn't have to move to Chicago and live with my aunt and uncle and finish high school there? Yes. Gian and Rose-Marie willingly became my legal guardians after my parents died. I was able to stay in River Cross. But I'm not in agreement with Gian reneging on a deal he made with Jewel, especially after I've seen her jump through hoops and stress out over bartering her way to that scotch. For your father."

"Yeah," Rogen said. He removed his hand from Vin's chest and rubbed the back of his neck where tension built. "I know she went through a lot of trouble to hold up her end of the transaction. Bay and Scarlet did, too. Because my dad told Jewel he'd follow through on the deal. When he never had any intention of doing so."

"Let's get this over with."

They continued on their way. Rogen rapped his knuckles on the frame of the opened double doors and asked his father, "Got a few minutes?"

Gian glanced up from his laptop. "I was wondering when you'd stop by. How was the deep-sea fishing?"

Rogen fought a wince over the lie he'd told. "Yielded excellent results. We have the scotch." Why beat around the bush? He could tell by his father's steely gaze he knew what his boys were up to.

That steely gaze slid from Rogen to Vin. Then landed on Rogen again. "In your back pocket?"

"In a manner of speaking, yes. It's with Jewel," Rogen said. "Until you agree to honor your handshake."

Rogen's father let out a sharp laugh. "I will admit that I'm impressed by her resourcefulness. But why are you helping her to acquire land that's rightfully yours as well, Rogen, by inheritance?"

"*Because* it's rightfully mine, by inheritance. And I have plans for it, since you and Anthony haven't come to terms with developing the property. As it happens, Jewel has a purpose for it, too. Both of our ideas complement each other. So we'd like to go into business together."

Gian stared. Hard. For several incredibly long, incredibly uncomfortable moments.

Finally, he snapped the lid of his computer closed and stood. "I believe I've made it abundantly clear that there will be no more Angelini-Catalano joint ventures. Business or otherwise."

Rogen sighed with exasperation. "With all due respect, you can't dictate what transpires between Jewel and me personally. Or professionally. Not when we've agreed to use our own funds for the entire transaction and leverage our lines of credit outside of Angelini, Inc, and Catalano Enterprises for the inn and winery."

His father looked taken aback. "An inn and a winery?"

"Those are the plans," Rogen told him.

Gian gave this consideration, then nodded. "Very intelligent decisions."

Some of Rogen's tension eased. "Then you'll release the land so she and I can move forward?"

"No."

The tension returned full force. "No?"

"No," Gian confirmed. Took his seat. Opened his laptop.

Anger flashed though Rogen. Why was his father being so damn obstinate? It couldn't possibly just be over Anthony Catalano wanting to build a marketplace that would have brought in more profits than Gian's desired concept for all that acreage.

Rogen said, "We're willing to buy the property—not even asking you to deed your portion outside of the trusts. You'll make a nice chunk of change on property that's just sitting there, costing you taxes and county assessments every year."

"I've already explained my reasoning. Don't ask me again."

Now Rogen stewed. His temper flared. "Then the decanter stays with Jewel. Angelini scotch in the hands of a Catalano."

He whirled around and stalked off. Knowing his father would stew over the parting shot.

Vin took a deep breath. Let it out slowly. Said to Gian, "They really do have a solid theory. They discussed it on our little adventure to get the scotch. Laid quite a bit of groundwork. Mapped out a strategy. Consulted on finances."

"All with your help?" Gian challenged.

"I stayed out of the conversation. Only answered legal questions. I told them it was a conflict of interest for me, so I didn't pen any agreements for them."

"I appreciate your loyalty," Gian commented. "Though I'm not pleased to know that you do have an involvement with their endeavor."

"I didn't think you would be," Vin admitted, his gut coiling. "But my presence on the trip has no bearing on Angelini, Inc., operations. We went for the scotch, as Jewel had told you she'd acquire it for you."

"And Rogen told her—and you—that I intended to keep the decanter, compensate Jewel for it, and end our arrangement there?"

"Yes, sir."

With a shake of his head, Gian said in a disgruntled tone, "That girl always was good at wrapping him around her finger." He let out a harsh breath. "Rumor has it, she has the same effect on you. Something I'm also not pleased about."

Vin's jaw set. He walked a very fine line with that loyalty he clung to. Considering all the gray area he'd dabbled in in the past week and a half. He said, "They have a sound business model. I happen to agree with it. I'd like to see them follow through and build their own legacies. It'd also be good for the community's economy and put River Cross more on a par with Sonoma and Napa Valley, bringing in more tourists and providing more venues for events and festivals. From every angle, I see it as a win-win."

"Except that I don't want my sons associating with Jewel Cata- lano."

It was a low blow for Gian to use the plural. Yes, Vin knew that Rogen's father also thought of Vin as a son. Even before Vin had come to live at the estate, because he'd spent so much time there with Rogen and Jewel as kids. Rose-Marie had treated Vin like family, too, doting over him because her own son was off in Manhattan and her daughter was buried in the River Cross cemetery.

Despite Vin's devastation over his parents' deaths and his sub- sequent black moods, he'd actually latched on to the support and affection given by Gian and Rose-Marie. There had always been an underlying current in the mansion, after Vin had moved in, that had almost made him feel as though they were all given a fresh start. It was that particular connection that had made them close. And had gotten them all through the horrific tragedies they'd ex- perienced.

As he thought about that time of his life, something elusive percolated in the back of his brain. But it was only a tiny notion, not strong enough for him to dissect or ruminate over. So he shoved it aside.

He told Gian, "Rogen and I both have deep affection for Jewel. In this instance, I don't think the sins of the fathers should be visited on the heirs. She has nothing to do with the family feud. Nor do Rogen or I."

"Understand that I once held Anthony and Sophia in high re- gard as well. They deceived me."

Vin's tightrope became a thin strand as he cautiously, though relevantly, asked, "And the answer is to sabotage their daughter? In the process keep Rogen from his dream as well?"

Gian shrewdly told him, "I didn't hire you as Chief General Counsel solely because you were a part of this family. I did it because you're a smart man. Logical. Practical. Someone who thinks things through before acting. I know it hasn't always been that way, but since you decided to forgo San Francisco State for Yale you've really stood on solid ground. I have deep respect for you, as I do for Rogen."

"But . . . ?"

"But"—Gian speared him with a resolute look—"trust me when I tell you my intentions are neither misguided nor unwarranted. If you take *my* counsel, the two of you just might come out of this 'little adventure' unscathed."

When Jewel arrived at the Catalano estate, she left her suitcase and laptop bag in her suite and locked the scotch in the safe in her dressing room, where she kept her most expensive jewelry.

She caught up on e-mails, then sought out her parents, since Cameron had informed her that Anthony was working from the mansion for the remainder of the week. She found him, along with her mother, on one of the patios, having lunch.

Jewel strolled along the pavers under a huge awning. Her mother glanced up at her approach, her fork midway to her mouth. Sophia dropped the utensil on her salad plate. Shoved back her chair. Stood. And marched off.

Jewel gaped.

Her gaze flitted to her father. "What was that all about?"

Anthony reached for his iced tea and took a drink. Then he said, "Give her a little time to digest."

Jewel's stomach knotted. "You're obviously not speaking of the food. She barely made a dent in that salad."

"She was in town this morning for coffee with her friends. They delicately gave her an earful of River Cross's latest gossip. *Scandal*, if you will."

*Oh, Christ.*

Jewel slipped into a seat across from her father at the round glass-topped table. "What'd she tell you?"

"That word on the street is you, Rogen, and Vin are spending your evenings together. And that *is* the delicate terminology."

"It was one evening at Rogen's house—just the two of us. I didn't even stay over," she huffed. "And how the hell would anyone know what we were doing, anyway, when we've been on a plane the last several days?" As an aside, she added, "By the way, I have the scotch. According to Rogen, his father is going to try to do exactly as you suggested. Keep the scotch and the land."

"Where is it now?"

"My safe."

"Excellent. And congratulations on pulling off the acquisitions."

"Thank you." She was pleased with her coup, too. But that didn't stop the churning of her stomach.

Her father tactfully asked, "Are you three . . . reunited?"

Jewel let out a soft laugh, despite her tension and the sensitive topic of conversation. "Daddy, I'm twenty-eight years old and we're not currently amidst polite society. It's acceptable for you to ask if we're all sleeping together."

Oh, but hearing those words out loud ratcheted the roiling of her insides a few notches.

"I'm not exactly interested in learning the gory details, Jewel. Just answer the question, so I know what we're dealing with here."

"I'm not sure exactly what Mother's friends told her, but Scarlet informed me of the rumors and I can verify that the *gory details* are fact. For the most part. I wouldn't be surprised if there are some embellishments. But Rogen, Vin, and I are sort of . . . dating."

"All at once?"

"Yes . . . ?" She cringed.

Her father set aside his glass of tea. He said, "Appearances are very important to your mother, Jewel. You know this. She doesn't like gossip that involves our family."

Now Jewel turned a bit exasperated. "Daddy. Your feud with the Angelinis has practically burned the rumor mill to the ground over the past fifteen years. Especially of late, with Rose-Marie hosting parties and making it publicly known Catalanos aren't invited. Gian gets a kick out of shunning us and having it come across as though he's sparing his guests from the bad apples."

"Yes, well." Her father let out a long breath. "In some respects, we *are* bad apples."

Very cryptic. Her brow knitted.

Anthony got to his feet. He hadn't finished his meal, either.

Jewel was running her family off?

"Daddy, stay and eat," she said as she pushed out of her chair, emotion swelling in her throat. "*I'll* leave."

"No, Jewel. Have some lunch. I have work to get back to." He gave her a quick kiss and sauntered off.

Jewel's heart sank.

*Damn that Holly McCormick and her big mouth.*

But then again, what had Jewel expected?

No, she really hadn't thought the threesome through beyond their international excursion. Now that they were in River Cross, what was to become of their new relationship? And exactly how were they supposed to justify it to everyone?

Not that Jewel typically subscribed to the need to explain herself. Yet her family did hold a high standing in the community, in River Cross society. As well as in San Francisco society. And yes, image was very important to her mother. Sophia was a very meticulous person who served as trusted friend, gracious hostess, dedicated volunteer, and a one-woman welcoming committee at the visitor's bureau numerous hours a week. That was all when she wasn't mingling with the tourists who stopped at the Catalano winery.

How must it look for someone like Holly McCormick, somewhat new to town since she'd reportedly been in Savannah the past several months, to be relaying tidbits about Jewel's love life? And outright claiming Jewel, Rogen, and Vin were engaged in a three-way sexfest?

Likely her mother feared for not only Jewel's reputation but also her own—and that of the family and the winery.

*Fuck.*

Jewel bypassed lunch and went in search of her mother, finding her on the tennis court, aggressively taking swings at balls flying out of the machine twenty feet away. Jewel waited off to the side while her mother got some of her angst out. Then Sophia pulled the tiny remote from the pocket of her white skirt and turned off the machine. She hadn't quite broken a sweat yet, but Jewel brought her a towel.

"Daddy told me you've heard the gossip about me," she said without preamble. What was the point of dipping a toe in? Might as well jump in with both feet, because she couldn't dispute what she'd learned thus far of Holly's ramblings.

"You realize we don't approve of you seeing Rogen."

"I'm a little too old for that directive, Mother," she gently said. "And neither of you ever took exception to him prior to the feud erupting. You were also both very fond of Vin."

"That was a long time ago." Sophia dabbed at her neck with the towel.

"They've turned out quite nicely. Very upstanding and handsome, and pretty much everything you've ever wished for me when it comes to a date."

"Jewel." Her arm lowered and she glared. "What I heard this morning isn't that you have casual flirtations going on. It is specifically implied that the three of you spend your evenings together."

Jewel's ire sparked. "Okay, that absolutely cannot be validated by anyone other than me, Rogen, or Vin. Just because Vin took Holly home and didn't follow her inside, instead returned to the Angelinis' gala, doesn't mean he joined me and Rogen. No one knows anything about our relationship besides the three of us. Well . . ." she amended, "Scarlet and Bay now know. But that's it!"

"I just don't . . . understand how . . ." Sophia shook her head.

"And you don't have to, Mother. You don't have to speculate or ponder the mechanics or the sleeping arrangements, or anything other than the fact that we all care for each other and we've just had a really hard time, since the night of the party, staying away from one another." She inhaled deeply and added, "Oh, and Rogen and I want to go into business together."

"You did *not* tell your father that?" Sophia questioned. Insisted?

"Didn't come up." That was a cowardly excuse. But . . . one crisis at a time. "Though I did procure the scotch."

"We won't allow—"

"Mother, please. Rogen and I are not asking to just be given the land. We'll purchase it with our own capital. We'll both be responsible for the endeavor. Its success or failure. We won't be a burden on anyone, because we'll hold full accountability."

"I'm not suggesting you'd be a burden." Sophia walked over to the towel bin and dropped hers in. Returning to Jewel, she said, "I'm not interested in any sort of repeat performances, history repeating itself, call it what you want. I don't believe it's wise to go into business with Rogen Angelini, and I most certainly do not want to hear anything further about you, him, and Vin seeing each other."

Jewel simmered, yet she forced some calm into her voice as she said, "Then I suggest you stop engaging in conversation with women who enjoy gossiping."

She spun on her heel and headed back to the house.

# TWENTY

"I don't get it," Jewel said to Vin as she layered a lasagna for dinner. They were at his house and she loved his gourmet kitchen almost as much as she loved hers. But that was mainly because she couldn't find anything in his, not yet knowing the placement of it all. "What purpose does it serve for Holly to spread rumors about us?"

Sitting across from Jewel at the wide island, Vin sipped wine and said, "What does it matter?"

"Uh, because my parents are freaking out? And I'm sure Rogen's are as well."

Vin nodded. "Yeah, you got me on that one."

She added flat noodles, ladled her homemade sauce over them, topped them with ricotta cheese, and repeated the process a few more times.

Vin said, "So Holly's not happy that I lost interest in her. I'm sorry for that, but . . . not exactly a reason to spout off to the world."

"Christ," Rogen interjected as he suddenly joined them in the kitchen, having told them he needed to run some errands on his way over. "Everywhere I went in town, people were staring and whispering. I even got a few pats on the back." He grinned mischievously. "Had to tell a couple of guys I don't go for Vin, so they haven't got the wrong impression. No offense, man."

Vin scowled.

"Rogen!" Jewel's eyes widened. "You did not say that!"

"Relax, sweetheart." He rounded the island and kissed her. Then asked, "Where's your Beamer?"

"I had Vin open the garage door and I snuck in." She lifted the baking dish and popped it into the pre-heated oven. "Very covert-like, just in case *someone*'s keeping tabs on us."

"So, how'd your parents take the news?" Rogen asked.

"Not well." Her heart wrenched at her mother's initial reaction to seeing Jewel. "Mom actually got up from the lunch table and walked away the second I arrived."

Vin winced. "That's harsh."

"We spoke later and, of course, she had grave warnings. Tons of misgivings. Pretty much wanted to lock me in a tower far, far away from the two of you."

"Yeah, my father would actually appreciate that gesture," Rogen lamented.

"This just keeps getting worse and worse," she said with dread in her voice. "And I don't know what we're supposed to do about it. Move to San Francisco? Or go have lunch at Bristol's tomorrow so that we're totally out in the open?"

"Lunch is a start," Vin offered. "Good suggestion."

"I think I was joking," Jewel mused. And reached for her wine.

Rogen poured himself a glass of the merlot and said, "The hot topic of our three-way aside, we're not making any progress on procuring that land."

"I don't know," Vin quipped. "After that bombshell you dropped on your father this morning, I'd say he might actually put some thought into how he can maneuver the deal. Still to his advantage, but I saw the look on his face when you told him his scotch was in Catalano possession."

"Rogen." She *tsk*ed. "That's pushing a very explosive button."

"What choice did I have?" he contended. "My father's playing hardball. I'm going to deflect. Find a way to get what we want."

Jewel smiled. Kissed him again. Softly. Sweetly. Against his lips, she said, "I love sheer determination. Turns me on."

He groaned sexily. "Too bad you started the lasagna already."

"Such bad timing on my part."

He kissed her, then asked, "So you'll stop obsessing over Holly and let us three be the only ones who give a rip over what goes on amongst us?"

"Of course not," she said. "I always obsess over drama. You know this about me. Runs in the family. Yours, too."

He smacked her on the butt and then went for the plates to set the table.

Turning to Vin, she asked, "Is it really wise to flaunt our relationship in public?"

"I don't consider it flaunting. There are very few people who don't already know, or who haven't just recently learned—thanks to Holly—of our pasts and how close we all were growing up. So it isn't exactly a new world order to see us together now. After all, it's not like we're going to be making out in a corner booth somewhere."

"No more fucking me in a public bathroom," she ordered.

"That I cannot guarantee." He winked.

Jewel's insides ignited. "You just love being wicked."

"You didn't exactly say no to two orgasms that day."

"So if you're going to break the rules, you'd better make it three of 'em next time."

He chuckled, low and deep. Keeping the heat rushing through her veins.

"We should uncork another bottle," she suggested. "I think we all need it."

Later, over dinner, Jewel still pondered her parents' reaction to the news of her, Rogen, and Vin. She said, "You know, my father didn't go into a fit of rage that an Angelini was on one of his planes, like I sort of thought he would. For that matter, he was really more contemplative than angry about what he'd heard of the three of us. I won't say he was the least bit understanding. He literally lost his appetite and walked away as well. I'm sure he's got some steel-caged mental block to keep out the intimate details. But there was something about the interaction that took me by surprise. I just don't know what it was."

With a nod, Vin said, "I had a kernel just dying to pop in my head, too, when I spoke privately with Gian. Almost as though . . . there's something about the feud we don't really know."

"For that matter," Jewel continued, "it was my mother who fumed this morning, more so than my father. Shouldn't that be the other way around? I mean, putting aside the hit to her reputation, my mother is a pretty frisky woman with her husband. She's not exactly a prude—I'd half-expect her to want juicy tidbits. Conversely, my father should have threatened to throttle both of you for defiling his daughter."

"*Defiling?*" Rogen scoffed with a pointed stare. "Who begs on a nightly basis?"

Her cheeks flushed. The corner of her mouth lifted. "Well, it's just that you're both so irresistible. I can't help myself."

"Yes," Vin chimed in, "and our willpower is so indestructible."

"No complaints there," she muttered playfully into her wineglass before taking a sip.

Rogen was quiet a few moments, then added, "You know, Jewel, I got the sense my mother was worried something might be wrong at your estate when you showed up unexpectedly at the party. Which struck me as odd, because my parents were clearly disturbed by your unwelcome presence. But somehow, I feel that might have changed if you'd actually been there to deliver bad news."

"Well, they were all best friends," Vin stated. "For most of their lives. As the three of us have discovered, that doesn't just go away because of time and distance."

"I think the answer is staring us in the face," Jewel said as she offered her glass to Rogen for him to pour more of the merlot. "It's just a little disconcerting we haven't been able to see it vividly."

"Something to do with the mothers?" Vin ventured.

"Yes," Jewel agreed. "They were like sisters. Since they were kids. Tragedy can alter the course of your life, certainly. But they're two very steady, strong-willed women who allowed their husbands to declare they could no longer be friends. That seems to go against the grain for them. Understandably, Gian could be furious with my father for circumventing him during a time when he was distracted, but what did that have to do with the wives? My mother doesn't have much say in the family business—her choice. And she usually gets a far-off look in her eyes when Daddy goes on and on about one investment or another. Like she's mentally contemplating her next charitable cause to conquer and finds that much more exciting."

"Can't say that my mother has ever taken much interest in distillery operations, either," Rogen said. "They both prefer to leave business to the men."

"So why do I feel as if we're not seeing the big picture?" Jewel asked.

"Because we haven't yet gone directly to the source?" Rogen speculated.

"*The mothers,*" Vin repeated.

"Yes." Jewel lifted her glass in toast for the breakthrough. "The mothers."

And a plan began to form in her head. . . .

The next afternoon, Jewel pulled into the parking lot of Bristol's ten minutes ahead of her scheduled meet-up with Rogen and Vin.

She sat in her convertible and stared at the stylish brick building before her.

Why had she agreed to this particular restaurant?

There were dozens in River Cross. Many of them much more low-key.

The problem with this particular establishment was that it was one of the most popular eateries and bars in town. Jewel couldn't make it through the lounge, the dining room, or the patio without running into a handful of people she knew.

And she was going to have lunch here with Rogen and Vin, amidst rumors the trio were scorching the sheets?

A few beads of perspiration popped along her hairline, and against the bare nape of her neck, since her blond hair was pulled into a high ponytail. She wore a daffodil-colored sheath and strappy sandals. Not exactly confining clothes. And it was a balmy spring day. Definitely not one that called for an extra layer of deodorant. Yet she was currently wishing she'd brought along the clear gel to freshen up.

Her throat felt dry and tight. Her palms were clammy. Her pulse beat a bit too fast.

Okay, so, facing the music was no easy feat. Knowing people would stare—and not for the usual reasons. She was accustomed to garnering attention, which mostly came from her family name and abundant stock portfolio. The envious gazes of women sometimes followed her. Flirtatious stares from men.

But this would be different.

She considered what one might speculate over when they heard the term *ménage à trois*.

Words such as *taboo* and *insatiable* and *slut* came to mind.

*Whoa.*

Where had that last one come from?

And *oh, my God.* Was that what people were saying about her?

Chances were very good few would even bat an eye at Rogen and Vin's participation in a threesome. They were quite devilish by nature . . . and men. But hers?

Was there a double standard that would leave the connotation of *loose* and *easy* in her wake?

Jewel choked on a humorless laugh. Until that night of the gala, she hadn't had sex in seven years! She'd rarely dated in the city. And, for God's sake, the only two men she'd ever slept with were Rogen and Vin.

*Come on, Jewel.* She goaded herself.

*Chin up. Shoulders squared.*

*Turn off the car and get out.*

She pulled in a deep breath. Exhaled slowly.

*Okay. Now turn off the car and get out.*

She didn't. Instead, she gave up her primo parking spot and drove away.

"Jewel's not meeting us," Rogen announced as he plopped into a chair on the patio and set his phone on the table.

Vin glanced up from the menu.

"Says she needs more time," Rogen told him.

Vin's brow quirked. "To have her nails done, or to be seen in public with us?"

Rogen smirked.

"Ah. The latter."

A cute brunette swooped in to take their orders, all perky and flirty, batting long lashes. Vin considered doing her the huge favor of telling her to save it for her other male customers. Neither he nor Rogen would nibble on the lure.

They each selected a burger and iced tea. Then Rogen said, "I get that it's probably different for a woman in this particular scenario. Especially in a town where you know so many people."

"She'll come around," Vin assured him. "Jewel's never been one for letting others' opinions derail her. This is just a unique situation and one that came about quickly. Unexpectedly. You and I are still working through it, right?"

"I don't know what's to work through anymore," Rogen admitted. "Even slugging you on a regular basis wouldn't change the fact that I'd give her whatever she wanted, including a relationship that involves you."

"I'm not sure whether to be flattered or offended," Vin deadpanned.

"Come on. This is what you and I want. There's no reason to beat around the bush. Sure, it irritated you when you thought she'd gone back to me years ago. It pissed me off to learn the two of you had been an item while I was gone. But the bottom line is and always will be that we want one woman who's *ours*. Yours and mine. And that woman is Jewel."

All the more reason Vin was unsettled that she'd bailed on lunch. He could understand it. But he worried over her being off somewhere convincing herself to call off the ménage.

Or being with someone—like her mother—who would do the convincing for her.

Yet he clung to his previous belief that Jewel might suffer self-doubt, but she didn't let anyone else tell her what to do and how to do it. So he had lunch with Rogen, who then headed back to the office.

Vin stuck around. He caught up on e-mails and texts on his

phone. Made a couple of calls. Was just about ready to pay the check and leave when Holly strolled over.

"All alone?" she asked in her husky southern drawl. "I can't imagine why Jewel Catalano would let you out of her sight."

Vin sat back in his chair. His temper simmered. "I didn't have lunch with Jewel today. I'm surprised you don't already know that."

"Now, Vin," she said as she slid into the seat across from him that Rogen had vacated. "I didn't mean to spill the beans on your new love life."

"Really?" He gave her a *don't bullshit me* look to go along with the one that no doubt warned: *I protect my own*. "Because that's exactly what you did."

"I was having cocktails with Francine Hillman, who'd seen the three of you together, right on this very patio. I had too much to drink and one thing led to another."

"Let me give you a piece of advice." He leaned forward, folding his forearms on the table. "The people of River Cross know Jewel and her reputation much better than yours. She might be feeling the digs at the moment, but I promise you, she'll bounce back twice as strong. You said of her grudge toward me, *Hell hath no fury?*" His gaze narrowed. "When it comes to Jewel, you're right. So I'd watch my back, if I were you."

She gaped.

Granted, Vin knew perfectly well Jewel would never stoop to slandering Holly to even the score. But Holly didn't know that.

For good measure, Vin added, "You don't have a clean slate yourself, Holly. You wouldn't want your own reputation dragged through the mud, now, would you? Since you seem to be playing the high-and-mighty card. Rogen and I can attest to how you like it in the bedroom."

He pushed back his chair and left her stunned into silence. He caught the server on the way out and handed over cash. Then Vin returned to work at the mansion.

Jewel was in the San Francisco office the next morning when the very unexpected happened. The very horrific.

"Rose-Marie Angelini is on the line for you," Cameron announced.

Jewel's heart nearly stopped.

What the hell did Rogen's mother want with her?

*Like you don't know.*

She stared at the phone. For how long she had no idea.

Cameron actually came into the office. "You gonna pick up?"

"I . . . don't know."

"She's waiting. And you are not a rude person, Jewel."

She swallowed hard. "No, I am not. But this is . . . complicated."

"Would you like me to tell her you went to a meeting?"

"No. I've been spineless enough lately." She still kicked herself for not being able to get out of her car at Bristol's. So she snatched the receiver and infused a shitload of confidence she didn't really feel at the moment into her voice. "Mrs. Angelini. What a pleasant surprise."

"I'm in the city," Rose-Marie said. "I wondered if you would meet me for lunch."

Jewel sucked in a breath. How much more awkward could this get? She'd already had to explain the threesome to her parents. Now to Rogen's mother?

*Damn it.*

Why hadn't she taken Cameron up on her offer to say she was in a meeting?

*Because that wouldn't make this confrontation go away.*

So Jewel bucked up. "Tell me when and where."

"Bayview in the Financial District. Not far from your office. It's by the Hyatt."

"I've been there many times. Excellent location."

"One o'clock?"

"I'll see you then."

"Thank you." Rose-Marie disconnected the call.

Jewel replaced the receiver in its cradle and tried to focus on work for the next couple of hours. But her mind whirled. She debated whether she should phone Rogen and fill him in. But decided she might as well find out what his mother wanted, what she had to say, before making anyone panic. Other than herself, that was.

Lunch rolled around a little too quickly. Jewel arrived at Bayview precisely at one; Rose-Marie was already seated.

Had Rogen's mother arrived early so that she had time to settle herself, relax, think through this face-to-face meeting?

A tactic Jewel realized *she* should have employed. Might have helped her to get a grip on her cyclonic thoughts and emotions.

She followed the maître d' through the lively restaurant. It was an elegant, upscale dining room with panoramic views of the San Francisco Bay and the Bay Bridge from the top of the high-rise building. It happened to be a sunny day and the rays sparkled on the capped waves.

Despite the warm ambience of candles on tables that were topped with formal full-length white-linen cloths, delicate china, and polished flatware, Jewel's pulse slowed to a paltry crawl. Her strides shortened as she dragged her feet to reach Rose-Marie, seated at the floor-to-ceiling windows, perusing a menu.

She apparently caught Jewel in her peripheral vision, because she rested the menu on the table and stood. Dressed all in white, she looked pristine and angelic. Was that on purpose? Because Jewel wore flashy red and it suddenly made her feel . . . risqué.

They did the polite double-cheek air-kiss thing—more for public effect than anything else—and then Jewel took the chair across from Rose-Marie. The maître d' placed a linen napkin in Jewel's lap and handed over a menu. She set it aside. She already knew what she was ordering. Not that she expected to be able to eat with her stomach twisted so tight and nervous energy coursing through her.

A server swooped in. With a subtle wave of Rose-Marie's manicured hand, she indicated for Jewel to order first.

"Iced tea with a mint leaf and the chicken Caesar salad," she said.

"Very good," the server confirmed with a nod. She turned her attention to Jewel's dining companion. "And for you, Mrs. Angelini?"

"Iced tea with lime and the grilled tuna Niçoise salad."

"Wonderful selections, ladies. I'll be right back with your tea and bread."

Jewel wondered if she should have requested a cocktail instead. Perhaps an extra-dirty martini to go with her scarlet letter? Not that she'd committed adultery. But the way Rogen's mother eyed her with a hint of wariness in her golden eyes suggested Jewel had done something equally immoral and offensive.

"Thank you for joining me," Rose-Marie said in her soft, cultured tone.

"It's nice to see you again, Mrs. Angelini."

"Please, call me Rose-Marie. You used to call me Aunt Rosie." Her head inclined slightly to the side. "Do you remember?"

"Yes, of course. That was a long time ago."

Rose-Marie's smile was a forlorn one. "An entire lifetime ago."

"Yes."

They paused as the tea and bread basket arrived. Jewel reached for her glass and took a big sip, hoping to wash down the emotion and anxiety bubbling in her throat.

Rose-Marie said, "You've grown into a very lovely woman."

Jewel stared at her over the rim of her glass. What was that inflection she heard in Rose-Marie's tone? Sadness? Remorse? Nostalgia? All three? Something entirely different?

Returning her tea to the table, Jewel cautiously said, "You're as beautiful as you've always been. In fact, you look almost the same as you did when I was twelve and you were teaching me how to wear mascara and lip gloss. A hint of blush on my cheeks to give me some color."

Tears burned the backs of Jewel's eyes, but she fought them. Her life had been intertwined with the Angelinis way back when. It'd literally been a culture shock to have the ties instantly severed. To be cut off from all of them. So suddenly. So harshly. Even Gian.

Which made her think once more of Rose-Marie's lifelong friendship with Jewel's mother. How must that have felt for the two of them to have been ripped from each other?

*Precisely how it felt for it to happen with you and Rogen. And Vin.*

Jewel's heart wrenched. The feud honestly could not have been strictly over land. But before she could begin to gently probe for answers, Rose-Marie got down to business.

She said, "I understand you and Rogen are back together. As a couple?"

*Do not gnaw your lip.*

Jewel lifted her chin and said, "It's a bit more complex than that."

"Yes, I can imagine. Since I've also heard that you're back together with Vin."

*Oh, boy.*

The salads arrived. Jewel picked at the romaine lettuce with her fork.

"Tell me," Rose-Marie encouraged. "How do you see this working out? With the three of you."

Jewel cut strips of chicken. Though she didn't take a bite.

She glanced up at Rose-Marie and admitted, "I don't have an answer for you. This all came about unexpectedly. It's been challenging, emotionally. But Rogen and Vin understand how I feel about them."

"How *do* you feel, Jewel? Are you in love with them? Both of them?"

"Yes." That didn't require a moment of consideration. She knew it to the depths of her soul. Jewel said, "I know Rogen and I falling in love when we were kids might seem inconsequential and immature. But the feelings only grew. Intensified over the years. And, for me, never fully went away."

"And what about Vin?" Rose-Marie quietly asked. Not accusatorily. More . . . curiously. "We didn't realize the two of you were an item until right around his high school graduation. Why was it a secret? Were you trying to keep it from Rogen?"

"Rogen and I had broken up by then. But, yes, that is one of the reasons we never went public, until a couple weeks before prom—and even that was very discreet. Mostly just Bay and Scarlet knew. I went to Trinity to explain it all to Rogen. Behind my parents' backs, and yours and Mr. Angelini's. Yet I never actually told Rogen, because I realized when I saw him that I still had feelings for him."

"And Vin."

"Yes. Another reason I didn't want anyone to know"—she gave Rose-Marie an earnest look—"was because I was afraid your husband might ship him off, too. Before he turned eighteen."

"Hmm." She pushed her salad around on the plate as well. But never raised the fork to her mouth. Her gaze returned to Jewel and she said, "That was never a consideration. Though our hearts broke for him following his parents' deaths, it was a blessing that Vin came to live with us. Having him there helped to heal our home. Our lives."

Jewel sensed there was much more meaning behind those words. She very respectfully, tentatively, asked, "Having Rogen there wouldn't have done the same?"

Rose-Marie's shoulders squared. Defensively. Her voice turned a bit darker as she said, "I regret that we insisted he go to Trinity. Every day after he left, I regretted it. I cried. I missed him terribly. But I was in no condition to be a mother to him after—"

*Taylor.*

She didn't have to say her daughter's name. Jewel instantly felt the woman's pain. It sliced right through her. Stealing her breath.

Rose-Marie glanced away. Sniffled. Worked to compose herself as she stared out the window.

Jewel reached across the table and covered Rose-Marie's hand with hers. "I'm sorry."

Rogen's mother nodded, her gaze still on the bay. "I know Trinity was a better environment for my son. Overnight, the mansion became like a mausoleum. Bleak. Cryptic. Somber."

"Fragile," Jewel added. "I felt it, too."

Rose-Marie's attention shifted to Jewel. Both their eyes were misty.

The other woman said, "Rogen needed to find some inner peace. Unfortunately, Gian sending him to school all the way across the country caused him to lose more of it. Because we sent him away from you."

Now were they getting to it? The real reason behind the exile?

Jewel brazenly asked, "Is it true that you and your husband wanted to separate us so that we'd fall out of love? Meet someone else. Never marry each other."

Vin had made that comment on their trip. It had stuck with Jewel.

Rose-Marie stared at her for several suspended seconds. Myriad emotions swirled in her pale-gold irises.

Jewel had no idea how long it took for Rogen's mother to respond. She waited with mounting anxiety, her heart constricting.

Eventually, Rose-Marie said, "Yes."

Jewel's gaze dropped. Her hand covering Rose-Marie's slipped away.

She swallowed down a hard lump of pain and asked, "Is it because you didn't think I was good enough for him? Not smart enough for him?"

"It had nothing to do with you personally, Jewel."

Now anger flashed through her. "It was all because of my last name?"

"Yes. Gian—" The other woman shook her head. "That's neither here nor there. What I'd really like to say to you is that I actually do understand your current predicament. With Rogen and Vin."

This piqued her interest, though Jewel was still a bit shredded and hung up on Rose-Marie's previous confession.

Jewel asked, "What do you mean, you understand?"

With a tight smile, she said, "I was once in love with two men at the same time."

*Whoa. Bombshell.*

Continuing, Rose-Marie insisted, "It was nowhere near as racy as what I've heard of your . . . *affair* . . . around town. You see, the first man I fell in love with, my freshman year of college, went to school at Oxford. I met him at a Christmas party—he was visiting friends who attended San Francisco State. We clicked instantly. Spent the entire break together. Were completely inseparable. I was crazy about him." She smiled softly at the memory. Then sighed. "But, of course, distance is never a true friend to anyone in love. We wrote regularly. Spoke on the phone. But about a year later, something had begun to change with mine and Gian's friendship."

*Well, well.* Wasn't this a familiar story?

"One day we were just teasing each other over silly stuff and the next . . . we were kissing. Just like that." She snapped her fingers for emphasis.

"I can relate," Jewel told her. "It's like kismet throws a switch and suddenly—electricity."

"Exactly."

They shared a knowing moment.

Then Rose-Marie said, "Of course, I was torn between the two. But I had to be practical about it. Alexander lived in England and had no intention of moving to the States. I never wanted to leave River Cross. So I deliberated over the situation. Vacillated between the two men. Weighed pros and cons. And then I realized that I loved one more than the other."

That was where the kindred spiritship shattered.

Jewel sat back in her chair, no longer enrapt. "You're telling me I should choose."

"It's only fair, don't you think? And, honestly, Jewel. What would your future be like, having a relationship with both of them? Where would you live? How would you explain your romantic scenario to people? Would you marry one of them? Both? What about children? How on earth could you manage that? Rogen and Vin are extremely territorial—do you believe they each could accept you carrying the other's child?"

Now Jewel couldn't breathe. She sipped her tea as her head spun. Christ, she hadn't gotten *that* far with agonizing over the love triangle.

She said, "This is all very new and—"

"My dear," Rose-Marie interjected, her tone soft again. Maternal. "I'm trying to protect you as much as I am Rogen and Vin. These things always end badly. Someone *always* gets hurt."

Jewel could hardly dispute that logic. The threesome had already experienced that. Many times over.

"The difficulty," the older woman said, "comes when you let it play out for too long. Until something—or someone—snaps."

Jewel waited for the server to refresh their glasses before she insisted, "The three of us have been very open with one another."

With a slight shake of her head, Rose-Marie told her, "It's not ideal, Jewel. Or suitable in any form. And quite frankly, I don't appreciate hearing the rumors. I'm sure your mother doesn't, either. Is it fair to hurt her as well?"

That was a strategic stab in the heart, so pleasantly veiled.

But Jewel latched on to her own weapon and said, "I'm surprised you care how any of this affects my parents. You hate my mother. After decades of friendship, you shunned her."

Rose-Marie's gaze turned hooded. Clouded. "I've never hated Sophia. Not a day in my life. What I feel, Jewel, is a much, *much* stronger, more loathsome emotion than hate."

Jewel stared at the woman sitting across from her, a look on her face that almost made Jewel wonder if Rose-Marie thought of herself as some sort of monster.

"What is it, then?" Jewel managed to ask, albeit with trepidation and a hint of fear.

Rose-Marie pinned her with a pained expression. And said, "Envy."

The breath rushed from Jewel's opened mouth. Her insides seized up. She continued to stare at Rose-Marie. Aghast.

The self-perceived monster sitting across from her gave a gentle smile. "Eat your salad, dear. I did invite you to lunch, after all."

# TWENTY-ONE

*How far are you willing to go?*

Jewel posed the query to herself for the umpteenth time that afternoon.

Regardless of the dire warning issued by Rogen's mother cloaked in emotional blackmail—and her own personal torment—the plain and simple truth was: The woman had a point.

Several of them, actually.

So now Jewel had to seriously consider how far she'd take her involvement with her two lovers, knowing this plain and simple truth.

While Jewel paced her office after a very uncomfortable, somewhat harrowing, lunch and stewed over . . . *everything* . . . her thoughts kept returning to what Rose-Marie had said about someone always getting hurt in these types of situations. All the questions she'd posed that Jewel had not previously considered and had not been able to answer. Lobbed on top of Rogen wondering whether she truly understood what it would really mean to be in a long-term, committed relationship with him and Vin.

She loved both men. To the depths of her soul.

But what sort of position were they really putting themselves in? If things went awry, if it didn't pan out for one or all of the reasons Rose-Marie had addressed, or for any other reason, how would it affect them all?

What about Rogen and Vin's friendship? Christ, they were like brothers.

Jewel had come between them once before. Albeit temporarily. Still, it could happen again. And this time it might be even more disastrous. Something none of them could recover from . . .

There was something else Rose-Marie had said that kept pecking away at Jewel's brain.

*I've never hated Sophia. Not a day in my life. What I feel, Jewel, is a much, much stronger, more loathsome emotion than hate.*

Jewel snatched her iPhone from the desk and called Rogen.

He wasn't exactly in a fantastic mood.

"I can*not* get my father to budge," he said crossly.

She groaned. "To be honest, I'm certain *my* father will never agree to the sale now, either. Not while my mother's still so upset over . . . us."

"Fuck!" he roared. "We were so goddamn close."

To the joint venture . . . and to a three-way happily ever after.

Jewel's eyes briefly closed.

Kismet and family forces had fucked them again?

*Maybe* . . .

Or maybe not.

Because they still had one more avenue to explore.

Perking up, she contended, "It's not over yet. Vin hit upon a valid point the other night. So get your mother to Tea and Sympathy at six P.M. tomorrow. The back room with the private entrance. I'll make a reservation for three—her, you, and Vin. In your name, in case she gets suspicious and calls the restaurant."

"What's cooking in that clever brain of yours?"

"Just play along. I have a plan."

*A unicorn, if you will.* . . .

Jewel walked into the cozy event room of Tea & Sympathy in River Cross and wanted very much to simply turn around and walk out.

Rogen and Vin were there—which made her blood sing.

But Rose-Marie was present as well, as Jewel had requested of Rogen. And the sight of her made Jewel's stomach plummet to her knees. Because this was not going to be a pleasant get-together.

Rose-Marie sat at the far end of the coffee table, sipping her tea. She gently placed the china cup on its saucer as Jewel rounded the squat table, Rogen in a chair on one side, Vin on the sofa opposite him. Today, Rose-Marie wore her trademark color, blue. A pale shade that complemented her delicate features, fair skin coloring, and unique golden irises.

Since Jewel had been the one to plan the rendezvous, she'd carefully selected her own attire—a bronze satin short-sleeved, off-the-shoulder mini. Elegant and subtle versus flashy and risqué.

Jewel left a quick kiss on Rose-Marie's cool cheek and said, "Lovely to see you again."

"You, as well. Although I wasn't expecting you for tea." Rose-Marie slid a glance from Vin to Rogen, who opened his mouth as though about to explain.

But then Jewel's mother—always one to make a grand entrance—came blowing into the room with her signature Giorgio Beverly Hills Red perfume surrounding her in an alluring cloud while she chatted animatedly on her iPhone.

She pulled up short when she saw the small gathering and stopped mid-sentence, her jaw instantly slacking.

Sophia, dressed in a semi-sheer leopard-print button-down blouse, and slim black pants and ankle boots, eyed Rose-Marie while saying to her caller, "I'll have to get back to you." She disconnected and dropped her phone into the beige leather handbag dangling in the crook of her arm at her side. Her palm up. She waggled a few fingers and said, "What the hell is this?"

Jewel returned to the entryway and closed the pocket doors to the main restaurant for privacy.

"I believe it's called a *Come to Jesus* meeting," Rose-Marie said in a tight voice. "Which I am not interested in attending." She got to her feet.

"Mother," Rogen countered, also standing. "Vin, Jewel, and I set this up. Because Dad reneged on his deal with Jewel."

"And you blame *me*?" Rose-Marie demanded.

"For the record," Sophia chimed in, "we're not signing, either."

"Mother!" Frustration tore through Jewel.

Rose-Marie said to Jewel, "I believe I was abundantly clear at lunch about mine and Gian's feelings regarding your . . . relationship. And it is no secret that we do not want an Angelini-Catalano business deal now or in the future."

*"Lunch?"* Sophia's wounded gaze shot to Jewel, now lingering by the sofa, close to Vin. Needing his silent reassurance, his commanding presence, to keep her steady. "Since when do you lunch with Rose-Marie Angelini?"

Jewel bit back a long-suffering sigh. "It was just the once, Mother. She invited me while she was in the city."

"In the city, my foot," Sophia scoffed. "Rose-Marie only goes into the city to shop, and that obviously wasn't the case—she went specifically to see *you*, Jewel—because that dress she's wearing is *not* new. I saw her in it two weeks ago when I passed by the Soroptimist luncheon in the dining room of Voltaire's on my way to the Junior League luncheon on the patio."

"Yes, well, it is a bit more appropriate for early-evening tea than leopard print," Rose-Marie snarled.

Jewel rolled her eyes. After fifteen years apart, they still bickered like sisters.

Oddly, she found that encouraging.

"Ladies, please," Vin interrupted as he stood, towering over the group, filling the space with his impossibly broad shoulders. Exciting Jewel, despite the tension hanging thick and palpable in the air. "We didn't get you together to clash over outfits."

Rose-Marie crossed her arms over her chest. "This is about the property, then?"

"Yes," Rogen said. "Maybe you can shed some light on why my father is so hell-bent on screwing Jewel over by not honoring his word and handshake, and plotting to trick her out of her bargaining chip."

"I knew it." Sophia *tsk*ed, full-on admonishment toward Rose-Marie and just shy of an *I told you so* to Jewel.

"Mother," Jewel quietly scolded.

"Fine," Sophia said. Though she pinned Rose-Marie with a stern look and suggested, "Why don't you tell them? Jewel, specifically. She has a right to know, doesn't she?"

Rose-Marie gave a slight shake of her head. "This has nothing to do with Jewel."

"It has *everything* to do with Jewel!" Sophia erupted, taking everyone aback. "It has *always* had everything to do with Jewel!"

Her mother's intensity rocked Jewel. She reached out a hand and latched on to Vin's dress shirt at his waist to stabilize herself. He placed a comforting solid hand at the small of her back.

"What the hell is going on?" Rogen slowly asked. As though he suddenly wasn't sure he wanted to know.

Jewel was feeling a little queasy herself over the prospect of hearing out Rose-Marie. If she chose to spill. Because the look on her own mother's face was one Jewel had *never* seen before. Full of sheer agony.

Yet Sophia quickly schooled her expression. Took several deep, calming breaths. Then said, "Tell them, Rose-Marie." Her voice was much smoother, softer. That was Sophia Catalano for you—ever the expert at composing herself after an outburst, which she rarely tempered when she felt it was warranted. "This has gone on much too long. Tell them everything. Tell them why you used the development of the marketplace on the land we jointly own as an excuse to sever ties with my family. When everyone involved agreed the profits generated would far exceed those of a viticulture center. And that the return on investment was meant solely for Angelini and Catalano heirs—*our* children, Rose-Marie. And their children, their grandchildren, and so on. We'd all agreed to it. But you claimed that when Gian turned his back during Taylor's illness, Anthony drove a knife in."

"Oh, Jesus," Jewel whispered. This was about to get ugly.

Actually, it already was.

Sophia continued. "The so-called family feud was nothing more than a dissolution of lifelong friendships and a successful business partnership." She still spoke at a reasonable decibel, though pain and anguish tinged her voice. "The Angelinis needed an excuse for the fallout, and the land dispute worked perfectly." With another hard glare toward Rose-Marie, she added, "And we let you use it."

"I don't understand," Jewel said, her brows knitting, her gaze on Rose-Marie.

Who very bitterly told her, "I didn't want you in my house, Jewel." She more deliberately iterated, "I didn't want you in my *home*."

Jewel's head snapped back as though she'd just received a physical blow.

"What the *fuck*?" Rogen boomed.

Vin pulled Jewel to his side, his arm protectively around her waist as she reeled.

Rose-Marie's eyes turned nearly translucent as tears flooded them. "It wasn't your fault," she assured Jewel. "It was all mine. From the very beginning."

Rogen grabbed some tissues from the box on the coffee table and handed them to his mother.

"What are you talking about?" he asked, notably trying to dial down his rage. It was his mother he was speaking to, after all.

Rose-Marie sniffled and told him, "I love you very much, Rogen. From the moment I found out I was pregnant, I was in love with the idea of having a child. So was your father. He was so proud of himself when he learned we were having a son that he passed out cigars and scotch before you were even born. And when that day came . . . When he held you in his arms for the very first time . . ." She smiled softly, albeit shakily. "There was a sparkle in his eyes and a look of absolute awe and wonderment on his face. He was hooked. Instantly."

There was an eerie resonation to Rose-Marie's voice. Precisely what Jewel had heard from her at Bayview. Only now it was darker. Much more ominous this time.

Rose-Marie said, "You and your father bonded from those first seconds together. It only strengthened from there. Even when you disagree on something. It's always been an unbreakable bond. Something you share. Something that's special just between father and son."

Jewel's gaze slid to Rogen, who appeared as perplexed as she felt. And both of them were quite concerned about his mother's cryptic tone and visibly unstable state. Vin was as well.

Rose-Marie glanced over at Sophia. She said, "A couple of months later, my best friend gave birth. To the most beautiful baby girl." Her attention shifted to Jewel. The tears streamed, tugging at Jewel's emotions, her heartstrings. "You were perfect." Another quivering smile. "Plump cheeks, wide eyes, the tiniest fists. You were a happy baby, always smiling, and cooing, and . . . hiccupping. You hiccupped a lot."

Perhaps it was the gradual change in Rose-Marie's tone to an almost trancelike cadence that caused Vin's arm to tighten around Jewel.

"Mother?" Rogen asked in a quiet voice. "Maybe you should sit."

Her gaze remained on Jewel, and she continued, as though she'd not heard her son. "Your mother was instantly addicted to you. Everyone was. The way you smelled, how adorable you were. How delicate. She took you everywhere—she was always in town showing you off. All bundled up in pink. And every time I saw the two of you together, I was . . . jealous." She choked on a half sob. "I was so very jealous. I wanted what Sophia had—a daughter of my own."

She finally tore her gaze from Jewel and it landed on Rogen. "I wanted to feel that special bond that you and your father shared. That Sophia and Jewel shared. Your father wanted another child, too, but it took us years to conceive. I grew more and more frustrated. More envious. The feeling clawed at me. Ate away at me." Her voice cracked with agony . . . and shame. "Eventually, I got pregnant. And Taylor was born. And I had my own perfect daughter bundled in pink."

Emotion rushed through Jewel. Along with the disturbing notion that she knew exactly where this was headed.

Sophia quietly said, "Taylor was precious. So inquisitive, and mesmerized by everything."

"Yes," Rose-Marie agreed, the fat drops still tumbling down her cheeks, unbidden. And she didn't bother to brush them away. She said, "For nine years, I was deliriously happy. The frustration vanished. The jealousy fled. Everything was blissfully normal. Peaceful."

"And then Taylor got sick," Sophia said on a broken breath, deeply affected no matter her current disassociation from her best friend—or her goading for Rose-Marie to reveal the truth to their children.

"When she died," Rose-Marie said in a distant voice, "it was like my own heart stopped beating. Like I couldn't breathe, couldn't think. But the evil fate of it all was that *my* heart actually was still beating and I *was* still breathing. And even though I balled my fists and pressed them to my temples, thoughts kept churning in my head. I'd press the heels of my hands to my eyes, but I could always see Taylor's fragile, lifeless body."

"Oh, God!" Jewel turned into Vin's chest and he wrapped his arms around her. Held her firmly.

"Mom," Rogen coaxed, "sit. Drink some tea."

"No," she said. "Sophia's right. I have to tell Jewel all of this. You, as well."

Jewel pulled away slightly, but Vin kept his arms around her. She looked over her shoulder at Rose-Marie, a bit distorted in her vision because Jewel's eyes were also filled with tears.

Rose-Marie said, "I was the one who sent Rogen away. Not my husband. I was the one who set it all up. I wanted Rogen out of the mansion. I was someplace so dark and terrifying in my mind and in my heart I didn't know how to deal with him. I didn't want him to see me like that. And, yes, I wanted to drive a wedge between the two of you. I didn't want the two of you to ever be together again."

Jewel turned to fully face Rose-Marie. Vin stayed close, his chest grazing her back so that she knew he was right there if she needed him.

She tentatively ventured, "You didn't want to see me because your daughter was gone and your best friend's was still alive. The best friend you'd envied so much."

Rose-Marie nodded. "With Taylor's last breath, all the jealousy returned. Tenfold. *More.*"

"Rose-Marie," Jewel gently said.

"You remind me of her," Rose-Marie told Jewel. "Remember strangers would think you were sisters? You both had blond hair and blue eyes. And she adored you. She followed you everywhere she could. Looked up to you."

"I loved her as though she was my sister," Jewel said, her heart wrenching.

"I shouldn't have done what I did to you. Or to your mother. I've lived with the guilt and the jealousy for so long, and all I can think," she said with reverberating agony as she clutched the gold necklace with Taylor's birthstone, at her throat, that she always wore, "is that the angels took my little girl because I never deserved her." She tore away the dainty chain, dropped it on the coffee table, and rushed out, flinging open the pocket doors with a heavy thud.

"Mom!" Rogen called.

"Wait!" Jewel lunged toward him, flattening her palms to his chest. "Just wait." Jewel turned to her stunned and clearly heart-stricken mother and said, "She's your best friend, and she is in a *lot* of pain. Go to her."

Tears flooded Sophia's eyes. It took her a few moments to come around. Then she hurried out of the room.

Jewel turned back to Rogen and threw her arms around him. Cried in his strong embrace. Not just for her, but for him as well. Rose-Marie and Gian. Her parents. Vin, who always got caught in the Angelini–Catalano drama. And steadily weathered the squalls.

It took some time, but Jewel eventually pulled away from Rogen. Asked, "Are you all right?"

"This isn't about me," he roughly said. "Are *you* all right?"

"I don't know. I think I might be in shock. And, yes, it *is* about you. That's your mother who's suffering so deeply." She faced Vin. "And someone you care about." She hugged him.

Vin whispered against her temple, "I know how much that hurt you. I'm so sorry."

"Me, too," Rogen told her.

She pulled in a few more deep breaths. The tears kept falling, but a bit slower now as she gradually came around. Though she trembled from head to toe.

To Rogen, she asked, "I need to go somewhere. Can you drive me?" She reached for her clutch on the sofa cushion and handed over her keys, since she wasn't wholly steady. Then looked over at Vin. "I need you with us."

His fingertips gently grazed her wet cheeks. "Of course."

Rogen snatched more tissues and gave them to her. "You're killing us here, Jewel."

She blotted her skin. It really didn't do any good.

They left through the back entrance; Jewel was grateful Tea & Sympathy had separate access to the event room. God forbid the crowd out front should bear witness to Rose-Marie dashing out with Sophia hot on her heels, followed by the three of them. All visibly wrecked by Rose-Marie's story.

Vin opened the passenger door of Jewel's convertible and she slid into the tan leather seat. Rogen climbed in on the driver's side and Vin sat directly behind her. She moved the seat up to give him more legroom.

"I don't see our moms," Jewel commented as she scanned the parking lot.

"I'm sure they're in Mother's car," Rogen said. "Her driver will get them safely to the estate."

"That's where I need to go as well."

Rogen glanced over at her. "Jewel . . ."

"It's not about your mother," she assured him. "There's something I have to do."

He frowned, not liking her secrecy. But he pulled out of the space and hit the road.

No one spoke. What was there to say at the moment? It was impossible to relive those twenty or thirty minutes of Rose-Marie's excruciating confession and the horrifying pictures she'd painted.

And who the hell wanted to mention how unnatural she'd sounded, so traumatized and resentful? Toward herself.

Jewel couldn't fathom existing with that sort of torment day in and day out. Year after year. Rose-Marie needed some serious help.

One thing Rose-Marie could count on, Jewel knew, was that her mother would lend the support needed. She'd perpetuated a lie for the Angelinis, after all. So that they could save face. Appear to be normal following their tragedy. Because Sophia knew the importance of appearances.

She would be able to commiserate and empathize with Rose-Marie's feelings related to her daughter's death, even if Sophia hadn't lost a child herself. Jewel was certain it was a maternal thing that lived and breathed in every mother. And Sophia had adored Taylor.

While Jewel's heart went out to Rose-Marie, Gian, and her own parents, she was a bit worried about Rogen. She rested a hand on his thigh. He covered it with his own hand. Gently squeezed.

They reached the porte cochere at the mansion and Rogen said, "There's Mother's driver."

Jewel breathed a sigh of relief.

Vin opened her door again and she asked Rogen, "Will you pop the trunk for me?"

He did, and she rounded the back of the car to retrieve her oversize Louis Vuitton tote, hitching the straps over her shoulder. Vin shut the trunk for her.

"Want me to carry your bag?" he asked.

"No, thanks. This is something I have to do myself."

They ascended the steps to the gorgeous terrace that ran the length of the front wing of the manor. A valet escorted them in, also asking if he could assist with Jewel's tote. She politely declined.

Rogen and Vin flanked her as she headed toward Gian's study.

His assistant, Elizabeth, had a massive desk outside the sanctuary. Jewel was quite familiar with her, given all the time she'd spent calling Gian's office directly to try to engage him in entertaining her offer on the land, prior to the gala. Which now seemed like a million years ago.

Elizabeth glanced up from her computer at the sound of Jewel's heels clicking on the marble floor.

"Gentlemen. Miss Catalano," the attractive chestnut-haired thirtysomething greeted them.

"I'd like to see Mr. Angelini." Jewel didn't wait for a response, just kept walking.

The assistant jumped up and rushed ahead of the trio by just a step so that she could dutifully announce, "Miss Catalano, Rogen and Vin to see you, sir."

His head snapped up from paperwork he was reviewing. "I didn't realize we had an appointment."

"I'm sorry," Jewel said, striving for a professional tone but not succeeding. She was still rattled to the core. "I didn't have a chance to make one."

"Then to what do I owe the honor?"

He didn't sound condescending, as she'd half-expected. Rather, he seemed intrigued by her presence. Perhaps a bit admiring of her verve. She suspected very few people barged in on him.

Jewel stopped in front of his desk and set her bag on the corner. Then she extracted a large box. Placed it in front of him. She simply said, "Open it."

Now he eyed her suspiciously. But he took the bait. He stood and unlatched the numerous sturdy clasps. Then folded back the lid. Another box was nestled inside, and he flipped the top. Peeled away layers of black velvet. Then let out a snort filled with distain.

"You've resorted to taunting me with the decanter?"

"Of course not," Jewel said. "That scotch is a part of Angelini history. Your heritage. It belongs in your hands, not mine."

"I don't understand." He gave her a quizzical look. "Rogen told you I had no intention of fulfilling my end of the transaction. That I'd find a way to keep the scotch, even though I'd compensate you for it."

"Yes."

"Then why bring it to me?"

"What purpose does it serve for a Catalano to keep it?"

One corner of his mouth jerked up. "To twist the knife, since I'd forever know it was in your possession."

"Ah, see, that's the thing, Mr. Angelini. There is no knife." She gave him a steady, challenging look. "Is there?"

Beside her, Rogen said, "Mother told us everything. What happened after Taylor passed. How the Catalanos let you blame the distance you needed from them on an underhanded business deal. A guise you attempted to keep up by double-crossing Jewel."

Gian Angelini stared at Jewel. She couldn't read the expression in his eyes. There wasn't a hint of him wanting to deny the truth. Nor was there full-on remorse. It was almost as though . . . he clung to survival instincts.

Jewel's heart constricted once more. The organ was getting more than its fair share of turns through the wringer. And it hurt.

Survival instincts she could understand and accept, though. This man was proud, and he was strong. And he was clearly willing to do whatever he had to in order to protect his wife—and her sanity. His family, as a whole.

Rogen was similar in so many ways. With the exception of the fact that he never would have lied about why the friendship and partnership had dissolved. That was where his DNA varied slightly, and Jewel knew it.

Finally, Gian said, "I'll write you a check."

"I don't want a check," she hastily told him. "This is a gift. From my family to yours."

She grabbed her tote, whirled on her heels, and marched out.

Jewel had only made it to the curving grand staircases that led to the upper floors when Gian's authoritative voice filled the cavernous foyer.

"Jewel."

She stopped. Pulled in a breath.

At that instant, Rose-Marie and Sophia came from the great room, Sophia's arm around the other woman's shoulders. Both mothers still teary-eyed.

"My God." Gian rushed over to his wife. Cupped Rose-Marie's wet and flushed cheeks.

Sophia's arm slid away and she approached Jewel, who gave her a monstrous hug.

"Are you okay?" Jewel asked.

"I will be. So will Rose-Marie. She needs more than the antidepressants and Valium she's been taking for years. She needs grief counseling and someone she can talk to on a daily basis about all these feelings she's held in for so long. Honestly, I can't imagine how she's kept this all to herself."

"She's resilient," Jewel said. "But no one's invincible."

Sophia pulled away. "You aren't upset with her?"

"What's to be upset about, other than how much pain she's in? We can't change the past. It happened. I just . . . I don't understand why you didn't tell me the real reason behind the 'feud.' That it didn't really exist."

Sophia stared at Jewel with watery eyes. "What would I have said to you, Jewel? That your Aunt Rosie, who you loved fiercely and spent so much time with, who loved *you* in turn, couldn't bear the sight of you? That she couldn't allow you and Rogen to be together—or, God forbid, marry—because she didn't want you in her presence during the most horrific time of her life? *Cara mia,*" Jewel's mother said, using the term of endearment for her daughter that she reserved for when she wanted to make a point. "How cruel would that have been to hear when you were just thirteen years old?"

Jewel swallowed down a lump of emotion. More tears burned. "Right. I would have been devastated." She shook her head. She'd been devastated anyway, because Rogen had been sent to Trinity. But there might have been a psychological blip over the scenario her mother presented. "I'm not sure I would have fully understood at that age."

Sophia kissed her on the cheek, then said, "You're a good person, Jewel. Especially for sending me after Rose-Marie. I'm going to be the one to talk to her every day, in addition to professional help. And we'd like you to join us from time to time. She still adores you so much."

Her mother swept away the tears on Jewel's cheek with her thumbs. More activity in the foyer drew their attention. Her father came barreling through the front doors.

"What's the emergency?" he demanded in an alarmed tone.

Jewel slid a private glance toward Rogen and smiled. He'd been right. Their parents still cared enough about one another to worry if something might be amiss at the others' estate.

Conversely, and with a scowl, Vin announced, "I didn't say it was an emergency, Mr. Catalano. I just told your assistant that it'd be a good idea for you to come over."'

"That would indicate an emergency, Vin," Anthony shot back. "It's good to see you, by the way. Been too long." His gaze shifted. "Rogen. You're looking well."

"As are you, sir."

"Little late in the day to be calling me that, don't you think? 'Anthony' is fine."

Rogen nodded and gave a shadow of a grin. Jewel's father wasn't about to throttle him. She sighed with relief.

As Sophia went into her husband's arms, Rose-Marie crossed to Jewel, taking her hands in hers.

"I'm so very sorry," the older woman said, choking on a sob. "For everything."

"I don't need you to apologize. I just want you to feel better. And let my parents be your friends again."

Rose-Marie folded her arms around Jewel. It was a fragile hug, but a comforting one.

When Rose-Marie eventually released her, Jewel added, "And try to understand that I love your son *and* the man you helped to raise. Not one more than the other. But equally. I always have."

"They're very fortunate for that." Glancing over at Jewel's parents, Rose-Marie told them, "You have a very beautiful and compassionate daughter. A woman with a heart big enough to offer double the love—to my two treasures."

"I think that's as much information as we need to know on the matter," Anthony dryly said. "Sometimes ignorance truly is bliss."

Jewel laughed softly.

Rose-Marie joined Rogen and Vin. "I couldn't be prouder of you two. And despite what I told you earlier, please know that you and Gian are what I live for. I love you all so much."

Rogen embraced his mother. Held her tight. Then stepped away so that Vin could get in his time with the maternal presence in his life.

"Jewel," Gian said. "Are you really serious about the inn and winery? Committed to them?"

"Absolutely. Fully."

His attention shifted to Rogen. "And you?"

"One hundred percent."

With a decisive nod, Gian announced, "Then I'll relinquish the Angelini portion of the property to both of you. Will you do the same, Anthony?"

Jewel held her breath. Her heart skipped several beats.

Anthony grinned. "Of course. I think their vision for that land is the best damn idea any of us have had in a long time."

"Agreed," Gian said. Then he closed the gap between him and

Jewel's father in three wide strides and extended his hand. "I'll never forget what you and Sophia did for us. I hope you know that we're appreciative. And sorry. Truly and deeply."

"It was necessary," Anthony contended, demonstrating his own compassion. And the lengths he'd go to for people in need. Jewel was immensely proud he was her father. "Especially for Rose-Marie. Her well-being was worth the sacrifice. Though . . . I have missed you, my friend."

"No more than I have you." They shook. Then clasped each other on the shoulder.

"This is lovely," Rose-Marie said with a sniffle. "Except . . . aside from the business aspect, I'm not quite sure Rogen, Vin, and Jewel have reconciled their issues."

Jewel told her, "I heard every word you said to me yesterday. I'm sorry I didn't have any answers to give you. The truth is . . . Those are things Rogen, Vin, and I have to work out. Together. Just the three of us." To her two men, she said, "I'll admit that in Paris I wasn't thinking of consequences or reality. But now I am. And I *do* understand what you were saying to me. . . . We'll have to make a lot of decisions. Fortunately, in the end . . . we all want the same thing."

"And you can handle that?" Rogen asked.

"I can do anything that keeps you both in my life. In my heart." She drew the line at saying *in my bed*. No need to antagonize her father further. Though she gave Rogen and Vin a wink.

They grinned.

*Nuff said*.

She still had one concern, though. To both parents, she asked, "Can you deal with the scandal?"

Gian said, "We've dealt with far worse. Or haven't you heard?"

Sophia nodded. "I'm sorry for the way I acted initially, Jewel. All I want is for you to be happy. And you're right. Both men did turn out nicely. Very upstanding and handsome, and pretty much

everything we've ever wished for you," she repeated Jewel's sentiment from days before. "And California is all about alternative
lifestyles, so . . ." She shrugged. Looked a bit hopeful over the entire scenario.

Jewel joined Rogen and Vin and said, "I'm pretty much over
the gossip already."

Rogen stepped forward and hugged her. Gave her a kiss on
the cheek. Though his eyes burned—he was clearly looking
forward to doing much more than that when they had some
privacy.

Vin repeated the gesture but whispered in her ear, "You won't
regret this. Rogen and I will make damn certain of it. *Every* night."

A ripple of excitement chased down her spine.

"I have no doubt." She squeezed him back.

Then Rose-Marie suddenly declared, "My manners! Good
Lord, I haven't offered anyone a cocktail."

Everyone laughed, relieved the tension had broken.

Gian said, "Shall we all retire to the patio? We have a new
cognac I'd like you to sample."

No one could argue with that.

Jewel linked arms with Rose-Marie and smiled at her. Sophia
joined Jewel on her other side and they strolled through the mansion. The men followed close behind, engrossed in business matters
pertaining to the release of the property next door.

She heard Gian say, "I'll expect your letter of resignation on
my desk first thing Monday morning, Vin. You're going to be busy
with legalities for the inn and winery."

Jewel shot a glance over her shoulder. Let out a small gasp
when she discovered Vin staring at her ass. He dragged his gaze
away and told Gian, "They did ask for my legal counsel."

"Offer still stands," Rogen assured him. "A bit modified, however. How about a third of the partnership?"

Jewel grinned. Now they were getting the numbers right.

"I accept," Vin said. To Gian, he added, "With all due respect, sir."

"The three of you have always been thick as thieves. Why would I expect anything different now?"

Jewel returned her attention to the mothers.

She said to Rose-Marie, "You know, I love doing all those girly mother-daughter things, like shopping, pedicures, a movie on a rainy Saturday, lunch in the city."

"I would like to think of you as my daughter-in-law," Rogen's mother said. Even though Jewel knew it would be a concept for Rose-Marie to gradually ease into, it offered hope.

Jewel teased, "That would entail twice-monthly Sunday jazz brunches on the terrace of the Scion Inn with me and my mother. That is, until our inn opens."

"I'd be delighted."

Sophia asked, "Do you have a name yet, Jewel?"

"DeVine Inn. Since we'll also have a vineyard on property." She spared a glance to her left, to her right. Then asked, "What do you think?"

"Heavenly," her mother said.

Rose-Marie laughed softly. "I can't think of a more appropriate word. Indeed . . . heavenly."

# TWENTY-TWO

"That was one seriously twisted path we traveled today," Jewel said as she sipped her martini. She sat near the foot of a double chaise-longue chair on Rogen's patio, which was alight with flames from the fireplace, the lava stone–filled planters, and a star-studded sky. She was situated between both men, her legs tucked under her. They flanked her with their hunky bodies. Exactly what Jewel preferred.

Rogen said, "It sure as hell wasn't easy seeing my mother that distraught."

"Not easy knowing I've played a huge part in her trauma, either," Jewel commented.

"It wasn't personal, Jewel," Vin reminded her, always the voice of reason. Which she adored. "You can't help that you shared some similarities to Taylor. Like Rose-Marie said, it was never your fault."

"Still, I feel bad about how life exploded around them. Everyone, really."

"What your parents did for mine," Rogen said. "That was something. To let my parents cover up all the emotional horror unfolding in our house by faking a feud . . . That's pretty serious stuff."

With a nod, Jewel said, "I'm still blown away by it. Except that I can see from your parents' side how hard . . . how excruciating . . . it would be to surround themselves with their nearest and dearest friends, who'd not encountered any tragedies. Who had precisely what your parents wanted—a healthy daughter. A family that wasn't shattered. To not have to send away their only son because of how tumultuous and tenuous the environment had become."

"I'll admit," Rogen said, "though it's painful to think of it, that I'd rather my parents sent me to Trinity than to have gone to the extreme of committing my mother to a mental health facility." He shook his head, as though his thought hadn't quite come out right. "I know she needs help, and I'm relieved she's getting it. But she's lived an extremely productive life—has devoted herself to charities and volunteering—because she could come and go, and live in her own home. Not some institution. Do I believe what they did was right by forsaking the relationship with your parents? No. But—"

"She's your mother, Rogen," Vin said. "All you want for her is to be healthy and happy."

"Yes."

"You can't justify their actions for them," Vin added. "And Jewel was right. We can't change the past. So let's stop trying. Let's cut it loose. Because now we have a future."

Jewel lifted her glass. *"Salut."*

They tapped rims.

She polished off her martini and handed over the glass to Rogen, who deposited it, along with his, on the small table next to the lounger. Vin did the same.

Jewel stretched between them, facing Rogen. She said, "I'm sorry I let all the gossip go to my head."

Rogen's fingers glided across her collarbone. "It was a bit in-our-face when we came back from Paris, with not much time to prepare for what we'd encounter from the rumors."

She kissed him. Then craned her neck toward Vin behind her. Kissed him, too. She breathed him in and said, "God, I've missed how you both smell. All the heat. The virility."

Returning her attention to Rogen, she fisted his tee at the waist and pushed it upward and over his arms and head, tossing it aside. Her hands skimmed his muscles and they flexed beneath her touch.

He sighed sexily. "Something tells me we're not going to have any trouble working out all the logistics of this arrangement."

"We're pretty creative people." She kissed him.

Then Jewel turned to Vin and toyed with the top button of his dress shirt. He gave her a devilish grin.

"I know you're dying to rip it open," he said. "Go ahead. I have a closetful of expensive shirts, remember?"

Heat blazed through her. She gripped the opening at his pecs and yanked forcefully, sending buttons flying.

"God, that just feels *so* good," she told him.

He kissed her. Wildly. Passionately. The way he always did.

Rogen worked the zipper on her dress and she wiggled out of it with his help while still kissing Vin. Then Rogen's hands were on her and she had to tear her mouth away and gasp for air as everything inside her ignited.

She unfastened Rogen's belt and jeans while he toed off his boots. Jewel dragged the denim and his boxer briefs down his legs. Then repeated the process with Vin.

Her tongue swept along exposed skin, rock-hard muscle, his cock. Then she did the same to Rogen. He pulled her on top of him and kissed her senseless. Sensually. Hungrily. Making her pulse skyrocket.

Vin shifted and twined his fingers in the sides of her lace thong. He eased the material over her hips and down her thighs. She maneuvered with him to get the scant lingerie off her. Then she straddled Rogen's hips. His hands caressed her breasts as she kissed him.

One of Vin's hands whisked over her belly, causing the flesh to quiver. He stroked her pussy lips, already moist from her escalating desire. His other hand covered her ass. Then his fingers traced along the cleft, taunting her with her very favorite thing—forbidden pleasures.

Jewel had a palm flattened on the cushion at Rogen's side. She licked the other and rubbed the head of his cock. Then closed her hand over it and slid down to the shaft, pumping slowly.

"Yeah," Rogen said on a sexy groan. "Like that."

Vin slid two fingers inside her and stroked while also rubbing her clit. He was on his knees beside Rogen's hip, positioned to set a quick, steady pace.

Rogen's mouth closed over her nipple and he sucked hard. Jewel let out a little squeal of delight.

"This really is too decadent for words," she said. "But I don't feel guilty anymore. I just . . . *feel*."

And how fucking wonderful *that* was!

Vin worked her faster. Rogen suckled her other nipple. And Jewel cried out when the radiant orgasm took hold of her.

While she still vibrated from the climax she guided Rogen's cock into her pussy. He plunged deep, gripping her hips to steady her as he fucked her.

"Yes," she told him, their gazes locked. "That's incredible." Her forearms rested along his chest as she leaned over him.

He shifted her hips away and pulled out of her. Vin squirted lube over her skin and then eased into her small, tight hole.

"Oh!" Jewel moaned loudly. The variance in sensation from Rogen in her pussy to Vin in her ass was exquisite.

He pumped slowly a few times. Then withdrew. Rogen entered her again.

"Oh, God." Her head dropped to Rogen's shoulder. All Jewel wanted to concentrate on was the difference in the pleasure her two lovers brought her, in two very different spots. The stroking of Rogen's cock. Then Vin's. Then Rogen's.

"Fuck," Vin murmured. "Those moans of yours drive me crazy."

"What you both do to me drives *me* crazy," she said.

While Vin gently pushed farther into her, Rogen coaxed her hips downward, so that his dick slid between her slick folds while Vin was inside her.

"Yes," she whimpered. "You can't imagine how good it feels to have you both stroking me. Making me wetter. Hotter."

Vin gave Rogen his turn and he thrust assertively, hitching her breathing and her pulse.

"Oh, yes," she moaned, barreling so quickly toward orgasm.

Rogen pulled out and Vin slipped in. Her folds glided along Rogen's thick shaft again. Then the head of his cock rubbed her clit with a quick tempo and just the right amount of pressure as her body rocked from Vin's pumping.

Fire roared through her veins. Beads of perspiration popped along her nape.

Jewel's breasts brushed over Rogen's pecs with every thrust, her nipples tightening against the sweep of his hot, smooth skin and chiseled muscles. She rode his cock while Vin continued to pump steadily.

Erotic sensations kept swelling within her. Searing. Tingling. Tempting.

"I want both of you," she told them on sharp pants of air. "Inside me."

Rogen's grip on her hips tightened to keep her in place. The tip of his cock nudged her opening.

"Are you sure?" Rogen asked.

"Yes, yes," she assured them. "I'm about to come. Give me what I need. Right now."

She was so wet. Opening to them. Ready for them.

Vin eased out just to the point of the head of his erection nestling within her. Rogen inched in that much as well.

Exhilaration exploded down Jewel's spine and deep in her core. "Oh, God." It was too much and yet somehow not enough. "More."

"Fuck," Vin all but growled. So heatedly. "It's good for us, too, baby. Take it slow."

Not heeding the warning, she rolled her hips.

"Jewel!" Vin scolded and encouraged at the same time.

Rogen pushed farther into her. So did Vin.

Jewel could barely breathe and her heart thundered. "Oh, Christ." The two of them filling her was like nothing she'd ever known, nothing she could ever have been prepared for. Vin was leaning over her. Her chest was pressed to Rogen's. They surrounded her, carefully moved within her. Stroking, pumping, thrusting.

Sending her to some incredibly primal, wicked place that made her lose touch with everything . . . except heat and sensation.

And when those sensations burst wide open, Jewel screamed.

"Oh, fuck!" Vin's cock throbbed and his body convulsed as he came.

Rogen drove deeper, faster. And then she felt him surge and explode inside her, filling her with heat and moisture.

"Yes," Jewel moaned, the rush of desire setting her off again with enticing ripples.

They stayed in that place for endless moments, Jewel crushed between the two of them in the most sinfully delicious way.

She could have stayed there forever.

Eventually, Vin withdrew. He flopped down beside her on his back. Jewel unraveled from Rogen and lay between them. They all still breathed a bit heavily.

Rogen told her, "I love you, Jewel. I always have and I always will."

She kissed his cheek. "I love you, too."

Then she rolled toward Vin. "And what about you, surly?"

He chuckled. "I suppose I love you a little bit."

She held up her hand, pinched her index finger and thumb together until there was just an inch of space between them. "About that much?"

His brow crooked. He used his own finger and thumb to push hers in a quarter of an inch. "Maybe that much."

Jewel let out a healthy laugh. "You asshole! Play nice. Or I'll slap you again."

"If that's the game you want to play, then expect me to smack that very fine ass of yours before I fuck it again."

Liquid fire replaced the blood in her veins. "You wouldn't tease a girl, would you?"

Vin pulled her onto him and said, "You are no girl, Jewel Catalano. And for the record, I am very much in love with you. Forever."

"Aww . . . he has a sensitive side." She kissed him.

Vin mumbled, "Don't tell anyone."

"As always," she said against his lips, "your secret is safe with me."

Another scorching kiss.

Then Jewel said, "I love you, too."

She'd finally found her destiny and her place in life. With the exception of one thing.

"Seriously, boys . . . where are we going to live?"

# EPILOGUE

*Okay, Jewel. This is simple.*

She sat in her convertible outside of Bristol's two weeks later. At lunchtime. The parking lot was packed, which meant the same could be said for the inside.

Jewel, Rogen, and Vin had spent the past two weeks in San Francisco, helping her pack up her house and do some touch-up work before she put it on the market. Her father kept a spacious apartment in the city, and he designated a room for her for when she needed to tend to business at Catalano Enterprises.

Now she'd returned to River Cross. Rogen and Vin were already inside the restaurant. Jewel was a few minutes late in joining them.

*Turn the car off.*

She did.

*Pull the keys from the ignition.*

She did.

*Unhook the seat belt.*

She did.

*All right. All good there.*

She took several deep breaths.

This would be the trio's first public appearance since returning from their whirlwind trip to procure the scotch. Jewel was now residing in Vin's house—with Rogen as well. The location easily decided upon because Vin's house had all the amenities Rogen's possessed but with a much larger master suite and a bigger kitchen. They all liked to cook together, after all. Plus it was on neutral territory. Not on the Angelini estate, not on the Catalano one.

That didn't matter in the grand scheme of things with the "feud" having ended, except that Jewel and Rogen had contended since they were all forging a new path and building a legacy for the three of them, they didn't want one last name dominating the other two.

Now Jewel was demonstrating *exactly* how far she'd go for her lovers. . . .

She opened the door. Stepped out of the car and closed the door. Locked it with the fob, which was a habit she'd always found ridiculous because the top was down, for God's sake.

She dropped the keys in her small handbag, hitched her chin, and marched across the parking lot to the entrance.

She'd purposely selected a red mini for the occasion. No need to cower in any corners.

Jewel wove her way through the crowded bar. Smiling at acquaintances and longtime friends. Ignoring the double takes, the lean-ins toward drinking buddies or dining companions that preceded whispers, likely along the lines of, *Oh, my God! There's Jewel Catalano! She's sleeping with Rogen Angelini and Vin D'Angelo. At the same time!*

She gave a friendly wave to Francine Hillman and a few of the inner circle Jewel had always been a part of. Francine waved back. Looked a little envious, if Jewel read her correctly.

And Jewel knew why.

Because as she stepped onto the patio there were Rogen and Vin, with blueprints of the inn spread out on the large table—and

Rogen poring over a book on viticulture—and she lost her breath. And knew the women stealing glances her way might be gossiping about her, but chances were damn good they all wished they were in her Jimmy Choo shoes.

Especially when Rogen caught sight of her and gave her his wicked grin, his vibrant blue eyes shimmering with lust and love. He got to his feet. As did Vin, looking devilishly handsome in all black. She accepted a kiss on the cheek from both of them. And couldn't help the *eat your heart out* smile that spread across her lips.

Because they were all hers.

And Jewel was more than happy to be shared by *these* angels.

Turn the page for a preview of

# THE BILLIONAIRES: THE BOSSES

coming in September . . .

As Christian lit the multiple fires and dimly set chandeliers, Bayli passed through glass doors to the terrace. Rory followed closely behind.

"He has a swimming pool," she drolly commented. "Why am I not surprised?"

"And a spa."

All sleek and stylish, with water features made of flat, polished obsidian stone, all artistically lit. Bayli stood at the railing and took in the scene once more.

"Not too shabby, eh?" Rory said from beside her.

"Your apartment is incredible, too. Remind me to *never* show you mine."

"Bayli."

"Shh." She kissed him. It was meant to be a quick kiss, but of course Rory took charge of it. His arms slid around her waist and he hauled her up against him.

Where Christian's kisses were intense and all-consuming, Rory's held the playful promise of wicked things to come, making her toes curl.

When she finally pulled away, she breathlessly said, "I had a point to make."

He grinned deviously. "So did I."

Unraveling from him—and fanning her flushed face with a hand—she took a couple of steps back so that she didn't fall into his embrace again.

She told him, "This is all extremely nice," she gestured toward the terrace and Christian's apartment, in general, "but it's not the reason I'm here. Yes, I want to someday be someone and maybe have my own swimming pool, too. You know this about me already, and it's one-hundred percent true. I want more for myself than I've ever had—I'm sure that's also how Christian felt from the time he was a kid. But . . . There's something much more enticing and poignant about all of this that has nothing to do with material desires."

Rory crossed his arms over his chest. Cocked his head to the side. "Tell me."

"It's like when you read a novel and the character has painted himself into a corner, and as the reader, you're wondering how the hell they'll ever free themselves. How they'll escape whatever drudgery or peril or cage they're facing with no obvious route in sight or in mind. And then something mysterious happens—they discover a secret or accidently flip a switch that reveals a private passage through the walls or they find a trap door. Whatever. And suddenly, a slew of new opportunities are laid out before them. It's a very heady sensation for the reader as much as for the character."

"You might be losing me on this one, babe."

She laughed softly. "Think about it. When I came to your restaurant it was because I needed a job. Would I have been content coming in three nights a week to seat people who'd look right through me—a nobody—because they're more interested in *seeing and being seen* in a roomful of VIPs?"

"Likely not. One of the reasons I didn't hire you."

"Smart of you. But I faced a corner because you turned me away. Luckily, I had the gig at the fund-raiser with the opportunity to impress Christian. He was my trap door . . . Except." She held up her finger as Rory started to speak. "Not in the way I'd anticipated. The show will be a fantastic break for me, and I'm eternally grateful for the chance to prove I can do this, for being chosen. But I got painted right back into the corner, because I came full circle with you."

"I'm your corner?"

She grinned. "*You're* my trap door, too."

"Why am I not getting that logic?"

With another laugh, Bayli said, "Because I'm high on champagne and aphrodisiacs and a really amazing orgasm. But, Rory, what I'm telling you is that I was living in fear of not landing the hostess job—because I really need the steady paycheck. And while I was all tangled up in that fear, the two of you were already working out my escape route. And the truth is, I don't care about this amazing view of Central Park. I mean, it *is* amazing . . . But my point is, for the first time in my life I'm understanding that what I want isn't just about *being* special in the eyes of strangers. It's about *feeling* special, and worthy, when I'm with people I care about. Who care about me." She got a little teary-eyed, but Rory didn't seem to mind.

He brushed his fingers over her cheek. His breath blew against her temple as he said, "Beautiful Bayli. Sometimes you're just too much in your head, honey." His finger and thumb gingerly pinched her chin and lifted it so that she stared him the eyes. "Christian and I aren't *your* escape route. You're ours. From the moment we saw you, even though it was separately, we both knew you were the answer to our problem with the show. And that we both wanted you. That you are what we *both* want."

His mouth crashed overs and he kissed her with the sort of hunger that clawed at her, made her instantly restless. Made her crave carnal pleasures she knew little about, but was more than eager to learn. With them.

Bayli couldn't stop herself from working Rory's tie as the kiss went on and on. She shoved the buttons through their holes. Yanked the belt from his pants. Then her hands splayed over his ridged abs and she got even hotter.

Breaking the kiss, Rory took her by the hand and slowly backed into the apartment, his smoldering gaze still on her. She tried to breathe normally, but that proved impossible. They entered the living room, the atmosphere warm and inviting.

Bayli gently pulled her hand from Rory's and crossed to where Christian watched them, a sexy grin on his face.

"What are you smiling at?" she asked before her lips swept over his.

"The two of you. I was getting a little worried that you were arguing again. But . . . clearly not."

"Definitely not. Though don't count on us to always be so well behaved with each other. He gets so easily agitated."

From behind her, Rory gave a half-snort. Bayli laughed quietly.

She told Christian, "He seems to think I have some complexities as well."

"Don't we all?" Christian offered.

"Indeed. Currently, yours is being too buttoned up." She had him out of his tie and shirt in record time, then admired his chest and the long grooves of his obliques. Sighed longingly. "You make me want to lick every single inch of you."

"Maybe we'll get to that later. At the moment, I think you're the one wearing too much clothing."

Rory was suddenly at her back. He slid the side zipper of her dress down its track, the slow zinging of metal filling the otherwise quiet room.

Christian's head dipped and he pulled her into one of his soul-stirring kisses that snagged her from reality. Meanwhile, Rory eased the silver material down her body and then knelt behind her. He dragged her panties away and palmed her ass, spreading her cheeks. His mouth was on her pussy in the next instant and she moaned into Christian's mouth.

Christian's arm wound around her waist to hold her steady. His other hand cupped her breast and kneaded a bit roughly, insistently as Rory tongued her clit and then her opening. He suckled her slit, and then pressed his tongue inside.

Bayli had to end her electrifying kiss with Christian in order to suck in some much-needed oxygen. And because her entire being was on fire.

She twisted slightly at the waist and combed her hand through Rory's hair. Christian drew her puckered nipple into his mouth while Rory continued to eat her pussy. The compounded sensations were scintillating and had her deeply aroused again. And stepping further away from the restrictive confines of a conventional sexual relationship.

When she was on the verge of coming, Rory stood. Her mind whirled. "Hey."

He gave her his cocky grin. "Not just yet," he told her. "You weren't begging for it." He kissed her.

"Not verbally," she complained. "But trust me, my body is screaming for another release."

"We'll make it scream louder," Christian assured her.

And an entire Fourth of July full of fireworks erupted inside her.

Rory took her hand and led her across the room, toward the elevated entryway and curving staircase. But they didn't make it that far. There was a long, ebony credenza that stretched along the short wall at the foyer and was partially tucked into a corner. Its purpose was primarily bar service, with fancy, intricately cut-glass decanters and matching glasses set out. Along with a silver-plated ice bucket with a lid. Though a large portion of the surface was devoid of items.

Christian stopped here and said, "This'll do nicely."

"Care to elaborate?" Bayli asked.

"You'll enjoy what I have in mind." He shot a look toward Rory. "What *we* have in mind."

"I can certainly improvise and make this work," Rory said. And freed the fastenings of his pants.

Bayli's fingers were at Christian's waist, quickly loosening his belt, then unbuttoning and unzipping him. She shoved his pants and briefs down his legs while he toed off his shoes. She admired him as he stepped out of the clothing and his socks. His cock was rock hard and his muscles were bunched.

Oysters and lobster bisque be damned, Christian and Rory were the *ultimate* aphrodisiacs.

She turned to Rory, who was naked as well. Her heart skipped some necessary beats.

For a few suspended seconds, Bayli wasn't the least bit sure what she should do. What she should do *with these men*, to be exact.

They were several steps ahead of her, though.

Christian took her hand, garnering her attention. He perched himself on the edge of the credenza and she stood between the vee of his parted legs. He kissed her as he wrapped her fingers around his steel erection.

Behind her, Rory lifted her leg and draped it over Christian's, opening her to them both. Rory's fingers slid into her moisture and heat from behind. Christian's rubbed her clit.

It was nearly impossible to keep up their sizzling kiss and slowly pump his cock while he and Rory were sending her into that blissful state again.

So Bayli decided to change things up. Take charge this time.

She broke her kiss with Christian and released his cock from her tight fist. She grabbed Rory's free hand and pulled it around her side, forcing him to coil his fingers around Christian's throbbing dick.

"Bayli," both men said in unison. With the same distinct edge of *oh, hell no*! in their voices.

"Do this for me," she said. "So I can concentrate on what you're doing to me. And, because . . . well, it's making me absolutely crazy, Rory, to see your hand on Christian's cock."

"This isn't what we do," Christian said in a strained voice.

Her brow crooked. "But for me . . . ?"

Rory let out a low growl. "That's a two-way street, honey."

Excitement rippled through her. When it really shouldn't, since she knew exactly what tripped through Rory's mind at that very moment.

She said, "Just give me this right now." Because good Lord, it was riveting to watch Rory's strong hand encircle Christian's thick cock. And pump heartily.

Her mouth was all over Christian's chest, her tongue flitting over his small nipples, her teeth lightly nipping his flesh, her lips dragging along his heated skin. All the while he rubbed her clit with a fervor that screamed *payback*. And she loved every second of it.

Rory's fingers withdrew from her and he grabbed a condom from the small stack he'd set on the ledge of the divider wall. He was sheathed in seconds and his cock teased her opening for a few moments.

Bayli studied Christian's face as Rory's hand still pumped, and he was about to enter her. The air was thick with sexual tension. With denial of what both men believed in, and the silent acceptance that they would do whatever Bayli asked of them. She was in control. Even as her body tightened and she wanted them both with a voracious appetite she'd never before imagined, let alone experienced, she understood that everything she didn't know and wasn't accustomed to didn't matter in the slightest.

They would give her whatever she wanted. Whatever she asked for.

Calista Fox

Calista is a former PR professional, now writing fast-paced, steamy books to set your pulse racing! She has won many reviewers' and readers' choice awards, as well as best-book awards. Calista has crossed the country many times over by corporate jet and travels internationally, always with her laptop in tow to capture intriguing story elements and exotic locales. She is a past president/adviser of the Phoenix chapter of the Romance Writers of America national organization.

The first two books in the sexy new billionaire ménage **Lovers' Triangle series** by

# CALISTA FOX

---

## THE BILLIONAIRES
Available April 2017

---

## THE BILLIONAIRES: THE BOSSES
Available September 2017

---

 St. Martin's Griffin

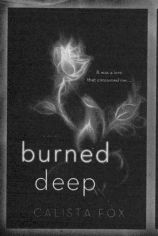